The City
of
Dreaming Books

A Novel from Zamonia by
Optimus Yarnspinner

Translated from the Zamonian
and Illustrated by

Walter Moers

whose German text was
translated into English by
John Brownjohn

THE OVERLOOK PRESS
New York

This paperback edition first published in the United States in 2008 by

The Overlook Press, Peter Mayer Publishers, Inc.
141 Wooster Street
New York, NY 10012

Cataloging-in-Publication Data is available from the Library of Congress

Manufactured in the United States of America
ISBN-13 978-1-59020-111-4
10 9 8 7 6 5 4 3 2

Part One
Dancelot's Bequest

Optimus Yarnspinner

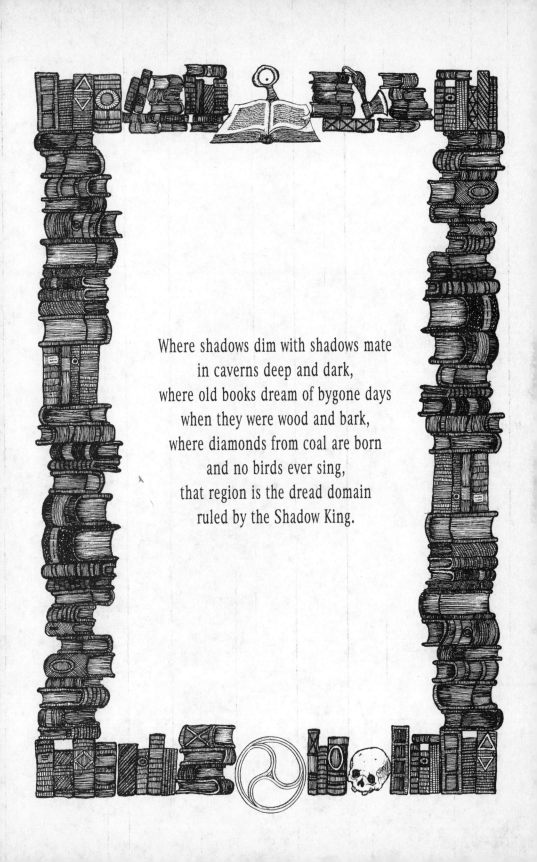

Where shadows dim with shadows mate
in caverns deep and dark,
where old books dream of bygone days
when they were wood and bark,
where diamonds from coal are born
and no birds ever sing,
that region is the dread domain
ruled by the Shadow King.

A Word of Warning

This is where my story begins. It tells how I came into possession of *The Bloody Book* and acquired the Orm. It's not a story for people with thin skins and weak nerves, whom I would advise to replace this book on the pile at once and slink off to the children's section. Shoo! Begone, you cry-babies and quaffers of camomile tea, you wimps and softies! This book tells of a place where reading is still a genuine adventure, and by adventure I mean the old-fashioned definition of the word that appears in the *Zamonian Dictionary*: '**A daring enterprise undertaken in a spirit of curiosity or temerity, it is potentially life-threatening, harbours unforeseeable dangers and sometimes proves fatal.**'

Yes, I speak of a place where reading can drive people insane. Where books may injure and poison them – indeed, even kill them. Only those who are thoroughly prepared to take such risks in order to read this book – only those willing to hazard their lives in so doing – should accompany me to the next paragraph. The remainder I congratulate on their wise but yellow-bellied decision to stay behind. Farewell, you cowards! I wish you a long and boring life, and, on that note, bid you goodbye!

So ... Having probably reduced my readers to a tiny band of reckless souls at the very outset, I should like to bid the rest of you a hearty welcome. Greetings, my intrepid friends, you're cut from the cloth of which true adventurers are made! Let us waste no more time and set out at once on our journey. For it is a journey on which we're embarking, a journey to Bookholm, the City of Dreaming Books. Tie your shoelaces good and tight, because our route will take us first across a vast expanse of rugged, stony terrain, then across a monotonous stretch of prairie where the grass is dense, waist-high and razor-sharp, and finally – along gloomy, labyrinthine, perilous passages – deep into the bowels of the earth. I cannot predict how many of us will return. I can only urge you never to lose heart whatever befalls us.

And don't say I didn't warn you!

♪

To Bookholm

In western Zamonia, when you've traversed the Dullsgard Plateau in an easterly direction and finally left its rippling expanses of grassland behind you, the skyline suddenly recedes in a dramatic way. You can look far, far out across the boundless plain to where, in the distance, it merges with the Demerara Desert. If the weather is fine and the atmosphere clear, you will be able to discern a speck amid the sparse vegetation of this arid wasteland. As you advance, so it will grow larger, take on jagged outlines, sprout gabled roofs and eventually reveal itself to be the legendary city that bears the name of Bookholm.

You can smell the place from a long way off. It reeks of old books. It's as if you've opened the door of a gigantic second-hand bookshop – as if you've stirred up a cloud of unadulterated book dust and blown the detritus from millions of mouldering volumes straight into your face. There are folk who dislike that smell and turn on their heel as soon as it assails their nostrils. It isn't an agreeable odour, granted. Hopelessly antiquated, it is eloquent of decay and dissolution, mildew and mortality. But it also has other associations: a hint of acidity reminiscent of lemon trees in flower; the stimulating scent of old leather; the acrid, intelligent tang of printer's ink; and, overlying all else, a reassuring aroma of wood.

I'm not talking about living wood or resinous forests and fresh pine needles; I mean felled, stripped, pulped, bleached, rolled and guillotined wood – in short, paper. Ah yes, my intellectually inquisitive friends, you too can smell it now, the odour of forgotten knowledge and age-old traditions of craftsmanship. Very well, let us quicken our pace! The odour grows stronger and more alluring, and the sight of those gabled houses more distinct with every step towards Bookholm we take. Hundreds, nay, thousands of slender chimneys project from the city's roofs, darkening the sky with a pall of greasy smoke and compounding the odour of books with other scents: the aroma of freshly brewed coffee and fresh-baked bread, of charcoal-broiled meat studded with herbs. Again we redouble our rate of advance, and our burning desire to open a book becomes allied with the hankering for a cup of hot chocolate flavoured with cinnamon and a slice of pound cake warm from the oven. Faster! Faster!

We reach the city limits at last, weary, hungry, thirsty, curious – and a trifle disappointed. There are no impressive city walls, no well-guarded gates in the shape, perhaps, of a huge book that creaks open at our knock – no, just a few narrow streets by way of which Zamonian life forms of the most diverse kinds enter or leave the city. Most of them do so with stacks of books under their arms – indeed, many tow whole handcarts laden with reading matter behind them. Were it not for all those books, the cityscape would resemble any other.

So here we are, my dauntless companions – here on the magical outskirts of Bookholm. This is where the city has its highly unspectacular beginnings. Soon we shall cross its invisible threshold, enter its streets and explore its mysteries.

Soon.

But first I should like to pause for a moment and tell you why I came here at all. There's a reason for every journey, and mine was prompted by boredom and the recklessness of youth, by a wish to break the bounds of my normal existence and familiarise myself with life and the world at large. I also wanted to keep a promise made to someone on his deathbed. Last but not least, I was on the track of a fascinating secret. But first things first, my friends!

Ψ

Lindworm Castle

When a youthful inhabitant of Lindworm Castle* becomes old enough to read, his parents assign him a so-called authorial godfather. The latter, who is usually some relation or close family friend, assumes responsibility for the young dinosaur's literary education from that time on. The authorial godfather teaches his charge to read and write, introduces him to Zamonian literature and tutors him in the craft of authorship. He makes him recite poems, enriches his vocabulary and undertakes all the steps required to ensure his godchild's artistic development.

My own authorial godfather was Dancelot Wordwright. A maternal uncle who might have been hewn from the primeval rock on which Lindworm Castle stands, he was over eight hundred years old when he became my sponsor. Uncle Dancelot was a workmanlike writer devoid of any exalted ambitions. He wrote to order, mainly eulogies for festive occasions, and was considered to be a talented composer of after-dinner speeches and funeral orations. More of a reader than an author and more of a connoisseur of literature than an originator thereof, he sat on countless juries, organised literary competitions, and was a freelance copy-editor and ghost-writer. He himself had written only one book, *The Joys of Gardening*, in which he expatiated in impressive language on the cultivation of cauliflowers and the philosophical implications of the compost heap. Almost as fond of his garden as he was of literature, Dancelot never tired of drawing comparisons between the taming of nature and the art of poetry. To him, a home-grown strawberry plant was the equal of an ode of his own composition, a row of asparagus comparable to a rhyming pattern and a compost heap to a philosophical essay. You must permit me, my long-suffering readers, to quote a brief passage from

---

* Translator's Note: Anyone fleetingly acquainted with Zamonian history or literature will know that Lindworm Castle is a hollowed-out rock projecting from the Dullsgard Plateau not far from Loch Loch in western Zamonia. The castle is inhabited by Lindworms that walk on their hind legs, are capable of speech and cherish a high regard for creative writing. As to how this came about, less well-informed readers should consult pp. 41–69 in *Rumo and His Miraculous Adventures.* They will not, however, find this essential to their further perusal of the present book.

LINDWORM CASTLE

his book, which has long been out of print. Dancelot's description of a common or garden blue cauliflower conveys a far more vivid impression of my authorial godfather than I could transmit in a thousand words:

The cultivation of the blue cauliflower is a rather remarkable process. What pays the price in this case is not the foliation, for a change, but the inflorescence. The gardener encourages the umbel's temporary obesity. Crowded together into a compact head, its countless little buds swell, together with their stalks, into an amorphous mass of bluish vegetable fat. Thus, the cauliflower is a flower that has come to grief on its own obesity before flowering; or, to be more precise, a multiplicity of unsuccessful flowers, a degenerate panicled umbel. How in the world can such a bloated creature, with its plump and swollen ovaries, propagate itself? It, too, would return to nature after an excursion into the realm of the unnatural, but the gardener gives it no time to do so: he harvests the cauliflower at the zenith of its aberration, the highest and most palatable stage in its obesity, when the taste of this adipose plant approximates to that of a rissole. The seed collector, on the other hand, leaves the bulbous blue mass in its corner of the garden and permits it to revert to its better self. When he goes to look at it after three weeks, instead of three pounds of vegetable obesity, he finds a very loosely freely flowering bush with bees and flying beetles humming round it. The unnaturally swollen pale-blue stalks have converted their thickness into length and become fleshy stems tipped with a number of sparsely distributed yellow flowers. The few buds that have proved durable turn blue and swell up, then flower and produce seeds. Honest and true to nature, these gallant little survivors are the saviours of the cauliflower fraternity.

Yes, there you have Dancelot Wordwright as he lived and breathed: in tune with nature, in love with language, unfailingly accurate in his observations, optimistic, a trifle eccentric, and – where the subject of his literary labours, the cauliflower, was concerned – as tedious as could be.

All my memories of him are pleasant, discounting the three months that followed one of Lindworm Castle's numerous sieges, during which a stone launched by a trebuchet struck him on the head and left him convinced that he was a cupboard full of dirty spectacles. Although I feared at the time that he would never re-emerge from his delirium, he did, in fact, recover from that severe blow on the head. Unfortunately, no such miraculous recovery occurred in the case of his final and fatal bout of influenza.

⟨

Dancelot's Death

When Dancelot breathed his last at the conclusion of a long and fulfilled dinosaurian existence spanning eight hundred and eighty-eight years, I was a mere stripling of seventy-seven summers and had never once set foot outside Lindworm Castle. He died of a minor influenzal infection that proved too much for his weakened immune system (an occurrence which reinforced my fundamental doubts about the reliability of immune systems in general).

On that ill-starred day I sat beside his deathbed and noted down the dialogue that follows. My authorial godfather had requested me to record his last words in writing. Not because he had grown so conceited that he wished his moribund sighs to be preserved for posterity, but because he thought it would provide me with a unique opportunity to gather authentic material in this special field. He died, therefore, in the execution of his duty as an authorial godfather.

Dancelot: 'I'm dying, my boy.'

I (*inarticulately, fighting back my tears*): 'Huh . . .'

Dancelot: 'I far from approve of death, either from fatalistic motives or with the philosophical resignation of old age, but I suppose I must come to terms with it. Each of us is granted only one cask and mine is tolerably full.'

(*I'm glad in retrospect that he employed the cask metaphor because it indicates that he regarded his life as rich and fulfilled. A person who looks back on his life and likens it to a brimming cask, not an empty bucket, has accomplished a great deal.)*

Dancelot: 'Listen, my boy. I have little enough to leave you, at least from the pecuniary aspect. That you already know. I have never become one of those opulent Lindworm Festival authors with sacks full of royalties piled high in their cellars. I intend to bequeath you my garden, although I know you aren't too keen on vegetables.'

(This was true. As a young Lindworm I had little use for the glorification of cauliflowers and hymns to rhubarb in Dancelot's treatise on gardening, and I made no secret of it. Dancelot's seed germinated only in later years, when I had established a garden of my own, grew blue cauliflowers and derived much inspiration from the taming of nature.)

Dancelot: 'I'm rather clammy at present . . .'

(I couldn't help laughing, despite the depressing situation, because 'clammy' is Zamonian slang for 'broke', and there was something unintentionally amusing about his use of that word in his present sweaty state. Had I myself employed this ill-judged resort to black humour in an essay, Dancelot would probably have red-pencilled it. I managed to smother my guffaw in a handkerchief and pass it off as tearful nose-blowing.)

Dancelot: . . . so I can't leave you anything from the material point of view.'

(I made a dismissive gesture and sobbed, this time with genuine emotion. Even at death's door, he was concerned about my future. It was touching.)

Dancelot: But I do possess something worth considerably more than all the treasures in Zamonia. At least to an author.'

(I stared at him with brimming eyes.)

Dancelot: 'Yes, not counting the Orm, it might be described as the most precious thing any author can acquire in the course of his existence.'

(*He was really making a meal of this. In his place I would have tried to get the requisite information off my chest with all due speed. I leant towards him.*)

Dancelot: 'I'm in possession of the most magnificent piece of writing in the whole of Zamonian literature.'

(*Oh dear, I thought. Either he's becoming delirious, or he wants to leave me his dusty library and is referring to his first edition of* Sir Ginel, *that hoary old novel by Doylan Cone, an author he found so admirable and I so unreadable.*)

I: 'What do you mean?'

Dancelot: 'Some time ago a young Zamonian writer from outside Lindworm Castle sent me a manuscript accompanied by the usual bashful blah-blah-blah: this was only a modest attempt, a hesitant step into the unknown, et cetera, and would I care to tell him what I thought of it – and many thanks in advance!

'Well, I've made it my duty to read all such unsolicited manuscripts, and I can justly claim that reading them has cost me a not inconsiderable proportion of my life and a certain amount of nervous energy.'

(*He emitted an unhealthy-sounding cough.*)

Dancelot: 'It wasn't a long story – only a few pages or so. I was seated at the breakfast table, having finished reading the newspaper and poured myself another cup of coffee, so I tackled it at once. My good deed for the day, I thought. Why not get shot of it right away, over breakfast? Many years of experience had inured me to the usual literary hiccups of a young writer wrestling with problems of style and grammar, pangs of unrequited love and cosmic despair, so I sighed and began to read.'

(*Dancelot heaved a heart-rending sigh. I couldn't tell whether it replicated his sigh on that occasion or heralded his imminent demise.*)

Dancelot: 'When I picked up my coffee cup some three hours later, it was still brim-full and its contents were stone-cold. But it hadn't taken me three hours to read the story; I had devoured it in less than five minutes. I must have spent the rest of the time in a kind of trance, sitting there motionless with the manuscript in my hand. Only a missile from a trebuchet could have dealt me a blow of comparable impact.'

(I was briefly but unpleasantly reminded of the time when Dancelot had thought he was a cupboard full of dirty spectacles. But then, I must confess, an outrageous thought occurred to me. What went through my head the next moment, and I quote it verbatim, was: 'I hope he doesn't kick the bucket before he's told me what was in the confounded manuscript!'

No, I didn't think: 'I hope he doesn't die!' or 'Please don't die, authorial godfather!' or anything of that kind. My thought was couched in the words cited above, and it still shames me, even today, that they included the phrase 'kick the bucket'. Having gripped my wrist like a vice, Dancelot sat up and fixed me with staring eyes.)

Dancelot: 'The last words of a dying man on the point of imparting a sensational revelation – make a note of that literary device, it's a guaranteed cliffhanger! No reader can resist it!'

(Although Dancelot was dying, nothing seemed more important to him at that juncture than to teach me a cheap trick favoured by trashy romantic novelists. This was godfatherly devotion to duty of the most consummate and touching kind. I sobbed, overcome with emotion, whereupon Dancelot relaxed his grip and sank back against the pillows.)

Dancelot: 'The story wasn't long, only ten handwritten pages, but I had never, never in my entire life, read anything even approaching its perfection.'

(Dancelot had been an obsessive reader all his life, perhaps the most industrious bookworm in Lindworm Castle, so I was duly impressed by that statement. He was fanning my curiosity into a blaze.)

I: 'What was it about, Dancelot? Tell me!'

Dancelot: 'Listen, my boy, I don't have time enough left to tell you the story. It's tucked into my first edition of *Sir Ginel*, which I intend to leave you with the rest of my library.'

(*Just as I thought! My eyes filled with tears once more.*)

Dancelot: 'I know you aren't particularly fond of the book, but I suspect that you'll grow into Doylan Cone some day. It's a question of age. When you get a chance, dip into it again.'

(*I promised to do so, nodding valiantly.*)

Dancelot: 'What I want to tell you is this: the story was so perfectly, flawlessly written that it wrought a drastic change in my life. I decided to give up writing, or largely so, because I knew I could never produce anything approaching its perfection. Had I never read that story, I should have continued to cling to my vague conception of great literature, which lies roughly in the Doylan Cone price range. I should never have discovered what perfect creative writing really looks like. As it was, I now held a sample of it in my hands. I resigned, yes, but I resigned gladly. I retired, not from laziness or fear or some other reprehensible motive, but in deference to true artistic aristocracy. I resolved to devote the rest of my life to the workmanlike aspects of writing and confine myself to subjects that are communicable. You already know what I mean: the cauliflower.'

(*A long silence ensued. I was just beginning to think he'd died when he went on.*)

Dancelot: 'And then I made the biggest mistake of my life: I wrote the young genius a letter in which I advised him to take his manuscript to Bookholm and look for a publisher there.'

(*He heaved another big sigh.*)

Dancelot: 'That was the end of our correspondence. I never heard from him again. He probably took my advice but had an accident or fell into the hands of highwaymen or Corn Demons on the way to Bookholm. I should have hurried to his side – I should have taken him and his work under my wing – but what did I do? I sent him off to Bookholm, that lions' den, that haunt of skinflints and vultures who make money out of literature! I ask you, a city teeming with publishers! I might just as well have sent him into a forest full of werewolves with a bell round his neck!'

(*My godfather's breath rattled in his throat as if he were gargling with blood.*)

Dancelot: 'I hope that I have compensated in your case for all I did wrong in his. I know you have what it takes to become Zamonia's greatest writer and acquire the Orm. Reading this story will help you to attain that goal.'

(*Dancelot still clung to the old belief in the Orm, a kind of mysterious force reputed to flow through many authors at moments of supreme inspiration. We young and enlightened writers used to laugh at this antiquated hocus-pocus, but respect for our authorial godfathers prompted us to refrain from making any cynical remarks about the Orm in their presence, though not when we were in the company of kindred spirits. I know hundreds of Orm jokes.*)

I: 'I'll read it, Dancelot.'

Dancelot: 'But don't be alarmed! You'll find it a terribly traumatic experience. It will dash all your hopes and tempt you to abandon a literary career. You may even consider doing away with yourself.'

(*Was he raving? No piece of writing on earth could possibly have that effect on me.*)

Dancelot: 'But you must surmount that crisis. Go travelling! Roam the Zamonian countryside! Expand your horizons! Get to know the world! Sooner or later the trauma will transform itself into inspiration. You'll sense a desire to pit yourself against that perfection and one day, if you don't give up, you'll match it. There's something within you, my boy, that no one else in Earthworm Castle possesses.'

(Earthworm Castle?! Why had his eyelids started to flicker like that?)

Dancelot: 'There's one more thing you must bear in mind, my boy: it doesn't matter how a story begins or ends.'

I: 'What *does* matter, then?'

Dancelot: 'What happens in between.'

(He had never given vent to such platitudes during his lifetime. Was he losing his reason?)

I: 'I'll make a note of that, Dancelot.'

Dancelot: 'Why is it so cold in here?'

(The room was sweltering because we had lit a big open fire for him in spite of the summer heat. The look he gave me conveyed that the Grim Reaper was already celebrating his triumph.)

Dancelot: 'So damnably cold . . . Could someone shut the cupboard door? And what's that black dog doing in the corner? Why is it looking at me like that? Why is it wearing spectacles? Dirty spectacles?'

(I looked, but the only living creature in the corner of the room was a small green spider lurking in its web beneath the ceiling. Dancelot drew a slow, stertorous breath and closed his eyes for ever.)

The Manuscript

It was several days before I investigated Dancelot's parting words, I was far too busy making funeral arrangements and settling his estate. Being his authorial godchild, I had to compose a funeral ode, an anthemic poem of not less than a hundred alexandrines. This I read aloud at his cremation in the presence of all the inhabitants of Lindworm Castle. After that it was my privilege to scatter his ashes from the summit of the castle rock. For a moment, Dancelot's remains hovered in the air like a wisp of grey smoke; then they dispersed into a fine mist that slowly subsided and finally disappeared altogether.

I had inherited his cottage, together with his library and garden, so I decided to leave my parental home at last and move into it. This took several days, but I eventually set about incorporating my own books in Dancelot's library. Sheets of manuscript came fluttering out of some of his volumes, having possibly been inserted between their pages to conceal them from prying eyes. They ranged from brief notes to rough outlines and whole poems. One of them read:

For ever shut and made of wood,
that's what I am. My head's no good
now that it by a stone was struck.
Old spectacles besmirched with muck
repose within me by the score.
I'm just a cupboard, nothing more.

Oh dear, I was quite unaware that Dancelot had been trying to write during his spell of mental derangement. Although I briefly considered removing this piece of doggerel from his literary legacy, I thought better of it – after all, an author owes a duty to the truth. Good or bad, Dancelot's efforts belonged to the reading public. Laboriously, I continued to sort through his books until I came to Doylan Cone's *Sir Ginel* and recalled my authorial godfather's mysterious statement on his deathbed: a sensational

manuscript was concealed between its pages. Afire with curiosity, I opened the book.

Sure enough, between the front cover and the title page was a folded sheaf of manuscript. Was this what my godfather had raved about so fervently? I removed the ten foxed, yellowish sheets and weighed them in my hand for a moment. Dancelot had not only whetted my curiosity but coupled his revelation with a warning. Reading the story might change my life just as it had changed his, he had predicted. Well, why not? I thirsted for change! I was still young, after all, having only just turned seventy-seven.

The sun was shining outside. Inside the house I felt oppressed by the lingering presence of my late godfather: the smell of his countless pipes, the crumpled balls of paper on his desk, a half-written after-dinner speech, a half-empty teacup and, on the wall, an ancient portrait of him as a youngster with eyes like saucers.

He was still omnipresent, and even the prospect of spending the night alone in the house unnerved me, so I resolved to find a quiet spot and read the manuscript in the open air. Sighing, I made myself a sandwich with some of Dancelot's home-made strawberry jam and went outside.

I will never, I'm sure, forget that day till I die. The sun had long passed its zenith, but it was still warm and most of the castle's inhabitants were out and about. The pavement cafés were crowded and sun-loving dinosaurs were lounging on the castle walls, some playing cards, others engrossed in books or reading their latest effusions aloud. The laughter and singing that filled the air were typical of a late summer's day in Lindworm Castle.

It was far from easy to find a quiet spot, so I strolled on through the streets until I finally began to peruse the manuscript while walking.

My first thought was that every word was in the right place. Well, there was nothing so special about that – every piece of writing makes the same initial impression.

It's only on closer inspection that one notices occasional solecisms: the misplacing of punctuation marks, the insidious spelling mistakes, the use of cock-eyed metaphors, the spurning of one word where two will do, and all the other blunders a writer can make. But that first page was different. Even without absorbing its contents, I gained the impression that it was a flawless work of art. It resembled the kind of painting or sculpture that tells you at a glance if it's kitsch or a masterpiece. No handwritten page had ever had that effect on me even before I'd read it. This one looked as if it had been inscribed by a calligrapher. The characters, each of them a work of art in its own right, were choreographed across the page like an enchanting ballet. It was quite some time before I could tear myself away from this captivating general impression and at last begin to read.

'Here, every word is *really* in the right place,' I thought after reading the

first page. 'No, not just every word but every punctuation mark, every comma.' Even the spaces between the words seemed to be of inalienable importance. And the text itself? I can divulge this much: it conveyed the thoughts of an author in a state of *horror vacui*, or fear of a blank page – an author paralysed by writer's block and desperately wondering what sentence would best begin his story.

Not a particularly original idea, I grant you. Many essays have been devoted to this classic, almost stereotypical bane of the author's profession. I must know dozens, a few of them written by myself. They usually testify to the writer's incompetence, not his greatness: he can't think of anything, so he writes about his inability to think of anything. He's like a trumpeter who has forgotten his music and toots away meaninglessly, merely because it's his job.

But *this* writer's treatment of a hackneyed idea was so brilliant, so ingenious, so profound and, at the same time, so amusing that I found myself in a state of feverish exuberance after only a few paragraphs. I felt as if I were dancing to heavenly music with a lovely girl dinosaur in my arms, slightly tipsy after imbibing a glass or two of wine. My brain seemed to be rotating on its own axis. Ideas rained down on me like spark-trailing meteors that landed with a hiss on my cerebral cortex. Giggling, they permeated my brain and made me laugh, made me loudly endorse or contradict them. Never had any piece of writing evoked such a lively reaction from me.

I must have made a thoroughly demented impression as I strutted up and down the street declaiming at the top of my voice, brandishing the letter, laughing hysterically now and then, or stamping my feet with enthusiasm. However, eccentric behaviour in public is the done thing in Lindworm Castle, so no one remonstrated with me. People may have thought that I was rehearsing for some play in which the protagonist had been smitten with insanity.

I read on. The author's way of writing was so absolutely right, so perfect, that tears sprang to my eyes – something that usually happens only when I'm listening to stirring music. There was an unearthly finality about its grandeur. Sobbing unrestrainedly, I continued to read through a veil of tears until a new idea of the writer's tickled me so much that my tears abruptly ceased and I roared with laughter. I guffawed like a drunken idiot and pounded my thigh with my fist. By the Orm, how funny it was! I gasped for breath, quietened briefly with one paw clamped to my mouth – and, despite myself, burst out laughing again. As if under some strange compulsion, I repeated the words aloud several times, interrupted by recurrent paroxysms of hysterical laugher. Ha, ha, ha! That was the funniest sentence I'd ever read! An absolute scream, a joke to end all jokes! My eyes now filled with tears of mirth. The punchline was quite spontaneous – I could never have thought of anything as witty, not in my wildest dreams. By all the Zamonian Muses, how stunningly good it was! It was a while before the last great tidal wave of laughter subsided and I

could read on, still gasping and wheezing with mirth, still shaken by occasional titters. I had wept buckets and the tears continued to stream down my face. Two distant relations came towards me. They raised their hats with a lugubrious air, believing me overcome with grief for my late godfather. Just then I involuntarily emitted another bellow of mirth, and they walked off quickly pursued by my peals of hysterical laughter. At last I quietened sufficiently to be able to continue reading.

The next page resembled a string of pearls, a series of associations so fresh, so relentlessly original and profound that I felt ashamed of the banality of every sentence I myself had written until then. They transfixed and illumined my brain like shafts of sunlight. I uttered a jubilant cry and clapped my paws several times, but I would sooner have underlined each sentence twice in red and written 'Yes! Yes! Precisely!' in the margin. I still remember kissing every word of every sentence that particularly pleased me.

Passers-by shook their heads as they saw me prancing exultantly through the streets with the manuscript in my hand. Those simple characters inscribed on paper had induced a state of sheer ecstasy. Their writer, whoever he was, had transported our profession to a realm that had hitherto been *terra incognita* from my point of view. I breathed heavily, overcome with humility.

Then came a paragraph that struck an entirely new note – a note as high and clear as that of a glass bell. The words suddenly transmuted themselves into diamonds, the sentences into diadems. These were ideas produced by concentrated intellectual high pressure, words ground and polished into gems of crystalline perfection reminiscent of the precise, unique structure of snowflakes. The cold emanating from them made me shiver, but it wasn't the mundane frigidity of ice: it was the grand, exalted, eternal chill of outer space. This was creative thought and writing in its purest form. I had never read anything even half as immaculate.

I will quote one sentence from this text, namely, the one with which it ended. It was also the sentence which finally dissolved the writer's block that had inhibited the author from starting work. I have since used it whenever I myself have been gripped by fear of the blank sheet in front of me. It is infallible, and its effect is always the same: the knot unravels and a stream of words gushes out on to the virgin paper. It acts like a magic spell and I sometimes fancy it really is one. But, even if it isn't the work of a sorcerer, it is certainly the most brilliant sentence any writer has ever devised. It runs: '*This is where my story begins.*'

I lowered the manuscript, my knees went weak, and I sank exhausted to the ground – no, let's be honest, dear readers: I lay down at full length. My ecstasy subsided, my rapture gave way to desolation. Icy rivulets of fear trickled through my veins, filling me with apprehension. Yes, Dancelot had predicted that this manuscript would traumatise me. I wanted to die. How could I ever have presumed to be a writer? What did my amateurish attempts to scribble ideas on paper have in common with the literary sleight of hand I had just witnessed? How could I ever soar to such heights without this writer's wings of purest inspiration? I began to weep again – bitter, despairing tears this time.

Compelled to step over my supine form, people anxiously enquired what the matter was. I paid them no heed. As if paralysed, I lay there for hours until darkness fell and the stars began to twinkle overhead. Somewhere up there my authorial godfather was smiling down at me.

'Dancelot!' I shouted up at the vault of heaven. 'Where are you? Come and bear me off to your kingdom of the dead!'

'Pipe down and go home, you drunken sot!' called an angry voice from a window.

Two nightwatchmen, who probably mistook me for a young and inebriated poet in the throes of creative endeavour (a not entirely false assumption), linked arms with me and conducted me home with many an encouraging cliché ('You'll feel better in the morning!', 'Time is a great healer!', et cetera). Once there I flopped down on the bed as if felled by a trebuchet. Not until the small hours did I notice that I was still clutching the jam sandwich, now squashed flat, in my fist.

The next morning I decided to leave Lindworm Castle. Having spent the whole night running through various ways of overcoming the crisis – hurling myself from the battlements, taking refuge in drink, abandoning my literary career and becoming a hermit, cultivating cauliflowers in Dancelot's garden – I resolved to follow my authorial godfather's advice and set out on a longish journey. I wrote my parents a consoling farewell letter in sonnet form and made up a bundle containing my savings, two jars of Dancelot's jam, a loaf of bread and a bottle of water.

Leaving the castle at dawn, I slunk through the deserted streets like a thief and did not breathe easier until I reached open countryside. I walked for many days, seldom resting because I had but one objective: to get to Bookholm and pick up the trail of the mysterious author whose artistry had filled me with such exaltation. In my youthful optimism I imagined him taking Dancelot's place and becoming my tutor. He would, I thought, bear me upwards to the sphere in which writing such as his originated. I had no idea what he looked like – I didn't know his name or even if he was still alive – but I was sure I would find him. Ah, the boundless confidence of youth!

That is how I came to Bookholm. So here I now am with you, my undaunted readers. And it is here, on the outskirts of the City of Dreaming Books, that my story really begins.

8

The City of Dreaming Books

Once I had grown accustomed to the overpowering smell of mildewed paper that arose from the bowels of Bookholm and survived some allergic sneezing fits occasioned by the ubiquitous clouds of book dust, and once my eyes had stopped watering in the acrid smoke from a thousand chimneys, I could at last begin to take stock of the city's countless marvels.

Bookholm had more than five thousand officially registered antiquarian bookshops and roughly a thousand semi-legal establishments that sold, in addition to books, alcoholic beverages, tobacco, and intoxicating herbs and essences whose ingestion was reputed to enhance your pleasure and powers

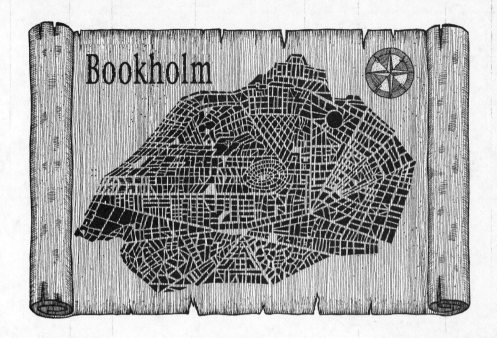

of concentration when reading. There was also an almost incalculable number of itinerant vendors with printed matter of every conceivable kind for sale in shoulder bags or on handcarts, in wheelbarrows and mobile bookcases. Bookholm boasted over six hundred publishing houses, fifty-five printers, a dozen paper mills and a steadily growing number of factories producing lead type and printer's ink. There were shops offering thousands of different bookmarks and ex-libris, stonemasons specialising in bookends, cabinetmakers' workshops and furniture stores filled with lecterns and bookcases, opticians who manufactured spectacles and magnifying glasses, and coffee shops on every street corner. Open for business twenty-four hours a day, most of the latter had inglenook fireplaces and were venues for authors' readings.

I saw countless fire stations in Bookholm, all extremely spick and span, with gigantic alarm bells above the entrances and horse-drawn engines towing copper water tanks. Disastrous fires had destroyed a substantial proportion of the city and its books on five separate occasions, for Bookholm was accounted the biggest fire hazard in Zamonia. Because of the strong winds that were constantly blowing through its streets, the city was cool, cold or icy depending on the time of year, but never warm, which was why its inhabitants preferred to remain indoors, heat their houses well and – of course – read a great deal. Their ever-burning stoves and the sparks that flew in the immediate vicinity of old and highly combustible books created a truly dangerous state of affairs in which a new conflagration might break out at any minute.

I had to resist the impulse to dash into the nearest bookshop and root around in its stock, for I would not have emerged before nightfall and first I had to find somewhere to stay. So I strolled past the windows with shining eyes, endeavouring to make a note of the shops whose wares seemed especially promising.

There they were, the 'Dreaming Books'. That was what the inhabitants of this city called antiquarian books because, from the dealers' point of view, they were neither truly alive nor truly dead but located in an intermediate limbo akin to sleep. With their existence proper behind them and the prospect

of decay ahead, millions upon millions of them slumbered in the bookcases, cellars and catacombs of Bookholm. Only when one of them was picked up and opened by an eager hand, only when it was purchased and borne off, could it awaken to new life. And that was what all these books dreamed of.

I spotted a first edition of *Tiger in My Sock* by Caliban Sycorax! *The Shaven Tongue* by Drastica Sinops – with Elihu Wipple's celebrated illustrations! *Hard Beds and Soiled Sheets,* Yodler van Hinnen's legendary, humorous travel guide – in mint condition! *A Village Named Snowflake* by Ivan Palisade-Honko, the much admired autobiography of an arch-criminal written in the dungeons of Ironville and signed in blood by the author himself! *Life Is More Terrible than Death*, the despairing maxims and aphorisms of Parsifal Gunk, bound in batskin! *The Ant Drum* by Semolina

Edam – the legendary mirror-writing edition! *The Glass Guest* by Zodiak Glockenspiel! Hampo Harrabin's experimental novel *The Dog that Only Barked Backwards*! All these were books I'd longed to read ever since Dancelot had sung their praises to me. I flattened my snout against each window in turn, groping my way along like a drunk and progressing at a snail's pace until I finally pulled myself together. I forbade myself to take note of any more titles and resolved to gain a general impression of Bookholm. I had failed to see the wood for the trees, or rather, the city for the books. After my cosy, dreamy existence in Lindworm Castle, which was enlivened at most by an occasional siege, the streets of Bookholm bombarded me with a hailstorm of impressions. Images, colours, scenes, sounds and smells – all were novel and exciting. Zamonians of every species passed me and each was a stranger. The castle had had nothing to offer but the same old procession of familiar faces, friends, relations, neighbours, acquaintances. Here, everything was alien and unfamiliar.

I did, in fact, run into one or two visitors from Lindworm Castle. When that happened we paused for a moment, said a polite hello, exchanged a few empty phrases, wished each other a pleasant stay and bade each other goodbye. We all cultivate this stand-offish manner when travelling, if only because no one goes abroad in order to meet others of his own kind.

On you go, I told myself, explore the unknown! Haggard poets were standing everywhere, loudly declaiming their own works in the hope that they would capture the attention of some passing publisher or wealthy patron. I noticed some singularly well-nourished individuals prowling round these street poets: corpulent Hogglings who listened attentively and made occasional notes. Far from being generous patrons of the arts, they were literary agents who bullied budding authors into signing cut-throat contracts and then subjected them to merciless pressure, using them as ghost-writers until they had milked them of their last original idea. Dancelot had told me about their kind.

Members of the Bookholmian constabulary were patrolling the streets on the lookout for illegal dealers operating without licences. Whenever they hove into view, handcarts were hurriedly wheeled off and books stuffed into sacks.

Live Newspapers – fleet-footed dwarfs dressed in their traditional galleys – hawked the latest literary gossip and scuttlebutt through the streets and charged passers-by a modest fee to read the reports on their strips of newsprint, for instance:

Heard the latest? *Gopak Trembletoes has auctioned his novella,* Lemon Icing, *to Nodram House, Inc.*

Believe it or not! *The editing of Ogdon Ogdon's novel,* Pelican in Pastry, *is going to take another six months!*

Outrageous! *The last chapter of* The Truth Drinker *by Fantotas Pemm was lifted from Kaira Prudel's* Forest and Folly!

Bookhunters were hurrying from one antiquarian bookshop to another, eager to convert their booty into cash or receive new orders. Bookhunters! You could recognise them by their miners' lamps and jellyfish torches, their martial attire of durable leather, their chain-mail shirts and pieces of armour, their weapons and equipment: cleavers and sabres, pickaxes and magnifying glasses, ropes, lengths of string and water bottles. One of them emerged from the sewers at my very feet, an impressive specimen wearing an iron helmet and wire-mesh mask. These protective devices were more than just a defence against the dust and dangerous insects in Bookholm's mysterious underworld. Dancelot had told me that Bookhunters not only competed for booty in the bowels of the earth but fought and even killed each other there. Seeing this fully armoured creature emerge from the ground, panting and grunting, I could well believe it.

But most of the passers-by were tourists attracted to the City of Dreaming Books by sheer curiosity. Many of them were being shepherded through the streets by guides with metal megaphones who loudly informed their charges, for instance, that Marduk Bussek had sold his *Valley of the Lighthouses* to such-and-such a publisher in such-and-such a building. Chattering and craning their necks like agitated geese, the tourists trailed after them, marvelling at the most trivial things.

My way was repeatedly barred by uncouth Bluddums who thrust flyers into my hand announcing which poet would be honouring which bookshop with his presence and reading from his works at 'timber-time' that evening. It was a while before I learnt to ignore this form of ambush.

Tottering around everywhere were small life forms dressed up as books on legs and advertising works such as *Mermaid in a Teacup* or *The Beetle's Funeral*. The book costumes tended to restrict their vision, so they sometimes bumped into each other, toppled over with a crash and strove to regain their feet amid roars of laughter.

I paused to marvel at the dexterity of a street entertainer juggling with twelve fat volumes at once. Anyone who has thrown a book into the air and tried to catch it will know how difficult that is – though I should add that this particular juggler possessed four arms. Other strolling entertainers, who were disguised as popular characters from classical Zamonian novels, would recite passages from the relevant works by heart if tossed a coin or two. On one street corner I spotted Janggli Patosh from *Men in Checked Jackets*, Oku

Okra from *The Weeping Stones* and Zanilla Sputum, the tuberculosis-racked protagonist of Mantho Snam's masterly novel *Sorcery in the Alps.*

'I am but an Alpine Imp,' the Zanilla impersonator cried dramatically, 'whereas you, my beloved, are a Troglotroll. We can never be united in matrimony. Let us end it all by jumping into Demon's Gulch!'

Those few words sufficed to bring tears to my eyes. Mantho Snam was an absolute genius! It was all I could do to drag myself away.

Move on, I told myself. Notices in shop windows, which I studied attentively, carried advertisements for poetry readings, literary salons, book launches and rhyming competitions. Itinerant dealers continually tugged at my sleeve and tried to foist dog-eared volumes on me, loudly quoting from their rubbishy wares as they followed me for streets on end.

While escaping from one of these importunate creatures I came to a black building with a wooden sign over the entrance stating that it was the *Chamber of Hazardous Books.* Slinking up and down outside was a Vulphead who addressed passers-by in a low growl, baring his fearsome teeth. 'You enter the Chamber of Hazardous Books at your own peril!' he rasped. 'No children or senior citizens admitted! Be prepared for the worst! We have books in here that can bite! Books with designs on your life! Toxicotomes, poisonous books that can strangle and fly! Genuine, every last one! This is no ghost train, ladies and gentlemen, this is for real! Make your wills and kiss your nearest and dearest goodbye before you enter the Chamber of Hazardous Books!'

Stretchers laden with bodies draped in sheets were being carried out of a side entrance at regular intervals. Despite this and the muffled screams that issued from the boarded-up windows, however, crowds of spectators were streaming inside.

'It's only a tourist trap,' I was informed by a flamboyantly dressed Demidwarf. 'No one would be crazy enough to make genuine Toxicotomes accessible to the public. How about something really authentic? Interested in an Orm trip?'

'Eh?' I said, mystified.

The Demidwarf opened his cloak to reveal a dozen little flasks inserted in the lining. He glanced around nervously and closed it again. 'That's the blood of genuine authors with the Orm circulating inside them,' he said in a conspiratorial whisper. 'One drop of it in a glass of wine and you hallucinate whole novels! Only five pyras* a flask!'

'No thanks,' I said dismissively. 'I'm an author myself.'

'You Lindworm Castle snobs think you're something special!' the dwarf called after me as I hurried off. 'Ink is all you write with, not blood! As for the Orm, very few of you ever acquire it!'

I was evidently in one of Bookholm's seamier districts. It was only now that I noticed how many Bookhunters were hanging around, engaged in shady business transactions with disreputable-looking characters. Jewel-studded volumes were produced from sacks and handed over in exchange for thick wads of pyras. I must have strayed into a kind of black market.

'Interested in books from the *Golden List*?' I was asked by a Bookhunter dressed from head to foot in black leather. He wore a mosaic mask depicting a death's-head, a belt with a dozen knives in it and two axes in his boots. 'Come down that dark alley with me and I'll show you some books you've never even dreamt of.'

'Many thanks!' I cried, beating a hasty retreat. 'Not interested!'

---

*Translator's Note: Zamonian exchange rates and units of measurement are such a complex subject that they merit a book of their own. This actually exists in the shape of the hundred-volume *Bunkle*, in which the druidical mathematician and economist Aristocious Bunkle meticulously listed and explained every one of Zamonia's relevant systems. It is only natural, in a continent whose inhabitants range in size from peas to trees, that the most varied forms of currency and units of measurement exist. The Bonsai Mite's *pyxl* is the Turniphead's *forzz*, and if I were to translate both words as a metre I would be wrong each time, even though the Bonsai Mite and the Turniphead both mean a unit of measurement which, relative to their average physical size, corresponds to a metre. And I haven't even mentioned the Hackonian *hakk* or the Voltigorkian *gork*! The inhabitants of Lindworm Castle – and, thus, Yarnspinner himself – employ an extremely complicated system of measurement that is strictly poetic in orientation, embodying units such as *hexameters* and *metaphorical density*.

There are races of Zamonian giants whose small change is as big as millstones, whereas life forms such as Nocturnomaths use a currency based on the telepathic exchange of doctoral dissertations. But, despite all these different conceptions of 'money', the pyra, a silver coin shaped like a tiny pyramid, is a universally recognised means of settling accounts, especially in commercial centres like Bookholm.

For descriptive purposes I have taken the liberty of translating Zamonian units of measurement into our own European units whenever Yarnspinner speaks of relative sizes, distances or weights. For authenticity's sake, however, I have chosen not to translate the pyra, which roughly corresponds in value to one Roman sestertius in the time of Virgil.

The Bookhunter uttered a demonic laugh. 'I don't have any books anyway!' he yelled at my retreating figure. 'I only wanted to wring your neck and cut off your paws, then pickle them in vinegar and flog them. Lindworm Castle relics are much in demand here!'

I left that nefarious neighbourhood as fast as I could. A few streets away all was normal again – no one to be seen but harmless tourists and buskers staging popular plays with puppets. I breathed a sigh of relief. Although the Bookhunter had probably been joking, I shuddered at the thought that mummified portions of a Lindworm's anatomy possessed a certain market value in Bookholm.

I plunged once more into the stream of passers-by. Some cute little Hackonian dwarfs on a school outing were toddling shyly along hand in hand, big saucer eyes on the lookout for their favourite poets.

'There! That's Mostyn Rapido!' they would cry, excitedly pointing someone out with their tiny fingers, or: 'Look! That's Namby the Sensitive having a coffee!' – whereupon at least one of the party would faint.

On and on I roamed, and I'm bound to confess that my powers of recall are overtaxed by all the marvels that met my eyes. I felt as if I were walking through the pages of a lavishly illustrated book in which each flash of artistic inspiration was surpassed by the next: walking letters advertising modern printing presses; murals portraying characters from popular novels; antiquarian bookshops whose old tomes literally overflowed into the street; multifarious life forms rummaging in bookcases and vying for their contents; huge Midgard Serpents hauling wagons full of second-hand rubbish driven by uncouth Turnipheads who pelted the crowd with trashy old volumes. In this city one was forever having to duck to avoid being hit on the head by a book. The hubbub was such that I caught only snatches of what was being said, but every conversation seemed to revolve around books in one way or another:

'... I wouldn't read a book by an Uggly if you paid me ...'

'... he's giving a reading in the Gilt-Edged Book Emporium at timber-time tonight...'

'... a first edition of Aurora Janus's second novel, the one with the two typos in the foreword, for only three pyras ...'

'... if anyone possessed the Orm, it was Aleisha Wimpersleake ...'

'... typographically speaking, a disgrace to the entire printing industry ...'

'... someone ought to write a footnote novel – just footnotes on footnotes, that would be the thing ...'

At last I paused at an intersection. Turning on the spot, I counted the bookshops in the streets running off it: there were no less than sixty-one of them. My heart beat wildly. Here, life and literature seemed to be identical: everything centred on the printed word. This was *my* city, my new home.

☌

The Hotel from Hell

I discovered a small hotel called the *Golden Quill*, an inviting and agreeably old-fashioned name suggestive of sound literary craftsmanship and a restful night's sleep in a feather bed.

I made my optimistic way into the gloomy lobby and across a strip of musty carpet to the reception desk, where, when no one appeared, I rang a copper bell. It was cracked and its discordant clangour filled the air. I turned, hoping to see some member of the staff hurrying towards me along one of the shadowy corridors that led off the lobby, but nobody came. Turning back to the counter, I was startled to find that the receptionist had materialised behind it like magic. He was a Murkholmer, I could tell from his pallid complexion. My knowledge of Murkholmers had been acquired from Sebag Seriosa's excellent novella on the subject, *The Damp Denizens*, and I had already encountered several of these rather weird Zamonian life forms in the streets.

'Yes?' he said, sounding as if he was at his last gasp.

'I'm, er . . . looking for a room,' I replied in a tremulous voice.

Five minutes later I was bitterly regretting not having taken to my heels on the spot. My room, for which I had paid in advance at the receptionist's insistence, turned out to be a lumber room of the most appalling kind. With unerring misjudgement, I had settled on what was probably the worst overnight accommodation in Bookholm. Not a sign of a feather bed, just a coarse, prickly blanket on a mildewed mattress with something rustling inside it. To judge by the noise coming from the room next door, which was occupied by a family of Bluddums, their children were using the furniture as xylophones. The paper was peeling off the walls and some creature was scampering around beneath the floorboards with a series of high-pitched squeaks. Dangling from the ceiling in an inaccessible corner, a white, one-eyed vampire bat seemed to be waiting for me to go to sleep so that it could begin its gruesome meal. Then I noticed that there were no curtains over the windows. The sun's merciless rays would be bound to shine in at five in the morning and prevent me from getting another wink, because the smallest glimmer of light prevents me from sleeping. (I've eschewed 'slumber masks' ever since I tried one out and forgot the next morning that I was wearing it. Panic-stricken in the belief that I'd gone blind overnight, I blundered around like a headless chicken, then tripped over a stool and landed so heavily that I dislocated my shoulder.)

I had no intention of spending the night at the hotel in any case. I was able to lay down my bundle at last and sluice off some of the dust from my travels with the brackish water in the washbasin – that would do for the time being. Bookholm's antiquarian bookshops were open twenty-four hours a day. Hungry, thirsty and itching to root around in their wares, I bade the bat and the Bluddums goodnight and hurried out into the bustling streets once more.

Only a small proportion of Bookholm – barely ten per cent, perhaps – is situated on the surface. By far the greater part of the city lies underground. Like some monstrous termite's nest, it consists of a system of subterranean tunnels that extends for many miles in the form of shafts, chasms, passages and caverns entwined into one gigantic, unravellable knot.

No one can say when or how this cave system came into being. Many authorities claim that it was indeed created by a race of prehistoric termites –

huge primeval insects that constructed it as a nest in which to hide their gigantic eggs. The city's antiquarians, on the other hand, swear that the system of tunnels was excavated over thousands of years by many generations of booksellers as a place in which to store old stock. This is certainly true of some parts of the labyrinth, especially those situated close to the surface.

Countless scholars have augmented this wealth of speculation with theories of their own. Personally, I favour a composite theory according to which the original system of tunnels was excavated by some form of prehistoric insect and then, over the millennia, enlarged by increasingly civilised creatures. The only certainty is that this subterranean world exists, that it has never been fully explored to this day, and that many parts of it are crammed with books that grow steadily older and more valuable the deeper into the catacombs one descends.

There was nothing to remind me, as I strolled through the streets, of the labyrinth beneath the cobblestones. I was delighted to note that I would not have to go hungry in Bookholm. In addition to the coffee houses and taverns there were many stalls selling inexpensive fare of all kinds: grilled sausages and stuffed poussins, bookworms baked in clay, fried mouse bladders, mulled ale, flying pancakes, roasted peanuts, cold lemonade. Every few steps I came to stalls where, for a small charge, you could dip a piece of bread in a cast-iron cauldron of melted cheese bubbling over a small brazier.

I bought myself a sizeable hunk of bread, dunked it liberally in melted cheese, wolfed it greedily and washed it down with two mugs of lemonade. After many days of deprivation on the road, this massive intake of food and drink assuaged my hunger and thirst as I'd hoped but also occasioned an unwholesome feeling of repletion. This rather worried me for a while. I was afraid it might portend some incurable disease – until, after walking off my meal for an hour or so, it vented itself in several ferocious expulsions of wind.

What *didn't* I see on my walk! I continued to repress the urge to enter a bookshop rather than stagger along laden with a huge pile of volumes, but the most incredible treasures could be had for the most ridiculous prices. *Where the Sea Wall Ends* by Ektro Backwater – an autographed copy for five pyras! *The Catacombs of Bookholm*, a critically acclaimed account of conditions in the Bookholmian labyrinth by Colophonius Regenschein, the legendary

Bookhunter: three pyras! *A Bed of Nettles*, the memoirs of Glumphrey Murk, the melancholy superpessimist: six measly pyras!

I was in a bibliophile's Elysium, there was no doubt about it. Even with the small sum Dancelot had left me I could in no time have acquired a whole library that would have been the envy of everyone in Lindworm Castle. For the time being, however, I simply drifted along.

Kibitzer's Warning

Once my wonderment at the bustle of activity in the streets had subsided a little, I began to resent being jostled by Bluddums and pestered by itinerant hucksters. It was also growing steadily colder with the advent of darkness, so I resolved to start exploring the second-hand bookshops. But which? A large one with a varied stock? A small, specialised establishment? If the latter, what should its speciality be? Poetry? Thrillers? Ugglian horror stories? Grailsundian philosophy? Florinthian Baroque? With their candlelit windows full of literary tit-bits, all the shops looked equally tempting. For simplicity's sake I plumped for the one I happened to be standing outside. Engraved on the door was a peculiar symbol: a circle divided into three by three curving lines inside it.

The lighting was so subdued that I couldn't decipher the titles of the books displayed in the window, but that only made it seem the most mysterious and alluring establishment in the street. In I went!

The discreet jangle of a bell announced my presence, the familiar scent of desiccated old tomes filled my nostrils and for a moment I thought I was alone in the shop. My eyes took a while to become accustomed to the gloom, but then I saw a humpbacked figure with enormous goggle-eyes emerge from the shadows cast by the bookcases. I heard a series of muffled, rhythmical clicks.

'Can I help you?' the gnome enquired in a thin, reedy voice. He sounded as if his tongue was made of parchment. 'Are you interested in the writings of Professor Abdul Nightingale?'

Good heavens, I'd wound up in a shop specialising in the effusions of that crackpot from the Gloomberg Mountains. Nightingale, of all people! Although I wasn't too well acquainted with his work, I knew enough to know that his scientific view of the world was far removed from my own poetic conception of it.

'Only superficially,' I replied coolly, anxious to get out fast before natural courtesy prompted me to let the gnome foist one of Nightingale's unreadable tomes on me.

'Superficiality implies a lack of profundity,' he rejoined. 'Perhaps you'd be interested in a secondary work devoted to Nightingale's scientific research into Zamonian labyrinthology? It's a fascinating treatise by Dr Ostafan Kolibri, one of his most gifted pupils. I'm not exaggerating when I say that it sheds considerable light on the decipherment of labyrinths in general.'

'I'm not particularly interested in labyrinths, to be honest,' I said, backing away. 'I fear I'm in the wrong shop.'

'Oh, aren't you interested in the sciences? You're looking for belles-lettres? Escapist literature for refugees from reality? You're looking for *novels*? Then you have indeed come to the wrong address. I sell non-fiction only.' There was no hostility or arrogance in his tone. He sounded politely informative, nothing more.

I grasped the door handle. 'Please forgive me,' I said stupidly, turning it. 'I'm new in this city.'

'You come from Lindworm Castle?'

I stopped short. One of the invariable constants in the life of a dinosaur that walks on two legs is that everyone can tell his birthplace at a glance. I had yet to discover whether this was an advantage or a disadvantage.

'I suppose that's obvious,' I retorted.

'Please forgive my somewhat derogatory generalisation on the subject of fiction. I had to devise a few stock remarks designed to shake off the tourists who keep barging in and asking for signed first editions of the *Prince Sangfroid* novels. Although this is a purely non-fiction establishment, I myself have devoured many a novel from Lindworm Castle.' The dwarfish figure bent over a book-laden table and lit a candle. 'And please forgive the subdued lighting. I think better in the dark.'

The ignited wick shed a dramatic light on the little creature's face. The flame danced nervously at first, then steadied and became less bright. The proprietor was a Nocturnomath – that I could tell without ever having seen one before. The shape of his cranium was unmistakable, as I knew from various encyclopaedias, and indicated that he possessed at least three brains. I now realised that the mysterious clicks emanated from his skull. A Nocturnomath's thought processes are audible.

'My name is Ahmed ben Kibitzer.' The Nocturnomath extended a bunch of twiglike fingers. I shook them gingerly.

'I'm Optimus Yarnspinner,' I said.

'Have you published anything?'

'Not yet.'

'In that case you'll forgive me for not having read anything of yours.'

I laughed stiffly, feeling an utter fool. I was a literary nobody.

'But, as I said, I've devoted a substantial proportion of my life to Lindwormian literature. My doctoral dissertation was an analysis of the effect of the poikilothermic circulation of dinosaurian authors on their stylistic concinnity.'

'Really?' I said, as if I knew what he was talking about. 'And what conclusion did you come to?'

'That a cold-blooded circulation can be quite compatible with stylistic harmony and elegance. Lindworms are born writers, I can prove it scientifically.'

'That's very flattering.'

'In fact,' the gnome went on, 'I'm of the opinion that, from the purely organic point of view, your species is positively made for writing. Your long lifespan is an important aid to mature craftsmanship and your three claw-tipped fingers are ideal for gripping pen and pencil. As for your thick saurian hide, it's the finest protection against poor reviews.' He tittered. 'Lindworms have produced some of the finest novels in the history of Zamonian literature. One has only to think of *The Ill-Starred Chamber* by Sarto Iambicus, or Vappid Rhymester's *Drunk on Moonlight*, or Hyldia Playtanner's *Blind Flamingo*, *Nocturnal Nonsense*, *Song of the Oyster* and *Brittle Bait*! Not to mention Doylan Cone's *Sir Ginel*!'

'You've read *Sir Ginel*?'

'Most certainly! Do you remember the passage where the knight's monocle falls into his breastplate and he has to joust almost blind? Or where his lower jaw is dislocated by a blow from a mace and he can only communicate in sign language for an entire chapter? How I laughed! A comic masterpiece!'

I hadn't got that far. I had tackled the boring old novel at Dancelot's insistence but gave up after the first hundred pages – they were wholly devoted to the care and maintenance of the medieval lance – and hurled it into a corner.

'Of course,' I lied. 'His lower jaw – an absolute scream!'

'You have to plough through the hundred-page introduction devoted to the care and maintenance of the medieval lance,' said Kibitzer, 'but the author really gets going after that. Take the chapter in which he dispenses with the letter E for a hundred and fifty pages – a brilliant feat of lipogrammatism! Remember Sir Ginel's jovial little drinking song?'

The Nocturnomath cleared his throat and quoted:

> *'Come, landlord, fill again my glass,*
> *and fill again my dish.*
> *Those things apart, a buxom lass*
> *is all that I could wish.'*

I gave a knowing smile. 'Ah yes,' I said, 'a stroke of genius.' I hadn't got as far as that!

'But forget about novels!' exclaimed Kibitzer, who now had the bit between his teeth. 'Lindworm Castle has also produced some excellent non-fiction – *The Joys of Gardening*, for instance. A milestone in the description of domesticated nature.'

I was taken aback. 'You know Dancelot Wordwright?' I said, at last letting go of the door handle.

'Know him? You must be joking. I could quote him in my sleep:

'Thus, nature is our only solace. Almost instinctively, we make our way out into the open air, out into our gardens. We breathe more freely and our hearts grow lighter amid the rustle of the trees and beneath the stars. From the stars we come, to the stars we go. Life is but a journey into the unknown.'

This little Nocturnomath was better acquainted with Dancelot's work than I. A tear oozed from my left eye.

'But I'm sure you share my admiration for him, if a quotation from his work has such an emotional effect on you. That makes up for your ignorance of *Sir Ginel.*'

I gave a start. Damnation, Nocturnomaths were mind-readers – I'd forgotten that! I resolved to be more careful what I thought about in future.

'Thoughts cannot be suppressed like speech,' Kibitzer said with a smile. 'But there's no need to exert yourself. I already know so much about you, I can dispense with mind-reading. You're personally acquainted with Dancelot Wordwright, aren't you?'

'He was my authorial godfather. He died recently.'

'Oh. Really? Please forgive my insensitive question and accept my sincere condolences. The man was a genius.'

'Thank you. He himself would not have claimed as much.'

'That renders him doubly important. To possess the potential inherent in *The Joys of Gardening* and then limit yourself to writing a single book – that is true greatness.'

If only Dancelot could have heard those words during his lifetime! More tears welled up in my eyes.

'But do sit down! You must be tired out if you've come all the way from Lindworm Castle. Would you care for a cup of nutmeg coffee?' The antiquarian tottered over to a coffee pot perched on a bookshelf.

Quite suddenly, my limbs felt as heavy as lead. Having been on my feet since dawn, I'd scarcely rested at the hotel and then roamed the streets for hours. His words made me realise how weary I was. I sat down on a chair and wiped the tears from my eyes.

'Don't worry, I promise I won't delve into your thoughts any more,' Kibitzer said as he handed me a temptingly aromatic cup of coffee. 'May I, therefore, enquire in the traditional manner what brings you to Bookholm? My question isn't prompted by curiosity. I may be able to help you.' He gave me a friendly smile.

Perhaps a kindly providence had guided me to this shop, I thought. The Nocturnomath was by way of being a fan of Dancelot's writing, so why shouldn't I begin my quest with him?

'I'm looking for an author.'

'Then Bookholm is definitely a better place to start than, say, the Graveyard Marshes of Dullsgard.' Kibitzer's laugh at his own little joke sounded like an attack of asthma. I produced the manuscript.

'Perhaps you'd read this. I'm looking for the person who wrote it. I don't know his name or what he looks like. I don't even know if he's still alive.'

'You're looking for a phantom?' The Nocturnomath grinned. 'Very well, let me see.'

First he checked the quality of the paper by rubbing it between finger and thumb, a procedure typical of his trade. 'Hm, high-grade Grailsundian wove,' he muttered. 'Timberlake Paper Mills, 200 grammes.' He sniffed the pages. 'Slightly overacidified. A peach tint. Birchwood with a hint of pine needles. The bleaching agent was insufficiently stirred. A trifle woody at the edges.' This was the sort of antiquarian jargon I'd already heard on the lips of itinerant dealers in the streets.

Kibitzer ran his forefinger along the edges of the sheets. 'Unevenly trimmed. A nick every five millimetres at least. The guillotine was already obsolete, probably a Threadcutter dating from the century before last. The watermark was applied with cuttlefish ink, from which I infer that—'

'Perhaps you should read it,' I ventured to suggest.

'Eh?' Kibitzer seemed to awaken from a trance and stared at the first page for a long time. He was probably marvelling, just as I had, at the manuscript's calligraphic beauty. At last he proceeded to read it.

After a few moments he began to hum to himself like someone reading a score, as if I weren't there at all. He emitted several hoarse laughs, cried 'Yes,

yes, exactly!' and made an extremely agitated impression. What followed might have been an imitation of my own response to the text at Lindworm Castle. He alternated abruptly between paroxysms of laughter and floods of tears, fought for breath, smote his brow with the flat of his hand, and gave vent to repeated cries of approval and delight: 'Yes indeed! Yes! How true! It's so . . . so perfect!' Then he lowered the manuscript and sat staring into the gloom for several minutes, utterly motionless.

I took the liberty of clearing my throat. Kibitzer gave a start and gazed at me with his big, glowing eyes. Their amber-coloured irises were quivering.

'Well?' I asked. 'Do you know who the author is?'

'It's fantastic,' he muttered.

'I know. Whoever wrote it is a literary giant.'

Kibitzer handed the manuscript back, his eyes narrowing to slits. The whole shop seemed to grow darker.

'You must leave Bookholm,' he whispered. 'You're in mortal danger!'

'What?'

'Kindly leave these premises! Return to Lindworm Castle at once! Go anywhere you like, but get out of this city at all costs! Don't stay at a hotel on any account! Show no one else this manuscript – no one, understand? Destroy it! Make good your escape from Bookholm as soon as possible!'

Every one of these recommendations was the diametrical opposite of what I really intended. In the first place I should have liked to spend a little longer in the shop and chat with the kindly Nocturnomath. Secondly, I was delighted to have shaken the dust of Lindworm Castle off my feet and was damned if I'd go back there so soon. Thirdly, I would naturally return to my hotel at some stage because I'd left my things there. Fourthly, I had every intention of showing the manuscript to anyone who cared to read it. Fifthly, I would never, of course, destroy the most flawless piece of writing I'd ever set eyes on. And, sixthly, I had no wish to leave this magnificent city, which promised to be the fulfilment of all my dreams. Before I could utter even one of my rejoinders, however, the gnome had hustled me out of the shop.

'Please take my advice!' he whispered as he thrust me out of the door. 'Leave the city as soon as possible! Goodbye – no, farewell for ever! Hurry! Escape while you still can! And steer clear of the Triadic Circle!'

Then he slammed the door, bolted it from the inside and hung a 'Closed' sign in the window. The shop's interior became even darker than before.

Colophonius Regenschein

Iroamed the surrounding streets in a daze. Thanks to the homeless and exhausted condition in which I now found myself, dear readers, these emotional ups and downs had proved too much for me. First the distressing reminder of Dancelot, then Kibitzer's hospitable reception and finally his brusque dismissal . . . What an unrefined, wizened little prune of a fellow he was!

I knew that antiquarian booksellers, and especially the Bookholmians among them, were given to eccentric behaviour – indeed, their professional reputation depended on it, so to speak. But what had Kibitzer meant when he told me to avoid the Triadic Circle? Had he been referring to the sign on his door? He was probably just an oddball afflicted by extreme mood swings – and no wonder, if he persisted in reading Professor Abdul Nightingale's crack-brained writings!

I strove to shake off my recollection of the incident by planning my future course of action. First I needed to know more about this city and its unwritten laws. I needed a guidebook and a street map – even, if such a thing existed, a printed list of the conventions to be observed when visiting antiquarian bookshops. It was possible that I had unwittingly broken certain rules peculiar to Bookholm.

While debating these points I recalled the shop window containing Colophonius Regenschein's *Catacombs of Bookholm,* a work that was said to plumb the city's mysteries. I resolved to acquire the book and digest its contents over a few cups of coffee in some well-heated café. By so doing I could become an expert on Bookholm overnight and kill time without having to spend it in the dubious company of the white bat and the rampaging Bluddums in the Golden Quill. I would collect my things in the morning and change hotels.

It didn't take me long to find the bookshop again. The book was still in the window, so I paid the paltry sum it cost, bought a street map and antiquarian guide as well, and bore my acquisitions off to a nearby coffee shop. A nocturnal reading was in progress, which meant that every half-hour some wretched poet would mount a table and deliver a recitation for which he would, at Lindworm Castle, have been tarred, feathered and hurled from the battlements.

I stood marvelling for a long time in front of a blackboard on which all the delicious fare one could order was listed in chalk. I was bewildered by the abundance of food and drink bearing names with literary associations: *Printer's Ink Wine* and *Blood and Thunder Coffee*; *Sweetpaper Sandwiches* (they could be not only eaten but written on); *Muse's Kiss Cocoa* and *Liquid Inspiration* (the latter a brutally high-proof spirit); *Horror Candies* (to be eaten while reading thrillers, many of them with surprise fillings of vinegar, cod liver oil or desiccated ants); and seventeen types of pastries named after various classical poets, for example, *Bethelzia B. Binngrow Buns* and *Ardelf Nennytos Cookies*. Those in need of more substantial fare could gorge themselves on dishes named after popular novelists or their heroes, for instance *Prince Sangfroid Pie* or *Risotto à la Evsko Dosti*, but there was also a light *Syllabic Salad* incorporating alphabet spaghetti and trombophone mushrooms. It was enough to make your head spin.

Having pulled myself together at last, I ordered a big jug of *Midnight Oil Espresso* and a pastry known as a *Poet's Ringlet*. Then I retired to a table right beside the crackling stove in the furthest corner of the establishment. I took a swig of coffee and a bite of my delicious Poet's Ringlet, got out *The Catacombs of Bookholm* and began to read.

A dwarf with an unpleasantly shrill voice was reading out a long-winded essay on his aversion to sponges, not that this impaired my concentration too much. If what I am reading has the power to grip me, I can read under the most difficult circumstances.

And *The Catacombs of Bookholm* surpassed my expectations in every respect. The book was not only informative but enthralling, and of a literary quality unusual in a work of non-fiction. After only a few paragraphs the dwarf's frightful voice became mere background noise and little more intrusive than the twittering of a bird. Meanwhile, eager to plumb Bookholm's amazing mysteries, I was descending into its hopelessly convoluted labyrinth of tunnels in the company of Colophonius Regenschein, the city's greatest Bookhunter and hero.

Regenschein hadn't always been Bookholm's greatest Bookhunter, dear readers. Oh no, there had even been a time when his name wasn't Colophonius Regenschein at all. A resounding pseudonym was part of every Bookhunter's stock in trade and Regenschein differentiated himself from his colleagues at the very outset by choosing one with no warlike connotations.

His real name was Taron Trekko and he was just a roaming Vulphead whose travels had brought him to the City of Dreaming Books quite by chance. Indeed, literature had meant nothing to him at first. Like most Vulpheads, Trekko possessed a prodigious memory and used that gift to earn a living in taverns by multiplying hundred-digit numbers in his head while juggling with raw eggs. However, he happened to arrive in Bookholm just as a dispute broke out between the adherents of druidical arithmetic and Old Zamonian mathematics. This divided the population of Zamonia into two irreconcilably hostile camps. The result was that mass brawls occurred nearly every time a 'memory artiste' put on a show, so a Vulphead had only to put his nose round a taproom door for the landlord to hurl a jug at him.

Thus, Taron Trekko found himself threatened with starvation in the midst of a city filled with taverns patronised by folk eager for entertainment, but he soon discovered a far more lucrative way of making money than performing numerical tricks for drunks, namely, dealing in rare books. This was no brilliant feat of deduction on his part, given that nearly everyone in Bookholm dealt in books. However, there existed some particularly rare specimens for which demand never waned. These were the books on the *Golden List*. The volumes on this list could not be purchased in any of the city's antiquarian bookshops. Very seldom offered for sale and promptly snapped up by wealthy collectors bidding in competition, they were literary legends coveted by all, rather like the gigantic diamond reputed to lie hidden in the heart of Lindworm Castle.

One particular type of adventurers – they were known as Bookhunters – had specialised in running these precious works to earth in the bowels of Bookholm and bringing them to the surface. Many Bookhunters were hired by collectors or dealers, others went prospecting on their own account. The sums offered for volumes on the Golden List were so astronomical that a single specimen could make a Bookhunter wealthy for life.

It was a dangerous occupation – the most dangerous in all Bookholm. You, my courageous readers, may conceive of going in search of some book as an antiquarian's boring spare-time hobby, but here in the depths of this mysterious city it was more perilous than hunting Crystalloscorpions in the glass grottoes of Demon Range. Why? Because the catacombs of Bookholm teemed with dangers of a very special kind.

The labyrinthine tunnels were said to be connected to *Netherworld*, the mysterious Realm of Evil reputed to extend beneath the whole of Zamonia. According to Colophonius Regenschein, however, the dangers lurking in the darkness below the city were real and lethal enough to be able to dispense with the support of old wives' tales.

It is impossible to ascertain precisely when the very first Bookhunters descended into the darkness, but the assumption is that it must have been roughly when professional antiquarianism first became established in the city. Bookholm had been the centre of the Zamonian book trade for many hundreds – indeed, thousands – of years: from the time when the first handwritten volumes appeared to the present age of mass production.

It was discovered at a very early stage that the catacombs' dry atmosphere rendered them ideal places in which to store paper. Whole national libraries were deposited in them. This was where princes hid their literary treasures, book pirates their booty, dealers their first editions and publishers their stocks.

Bookholm wasn't really a city at first. It existed almost entirely below ground in the form of inhabited caves linked ever more closely by artificial tunnels, shafts, galleries and stairways, and occupied by tribes and communities of the most diverse life forms. All that existed on the surface were the mouths of the caves and a few huts. From these the city continued to develop above ground until it attained its present size.

There was a wild and anarchic period in Bookholm's history, a time devoid of law and order during which raids and forays, mayhem, murder and thoroughgoing wars were of daily occurrence below ground. The catacombs were ruled by warlike princes and ruthless book pirates who fought to the death and were forever wresting literary treasures away from each other. Books were carried off and concealed in the ground, whole collections deliberately buried by their owners to hide them from the pirates. Wealthy dealers had themselves mummified after death and entombed with their literary gems. There were one or two valuable books for the sake of which whole sections of the catacombs were converted into death traps with converging walls, spear-lined pitfalls and spring-operated blades capable of transfixing or beheading incautious thieves. Intruders who activated a tripwire might instantly flood a tunnel with water or acid, or be crushed to death by falling beams. Other tunnels were purposely infested with dangerous insects and animals that bred unchecked, rendering the catacombs more hazardous still. The Bookemists, a secret society of antiquarians with alchemistic tendencies, celebrated their grisly rites down below. It was believed that the so-called *Hazardous Books* originated during this lawless period.

All of the catacombs' rational inhabitants were driven from them by the epidemics and natural disasters, earthquakes and subterranean volcanic eruptions that followed, and only the toughest and most stubborn remained behind.

This marked the true beginning of civilised life in the city and the birth of Bookholm's professional antiquarianism. Many treasures were brought to the surface, bookshops and dwellings arose, guilds were founded, laws enacted, crimes proscribed and taxes raised. Some of the entrances to the subterranean world were built over and others bricked up; those that remained were sealed off with doors and manhole covers, and rigorously guarded. From then on, only those parts of the catacombs that had been surveyed, mapped and pronounced safe could be entered, and then only by dealers who had obtained licences granting them access to the areas in question. They were entitled to exploit licensed tunnels and sell any books they found there. They were also at liberty to explore deeper levels, but it was not long before none of them ventured to do so after the boldest of their number had either returned more dead than alive or failed to return at all. This was how the first Bookhunters appeared on the scene.

They were audacious adventurers who had been commissioned by dealers or collectors to find rare books for them. Although no Golden List existed at this time, legends arose concerning very rare items. The Bookhunters began by looking for scarce and valuable works at random, often proceeding on the simple assumption that a book was older and more valuable the deeper it was located. Most of them were uncouth, insensitive souls, ex-mercenaries or criminals with little knowledge of literature and antiquarianism – in fact, some couldn't even read. Their principal qualification was an absence of fear.

Then as now, the Bookhunter's trade was governed by a few simple laws. Since those who had entered the catacombs could never be certain whether or where they would emerge, the following rule applied: the bookseller via whose premises Bookhunters regained the surface was entitled to sell their haul and retain ten per cent of the proceeds. Another ten per cent went to the Zamonian exchequer and the lion's share to the Bookhunters themselves. It was, however, an open secret that they also used other, illegal routes – sewers, ventilation shafts or tunnels of their own – and sold their booty on the black market.

As time went by the Bookhunters developed various methods of finding their way back to the surface. They marked bookshelves with chalk, unreeled balls of twine behind them or laid trails of confetti, rice, glass beads or pebbles. They drew primitive maps and illuminated many stretches of tunnel with lamps in which phosphorescent jellyfish were immersed in nutrient fluid. They staked out their territories, hewed springs of drinking water out of the living rock and established supply depots. It might be said that, in their own modest way, they brought a touch of civilisation to the catacombs of Bookholm.

For all that, bookhunting remained a hazardous form of livelihood. Successive generations of Bookhunters had to conquer new areas of the catacombs, and the deeper they went the greater the dangers became. Their work was made no easier by hitherto unknown life forms, huge insects, winged bloodsuckers, volcanic worms, fanged beetles and poisonous snakes. But every Bookhunter's most dangerous foe continued to be his own kind.

The rarer the really valuable books became, the fiercer the competition for them. Where Bookhunters had once been able to help themselves to a superabundance of literary treasures, several of them would now go hunting for the same long-lost library or the same rare item on the Golden List. This often triggered a cut-throat contest of which there could be only one winner. The catacombs of Bookholm were strewn with the skeletons of Bookhunters with axes embedded in their bleached skulls. The more refined manners became in the city overhead, the cruder and more brutal they became in the world beneath. In the end a permanent state of war prevailed there – a lawless, merciless conflict of each against all. Taron Trekko could not have chosen a less favourable moment to assume the professional name Colophonius Regenschein and become a Bookhunter.

He was, in fact, the first of his kind to become one. Being a Vulphead, he was positively predestined for that profession. Vulpheads are tough and in prime physical condition. They possess excellent powers of recall, an above-average sense of direction and a wealth of imagination. Most Bookhunters were distinguished by their fearlessness and brutality alone, whereas Regenschein brought a new attribute into play: his intelligence. He found it harder than they did to master his fears, was not as strong and ruthless, and did not possess the same criminal energy. But he did have a well-laid plan and was determined to become the most successful Bookhunter of all time. In this respect his phenomenal memory would prove to be his most important asset.

While still living on charity (and, as he himself confessed, on petty theft and stolen food), he acquired the knowledge he deemed indispensable to his aims by spending long hours in the municipal library and numerous bookshops. He learnt dozens of ancient languages, memorised old maps of Bookholm's underworld and combined the information he gleaned into a grand plan of action.

He studied the history of book manufacture from the handwritten manuscript to the modern printed volume and found temporary employment at a printing works and a paper mill. He learnt to distinguish between different papers and inks blindfolded, so as to be able to identify them by touch and smell in total darkness. He attended lectures on geology, archaeology and mining at Bookholm University, studied books on subterranean flora and fauna and made a note of which of the catacombs' plants, fungi, sponges, reptiles and insects were edible and which poisonous, which harmless and which dangerous. He learnt how to stave off starvation for days by chewing certain roots, how to recognise the most nutritious species of worms and catch them, and how to detect veins of drinking water in the rock by means of geological features.

Next, Regenschein became apprenticed to one of Bookholm's ex-libris perfumers. This was a profession unique to the city. For hundreds of years, wealthy collectors had made a practice of impregnating their books with perfumes manufactured to order. This lent their treasures an olfactory stamp of ownership, an aromatic ex-libris that was not only detectable and unmistakable, even in the dark, but invaluable to anyone concealing his books beneath the surface.

Colophonius Regenschein was equipped with a good sense of smell. Although Vulpheads' noses are not as sensitive as those of Wolpertings, or even of dogs, because their canine instincts and faculties have atrophied over the generations, they can nonetheless recognise olfactory nuances undetectable by other Zamonian life forms. Regenschein sniffed his way through the whole library of scents belonging to Olfactorio de Papyros, an ex-libris perfumer whose family business had helped to endow legendary collections and rare volumes with their unique fragrances for many generations. He memorised the books' titles and their authors' names, the details of where and when they had disappeared, and any other particulars about them he could find. He sniffed leather and paper, linen and pasteboard, and learnt how these different materials reacted to being steeped in lemon juice, rosewater and hundreds of other aromatic essences.

The *Smoked Cookbooks* published by the Saffron Press, the balm-scented manuscripts of the naturopath Dr Greenfinger, the *Pine-Needle Pamphlets* of the Foliar Period, Prince Zaan of Florinth's autobiography (rubbed with almond kernels), the *Rickshaw Demons' Curry Book*, the ethereal library of mad Prince Oggnagogg – Colophonius Regenschein became acquainted with every book perfume ever made. He learnt that books could smell of soil, snow, tomatoes, seaweed, fish, cinnamon, honey, wet fur, dried grass and charred wood, and he also learnt how these odours could change over the centuries, mingling with the aromas of the catacombs to such an extent that they often underwent a complete transformation.

In addition to this, of course, Regenschein studied Zamonian literature. He read everything that came his way, whether novel, poem or essay, play script, biography or collection of letters. He became a walking encyclopaedia. Every last corner of his memory was crammed with texts and particulars relating to Zamonian creative writing and the life and works of the most varied authors.

Colophonius Regenschein trained his body as well as his mind. He developed a breathing technique that enabled him to survive even in the most airless conditions. He also went on a slimming diet that reduced his weight sufficiently for him to squeeze through the narrowest of passages and fissures in the rock. In the end, when he felt thoroughly qualified to embark on a career as a Bookhunter, he decided to do so with a bang that would be heard all over Bookholm.

He did not choose any old bookshop for his first excursion, nor did he set off on an aimless quest. No, he turned his expedition into a venture that evoked scornful accusations of megalomania from everyone in the city. Through the medium of the Live Newspapers he announced exactly when and where he would descend into the catacombs and when and where he would reappear on the surface. He also gave advance notice of the three books he intended to unearth:

Princess Daintyhoof, the only surviving signed first edition of Hermo Phink's legendary account of how the Wolpertings originated, bound in Nurn leaves;

Treatise on Cannibalism, an account of the customs and conventions of mad Prince Oggnagogg's Cadaverous Cannibals by Orlog Goo, who was devoured by his objects of study on completing the book; and

The Twelve Thousand Precepts, the Bookemists' abstruse list of rules, possibly the most scandalous book in the whole of Zamonia.

Regenschein's announcement was somewhat presumptuous, given that the three books in question had for many years been regarded as lost and stood high on the Golden List, so even one of them would have made its discoverer wealthy. Last but not least, Regenschein further announced – doubtless so as to render his venture more spectacular still – that he would publicly commit suicide if he failed to bring the above-named works to the surface within a week.

Everyone in Bookholm agreed that the Vulphead had lost his wits. It was thought absolutely impossible to do what no other Bookhunter had succeeded in doing over the years, namely, to snaffle three Golden List books at once, let alone to do so within the space of a single week.

Amid roars of sarcastic laughter from a large crowd of spectators, the audacious Vulphead descended into the catacombs of Bookholm at the appointed hour. Bets were laid against his chances of success as the week went by. On the predicted day a vast crowd assembled round the bookshop from which he proposed to emerge after regaining the surface. Just before noon Colophonius Regenschein staggered out of the main entrance and into the street. Sodden from head to foot with blood, he had an iron arrow protruding from his right shoulder and was carrying three books under his arm: *Princess Daintyhoof*, *Treatise on Cannibalism* and *The Twelve Thousand Precepts*. He smiled, waved to the marvelling crowd – and collapsed unconscious.

In the next chapter of his book Regenschein described in every detail how he had planned this expedition, made long-term preparations for it and finally carried it out. He had begun by combining numerous descriptions of various parts of the catacombs into a complete mental picture of their layout. Then he assembled all the facts he had learnt while studying the three books he was after. He knew exactly when they had been printed, who had printed them and the addresses of the bookshops that had taken delivery of the first editions. Next, he traced their subsequent history with the aid of documentary records. He discovered that part of the first printing had been destroyed by a big fire, that some salvaged copies had been sold to another bookshop, that unsaleable stocks had been pulped, that individual copies had survived, and so on and so forth. He knew from diaries, letters and publishers' financial accounts how well or badly the books had sold and why, and where they had been consigned to the rubbish dump. The same sources yielded other useful items of information, for instance that a copy of the first edition of *Princess Daintyhoof* had turned up in the window of a certain bookshop, that it had eventually fetched an immense sum at auction and that it had disappeared after the purchaser had been robbed on the way home. Regenschein discovered that the putative thief, a celebrated book pirate whose sobriquet was Gory Hands, had been walled up alive by a fellow criminal named Blorr the Bricklayer. While examining the latter's papers, he further discovered a map on which Blorr had marked all the places where he had stored his victims complete with their possessions.

Once in the catacombs, Colophonius Regenschein was greatly assisted by his study of Zamonian literary history and book printing. He could classify every author and literary school, knew which antiquarian booksellers devoted themselves to certain writers or specialised fields, and could determine from a book's binding and the condition of its spine which edition it belonged to, when this had been published and how many copies had been printed. Regenschein had no need to ferret systematically through each stack of volumes like other Bookhunters. Armed with his jellyfish lamp, he had only to hurry along the passages glancing swiftly to left and right. He even derived valuable information from the order in which various subterranean collections had been stored and this guided him to the treasures he was seeking.

His apprenticeship with the ex-libris perfumer now paid off. One sniff sufficed to tell him that a whole roomful of books had once belonged to a collector who had imbued all his volumes with the aroma of freshly brewed coffee. Regenschein could tell for sure that the copy of *Princess Daintyhoof* he sought was not among them because it had belonged to an eccentric with such an insane love of cats that he impregnated his entire collection with the unpleasant odour of feline urine. A less proficient Bookhunter would now have gone sniffing for this everywhere, but Regenschein knew that the olfactory components of cat's piss took on the unique and penetrating smell of rotting seaweed after a century at most underground. When he was at last confronted by a time-worn brick wall in the depths of the catacombs and detected a smell of the sea, he knew that he had found his first book.

Where *The Twelve Thousand Precepts* was concerned, Regenschein's study of literary history had acquainted him with the year in which it had been banned and burnt by the Atlantean vice squad. As always in such cases, one copy had been ceremoniously conveyed into the catacombs and walled up there. Discovered by Bookhunters a century later, it changed hands several times before being destroyed by a bookshop fire – or so the authorities claimed. Regenschein, who had scoured the municipal records for that year, came across a bankruptcy petition lodged by the dealer who had owned the relevant bookshop. Further research in Bookholm's municipal library had enabled him to unearth the diary of the dealer's wife, in which she confessed that her husband had torched the shop himself and hidden his most valuable books in the catacombs. Having helped him to make away with them, she was able to give a precise description of their whereabouts.

Regenschein found the *Treatise on Cannibalism* by employing a similar process of detection. However, dear readers, I will spare you a full account of this and confine myself to saying that it entailed a detailed knowledge of paper manufacture in ancient times, of the microscopic technique required to cast lead type for footnotes, of the decline of Ornian isosyllabism during Zamonia's Singing Wars and the preservation of goatskin covers by means of linseed oil.

In short, Colophonius Regenschein found the books he was after even before the appointed week had elapsed, or within three days, so he had to stick it out in the catacombs for the remaining four in order to meet his self-imposed deadline exactly.

When he finally made for the surface he was attacked by another Bookhunter. As I already mentioned, the only professional qualification Regenschein lacked was the criminal initiative possessed by his colleagues. He simply hadn't considered the possibility that someone might try to rob him of his haul.

That someone was Rongkong Koma, Bookholm's most notorious and dangerous Bookhunter, an evil individual who owed all his successes to the fact that he never went looking for rare books himself but stole them from others on principle. Having learnt of Regenschein's grandiloquent announcement, he lay in wait beneath the bookshop from which his prospective victim was due to emerge. That was all he had to do apart from spearing Regenschein in the back with an iron javelin.

Fortunately for Regenschein, Rongkong Koma missed his heart and merely pierced his shoulder. A ferocious duel ensued. Although unarmed, Regenschein managed to inflict so many wounds on Koma with his canine teeth that the rapacious Bookhunter lost a great deal of blood and took to his heels, but not without swearing eternal enmity.

The Vulphead only just made it to the surface before passing out and did not regain consciousness for a week. He had lived up to his ambitious predictions, however, and the Live Newspapers were quick to spread the word. Overnight, Colophonius Regenschein had become the most famous Bookhunter of all.

He could also have become the best-paid Bookhunter of all, because collectors and dealers bombarded him with offers. But Regenschein turned them all down. Although he resumed bookhunting when he had recuperated – this time armed and forever on his guard against Rongkong Koma – he kept most of the books he acquired for himself. His ultimate intention soon became clear: Colophonius Regenschein aimed to collect one copy of every last book on the Golden List. He managed to do this in an incredibly short space of time and he also returned to the surface laden with other books which, although not on the list, were valuable in the extreme. These he sold, using the proceeds to purchase one of the handsomest old buildings in Bookholm, where he set up the *Library of the Golden List* as a place in which rare works could be studied under supervision for scholarly purposes. Colophonius Regenschein thus became Bookholm's greatest hero: a combination of adventurer, patron and paragon.

Despite his wealth and fame, however, and although his expeditions became ever more hazardous, Regenschein could not resist the lure of the catacombs. He was as hated down there as he was popular in the world above. Some of the most brutal Bookhunters dogged his footsteps and tried to steal his finds. They included Nassim Ghandari, nicknamed 'The Noose' because he crept up behind his victims and garrotted them with cheese wire; Imran the Invisible, so called because he was thin enough to be mistaken in the dark for a pit prop – until you were suddenly transfixed by a poisoned arrow from his blowpipe; Reverberus Echo, whose talent for vocal and acoustic mimicry led his victims astray and lured them into death traps, after which he cannibalised them to cover his tracks; and Lembo 'The Snake' Chekhani, a Bookhunter who had sunk so low, morally speaking, that he wriggled along on his belly camouflaged in manuscripts, as supple and attenuated as his nickname implied. Tarik Tabari, Hunk Hoggno, Erman de Griswold, Hadwin Paxi, Azlif Khesmu, Horgul the Hairless, 'Blondie' Snotsniff, the Toto Twins – Colophonius Regenschein became involuntarily acquainted with all of these Bookhunters and several more besides, but none of them managed to rob him of a single book and most sustained severe injuries in the course of their encounters with him. Some abandoned the profession and others steered well clear of him in the future. Only one repeatedly and deliberately challenged his supremacy: Rongkong Koma the Terrible. The most fearsome of all Bookhunters lay in wait for Regenschein again and again, doggedly thirsting for revenge, and the two of them fought almost a dozen strenuous duels from which neither emerged a clear winner, usually because they broke off hostilities by reason of exhaustion. One such confrontation mentioned by Regenschein was a crossbow duel after which, riddled with poisoned arrows, he just managed to reach the safety of the bookshop owned by Ahmed ben Kibitzer, who nursed him back to health. I'm sure, dear readers, that you can imagine how astonished I was, while reading Regenschein's book, to come across the name of the crotchety little Nocturnomath who had tried to send me packing.

But Bookhunters weren't the only danger that lurked beneath Bookholm. No one had ever descended as far into the catacombs as Colophonius Regenschein, and no one had set eyes on as many of its marvels and monstrosities. He wrote of miles-deep caverns filled with millions of ancient volumes in the process of being devoured by phosphorescent worms and moths. He wrote of tunnels infested with blind and transparent insects that hunted anything within reach of their yards-long antennae; of frightful winged creatures – he called them *Harpyrs* – whose frightful screams had almost robbed him of his sanity on one occasion; of the *Rusty Gnomes' Bookway*, an immense subterranean railroad system said to have been constructed thousands of years ago by a dwarfish race of very skilful craftsmen. He also told of *Unholm*, the catacombs' gigantic rubbish dump, where millions of books lay mouldering away.

Regenschein firmly believed in the existence of the *Fearsome Booklings*, a race of one-eyed creatures dwelling deep in the bowels of Bookholm and reputed to devour (alive) anything that came their way. He even entertained no doubts about the popular myth of a race of giants said to have lived in the deepest and biggest of all the subterranean caverns, where they stoked Zamonia's volcanoes. He had seen so many incredible sights in the catacombs that he regarded nothing, absolutely nothing, as being beyond the bounds of possibility.

Although his book had been accused of transgressing the frontier between truth and fiction, it did so in such a subtle way that I didn't care which page I was on. Regenschein's writing utterly enthralled me. I devoured chapter after chapter as Bookholm's nightlife raged around me, pausing only occasionally to signal for another pot of coffee before avidly reading on. Alas, dear readers, I cannot possibly summarise all the details Regenschein disclosed about the world beneath my feet, there were simply too many of them.

I will, however, make mention of one chapter, for it was in that one, the last of all, that Regenschein's book really took off. It was devoted to the *Shadow King*.

The story of the Shadow King was one of the more recent legends – only a few score years old – about the Bookholmian underworld. It told of the birth of a being said to have established a reign of terror in the catacombs far surpassing any of the Bookhunters' atrocities. The legend went as follows:

Many shadows exist in the gloom of the catacombs. Shadows of living creatures, of dead things, of vermin that creep, crawl and fly, of Bookhunters, of stalagmites and stalactites. A multifarious race of silhouettes dancing restlessly over the tunnel roofs and book-lined walls, they strike terror into many intruders or drive them insane. One day in the not too distant past, so legend had it, these incorporeal beings grew tired of their anarchic living conditions and elected a leader. They superimposed one shadow, one silhouette, one shade of darkness on another until all these became amalgamated into a demicreature. Half alive and half dead, half solid and half insubstantial, half visible and half invisible, he became their ruler and spiritual executor. In other words, the Shadow King.

This was only the popular version of the legend, for there were several different theories about who or what the Shadow King really was. Bookhunters claimed he was the wrathful spirit of the Dreaming Books, their incarnate anger at having been forgotten and buried in the catacombs. They believed that this spirit had come to wreak revenge on all living creatures, and that he dwelt in a subterranean abode named *Shadowhall Castle*. Such was the Bookhunters' version.

Those booksellers who still ventured some distance into the catacombs asserted that the Shadow King was nothing more than a monstrous parasite, a cross between an insect and a bat produced by the labyrinths' unwholesome atmosphere, and that its sole aim was to destroy their precious books. Such was the booksellers' version.

Scientists, on the other hand, endeavoured to prove that the Shadow King was a very ancient life form that had finally made its way upwards from the nether regions of the cave system. Far from pursuing a definite objective, they declared, it blindly followed its animal instincts and attacked anything it encountered because it needed sustenance. Such was the scientists' version.

The Ugglies believed that the Shadow King would spell the end of Bookholm. They predicted that he would unleash a catastrophe so immense and all-encompassing that it would wipe the city from the face of the earth. Such was the Ugglies' version.

The children of Bookholm, by contrast, were convinced that the Shadow King was an evil spirit that made horrific noises in their clothes cupboards at night. Such was the demon-in-the-wardrobe version.

The one point on which all agreed was that the Shadow King really existed. Whatever he was, whether phantom, animal or monster, many had heard him, some had been hunted by him and a few even killed by him. Those who had heard him likened his voice to the rustle of a book's pages fluttering in the wind. As for those who had seen him, they were now dead.

Many a Bookhunter's bloodstained and horribly mutilated corpse had been found, often with tiny pieces of paper lodged in the hundreds of cuts inflicted on it. The popular explanation of this phenomenon was that the Shadow King slew his victims with a weapon made of paper, possibly with one of the so-called Hazardous Books. And sometimes, on exceptionally windless nights, the whole of Bookholm could hear his spine-chilling howls rising from the depths.

Colophonius Regenschein, too, was firmly convinced of the Shadow King's existence, but not, like most other people, of his fundamentally evil disposition. He even believed that this mysterious creature had once saved his life when he fell into a trap laid for him by Rongkong Koma. The latter had meant to crush him to death beneath a huge bookcase, but someone had thrust the massive piece of furniture aside before it could land on him. Although Regenschein's saviour had disappeared by the time he scrambled to his feet unscathed, he felt sure it was the Shadow King.

He had been obsessed with this living legend ever since. He aimed to prove his theory that the Shadow King was an intelligent, benevolent being, not savage and malign, by hunting and capturing him, but not in order to kill him or put him on show: he wanted to gain the Shadow King's friendship and then release him.

Regenschein had part of his house converted into a barred enclosure got up to resemble the catacombs, complete with subdued jellyfish lighting and book-lined walls. He believed that the Shadow King would feel at home there and become habituated to Overworld, and one day, when he had been submitted to thorough scientific research, he would be granted his freedom.

In the last few pages of his book Regenschein described his preparations for the expedition and announced his intention of writing a sequel documenting his quest for the Shadow King. His research had led him to contact a collector and literary scholar named Pfistomel Smyke, who was reputed to have an extensive knowledge of the legends about the Shadow King and the books devoted to him. An acknowledged expert, Smyke was so taken with Regenschein's project that he helped him as much as he could and invested some of his own money in it. It was Pfistomel Smyke's old house in the heart of the city from which Colophonius Regenschein was said to have set off on his expedition into the catacombs.

But the final words in *The Catacombs of Bookholm* had been written by his publisher. He appended a melancholy postscript in which he reported that Colophonius Regenschein's descent into the catacombs from the home of Pfistomel Smyke was the last occasion on which the greatest of all Bookhunters had been seen. Sad to relate, my intrepid readers, his quest for the Shadow King was a venture from which he never returned.

Mulled Coffee and Bee-Bread

I shut the book and drew a deep breath. An explorer and adventurer, scholar and bibliophile – one who had, to crown everything, met a mysterious end in the service of literature . . . Colophonius Regenschein was indeed a hero after my own heart.

The poetry reading had ended long ago. The audience had dispersed and only a few tables were still occupied by a handful of customers drinking coffee or chatting together. One of them, seated alone at the table opposite mine, was unashamedly grinning at me. He was a Hoggling, a wire-haired, well-fed specimen of the breed wearing a black overcoat. He raised his coffee cup. 'To Colophonius Regenschein!' he said. 'The greatest Bookhunter of all!'

He screwed up his porcine eyes and winked at me. 'May I stand you a mulled coffee?' he asked amiably. 'And a slice of bee-bread to go with it, perhaps?'

I had no objection. I'd finished the book, my coffee pot was empty and I was hungry again. Any form of refreshment that didn't deplete my slender purse was only too welcome. I thanked him and sat down at his table.

'To what do I owe the honour?' I asked.

'Anyone who takes an interest in Colophonius Regenschein deserves a mulled coffee. And a slice of bee-bread.'

He signalled to a waiter.

'I had no idea he was such an interesting character,' I said.

'The most glamorous in the history of Bookholm, believe me. Will you be staying here long?'

'I only just got here.'

'*I only just got here* – a good title for a book,' said the Hoggling, jotting something down on a notepad in front of him. 'Forgive me, it's an occupational disease of mine: I have a compulsion to think up saleable book titles. You're from Lindworm Castle?'

I sighed. 'How did you guess?'

The Hoggling laughed. 'I'm sorry. I'm sure it must get on your nerves, having your address tattooed on your forehead, so to speak.'

'Oh well, there are worse things.'

'There certainly are, especially when the address is such a distinguished one. Authors are highly esteemed in this city.'

'I've yet to become one.'

'*I've yet to become one* – another good title! Interesting. So you're a talent on the point of bursting into flower. That must be the finest moment in any literary career. Your heart is overflowing with emotional vitality, your mind ablaze with ideas.'

'Mine isn't, I'm afraid. Those are stereotyped notions of the creative urge. At this moment, for instance, my mind is a complete blank.'

'Why not write about *that*? Your fear of the virgin sheet of paper, your dread of becoming a burnt-out case before your time – a fantastic subject!'

I remembered the manuscript in my pocket and couldn't help laughing. 'That's a cliché too,' I said.

'You're right.' The Hoggling chuckled. 'What do I know about writing? I'm only good at figures. Permit me to introduce myself: Claudio Harpstick, literary agent.' He produced a business card and handed it to me.

Claudio Harpstick

Impresario · Literary Agent · Legal Adviser

Legal and Mediatory
Services of All Kinds
We Complete Your Tax Returns!

7 Cinnamon Lane, Bookholm

'You advise authors?'

'That's my job. You need some advice?'

'Not right now. I've yet to write anything I might need advice on.'

'Give it time, give it time. Maybe you'll remember my card when the moment comes.'

The waiter brought our order: mulled coffee scented with nutmeg and huge doorsteps of rye bread liberally daubed with butter and liquid honey in which dead bees were floating. I stared at them in astonishment. Harpstick grinned. 'A local speciality,' he said. 'It takes a bit of getting used to, but in time you can't have enough of it. Rye bread warm from the oven spread with peppered butter and honey with roasted bees in it. The bees are detoxified and have their stings removed prior to roasting, so don't be afraid. They're deliciously crisp and crunchy.'

I picked up my slice of bread.

'Take care for all that!' Harpstick warned. 'Once in a blue moon a bee's sting *hasn't* been removed. If the poison gets into your bloodstream you may be in for a few really nasty weeks of lockjaw and delirium. The bees are Demonic bees from Honey Valley, an exceptionally aggressive variety. Still, that's one of the attractions of Bookholmian bee-bread: the subliminal danger, the hint of uncertainty – the buzz, so to speak. It helps if you chew slowly and watch out for stings. You get more out of it that way.'

Gingerly, I bit off a morsel and chewed it with care. The bees tasted delicious, rather like toasted almonds. I glunked* my teeth appreciatively.

'Really excellent,' I said.

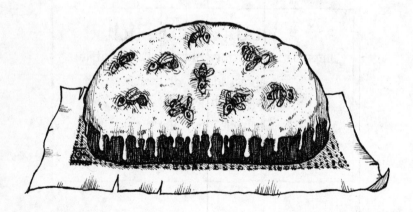

---

* Translator's Note: My apologies, dear readers, but I can only guess at the meaning of the verb 'glunk'. I devised the neologism myself as a translation of a Zamonian word I had never met before. Probably drawn from Lindworm Castle dialect, it almost certainly describes something which only Lindworms do with their teeth in order to produce a sound expressive of appreciation. I myself spent several days trying to make appreciative noises with my teeth, but to no avail.

'Try the mulled coffee,' said Harpstick. 'It's the best in the city.'

I took a sip. The hot, strong beverage suffused my stomach with an agreeable sensation of warmth. The blood shot to my head, rendering me slightly euphoric.

'There's a good dash of *ushan* in it – that's a fifty-five per cent proof spirit from the DeLucca district – so treat the coffee with caution too,' Harpstick said with a chuckle.

I nodded. I had never in my life drunk anything stronger than wine. Fifty-five per cent! These city folk certainly knew how to live. Far from home and slightly tipsy, I felt wild and free.

'Were you personally acquainted with Regenschein?' I asked, loquacious all of a sudden. 'What's he like?'

'I was invited to several parties at his home, so I was able to admire his library. I was present when he returned from his first expedition and collapsed before our very eyes, and also when he went in search of the Shadow King.'

'Do you believe he's dead?'

'I hope so.'

'I don't understand.'

'I hope so for *his* sake. Nobody knows exactly what goes on beneath this city' – Harpstick stamped the floor twice – 'but one thing's for sure: it isn't very pleasant. Regenschein disappeared five years ago. He's entombed in books, so to speak.'

'Good title,' I blurted out. '*Entombed in Books.*'

Harpstick stared at me in surprise.

'True,' he said, jotting it down on his notepad. 'If he's still alive,' he went on in a low voice, more to himself than to me, 'he'll have been down there for five long years. Not an enviable fate.'

'You believe in all those legends?' I asked with a smirk. 'The Shadow King, the Fearsome Booklings, Shadowhall Castle and so on?'

He looked at me gravely.

'No one in this city doubts that things exist down there which Bookholm would be better off without,' he said. 'Lawlessness, anarchy, chaos. Don't run away with the idea that we spread these rumours to attract tourists. Just imagine what we could make of the catacombs if they were fully accessible! Eighty to ninety per cent of the city is unexploited – out of bounds and controlled by who knows what weird creatures. You think that's desirable from a commercial point of view? Far from it!'

Harpstick was growing agitated. His face registered genuine indignation.

'On the other hand, we can't shut our eyes to what keeps happening there. I've seen a few of those who have ventured into the catacombs and made it back to the surface again. People with limbs torn off, people covered with bites and incapable of doing more than scream or babble inanities before they died. One of them drove a knife into his heart before my very eyes.'

Harpstick's porcine eyes were unnaturally big and bright. They seemed to look right through me at the frightful scene he had just recalled. Feeling embarrassed, I sipped my coffee and stared at my distorted reflection in its surface.

Harpstick gave himself a little shake and swigged at his own cup. Then he leant over, punched me playfully on the arm and grinned.

'But enough of that. Bookholm has its good sides too. What brings you to our city?'

I didn't feel like talking about my sad bereavement.

'I'm looking for someone,' I said.

'I see. A publisher?'

'No. An author.'

'Name?'

'I don't know.'

'What has he published?'

'Nothing.'

'What does he look like?'

'No idea.'

'Aha, then you can't fail to find him.' Harpstick gave a jovial laugh.

I briefly debated the Nocturnomath's warning. Then I fished out the manuscript.

'This is a short story of his.'

'Fine, that's almost as good as a calling card. May I see it?'

I hesitated for a moment, then handed it over. Harpstick began to read. Unobtrusively, I leant forward so as to study his reactions. He betrayed no emotion at all, humming softly to himself. He read quickly, joylessly, with the corners of his mouth turned down, like most people whose profession entails

74

a great deal of reading. I searched his face for signs of amazement or enthusiasm but could detect nothing of the kind. Halfway through the story he broke off and stared at me uncomprehendingly.

'Well?' he said. 'Why are you looking for him?'

'Surely you can see why?'

He gave the manuscript another glance.

'No. Have I missed something?'

'Don't you find the writing exceptional?'

'Exceptional in what way?'

'Exceptionally good.'

'This? No.' He handed the manuscript back.

I was speechless.

'I'll let you in on a secret,' said Harpstick. He looked around furtively and lowered his voice as if about to make some compromising confession.

'That story may really be exceptionally good. It may also be the worst trash ever written. If there's one person *utterly and completely* incapable of judging which it is, it's me. I can't tell good writing from a slice of bee-bread. I dread to think how much great literature I've held in my trotters without realising it. You want to know what really interests me?'

'Yes,' I lied politely.

'Bricks.'

'Bricks?'

'Bricks and mortar. I adore bricklaying. Every evening I go out into my garden and build a little brick wall. It's my way of unwinding. Next morning I knock it down, the following evening I rebuild it and so on. I love the smell of damp mortar, the fresh air, the exercise, the aching muscles. I get nice and tired, that's why I sleep so well.'

I nodded.

'In my profession it isn't a question of telling good literature from bad. Really good literature is seldom appreciated in its own day. The best authors die poor, the bad ones make money – it's always been like that. What do I, an agent, get out of a literary genius who won't be discovered for another hundred years? I'll be dead myself by then. Successful incompetents are what I need.'

'That's honest of you.'

Harpstick looked at me anxiously.

'Have I been *too* honest?' He sighed. 'I'm far too quick to speak my mind – it's my weak point. Many people find the truth hard to stomach.'

'I'm determined not to let the truth spoil the pleasure I take in my work,' I said. 'Writers have a hard time and very seldom get their due, I realise that.'

'An admirable attitude. Stick to it and you'll save yourself a lot of grief. Me, I'm good with people. That's my principal asset. I'm as good at dealing with sensitive authors as I am with hard-nosed publishers. I'm like a lubricant: almost unnoticeable and invisible but ubiquitous and indispensable. Nobody thinks I matter and plenty of people despise me – even a few of my best clients! – but the printing presses wouldn't roll without me. I'm the oil in the works.'

Harpstick took another hefty swig of coffee and dabbed his lips.

'This could be the finest short story in Zamonian literary history,' he said, tapping the manuscript. 'It could also be the maunderings of an untalented hack – I've no idea. I can read the words but I can't assess them. To me, every manuscript is the same: blah-blah-blah, just words strung together, nothing more. It could be my wife's shopping list or the most exquisite poem by Photonion Kodiak, I couldn't care less. And do you know what that means to someone in my profession? It's a boon. If I were capable of it, I might fall in love with this story, just as you have, and devote my life to tracing its author. I might even find him and make an unsuccessful attempt to market him. Then I wouldn't do what I'll be doing tomorrow morning, which is to secure Sandro Trockel a lucrative contract for three more books in his *Illiterate* series.'

I was familiar with Trockel's work. His books, which contained no text whatsoever, bore a large, simplified line drawing of some object or animal on every page. They were extremely popular with illiterates and sold in vast numbers.

'I may possibly – *possibly* – be able to help you even so,' Harpstick went on. 'I can give you the address of an antiquarian bookshop in the city centre. The owner is Bookholm's foremost expert on manuscripts. Here.'

He handed me another business card. It read:

'Pfistomel Smyke?' I asked in surprise. 'You mean . . .?'

'Exactly. The person from whose premises Regenschein descended into the catacombs. One of Bookholm's most distinguished citizens. His shop is really worth seeing. Pay him a visit and you'll be setting foot on historic ground.'

'I'll make a point of it,' I said.

'Go there tomorrow. He doesn't open till noon and closes early as a rule. The antiquarians in the city centre can afford to indulge in such whims. Take a look at his stock while you're there, it's truly unique.'

'Many thanks for the advice – and, of course, for the delicious snack.'

'It was a business investment. Buy a budding author a meal and he may pave the rest of your journey through life with gold. That's a literary agent's motto. In my case, alas, it has yet to prove well-founded.'

I hurriedly popped the last morsel of bee-bread into my mouth and was just about to get up and say goodbye when I felt a stab of pain in my gum.

'Akk!' I said.

'Is anything the matter?' asked Harpstick.

I pointed to my mouth. 'Akk!' I said again.

The Hoggling gave a start. 'A bee sting? Don't move! Open your mouth wide! Don't panic! The bee is dead, so it can't inject any more of its poison, but the slightest pressure on its body could be enough to force the toxin into your bloodstream and turn you into a blithering idiot! Let me take a look!'

I opened my jaws to their fullest extent to enable Harpstick to reach inside. My face was streaming with sweat. Grunting, he fumbled around inside my mouth. I held my breath and didn't move. Then I felt another brief stab of pain in my gum and the Hoggling sat back. He was holding up the dead bee and grinning again.

'You won't forget this bee-bread in a hurry,' he said. 'But I did warn you. The risk is part of the pleasure.'

I mopped my face. 'Many thanks,' I gasped. 'I don't know how to—'

'You must excuse me now,' Harpstick said abruptly, flicking the bee onto the floor. 'It's been a long night, the poetry reading was execrable and I could use a wink or two of sleep. Perhaps we'll meet again.'

I shook him by the trotter. He gazed into space and muttered: 'Hm, *A Wink or Two of Sleep*. A good title, don't you think?'

'To be honest,' I said, 'no. It sounds boring.'

'You're right.' He laughed. 'I really must be overtired.'

I sat on for a while after he left, checking my pulse for palpitations in case some of the apian poison had found its way into my bloodstream after all, but my heart continued to beat with metronomic regularity.

Out of the Frying Pan

I walked back to my hotel. Although the hour was late, many of the bookshops were still open and a lively atmosphere prevailed in the streets. Knots of people were standing on every corner, reading aloud to each other, laughing, chatting and drinking wine, mulled beer or coffee. I looked at a few shop windows and could scarcely resist the temptation to go inside and start rummaging.

It was quite an effort to leave this animated scene behind and return to my hotel room. The Bluddums next door seemed to have calmed down, because they were snoring and wheezing like congested bagpipes. I lay down on the bed, intending to put my feet up and grab a few minutes' repose. I stared at the bat in the corner and it stared back. Then I fell asleep.

In my dreams I was wandering along an endless tunnel whose walls were lined with shelves full of ancient tomes. Dancelot, a transparent phantom, was flitting restlessly along ahead of me. 'Down!' he kept calling. 'Down into the depths!'

We passed all kinds of characters from books I'd read: my boyhood hero Prince Sangfroid, who galloped past on his horse Blizzard; Prospopa Thonatas, the consumptive carpet dealer from *The Rajah's Ravioli*; Koriolanus Korinth, the smuggler-philosopher from *Pomegranates and Pumice Stone*; the twelve brothers from *The Twelve Brothers* and many other figures from popular novels. 'Back! Back! Go back!' they all cried, but Dancelot floated straight through them and so did I, because I too had become a disembodied spirit. Out of the depths of the tunnel came a huge, white, screeching one-eyed bat accompanied by a swarm of angrily buzzing roasted bees. The bat opened its hideous jaws and prepared to devour me. I remember thinking, 'Hey, you can't possibly eat me, I'm a disembodied spirit!' – but by that time it had.

I awoke. The bat was still dangling motionless in its corner, staring at me. It was probably dead, having died with its single eye open and hung there like that for ages. The Bluddums in the room next door were making a rumpus again. They had just woken up and engaged in another noisy free-for-all, smashing furniture and dislodging a picture from my wall. I got up with a groan, drowsily repacked my bundle and left this house of horrors.

The cool morning air cleared my head and refreshed me as I strolled through the streets. Feeling like a bite of breakfast, I betook myself to a café for a cappuccino and a bookling, a book-shaped pastry filled with apple purée and topped with almonds and pistachio nuts. Strangely enough, this local speciality bore the same name as the fearsome creatures rumoured to have established a reign of terror beneath the city. Before handing me the oven-warm pastry, the proprietor of the café deposited it on a page torn from some old book and thrust a long skewer into the side. The little ribbon of cinnamon-scented filling that oozed out resembled a liquid bookmark.

Also sitting in the café was another inhabitant of Lindworm Castle, Pentametros Rhymefisher, a former classmate of mine. I informed him of

Dancelot's death and he expressed his sympathy. When I told him what a lousy dump my hotel was, he gave me the address of another, assuring me that it was well kept and inexpensive. We wished each other a good trip and went our separate ways.

A little while later I found the recommended hotel in a narrow side street. Some Norselanders were just emerging from it. They looked well rested and in good spirits. If those fastidious, law-abiding and reputedly tight-fisted individuals favoured this establishment, I told myself, it really must be clean and cheap – quiet too, in all probability, because no Norselander would shrink from summoning the forces of law and order if someone disturbed his night's rest.

I asked to be shown a room. It proved to be completely bat-free, the water in the washbasin was clear as glass, the towels and bedlinen were clean, and no disturbing noises were issuing from the adjacent rooms, just the subdued voices of some civilised fellow guests. I booked the room for a week and had a really thorough wash for the first time since my arrival in the city. Then, refreshed and filled with curiosity, I set off on my next excursion.

Books, books, books, books. Old books, new books, expensive books, cheap books, books in shop windows or bookcases, in sacks or on handcarts, in random heaps or neatly arrayed behind glass. Books in precarious, tottering piles, books parcelled up with string ('Try your luck – buy our surprise package!'), books displayed on marble pillars or locked away behind grilles in dark wooden cabinets ('Signed first editions – don't touch!'). Books bound in leather or linen, hide or silk, books with clasps of copper or iron, silver or gold – even, in one or two shop windows, books studded all over with diamonds.

There were adventure stories supplied with cloths for mopping your brow, thrillers containing pressed leaves of soothing valerian to be sniffed when the suspense became too great, and books with stout locks sealed by the Atlantean censorship authorities ('Sale permitted, reading prohibited!'). One shop sold nothing but 'half' works that broke off in the middle because their authors had died while writing them; another specialised in novels whose protagonists were insects. I also saw a Wolperting shop that sold nothing but books on chess and another patronised exclusively by dwarfs with blond beards, all of whom wore eye-shades.

The big bookstores did not specialise, however, and usually displayed their wares in no kind of order – a system clearly favoured by their customers, as one could tell from the gusto with which they rooted around in them. There were no bargains to be had at the specialist bookshops, so it was almost impossible to find a well-known author's signed first edition at a reasonable price. The surprise packages on offer at the big antiquarian bookshops, on the other hand, might well contain a volume worth many times the rest of the package put together, and anyone who ventured downstairs into the basement of one of these huge establishments dramatically increased his chances of discovering some item of real value.

An unwritten rule prevailed in Bookholm: 'The price pencilled inside the cover is valid, and that's that!' In view of the vast numbers of old volumes transported into the city every day, it was inevitable that dealers and their assistants were often too pressed for time to assess the true value of items while sorting through them. Indeed, they were sometimes so harassed that they didn't even look at them, just sold off whole crates and sacks at knockdown prices. The result was that valuable books, too, came on the market and were wrongly classified, then banished to dark cellars or buried under stacks of cheap trash. They fell behind bookcases, slumbered in boxes under faded publishers' lists or languished on high, inaccessible shelves and were nibbled by rats and woodworms. These treasures were the main reason why Bookholm exerted such an attraction. The tourists who visited it were amateur Bookhunters, so to speak. Anyone could strike gold if only he looked for long enough.

Most visitors were collared on arrival by tourist guides who steered them into huge bookstores displaying stacks of largely worthless rubbish. The staff made a practice of mingling a few little gems with the cheap stuff, however, so a lucky tourist could make the occasional discovery even there. When he brandished the book in triumph and loudly rejoiced at the ludicrous price inside the cover, that was the most effective advertisement of all. Word that someone had paid a few measly pyras for a first edition of Monken Maksud's *Beacon in the Gloaming* would spread like wildfire and the shop would be besieged all night long by customers in search of similar lucky finds.

The bookstores that catered for a mass clientele had either bricked up their entrances to the catacombs or concealed them behind bookcases to prevent their customers from straying inside. Only a few streets away from the big

bookstores and cheap cafés, however, things became more interesting. The shops were smaller and more specialised, their shopfronts more artistic and individual, their wares older and more expensive. They also granted access to certain areas of the catacombs – *certain* areas, mark you, because they allowed their customers to descend only a few storeys, after which the entrances were bricked up or sealed off in some other way. It was quite possible to get lost in these subterranean passages for several hours, but everyone found their way out in the end.

The further into the city you went, the older and more dilapidated the buildings, the smaller the shops and the fewer the tourists became. In order to enter some of these antiquarian bookshops you had to ring a bell or knock. From them you could *really* descend into the catacombs without restriction but at your own risk. If the customer was a new and unknown Bookhunter the staff would issue exhaustive warnings, informing him of the dangers and drawing attention to the fact that torches, oil lamps, provisions, maps and weapons were on sale in the shop, as well as balls of stout string for attaching to hooks on the premises – a device that enabled you to venture into the depths in relative safety. Other bookshops offered the services of trained

apprentices who were well acquainted with certain parts of the catacombs and would take you on guided tours.

I had learnt all these things from Regenschein's book, so my knowledge of them made those inconspicuous little shops seem to me like doorways into a mysterious world. For the moment, however, I was uninterested in leaving the surface of the city. I was engaged on a very special mission: bound for Pfistomel Smyke's antiquarian bookshop at 333 Darkman Street.

I came to a spacious square – an unusual sight after all those narrow lanes and alleyways. What struck me as more unusual still was that it was unpaved and dotted with gaping holes among which tourists were strolling. It wasn't until I saw that these pits were inhabited that the truth finally dawned: this was the celebrated or notorious *Graveyard of Forgotten Writers*!

Such was the popular name for it, its official, more prosaic appellation being Pit Plaza. It was one of the city's less agreeable sights and one of which Dancelot had always spoken in hushed tones. It wasn't a genuine graveyard, of course. No one was buried there – or not, at least, in the conventional sense. The pits were occupied by writers too impoverished to afford a roof over their heads. They wrote to order for any tourist willing to toss them some small change.

I shivered. The pits really did look like freshly dug graves, and vegetating in each of them was a failed writer. Their occupants wore grimy, tattered clothes or were swathed in old blankets, and they wrote on the backs of used envelopes. The pits were their dwellings, a few tarpaulins being their only makeshift protection at night or when it rained. They had reached the bottom of the professional ladder, the very lowest point to which any Zamonian author could sink and the nightmare that haunted every member of the literary fraternity.

'My brother's a blacksmith,' a tourist called down into one of the pits. 'Write me something about horseshoes.'

'My wife's name is Grella,' called another. 'A poem for Grella, please!'

'Hey, poet!' yelled a Bluddum. 'Write me a rhyme!'

I quickened my step and hurried across the square. Aware that many a writer with a brilliant past had been stranded there, I did my utmost not to look down, but it was almost impossible. I glanced to left and right. Smirking youngsters were scattering sand on the poor fellows' heads. A tipsy tourist had tumbled into one of the holes and was being helped out by his friends, who were roaring with laughter. Meanwhile, a dog was cocking its leg on the edge of the pit. Its occupant, who took no notice of these goings-on, continued to jot down a poem on a scrap of cardboard.

And then the worst happened: I recognised a member of my own kind! Languishing in one of the graves was Ovidios Versewhetter, a boyhood idol of mine. I had sat at his feet during his well-attended readings in Lindworm Castle. Later he had left to become a famous big-city writer, but little had been heard of him thereafter.

Versewhetter had just composed a sonnet for some tourists and was now reciting it in a hoarse voice. They giggled and tossed him a few coppers, whereupon he thanked them effusively, baring his neglected teeth. Then, catching sight of me, he likewise recognised one of his own kind and his eyes filled with tears.

I turned away and fled from the appalling place. How terrible to have sunk so low! In our profession we were always threatened with an uncertain future – success and failure were two sides of the same coin. I strode off – no, I broke into a run – and left the Graveyard of Forgotten Writers behind me as quickly as possible.

When I finally came to a halt I was in a seedy little side street. I had evidently left the tourist quarter, because there wasn't a single bookshop in sight, just a row of shabby, ramshackle buildings with the most noxious smells issuing from them and muffled figures lounging in the doorways.

One of these hissed an invitation as I went by: 'Hey, want someone panned?'

Oh, my goodness, I'd strayed into *Poison Alley*! This was no tourist attraction; it was one of the places in Bookholm to be shunned on principle by anyone with a vestige of common sense and decency. Poison Alley, the notorious haunt of reviewers who plied for hire! Here dwelt the true dregs of Bookholm, the self-appointed literary critics who wrote vitriolic reviews for money. This was where anyone unscrupulous enough to employ such methods could hire venomous hacks and unleash them on fellow writers he disliked. They would then pursue his *bêtes noires* until their careers and reputations were utterly ruined.

'Sure you don't want a thorough hatchet job?' the hack whispered.

'No thanks!' I retorted. I only just resisted the urge to fly at his throat, but I couldn't refrain from passing a remark. I came to a halt.

'You guttersnipe!' I snarled. 'How dare you drag the work of honest writers in the mire where you yourself belong?'

The muffled figure blew a disgusting raspberry.

'And who are you to insult me like that?' he growled back.

'I'm Optimus Yarnspinner,' I replied proudly.

'Yarnspinner, eh?' he muttered. He produced a pad and pencil from his cloak and jotted something down. 'You haven't published anything yet or I'd know it – I keep a close check on contemporary Zamonian literature – but coming from Lindworm Castle you're bound to sooner or later. You goddamned lizards can't hold your ink.'

I walked off. What had possessed me to bandy words with such scum!

'I'm Laptantidel Latuda!' he called after me. 'No need to make a note of my name, you'll be hearing from me in due course!'[*]

Two Bookhunters were standing in a gloomy doorway, loudly haggling over some black market wares. Poison Alley was a dead end, of course, so I had to turn and walk all the way back past those ramshackle buildings and that muckraker, who bleated with laughter as I went by. I shook myself like a wet dog when I finally left him and his rat's nest behind.

I traversed the compositors' quarter, where the buildings were faced with worn-out lead type, and walked along *Editorial Lane*, which rang with the groans and curses of the copy-editors at work there, many of whom were clearly being driven to despair by lapses of style and punctuation. From one first-floor window issued a bellow of rage followed by a stack of handwritten sheets, which came fluttering down on my head.

I left the tourist quarter behind at last and proceeded ever deeper into the heart of Bookholm. According to Regenschein's book, this was where the oldest antiquarian bookshops were situated. Half-timbered and steeply gabled, the ancient buildings resembled elderly sorcerers huddled together for mutual support as they gazed down at me through their dark window embrasures.

Picturesque though the neighbourhood was, very few tourists frequented it. There were no street traders or loudly declaiming poets, no Live Newspapers or vendors of melted cheese, just age-old buildings whose windows were coated on the inside with soot to keep out harmful rays of sunlight. Shop signs were few and far between, so I could only guess which the bookshops were. Antiquarianism of the highest order was carried on here. Seated behind those blackened window-panes, for all I knew, might be wealthy collectors and celebrated dealers engaged in negotiating the sale of books worth as much as a whole row of houses. In this part of Bookholm one instinctively walked on tiptoe.

It wasn't midday yet and Pfistomel Smyke's establishment would still be shut, so I paused at an intersection and debated whether to kill time in some bookshop or other. On the door of one establishment, which had some

---

* Translator's Note: Those who are unacquainted with Optimus Yarnspinner's biography may be interested to know that this was a fateful encounter destined to have important repercussions on his subsequent career. Laptantidel Latuda, who was to become Yarnspinner's arch enemy, persistently harried him with scathing reviews when he began to be published.

gruesome faces carved on the half-timbering above its blackened window, I noticed the Triadic Circle I had first seen displayed on the door of Kibitzer's shop. The minuscule sign below it read:

INAZIA ANAZAZI
Ugglian Literature · Curses · Spells

Wow! An Ugglian bookshop, probably run by a genuine Uggly! It had been a long-standing childhood wish of mine to encounter a real live Uggly. The creatures abounded in the children's books and old fairy tales Dancelot had read me at bedtime – and, of course, in my subsequent nightmares. I now had an opportunity to see one in the flesh and was old enough not to run off screaming at the sight, so why wait? With a pleasurable shudder, I turned the door handle.

My presence was announced by the metallic screech of hinges left unoiled for an eternity. The interior of the shop was dimly illuminated by one or two little oil lamps. The book dust stirred up by my abrupt entrance danced round me and infiltrated my nostrils. I sneezed despite myself.

A tall, thin figure attired in black shot up from behind a stack of books like a jack-in-the-box. 'What do you want?' it shrieked.

'Er, I don't want anything in particular,' I said haltingly. 'I'd simply like to browse a bit.'

'You'd simply like to browse a bit?' the Uggly repeated as loudly as before.

'Er, yes. May I?'

The gaunt creature tottered towards me, nervously interlacing her spindly fingers.

'This is a specialised antiquarian bookshop,' she croaked malevolently. 'I doubt if you'll find what you're looking for.'

'Really?' I retorted. 'What do you specialise in?'

'Ugglian literature!' the hideous bookseller crowed triumphantly, as if those words alone would drive me out of the shop.

Looking deliberately unimpressed, I scanned the backs of the books nearest me. Soothsayers' prophecies, wart-curers' incantations, maledictions – nothing suitable for an enlightened Lindworm like me. I really wanted nothing more to do with this psychic scarecrow, but her unfriendly manner had provoked me. Instead of leaving the shop at once I lingered there and made my way along the shelves.

'Oh, Ugglian literature!' I crooned. 'How exciting! I'm passionately interested in predictions based on toads' entrails. I must root around in your treasures a while longer.'

I had resolved to teach the old crone some manners. From now on I would treat her with breathtaking condescension. I removed one of the books from a bookcase.

'Hm, Looba Gordag's *How to Foretell the Future by Interpreting Nightmares.* That's my kind of book!'

'Kindly replace it on the shelf. It's reserved.'

'For whom?' I asked sharply.

'For, er . . . I don't know the customer's name.'

'Then it could, purely in theory, be reserved for me. You don't know my name either.'

The Uggly wrung her spindly fingers in despair. I flung the book at the bookcase. It sailed past and landed on the floor, losing its back in the process.

'Whoops!' I said.

With a groan, the Uggly bent down to retrieve the book.

'What's this?' I exclaimed in delight, pointing to a big fat tome. 'Ah, a collection of Ornian curses!'

I leafed through the valuable book, clumsily dog-earing a couple of pages, and proceeded to read from it in a loud, resonant voice. At the same time I waved my free hand portentously in the Uggly's direction.

> *'Where slender stems of green bamboo*
> *rise high above the spectral plain*
> *and lifeless eyes peer blankly through,*
> *there hover spirits racked with pain . . .'*

The Uggly shielded her face with one arm and ducked down behind the counter. 'Stop that!' she screeched. 'Those curses are most effective!'

What a hoot! She actually believed in this stupid mumbo-jumbo! I tossed the book aside. It landed in an old wooden box, sending up a cloud of the finest book dust. An idea occurred to me.

Slowly turning to the Uggly, I levelled my forefinger at her in an inquisitorial manner and spread my leather wings a trifle. This made my cloak bulge in the shoulder region.

'I have another question,' I said.

This was an old Lindworm trick. My wings – they're just a bequest from some pterodactylic member of my ancestral line – are incapable of flight but admirably suited to spreading. It always amuses one to observe the intimidating effect this has on the unwary. Producing Dancelot's manuscript from my cloak, I held it under the Uggly's nose – near enough for her to read the text.

'Do you by any chance know the author of these lines?' I asked sharply.

The Uggly's face froze. She stared at the manuscript as though hypnotised, uttering a series of squeaks, then staggered backwards, bumped into a bookcase and clung to it like someone in the throes of a heart attack. Her violent reaction surprised me.

'You *do* know the author, don't you?' I said. There was no other explanation for her behaviour.

'No, I don't,' the Uggly croaked. 'Leave my premises at once!'

'I simply must find out who wrote this,' I insisted. 'Please help me!'

The Uggly took a step forward and struck a pose. Narrowing her eyes to slits, she spoke in a dramatic whisper: '*He will descend into the depths! He will be banished to the realm of the Animatomes, the Living Books! He will consort with Him whom everyone knows but knows not who He is!*'

I was aware that Ugglies employed such cryptic utterances to impress potential customers. They didn't work with me.

'Was that a threat or an Ugglian prophecy?'

'It will come true unless that manuscript is destroyed at once, more I cannot say. And now get out of my shop!'

'But you obviously know who—' I persisted.

'Get out!' screeched the Uggly. 'Get out or I'll summon the Book Police!' She dived behind the counter and grabbed a cord connected to a large bell suspended from the ceiling.

'Out!' she snarled again.

There was nothing for it. I turned to go.

'One more thing,' I said.

'Leave!' the Uggly gasped. 'Just go!'

'What's the significance of that peculiar sign on your door?'

'I don't know,' the Uggly replied. 'Goodbye for ever. Never dare to set foot in this shop again.'

'I thought Ugglies were omniscient, but you know surprisingly little,' was my parting shot. Opening the door provocatively slowly, I sauntered out to a squeal of hinges.

Slightly dazed, I stood there in the sunlight and listened to the sounds emanating from the bookshop. The Uggly was swearing unintelligibly to herself and fiddling with a bunch of keys. A lock clicked behind me for the second time in a few hours.

Great! I was getting nowhere fast. I hadn't been two days in Bookholm and already two booksellers had given me my marching orders.

Pfistomel Smyke's
Typographical Laboratory

Seventy-seven, seventy-eight . . . I was familiar with the antiquated numerals peculiar to Bookemistic numerology, as luck would have it, or I would have been unable to decipher the house numbers. Darkman Street was the oldest thoroughfare in Bookholm. The buildings here were so old and dilapidated that they had half subsided below ground level and their crooked roofs resembled alchemists' hats that had slipped sideways. Thistles were sprouting from their walls and birds nesting in the grass that thickly carpeted their shingled roofs. The eaves of these decrepit old buildings almost met overhead, they canted forward at such an angle. Indeed, they seemed to be pressing ever closer for the purpose of appraising me, their uninvited guest. Although it was noon and the sun was shining, I had made my way through the narrow streets almost entirely in shadow. I had a sneaking sensation that the houses formed a single building into which I'd stolen like a thief. There was no sound save the hum of insects and the squalling of cats. The cobblestones had cracked open in numerous places, forced apart by weeds, and I occasionally saw emaciated rats flit across the street. Did anyone live here? It was hardly surprising the streets received no normal visitors. I felt as if I had walked through an invisible gate into another age hundreds or even thousands of years in the past, a long forgotten epoch when decay reigned supreme.

A hundred and twenty-seven, a hundred and twenty-eight . . . I shivered, involuntarily reminded of a chapter in Regenschein's book in which he had written of this district and its sinister history – and recounted the legend of the Darkman of Bookholm. This was where, centuries ago, the Bookemists had lived and largely controlled the destinies of the city. Bookemism was a Bookholmian species of alchemy. Part scientists, part physicians, part charlatans and part antiquarians, the Bookemists had founded a guild devoted to typography, antiquarianism, chemistry, biology, physics and literature. These branches of knowledge had combined with conjuration, divination, astrology and other hocus-pocus to form a baneful amalgam sufficient to fill whole libraries with horror stories.

Two hundred and four, two hundred and five . . . In these old buildings, bizarre attempts had been made – for whatever reason – to transform printer's ink into blood and blood into printer's ink. Indescribable scenes must have occurred when the Bookemists assembled in the narrow street under a full moon, there to celebrate the rites laid down in *The Twelve Thousand Precepts* and carry out their gruesome experiments on animals and other life forms. This was in the period after the Bookholmians had been driven from the catacombs by epidemics and natural disasters, a time when civilisation was just beginning to burgeon: a transitional phase midway between barbarism and the rule of law, sorcerous cults and genuine culture.

It was in Leyden Lane, one of the streets leading off Darkman Street, that the first Leyden Manikin had come into being. This was also where the Bookemists had bred cats with wings and even, so it was said, the living books known as Animatomes. They had pursued their frightful experiments in the megalomaniac belief that anything capable of being imagined and committed to paper could also be created in reality, with the result that the neighbourhood had long abounded in hybrid creatures so bizarre as to defy description.

Two hundred and forty-eight, two hundred and forty-nine . . . One day, according to Regenschein, the Bookemists had set out to create a giant, a huge paper colossus that would defend Bookholm against all its enemies. Having boiled up some books, mixed printer's ink with herbs and performed various rituals, they fashioned a figure three times the height of a house out of pulped paper, minced animals and mashed peat from Dullsgard. This figure they steeped in printer's ink to render its appearance even more frightful and christened 'the Darkman'. Then, in a spirit of self-sacrifice, ten Bookemists had committed suicide so that it could be transfused with their blood.

Last of all, the figure had an iron rod inserted in its head and was exposed to a thunderstorm with its feet immersed in two tubs of water. An immense shaft of lightning is said to have raced down the rod and brought the Darkman to life. He uttered a terrible cry and, with electrical charges flickering round him, stepped out of the water. The Bookemists cheered and hurled their conical hats into the air – until the Darkman bent down, grabbed one of them and swallowed him whole. Then he stalked through the city, snatching up screaming inhabitants at random and devouring them. He even ripped the roofs off houses, reached inside and gobbled up anything that moved.

Eventually, so the story ran, one courageous citizen of Bookholm set the Darkman on fire with a torch. But the blazing giant staggered off through the

streets, bellowing with pain. The flames ignited house after house and street after street until he was finally reduced to a mound of grey ash. That was how Bookholm's first great conflagration is said to have started.

Three hundred, three hundred and one . . . The real truth, in all probability, was that some scatterbrained antiquarian had knocked over an oil lamp and that this hair-raising horror story was a figment of the imagination centuries in the making.

Three hundred and eleven, three hundred and twelve . . . Nevertheless, that old wives' tale seemed quite plausible to anyone who, like me, was tiptoeing through those coal-black ruins. If printer's ink had ever been transformed into blood and paper into a living creature anywhere in Zamonia, it was here in the heart of this crazy city.

Three hundred and twenty, three hundred and twenty-one . . . The urban heart of Bookholm was a place on the frontier between delusion and reality, a world of alchemy transmuted into architecture.

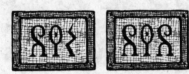

Three hundred and thirty-two . . . Three hundred and thirty-three! I came to a halt. I had at last reached the address I was looking for – 333 Darkman Street – and was standing outside Pfistomel Smyke's bookshop.

But what a disappointment! The building was probably the smallest I had so far seen in Bookholm. More of a witch's cottage than a genuine antiquarian bookshop, it was hemmed in by two blackened ruins whose sole remaining occupants, I suspected, were bats. Its only remarkable feature was that it was still standing after so many centuries. For No. 333 Darkman Street must have been many centuries old. The half-timbering, which seemed to have grown into position naturally, had never been planed or stripped of its bark – one of the characteristic features of early Bookholmian architecture. The bent and misshapen timbers meandered through the masonry, the wood was petrified and black as charcoal. The courses of stones between the timbers had apparently been laid without mortar, a technique no longer practised today. Granite and marble, tiny pebbles and fragments of pumice, iron ore, semi-precious stones, topazes and opals, quartz and feldspar – all had been so carefully selected, neatly trimmed and skilfully fitted together that none of them was in the wrong place and each supported its immediate neighbours. Mortar would have become friable over the years, causing the house to collapse long ago, but this early method of construction had triumphed over the march of time. Feeling ashamed of my overhasty verdict on the house, I looked at it rather more closely. It was indeed a work of art, a three-dimensional mosaic constructed with microscopic precision. I discovered that the little stones had even smaller stones between them, and so on and so forth until the tiniest were the size of

grains of rice – and all assembled firmly enough to withstand the passage of millennia. I bowed my stupid head in profound respect. That was how timeless art was created, I thought. That was how one ought to be able to write.

'Yes, this building is an architectural gem. One doesn't see that at first glance,' said a deep voice. I was jolted out of my reverie.

The door had opened without a sound, and leaning against the jamb was a Shark Grub. Although I had already seen a few representatives of that life form in Bookholm, this one was an exceptionally impressive specimen. The maggotlike torso looked grotesque with its fourteen skimpy little arms, and the neckless head was equipped with a set of shark's teeth. The peculiarity of the creature's appearance was not diminished by the fact that it was wearing a bee-keeper's hat and veil and carrying a smoke gun.

'Smyke's the name, Pfistomel Smyke. Are you interested in early Bookholmian architecture?'

'Not really,' I admitted, somewhat bemusedly groping in my pocket for the business card the Hoggling had given me. 'I got your address from Claudio Harpstick.'

'Ah, dear old Claudio! You want to buy some books?'

'Not that either, to be honest. I own a manuscript which—'

'You want an expert opinion?'

'Precisely.'

'Wonderful! This is a welcome distraction. I was just cleaning my beehive out of sheer boredom. Do come in.' Pfistomel Smyke retreated into the house and I followed, bowing politely.

'Optimus Yarnspinner.'

'Delighted to make your acquaintance. You're from Lindworm Castle, aren't you? I'm a great admirer of Lindwormian literature. Please follow me to the laboratory.'

Smyke undulated ahead of me down a short, dark passage.

'Don't let my hat and veil mislead you,' he went on chattily, 'I'm not a genuine bee-keeper, it's just a hobby. When the bees stop producing I roast them and bottle them in honey. Do you think that's heartless of me?'

'No,' I replied, running my tongue over my gums. The spot was still slightly inflamed.

'It's ridiculous, of course, going to all that trouble for one jar of honey in springtime. I only wear the hat because I think it's chic.' Smyke emitted a guttural laugh.

At the end of the passage was a bead curtain composed of lead type strung like beads on lengths of thin cord. Smyke parted it with his massive body and I followed him inside.

For the third time that day I entered another world. The first had been the Uggly's dusty, airless bookshop, the second the sinister, historic heart of Bookholm. I was now admitted to a world of letters, a room completely given over to writing and its exploration. Hexagonal in shape, it had a ceiling that tapered to a point. The large window was obscured by red velvet curtains. The other five walls were lined with shelves on which reposed stacks of paper in a wide variety of formats and colours; retorts, flasks, alembics and vessels of all kinds containing liquids and powders; hundreds of goose quills neatly arrayed in small wooden racks; an assortment of metal-nibbed pens in little mother-of-pearl boxes; inks of every conceivable colour including black, blue, red, green, violet, yellow, brown and even gold and silver; rubber stamps and ink pads, sealing wax, magnifying glasses of various sizes, and microscopes and chemical apparatus of a kind I'd never seen before. All these things were bathed in the mellow, fitful light of flickering candles standing here and there on the shelves.

'I call this my typographical laboratory,' Smyke said with a touch of pride. 'I conduct research into words.'

What surprised me most of all was the room's size. The building had looked so small and skimpy from the street, I could hardly believe that this spacious laboratory fitted inside it. My respect for Bookholm's ancient architecture increased by leaps and bounds as I strove to memorise as many details of these remarkable premises as I could.

There was writing everywhere. The velvet curtains over the window were printed with the Zamonian alphabet. Hanging between the bookcases were opticians' charts in various typefaces and framed diplomas and slates inscribed with jottings in chalk, and pinned to the wall were tiny memos. A huge, free-standing lectern was cluttered with manuscripts, inkwells and magnifying glasses. Printer's type of all sizes, either of wood or cast in lead, lay around on small tables beside bottles of printer's ink, each of which was labelled – like a vintage wine – with its year and place of origin. Suspended from the ceiling were strings in various forms of quipu, or knot-writing, from which dangled small plaster tablets engraved with hieroglyphs. Standing here and there were strange mechanical contraptions whose purpose utterly defeated me. The floor was tiled with slabs of grey marble skilfully engraved with various alphabets: Druidical Runic, Ugglian Gothic, Old Atlantean, Palaeo-Zamonian and so on.

In the middle of the floor was a large closed trapdoor (the entrance to the catacombs?) and standing in a corner was a small crate filled with ancient tomes – the only books I had so far seen on the premises. Hardly a lavish display for an antiquarian bookshop. Was there a library next door?

'I also have a small kitchen and a bedroom, but I spend most of my time in here,' said Smyke, as if he had read my thoughts. No library? So where were his books?

It was only then that I noticed the shelf with the Leyden Manikins on it. Six of the little artificial creatures were romping around in their jars and tapping on the glass.*

'I'm using those Manikins to test the acoustic quality of various types of literature,' Smyke explained. 'I read them poetry and prose. They don't understand a word, of course, but they're extremely sensitive to intonation. Bad verse makes them double up as if they're in pain, good verse starts them singing. They recognise a sad piece of writing by its sound and burst into tears.'

We paused in front of one of the bizarre machines, a wooden sphere resembling a terrestrial globe but engraved with letters of the Zamonian alphabet instead of a map. It could evidently be rotated by depressing a pedal.

'A novel-writing machine,' Smyke said with a laugh. 'An ancient device once believed to be capable of producing literature by mechanical means – a typical example of Bookemistic idiocy. The sphere is filled with syllables cast in lead. When you operate the pedal they fall out and form a row. Naturally, all they ever produce is sentences like "Pilgeon sulfriger fonzo na tuta halubraz" or something similar. The results are worse than the phonetic verse of the Zamonian Gagaists! I've a soft spot for useless junk of this kind. That's a Bookemistic inspiration battery over there, and that's an idea refrigerator.'

Smyke pointed to another two grotesque contraptions.

'If those things were regarded as technologically advanced, it must have been a very unsophisticated age. All those legends about sinister rituals and sacrifices are utter rubbish. The Bookemists were like children playing with type and printer's ink. When I compare the products of our modern literary industry. . .' Smyke cast his eyes up at the ceiling.

---

* Translator's Note: Among Zamonian scientists, Leyden Manikins are a favourite means of testing the effects of chemicals and medicaments without having to experiment on living life forms. A Leyden Manikin consists largely of peat from the Graveyard Marshes of Dullsgard with an admixture of Demerara Desert sand, adipose tissue, glycerine and liquid resin. These components are moulded into a manikin and animated with the aid of an alchemical battery.

If inserted in a glass receptacle and immersed in nutrient fluid, a Leyden Manikin will keep for about a month. It displays all the behavioural characteristics of a live creature, reacting to heat, cold and all manner of chemical compounds.

I nodded in agreement.

'If you ask me,' he said, 'I'd sooner be alive today than in the Zamonian Dark Ages.'

'Except that there weren't any corrupt reviewers in those days,' I said.

'True!' Smyke exclaimed. 'I see we speak the same language.'

I pointed to the trapdoor.

'Is that . . . ?' I asked.

'Yes, it is!' Smyke replied. 'My own private entrance to the catacombs of Bookholm – my stairway to the underworld. Wheee!' He waved all fourteen of his little arms at once.

'Is that where Regenschein . . . ?'

'Correct.' Smyke cut my hesitant question short. 'This is where Colophonius Regenschein embarked on his quest for the Shadow King.' He looked grave. 'I still cherish the hope that he'll return some day, even after five years.' He sighed.

'I've read his book,' I said. 'Since then I've been wondering where fact ends and fiction begins.'

An impressive change came over Smyke's physique. Previously so flabby and vulnerable-looking, his maggotlike body tensed and grew taller. His expression became stern and piercing, and he clenched his numerous fists.

'Colophonius Regenschein's credibility is beyond dispute!' he thundered at me, so loudly that he set the retorts on the shelves around us jingling. 'He was a hero – a genuine hero and adventurer! He had no need to fabricate his adventures. He underwent them all in person and paid a heavy price.'

The Leyden Manikins trembled at his tone of voice and some of them burst into tears. I recoiled, intimidated by his sudden transformation. Noticing this, he promptly reverted to his former manner and subsided, both physically and vocally.

'Forgive me,' he said, every inch the literary scholar, 'but this is still a very painful topic from my point of view. Colophonius Regenschein was a personal friend.'

I searched for something to say that would enable me to change the subject discreetly.

'Do you believe in the existence of the Shadow King?' I asked.

Smyke debated this for a moment. 'That's not a valid question,' he said quietly. 'No one who has lived in Bookholm for any length of time seriously doubts his existence. I myself have often heard him howling on windless nights. What interests me far more is another question: is he good or evil? Regenschein believed in his essential benevolence. Others assert that the Shadow King killed him.'

'Which view do you take?'

'A million dangers exist down there and any one of them could be responsible for his disappearance. They include Spinxxxxes that can grow to the size of horses, Harpyrs, Fearsome Booklings, vengeful Bookhunters – merciless creatures of all kinds. Why does it have to be the Shadow King who's responsible for Regenschein's disappearance? One could speculate on the matter ad infinitum.'

'Do you know how the Fearsome Booklings got their name?' I asked. 'Are they really so fearsome?'

'The Bookhunters called them that because they don't shrink from devouring even the most valuable books. They're reputed to feed on them when there's no live prey available.' Smyke chuckled. 'To Bookhunters, devouring a valuable book is far more reprehensible than killing a living creature.'

'Bookhunters seem to live by rules of their own.'

'They're dangerous, so for goodness' sake beware of them! I occasionally have dealings with them for professional purposes, but I try to limit those contacts as far as possible. Every encounter with a Bookhunter leaves one feeling reborn. Why? Because one has survived!'

'Shall we get down to business?' I asked.

Smyke grinned. 'You have a job for me? Would you care for a cup of tea first? A slice of bee-bread, perhaps?'

'No thank you!' I said hastily. 'I've no wish to presume on your hospitality. I'm looking for the author of a manuscript. It must be somewhere here . . .' I felt in my cloak but couldn't find it at once. I had stuffed it into a pocket at random after my dramatic visit to the Uggly's bookshop.

'Right, let's take a look,' said Smyke, reaching for the manuscript when I finally produced it. He screwed a thick-lensed monocle into his right eye and unfolded the sheaf of paper.

'Hm . . . High quality Grailsundian wove,' he muttered. 'Timberlake Paper Mills, 200 grammes. Unevenly trimmed, probably by an obsolete Thread-cutter guillotine dating from the century before last. Overacidified.'

'I know all that,' I said impatiently. 'It's the text that interests me.'

I couldn't wait to see what his reaction would be. If he knew anything at all about literature, he would be bound to display some emotion.

Pfistomel Smyke raised the manuscript until it was within range of his monocle. Even as he read the first sentence, his flabby body seemed to be transfixed by an invisible shaft of lightning. He reared up, trembling, and wavelets of emotion rippled across his masses of adipose tissue. He emitted a sound of which Shark Grubs alone are capable: a high-pitched whistle superimposed on a dull, booming note. Then he drew a deep breath and read on in silence for a while. All at once he gave a roar – of laughter. It was a prolonged paroxysm of mirth that made his torso wobble to and fro like a toy balloon filled with water. He quietened, then squeaked and gasped and giggled inanely. His growls of approbation alternated with phases of mute emotional turmoil.

I had to smile. Sure enough, he was displaying the whole range of emotions this same short story had evoked in me and Kibitzer. The corpulent creature not only knew something about literature but possessed a sense of humour as well.

Eventually he lapsed into dull, brooding silence. As far as he was concerned, I didn't exist. His eyes glazed over and he remained motionless for several minutes. At last he lowered the manuscript and seemed to emerge from a profound trance.

'My goodness,' he said, gazing at me with tears in his eyes, 'it's truly sensational. The work of a genius.'

'Well,' I asked eagerly, 'do you know the author? Can you at least point me in the right direction?'

'Not so fast, my friend.' Smyke smiled as he re-examined the manuscript, this time with a magnifying glass. 'First I have to conduct a syllabic analysis and draw up a graphological parallelogram. Stylistic mensuration will be necessary, and I must work out the ratio of metaphors to the number of characters, calligraphically calibrating the text with my alphabetic microscope. Next will come an acoustic test with the Leyden Manikins and an analysis of the cutaneous scales adhering to the paper – the full programme, in other words. That will take, let's see . . . the whole night at least. If you leave the manuscript with me now I shall be able to tell you more by noon tomorrow. Probably not the author's name, but one or two things about him: whether he's right- or left-handed, how old he was at the time of writing, what part of Zamonia he comes from, his weight, his personal traits and temperament, the authors that influenced him, the ink he uses, where it comes from and so on. I'll be able to ascertain his name if he has become a well-known author since writing this, but that will take longer. I should have to do some research in the manuscript library. Will you be staying in Bookholm for a little while?'

'It depends how much your expert opinion costs.'

Smyke grinned. 'Don't worry about that, it's on the house.'

'I really couldn't accept,' I said awkwardly.

'But I work for nothing on principle. It's the shop that provides my income.'

I'd quite forgotten about that. What shop did he mean? The crate of books in the corner?

'What I can already tell you is this,' Smyke went on. 'We're dealing with a valuable manuscript here. *How* valuable remains to be seen, but you must refrain from mentioning it to anyone. There are a lot of shady individuals in Bookholm. People have been knifed for an unsigned second edition before now.'

'You propose to hang on to the manuscript?'

'If you want quick results, yes. Of course, if you'd prefer to consult someone else . . .' He held out the manuscript. 'I can give you the addresses of several eminent colleagues.'

'No, no,' I said. 'By all means keep it overnight. I'm in rather a hurry.'

'I'll give you a receipt,' he said.

'That won't be necessary,' I told him sheepishly. 'I trust you.'

'No, I insist. I'm a member of the Bookholm Graphologists' Guild. We do everything by the book.' He wrote out a receipt and handed it to me.

'There,' he said. 'That was business, now comes pleasure. Would you care to glance at my stock?'

'Certainly,' I replied. What stock did he mean? His stock of Leyden Manikins?

Smyke indicated the crate of books.

'Help yourself, ferret around to your heart's content. Perhaps you'll find a bargain.'

He was probably hinting that I ought to recompense him for his unpaid endeavours by buying something. Well, perhaps I would find a book I could pretend to be enthusiastic about. I went over to the crate, knelt down, took out the first one that came to hand – and almost dropped it. It was *The Bloody Book*!

Smyke was pretending to take no notice of me. Humming to himself, he smoothed out the sheaf of manuscript with a heavy paperweight.

I stared at *The Bloody Book*. Incredible! It really was the edition bound in Kackertratts' wing membranes and allegedly written in demonic blood! One of the most sought-after items on the Golden List! Unique! A museum piece! This book was not just worth a row of houses, it exceeded a whole urban district in value.

'Look inside,' Smyke told me with a grin.

I opened the big book with trembling hands. My eyes lighted on the following sentence: '*Witches always stand amid birch trees . . .*' I can't explain why, but those few words filled me with a terror such as I had never experienced before. Beads of cold sweat broke out on my forehead.

I shut the book and laid it aside.

'Interesting,' I said in a tremulous voice.

'Demonistics isn't everyone's cup of tea,' said Smyke. 'I myself find it too grim a subject. I never dip into the book, I simply own it. Go on looking, perhaps you'll find something suitable.'

I removed the next book from the crate, read the title – and gave another start. It was *Silence of the Sirens* by Count Klanthu of Kinomaz – the signed first edition, what was more. Light fiction, to be sure, but *what* light fiction! Klanthu's first novel was his only commercial flop, so the whole of the first edition had been pulped – with the exception of this one copy. Then Klanthu became a success and its value rocketed. The book was later reprinted, of course, but this copy of the first edition with illustrations by Werma Tozler was worth an absolute fortune. I ventured to look for the price inside the front cover. There it was, pencilled in the corner in tiny numerals, a sum so astronomical it made my head spin. I carefully laid the book aside.

'Don't you care for light fiction?' asked Smyke. 'Ah well, it's more for green youngsters. Try another.'

I removed another big book from the crate.

'But . . .' I gasped. 'This is *The Solar Chronicles*, one of the most valuable books in existence!'

'Yes,' Smyke said with a grin, 'but only because the printer's ink was mixed with ground-up dust from the Lunar Eclipse Diamond. It's worthless from the literary aspect, but the print sparkles beautifully in candlelight.'

'I'm afraid these books are out of my financial league,' I said, rising to my feet. I'd never seen such treasures before.

'You're right,' said Smyke. 'It was only a little joke on my part. I wanted to show off a bit. Those are the minor joys and compensations of my lonely profession. Delve deeper and you'll find another seven titles, all of which appear on the Golden List – near the top, too.'

'You weren't exaggerating when you said your stock was worth a look.'

'Hm, well,' said Smyke. 'Some antiquarians fill vast premises with umpteen thousand books and employ armies of sales assistants. I prefer to work alone. I'm more of a specialist. Strictly speaking, this is the most highly specialised antiquarian bookshop in the city. I'm sure you now see why I can afford to dispense with a fee.' So saying, he ushered me out.

'May I make a suggestion?' he asked when I was already outside in the street.

'By all means.'

'If you've nothing better to do this evening, try this.' He handed me a leaflet.

Invitation

'From the Primal Note to Moomievillean Ophthalmic Polyphony'
A Historic Trombophone Concert at the Bookholm Bowl
performed by
The Murkholm Trombophone Orchestra
Sponsor: Pfistomel Smyke

At Sunset in the Municipal Gardens

Admission Free!

Bring a warm shawl with you!

'What is it?' I asked. 'A musical mystery tour?'

'You could call it that, but it's more than just a concert. Believe me, it would be worthwhile going. It's a genuine cultural experience, not a tourist attraction.'

'To be honest, I'd meant to attend a literary function this evening. At timber-time, if you know what I mean.'

'Timber-time shmimber-time!' Smyke made a dismissive gesture. 'Timber-time in Bookholm is a nightly occurrence. You won't get to hear a performance by the Murkholm Trombophone Orchestra every day of the week. It's an event! Still, don't let me talk you into it – perhaps you're allergic to trombophone music.'

'I couldn't say. I've never heard any.'

'You should definitely go, then. It's an acoustic adventure. I wish I could go myself, but . . .' Smyke shrugged. 'Duty calls . . .' He tapped the manuscript and sighed.

'Au revoir,' I said. 'I'll come back at noon tomorrow.'

'Good, see you then.' He waved me goodbye and quietly closed the door.

It wasn't until I had quit the heart of the city and returned to its busier neighbourhoods – this time making a big detour to avoid Poison Alley and the Graveyard of Forgotten Writers – that I noticed something: Darkman Street described a series of spirals round the geographical centre of Bookholm, so Pfistomel Smyke's house, which stood at its focal point, must have been among the very first of the city's buildings to be constructed above ground.

Timber-Time

Timber-time was what Bookholmians called the tranquil evening hours, that snug sequel to a busy day of selling books or writing them. When thick balks of timber blazed in open fireplaces and pipes were lit, when heavy wines developed their bouquets in big-bellied glasses and the Master Readers embarked on their public recitations – that was timber-time. That was when billets of firewood crackled on the hearth, bathing the various venues in a warm yellow glow, when ancient tomes and first editions hot off the press were opened, and when audiences crowded closer to listen to the old and tried or the new and outré, to essays or short stories, novels or collections of letters, poetry or prose. Timber-time was when the body came to rest and the mind sprang to life, when phantoms born of a literary imagination arose from the pages and danced about the heads of listeners and readers alike.

Timber-time was also – let's face it – a time for advertising and promotion. It was a regrettable but undeniable fact that Zamonian literature, too, was subject to the law of supply and demand. Bookholm, the city of innumerable books, was a particularly difficult place in which to drum up public interest in a new work, and timber-time readings were directed mainly to that end.

The Master Readers of Bookholm belonged to a guild that had existed for hundreds of years. Its rules and regulations were stringent and its entrance examinations rigorous. Professional readers had been through the mill and knew their trade, many of them being former actors or singers endowed with powerful vocal cords and exceptional dramatic skill. It was common knowledge that Bookholm produced the finest readers in Zamonia. When a text demanded it, their voices effortlessly alternated between the highest soprano and the deepest bass. They could sing extempore like nightingales, howl like werewolves, snarl like wildcats and hiss like hobgoblins. They could fill their audiences with terror or move them to hysterical laughter.

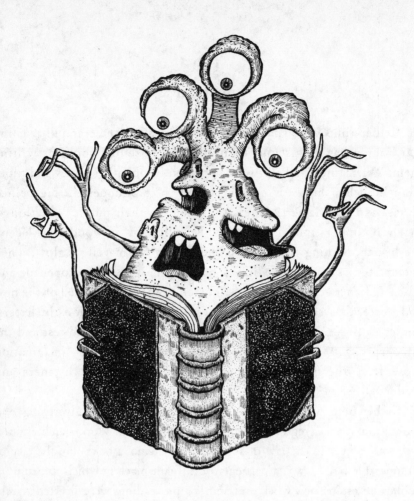

All Zamonian authors dreamt of having their work read aloud by the Master Readers of Bookholm, but not all were granted that privilege. The Master Readers were a capricious, choosy bunch, and any writer spurned by them was considered to be second-rate, no matter how many prizes he had won or books he had sold.

I paused in front of a slab of black slate on which the evening's readings were listed in chalk. I could choose between *Infanticide* by Hethlebem Deroh, *Air Face* by Rabocca Orkan, Rimidalv Vokoban's *Love and the Generation Gap*, and *Thanks But No Thanks* by Goliath Ghork. Other offerings included *The House of a Hundred Feet*, *Whispers and Shadows*, *Gone with the Tornado*, *A Pig for Two Pyras* and *The Unhilarious Sight Gag* – and all in a single street, together with twenty other not quite so high-grade readings for which no charge was made, some of them even with free beer thrown in.

I darted from window to window, peering in at all the people gathered round the crackling fires with teacups or wineglasses in their hands, filled with eager anticipation. Ought I really to pass up such an opportunity for a trombophone concert?

'*Timber-time shmimber-time!*' Pfistomel Smyke's voice re-echoed in my head. '*Timber-time in Bookholm is a nightly occurrence. You won't get to hear a performance by the Murkholm Trombophone Orchestra every day of the week.*'

It was true: timber-time really was a nightly occurrence in Bookholm and I had every intention of staying on for a while. Smyke's allusions to the concert had aroused my curiosity. 'An event', he'd called it, 'not a tourist attraction.' That I found particularly appealing for the very reason that I myself was a tourist. Timber-time was something for the masses; I was destined for higher things, having been personally invited by one of the city's most distinguished inhabitants. I tore myself away from the café windows and almost instinctively headed in the direction of the Municipal Gardens.

The sun had set some time ago, the air was fresh and cool. I shivered a little, having forgotten to bring a warm shawl as the invitation advised. Almost everyone else was wearing one, which made me feel even more out of place, especially as I was the only Lindworm in the audience. The concertgoers were seated in the open air on folding chairs arranged in long rows in front of a conchiform stage. I could have been seated beside a roaring fire in some warm café or bookstore, a free glass of mulled wine in my hand, listening to some legendary performer reading aloud from *A Pig for Two Pyras* – a novel in which the subject of missed opportunities was addressed with exceptional skill.

Missed opportunities, I thought ruefully. At that moment I was missing a reading in three voices of *The Unhilarious Sight Gag*, the sensationally amusing memoirs of the great humorist Ribbald Larph, or a feast of verse by Zepp Hippo, a poet I idolised. Instead of that I was waiting, frozen stiff, for a concert of music for wind instruments that would probably bore me even stiffer. If it didn't begin this minute I would simply stand up and – ah, the musicians were filing onto the stage at last! But my heart sank still further at the sight of them. I'd quite forgotten: they were Murkholmers – musicians from Murkholm, of all places! Not that I subscribed to the prejudices circulating about the inhabitants of that city, it was a well-known fact that the climate prevailing there tended to make them more melancholy than most. They were a bunch of depressive individuals afflicted with a deep-rooted death wish. They were even credited with criminal activities such as luring ships to their doom and looting them. No lively or uplifting music was to be expected from performers like these.

Nor was the Murkholmers' mere appearance calculated to raise my spirits. What with their spongy, bloated faces, pallid skin and mournful eyes, they resembled rain clouds stuffed into black suits. They gazed sadly at the audience as if they might burst into tears or commit collective suicide at any moment. Feeling more and more as if I were attending a wake, I impatiently scanned the audience. Then I caught sight of Ahmed ben Kibitzer in the front row, his yellow eyes staring at me reproachfully, and seated beside him was Inazia Anazazi, the Uggly from that appalling bookshop! She was talking vehemently to Kibitzer and pointing an accusing finger at me. I sank still deeper into my uncomfortable folding chair. This promised to be a bundle of laughs.

The concert began with a toe-curling overture. The musicians blew out their cheeks, which made them look even more froglike, and the opening notes emerged from their instruments in a series of discordant toots utterly

---

* Translator's Note: It may be helpful at this point if I give a brief description of the trombophone, an instrument with which Yarnspinner rightly assumed his Zamonian readers to be thoroughly conversant.

Trombophones are the only musical instruments capable of being bred. The trombophone shellfish, which derives its name from its distant resemblance to the trombone and euphonium, lives in coral reefs off the western shores of Zamonia, but especially in the vicinity of the city of Murkholm. It has an extremely long, tubular shell that develops into a convoluted knot, and it fills the depths of the sea, for as long as it survives there, with a ghostly kind of music not unlike the singing of whales.

Murkholmian beachcombers were the first to hit on the idea of using empty trombophone shells, which were regularly washed ashore on their coast, as musical instruments. Having fitted these with mouthpieces and valves, they developed in time into virtuosi who could coax the most delicate notes from their trombophone shells. Later they took to breeding trombophones and converting their shells into musical instruments for sale throughout Zamonia.

devoid of harmony.* They even seemed to be playing out of tune on purpose, and many of them produced nothing but breathy sounds. I could scarcely believe my ears. Their playing was not only bad, it was a deliberate insult to their audience and, as far as I was concerned, the last straw.

I gathered my cloak together and was just about to ask my immediate neighbour to let me pass when the first harmonies came rippling through the chilly air and a few of the musicians played duets. The orchestra had merely been tuning up, it seemed, so I decided to give it another chance.

One trombophonist struck up an extremely charming, airy theme and the others joined in by degrees. All of a sudden they sounded perfectly coordinated. I looked around to see how my fellow concertgoers were responding: they had all closed their eyes and were swaying in time to the music. Perhaps this was good form here – at least it spared one the sight of those doleful, froglike faces – so I shut my eyes likewise and concentrated on the music.

In my mind's eye I saw a lively swarm of Elf Wasps cavort through the air across an undulating landscape bathed in spring sunshine. The trombophone theme that conjured up the vision of those fluttering insects sounded almost harplike, it was so ethereal and melodious. The wasps formed up like dancers, and at each little variation in the music the scene changed: brimstone butterflies came flying along, a flock of hummingbirds joined in the Elf Wasps' dance, dandelion seeds whirled through the air. I was overcome by springtime emotions and my black mood was blown away – in the literal sense. One of the trombophones emitted a new note, clear as a bell, and a many-coloured rainbow arched across the landscape.

I opened my eyes, somewhat embarrassed by the sentimental scenes that were flitting through my head. Rather sheepishly I looked around to see if anyone had noticed my brief spell of rapture. A surprising sight met my eyes: the entire audience was in a state of collective ecstasy. Everyone was humming the melodies and swaying in time to them like live metronomes. Then – quite without warning – the trombophonists lowered their instruments and the concertgoers awoke from their trance. Throats were cleared, feet shuffled, the musicians cleaned out their mouthpieces with elongated bottle brushes and leafed through their scores. And that hadn't even been the overture. The concert itself had yet to begin.

18

The Trombophone Concert

An exceptionally fat Murkholmer rose to his feet, drew a deep breath, blew a clear note and held it.

For a long time.

A very long time.

A sensationally, impossibly long time from the pulmonary aspect. Without replenishing his lungs, without allowing the note to waver or fade, he held it for minutes on end. It wasn't a particularly remarkable note, neither low nor high but middling.

Shutting my eyes again, I saw an endless, absolutely straight ray of black light traversing an empty white void. I knew at the same time – don't ask me how, dear readers! – that this was the legendary *Baysvillean Primal Note*, the first officially recognised note in Zamonian musical history.

As it rang in my ears, warm as milk, a story surfaced in my mind. A memory from my schooldays? A vague recollection of something I'd read? It was the legend of the primal note which the then ruler of Baysville, Prince Orian, had commissioned his court musicians to discover. In accordance with his wishes, this note was to form the basis of all Zamonian music, the yardstick against which all future compositions and performances were to be measured. Neither pretentious nor unduly self-effacing, neither radical nor borderline, it had to be a note which could – without sounding vulgar – be appreciated by all and sundry. Orian gave orders for this note to be found without delay.

The court musicians of Baysville fanned out in all directions and tested all manner of notes from the ear-splitting crash of a blacksmith's hammer on the anvil to the mute cry of fear uttered by an oyster whose shell has been prised open. But they were all either too loud or too soft, too piercing or too muffled, too high or too low, too thin or too full, too clear or too dull. The court musicians were in despair because their prince was notoriously merciless by nature. Any underlings who failed to obey his orders promptly enough were made to eat slivers of Florinthian glass.

At the end of his tether, one of the court musicians passed a house from whose windows was issuing just the note he and his colleagues had been

looking for: neither too high nor too low, but clear, sustained and steady as a rock. A wholly irreproachable, straightforward note on which whole symphonies could be constructed.

The court musician, a young unmarried Norselander with a fine physique, entered the house. There he found a beautiful girl Norselander – likewise blessed with a perfect figure – playing on a recorder. He fell madly in love with her, just as she did with him, and took his beloved to see the prince, who, having heard her play the note in question on her recorder, proclaimed that the primal note had been found and officially recognised.

But that wasn't the end of the matter, as you, dear readers, have doubtless guessed, for all Zamonian legends must have an unhappy ending. The prince, who also fell in love with the girl, made his rival eat a plateful of glass daggers which choked him to death on his own blood. The girl was so overcome with grief that she swallowed several sharp-edged objects and also died a most atrocious death. Last of all, smitten with an unendurable sense of guilt, Prince Orian of Baysville devoured his own crown jewels and likewise died in agony, a victim of severe internal bleeding. Ever since then, however, the primal note has formed the basis of all Zamonian music.

It was this brief but highly dramatic tale that unfolded before my mind's eye as vividly as a theatrical production, having been summoned up by that sustained note on the trombophone, which now faded gradually away.

I opened my eyes. The fat instrumentalist removed the trombophone from his lips and sat down. I leant back in my chair. It was incredible: music capable of conveying a narrative without words! This was better than being read to; it was also better than any traditional music. Yes, it was a new artistic discipline: *literary* music!

Five more trombophonists rose to their feet. They quickly filled their lungs and blew five notes, only one apiece and always in the same order. It was a pentatonic scale, the simplest form of early music, the beginning of all tonal sequences, primitive but pure, and as touching as a delightful children's song, as the singing of our distant ancestors.

Closing my eyes once more, I was immediately confronted by a primeval panorama. The red glare of the setting sun was bathing the volcanic landscape in a glow that made the rocks look like molten lava. And rocks were all there was; nothing – not a single living creature, not even a plant – obtruded its presence on the pure geology. Profound serenity overcame me. The sun had quickly set and the rocks were now overarched by a dark-blue sky. Little by little, new notes infiltrated the trombophonists' playing, and at each one a star flared up in the sky, white and sparkling. Meteors went hissing through the darkness as the musicians proceeded to manipulate their valves more subtly still. Then a deep bass note rang out and an entire comet thundered across my imaginary firmament, trailing a pale-green tail. Trombophone after trombophone joined in, and the more the music swelled the greater the agglomerations of incandescent suns became until they formed whole galaxies and I knew, all at once, what kind of music was being played.

It was *astronomical systemic polyphony*, a bizarre aberration in the musical history of our continent ordained by an early Zamonian dictator named Slendro Pellogg the Enlightened. Feeling that his authority was threatened by the unbridled creative freedom inherent in the art of music, that pathologically bureaucratic despot aspired to subject it to as strict a set of rules as possible. Because the cosmic order struck him as the most suitable system, Pellogg decreed that the whole of Zamonian music should conform to the music of the spheres. As a result, musicians were compelled to spend years modifying and retuning their instruments in accordance with celestial maps and constellations, cometary orbits and phases of the moon. This musical and astronomical anomaly did not, of course, give birth to any cosmically harmonious music. Instead, because art and astronomy were mutually incompatible, it produced an insufferable din. To cut an unedifying story short, the leading musicians of the period stormed the tyrant's palace and stabbed him to death with their tuning forks.

All this my mind's eye saw enacted in images as clear as crystal: Pellogg staggered through the grounds of his palace, bleeding from dozens of tuning-fork wounds, and ended by tumbling into a goldfish pond whose waters turned pink. The trombophone music swelled to an almost unbearable cacophony and from the despot's corpse my gaze once more travelled upwards to the sky above, where chaos raged, planets and stars danced wildly to the blare of the orchestra, and the entire universe became distorted into a maelstrom of stars and planets that went whirling off into a black void. At that moment the trombophone music abruptly ceased.

My eyes shot open. I was seated on the very edge of my chair, panting and bathed in sweat despite the chill evening air.

All the concertgoers were talking excitedly. I saw the Uggly dabbing Kibitzer's brow.

'That was simply magnificent,' gasped the dwarf beside me. 'I've heard it dozens of times and it still works. No, what am I saying? It gets better and better!'

'It becomes stronger every time, the sensation of being whirled along in a vortex of stars,' someone behind me exclaimed. 'For one glorious moment I thought I was a star myself!'

It was incredible: we had all shared the same vision. These concertgoers were obviously regular attenders who heard the same music, saw the same images and dreamt the same stories again and again. Had I not been there myself, I would never have believed such a form of artistic mediation possible. Then, if not before, I ceased to regret having come and resolved to thank Pfistomel Smyke in person the next morning.

The orchestra struck up once more. The notes sounded flutelike, almost nasal, and I readily shut my eyes. I saw granite castles silhouetted against grey, overcast skies; pennants fluttering in the wind above mounds of slain warriors clad in blood-encrusted armour; quarrelsome ravens perched on gibbets with corpses dangling from them; charred skeletons on smouldering pyres. I had evidently been transported to the Zamonian Middle Ages.

It was a mystery to me how the musicians managed to coax such notes from their trombophones. They sounded like the primitive wind and string instruments of those days: squawks and monotonous wails, discordant caterwauling and the mournful drone of bagpipes. All at once I was looking out across a delightful landscape, an endless expanse of vineyards under a radiant summer sky, and in their midst a mountain that resembled the cloven skull of a giant filled with dark water.

This could only be Grapefields, Zamonia's largest wine-growing area, and the mountain was the Gargyllian Bollogg's Skull. Once again I knew something without knowing how I had learnt it. This was the story of Ilfo Guzzard and his legendary *Comet Wine*. Until then I had known it only through the medium of Inka Almira Rierre's poem 'Comet Wine', but now my brain became filled with all the details of that gruesome medieval drama.

Once every thousand years the Lindenhoop Comet travels through our solar system and comes so close to our planet that its light transforms a whole summer into one long, brilliantly illuminated day.

Ilfo Guzzard, the most influential wine grower of the Zamonian Middle Ages, owner of numerous vineyards in Grapefields and an amateur alchemist, was convinced that vines planted shortly before this nightless summer were bound to yield a wine more mature than any that had ever been bottled. In short, he aimed to produce a Comet Wine.

The comet drew nearer, the longest of all days dawned, and the heat of the sun and the light from that celestial body lent Ilfo's vines a quality surpassing all his expectations. They grew far more quickly and their grapes attained the size of watermelons – the pickers had to pluck them with both hands, one at a time, and carry them, groaning, to the wine press. Their juice was viscous and heavy, full-bodied and delicious, and the wine they yielded was the best of all time. And Ilfo Guzzard possessed a thousand barrels of it! One day he summoned all his employees – vine pruners and grape merchants, planters and pickers and coopers – to a meeting in his courtyard. Then the gates were shut. Taking an axe, Ilfo proceeded to chop holes in every last barrel. His employees thought he had lost his wits and tried to restrain him, but Ilfo would not be restrained. He didn't rest until the last barrel was smashed, the last drop had seeped into the ground and the whole courtyard was awash with Comet Wine.

Finally, Ilfo held up a bottle. 'This, my friends,' he announced triumphantly, 'is the last remaining bottle of Comet Wine, the finest and most delicious, rarest and most valuable wine in Zamonia. I've no need to house and tend any more bottles and barrels, no need to pay any more taxes and wages, nor will I need to go in fear of the Zamonian customs and excise authorities. All I shall need is this one bottle of wine, which is now worth a fortune, and all I shall have to do is watch it appreciate in value every day. I'm retiring.'

'What about *us*? What's to become of *us*?' asked one of his minions.

Ilfo Guzzard eyed him sympathetically.

'You?' he said. 'What's to become of you? You'll be unemployed, of course. I'm firing you all as of now.'

Not until that moment, as he stood there in the midst of hundreds of unemployed workers with history's most valuable bottle of wine in his hand, did it dawn on Ilfo Guzzard that it might have been wiser to give them notice of dismissal in writing. Their eyes were blazing with murderous intent – and also with a desire to own that priceless bottle of wine. They slowly and steadily converged on him.

'Very well,' thought Ilfo, who may have been a rotten employer but was certainly no coward, 'if I must die, at least I'll die drunk. No one's going to own my Comet Wine but me.'

He knocked the top off the bottle and drained it at a gulp. Then he was lynched by his workers. But he had underestimated the greed his speech had kindled in them. Having carried his corpse to the biggest wine press on the estate, they threw him into it and juiced him. They squeezed Ilfo until the last drop of Comet Wine had been extracted from his corpse, along with his blood, and bottled the frightful liquid in a jeroboam. It was now indeed the rarest and most valuable wine in Zamonia.

But the truly horrific story of Comet Wine was only just beginning, because it brought its successive owners nothing but the worst of bad luck.

Ilfo Guzzard's workers were executed for his murder, the next owner of the bottle was struck by a meteor and the one after that devoured by ants while asleep. Wherever the bottle went, murder and mayhem, war and madness soon followed. Many people believed that Comet Wine could restore the dead to life, so it was greatly coveted in alchemistic circles. The jeroboam passed from hand to hand, leaving a trail of bloodshed throughout Zamonia, until one day the trail suddenly ended and the receptacle containing Ilfo Guzzard's wine and blood seemed to vanish from the face of the earth.

The musical epilogue was a quivering tremolo that embodied the full horror of the story. Absolute silence followed.

I awoke from a state akin to hypnosis. The concertgoers around me were murmuring excitedly, the trombophonists bottle-brushing their mouthpieces with a satisfied air.

'That was new,' exclaimed the dwarf beside me. 'The Comet Wine piece wasn't on last week's programme.'

Aha, so they didn't always perform the same pieces. I felt privileged to have been present at a kind of première and closer in spirit to the admirers of Murkholmian trombophone music. By now, ten Midgard Serpents wouldn't have dragged me from my seat. I was eager for more of the same.

The murmurs died away, the musicians raised their instruments once more.

'Next comes some gruesic, I reckon,' the dwarf said with obvious pleasure. 'It'll go well with that gory tale of the Comet Wine.'

'What's gruesic?' I enquired.

'Wait and see,' the dwarf replied mysteriously. 'Now things will get really weird.' He broke off in mid chuckle. 'Hey, didn't you bring a shawl? You'll catch your death.'

I couldn't have cared less. I was willing to make any sacrifice for the sake of some more trombophone music.

Several of the Murkholmers projected shimmering notes high into the night sky while others blew discreetly in the bass register. I shut my eyes again, but this time I saw no overwhelming panorama. Instead, my head became filled with a profound understanding of the Dervish music of Late Medieval Zamonia – of which I'd known absolutely nothing until then.

Dervish music, I suddenly knew for certain, was based on a heptametrical scale whose intervals were measured in units called *shrooti*. Two *shrooti* equalled a semitone, four *shrooti* a whole tone and twenty-two *shrooti* an octave. That an interval should have taken its name from a musician was an honour unique in Zamonian musical history. Octavius Shrooti, the legendary Dervish composer of the Late Middle Ages, had evolved a gruesome form of music, or 'gruesic', capable of being blended with any composition. It was based on sounds calculated to inspire dread: dogs howling in the night, creaking hinges, the cry of a screech owl, anonymous voices whispering in the dark, rumbles from beneath the cellar stairs, malevolent titters in the attic, women weeping on a blasted heath, screams from a lunatic asylum, fingernails scratching slate – whatever made a person's hair stand on end and could be imitated by musical instruments. Shrooti blended this gruesic with popular contemporary music in an extraordinarily successful manner. In his day people went to concerts mainly for the purpose of being scared out of their wits. Ovations took the form of cries of horror, mass fainting fits equated to requests for encores, and when panic-stricken members of the public jostled their way to the exit, screaming, the concert had been a complete success. Coiffeurs styled their clients' hair so that it stood on end, chewed fingernails were considered chic, and concertgoers who chanced to meet in the street would greet each other with an affected 'Eeek!' and throw up their hands in simulated horror. A whole series of musical instruments originated at this time, among them the gallows harp, the devil's bagpipes, the trembolo, the ten-valved macabrophone, the death saw, the dungeonica and the throttleflute. Not for nothing was Octavius Shrooti's heyday known as the *Gruesome Period*.

The music died away and I opened my eyes. The dwarf beside me grinned.

'Now you know: that was gruesic. But this is when it really hots up. Be prepared for anything!' He sat back and closed his eyes with a sigh of anticipation.

Four trombophonists produced a chorus of howls that put me in mind of bloodhounds drowning in a castle moat. Two more imitated the bleating laughter with which Mountain Demons unleash avalanches. The fattest trombophonist seated in the middle of the orchestra persuaded his instrument to emit a despairing sigh like the final exhalation of someone being strangled by a garrotte. I also seemed to hear the pitiful cries of people buried alive and the screams of Ugglies burning to death.

Somewhat perturbed, I shut my eyes again. What horrific scenes would this music summon up in my mind? What terrible story would it recount?

At first I saw nothing but books. I was looking down an endless passage lined with shelves and old books. Surely nothing untoward could happen in an antiquarian bookshop? I studied the backs of the books more closely. Heavens, they weren't just old, they were *very* old – so ancient, in fact, that I couldn't decipher the titles. Several curious ceiling lights dispensed a ghostly, pulsating glow. Something was moving inside them. Were these the jellyfish lamps described by Regenschein?

At last I caught on: these were the catacombs of Bookholm – the labyrinth beneath the city, and I was in the midst of it! How fantastic, a subterranean journey into that mysterious, perilous world devoid of any personal risk! I need only listen to the music and devote myself to the scenes as they unfolded.

I opened my eyes briefly and closed them again, then repeated the procedure several times in succession. Sure enough, I could effortlessly alternate between the Municipal Gardens and the catacombs. Eyes open: Municipal Gardens. Eyes shut: catacombs.

Gardens.

Catacombs.

Gardens.

Catacombs.

Gardens.

Catacombs.

In the end I kept my eyes closed. Although I was actually seated on an uncomfortable folding chair in Bookholm's Municipal Gardens, I was stealing along a dimly lit, book-lined passage far below ground. Amazing, what this trombophone music was capable of. Everything looked so real, too! There was an overpowering smell of old paper – incredibly enough, I could even *smell* this scene! Not all the jellyfish ceiling lights were working properly – the creatures imprisoned in them shed a fitful glow – and some of the glass containers had cracked, releasing their occupants from captivity. A few of the phosphorescent invertebrates had clung to the shelves while escaping, whereas others had fallen to the floor and dried up.

What a weird place! There was a ubiquitous crackling noise, probably made by bookworms munching their way through paper. I could hear rats squeaking, beetles scuttling around and, overlying every other sound, a kind of whisper. I suddenly became aware that I could no longer hear any trombophone music.

I tried to open my eyes and catch a reassuring glimpse of the Municipal Gardens, but it was no use, my eyelids might just as well have been sewn shut. I could distinctly see the ominous scene in the catacombs, though. What a strange state of affairs, being able to see with my eyes shut! It no longer gave me a pleasurable thrill. My sole emotion was stark terror.

I tried to calm down by persuading myself that this was just another variation, a new and exciting addition to the concert programme. Now I was in the midst of the story – indeed, I might even be its principal character. But what kind of story was it and who exactly was I?

I stole further along the passage, looking nervously to right and left, up and down and back again. And then I was suddenly overcome by a strange sensation: I could *smell* which books were on the shelves. I had no need to waste time examining them, I could detect the lemony scent of the long-lost collection belonging to Prince Agoo Gaaz the Well-Read, not that his library held any present interest for me because – it abruptly dawned on me whose skin and story I now occupied – I was Colophonius Regenschein the Bookhunter!

How incredible! No, on the contrary, it was all too believable – it was frighteningly true! I had lost my ability to distinguish between dream and reality. I had become another person so completely that I was thinking his thoughts and sensing his fear. Now I knew why those precious volumes held no interest for me. I, Regenschein, was not alone in this labyrinth. I, Regenschein, was trying to escape from someone. I, Regenschein, had ceased to be the hunter and become the quarry: I was being hunted by the Shadow King.

I could hear him rustling and panting behind the books, and I sometimes fancied I could feel his hot breath on my neck, his sharp claws grazing my back. I made another desperate attempt to open my eyes, but in vain. I was imprisoned in Regenschein's body, held captive in the catacombs of Bookholm.

Was it possible to die in an imaginary scenario? In a dream? What if Regenschein were killed? Was this still a story or the real thing? I could no longer tell. I knew only that I could feel Regenschein's exhaustion in every limb – feel his aching muscles and burning lungs, his wildly beating heart. Then the passage ended abruptly and I was confronted by a wall of paper. My path was barred from floor to ceiling by a stack of manuscripts piled up at random. It was a dead end.

Feverishly, I debated what to do, retrace my steps and blunder into the arms of the Shadow King or try to demolish the wall of paper? I decided on the latter course of action and was about to set to work when the manuscripts began to stir. Nobody moved them – they moved of their own accord, slithering over each other like serpents, rustling as they crumpled up, straightened out again and eventually assumed the shape of a figure, a figure so horrific in appearance that –

'*Eeeeeeeee!*'

Someone was shrieking at the top of his voice.

'*Eeeeeeeee!*'

Was that Regenschein screaming in mortal terror?

'*Eeeeeeeee!*'

No, it was I, Optimus Yarnspinner, the cowardly lizard, who had flung himself to the ground and was begging for mercy.

'Please!' I entreated, sobbing. 'Please spare me! I don't want to die!'

'You can open your eyes,' said a voice, 'the music has stopped.'

I opened my eyes. I was lying face down on the grass, just in front of my chair, with the dwarf and several other concertgoers bending over me.

'Is he a tourist?' asked someone.

'Looks like a visitor from Lindworm Castle,' said someone else.

It was really embarrassing. I scrambled to my feet, brushed the grass from my cloak and sat down again. The entire audience was staring at me. I could sense the eyes of Kibitzer and the Uggly boring into me. Even the musicians were looking my way.

'They were bound to enjoy your discomfiture,' the dwarf whispered sympathetically, 'but you aren't the first by any means. It's a very intense experience, living out Colophonius Regenschein's last few minutes in person.'

'That's one way of putting it,' I whispered back, trying to sit as low in my chair as possible. I naturally couldn't help being repelled by the notion that I'd screamed and whimpered and rolled around on the ground – for how long, I wondered? – so I was overjoyed when the Murkholmers raised their instruments and reclaimed everyone's attention.

It sounded almost as if they were checking their valves again. One or another trombophonist blew a single note, seemingly at random, but that was all. Was the concert over? Was this a ritual of some kind? Even more gingerly and apprehensively than before, I experimented by shutting my eyes.

The image I saw this time was rather abstract. No landscape, no figures, no passages, just luminous little specks of various colours – yellow, red, blue – arranged in a circle. They lit up one after another, slowly at first, then at steadily decreasing intervals. The notes didn't fit together or produce a harmonious melody. Yellow, red, blue, yellow, red, blue – the sequence continued without a break, round and round. It was the first time trombophone music had infused me with no emotion of any kind, neither euphoria nor fear. No story began to unfold.

'The Optometric Rondo!' gasped the dwarf beside me. 'They're going to play some Moomievillean Ophthalmic Polyphony.'

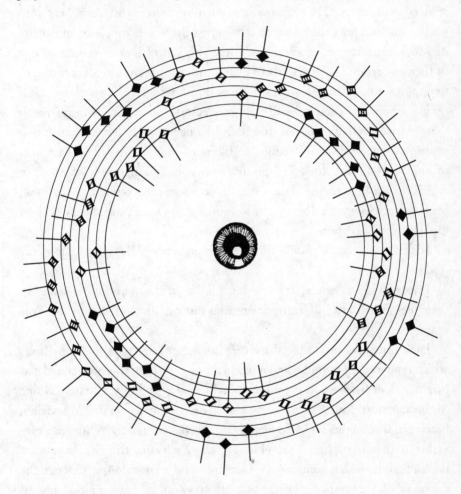

I knew this too, strangely enough, even though I had never before heard of Moomievillean Ophthalmic Polyphony. Yes, I was suddenly an expert on this esoteric branch of music and knew everything about it – for instance, that Moomievillean oculists had developed a diagnostic technique in which the interior of the eye was examined with a kaleidoscopic crystal of the kind found in the Impic Alps. In order to view every corner of the eye through the pupil, the oculist instructed the patient which way to look: straight up, up and to the right, right of centre, down and to the right, straight down, down and to the left, and so on until the eye had described a complete circle. Moomievillean oculists were Moomies, of course, and Moomies, as everyone knows, have six ears capable of picking up frequencies only spiders can detect. Their brains immediately convert all they hear into music, which is why they hum to themselves the whole time – as, of course, do Moomievillean oculists while at work. This is how it came about that one of them, a certain Dr Doremius Fasolati, noticed that the circular motion of the pupil, in conjunction with his musical humming, had a soothing effect on his patients. It even induced a slightly ecstatic sensation, with the result that – however shattering his diagnosis had been – they left his consulting room in a cheerful, almost euphoric frame of mind. This led to Fasolati's invention of Ophthalmic Polyphony, a circular arrangement of notes in which the musical theme always returns to its starting point and begins all over again. So much for my new-found knowledge of Moomievillean Ophthalmic Polyphony.

'The *Optometric Rondo*!' shouted the audience. 'Play the *Optometric Rondo*!'

I opened my eyes and saw the Murkholmian trombophonists rising to their feet. Shrill cries of enthusiasm rang out on all sides. I shut my eyes again.

Each note was now played by three trombophonists at the same time, which rendered it far louder and more piercing. The light this occasioned was brighter than before and the sound waves made my body vibrate. As one triplicated note followed another, the lights began to rotate. My vision, hearing and thoughts had also begun to revolve ever faster. Yellow-yellow-yellow, red-red-red, blue-blue-blue . . . I saw a whirling trinity of colours, a flaming rainbow that contracted into a circle and went spinning through the darkness of outer space. Discarding all my doubts, I abandoned myself entirely to the rapture those abstract notes induced in me. We had entered a realm far transcending that of literary music – one in which stories and images, persons and their destinies had ceased to be important. All that I had heard hitherto seemed a mere preliminary to what I was now experiencing, whose immensity was such that I can summarise it in only three words: *I became music.*

I began by evaporating. Steam must experience that sensation when it escapes from boiling liquid and rises into the cooling air. For the first time in my life I felt free, truly free from all mundane constraints, disburdened of my body and liberated from my own thoughts.

Then I became sound, and anyone transmuted into sound becomes a wave. Indeed, I venture to say that anyone who knows what it's like to become a sound wave is well on the way to fathoming the mysteries of the universe. I now understood the secret of music and knew what makes it so infinitely superior to all the other arts: its incorporeality. Once it has left an instrument it becomes its own master, a free and independent creature of sound, weightless, incorporeal and perfectly in tune with the universe.

That was how I felt: like music dancing with a flaming circle high above all else. Somewhere down below lay the world, my body, my cares and concerns, but they all seemed quite insignificant now. Here was the fiery wheel whose presence alone mattered. On and on it spun until its multicoloured luminosity

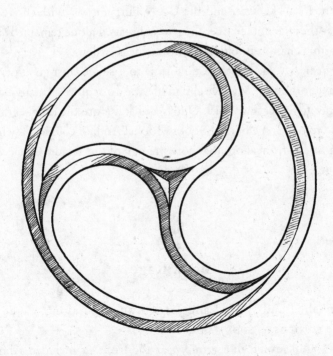

seemed to flow into its interior as well, in three curving trajectories that united at its central point.

And then I saw it: the *Triadic Circle.*

The Triadic Circle, the mysterious symbol emblazoned on the doors of Kibitzer's and Inazia Anazazi's bookshops . . . It glowed before my inner eye, conjured up by the power of the trombophone music, which was now blaring at maximal volume. That fiery circle was the loveliest, most flawless and magnificent thing I had ever seen. My one desire was to serve and obey it.

Then everything ceased abruptly. The music stopped, the mysterious symbol faded and I plummeted into the depths. I returned to earth, to Zamonia, to my own body. Click! So emancipated only moments before, my spirit had inexorably re-embedded itself in my flesh and was sandwiched between my molecules.

I opened my eyes. The Murkholmers had lowered their trombophones and begun to replace them in their instrument cases. Everyone stood up. No applause. I looked around in bewilderment. What a strange end to such a sensational concert! I turned to ask the dwarf some questions, but he had already left. I saw Kibitzer and the Uggly hurrying off with the rest of the audience as they scrambled over the rows of seats. I alone remained sitting on my collapsible chair in Bookholm's Municipal Gardens.

Then it came to me: I, too, had no time to lose – I must go at once! How could I have forgotten? My sole aim in life was to acquire as many books as I could gather together and carry. Quick, quick, before the others got there! I simply had to buy some books! Books! Books! And, of course, they had to be Dreaming Books from shops that bore the sign of the Triadic Circle. I dashed off after the rest.

♀I♂
Book Rage

We pushed and shoved and jostled our way along, eager to quit the gardens as soon as possible.

I soon found myself in a group near the front. It included Ahmed ben Kibitzer and the Uggly, but we barely noticed each other. I was engaged on a mission: I had to buy books, masses of them, and nothing else mattered. As if the trombophone music had emptied my brain of everything but that one overriding thought, I strode along as smartly as a soldier, repeating it to myself again and again: *Books, books, I must buy some books! Books, books, I must buy some books!*

We came to a street at last, but it didn't boast a single bookshop. We'd happened on what was probably the only street in Bookholm without one! What a waste of time! I panted with impatience, others swore. On, on!

The next street . . . Four second-hand bookshops, but none of them bore the sign of the Triadic Circle. Damnation, they were no use! On we went!

The next street . . . A dozen bookshops, two with the Triadic Circle. Impetuously, we charged into them like a horde of drunken barbarians, uttering such loud, triumphant cries that the other customers beat a hasty retreat and the proprietors took refuge behind their counters, looking apprehensive.

I peered around feverishly. Books at last! Which ones should I buy? No matter! They were books, that was the main thing! I must buy, buy! I seized a large shopping basket and filled it indiscriminately, sweeping books off the shelves regardless of title or author, price or condition. I couldn't have cared less if they were valuable first editions or cheap trash, if they concerned my fields of interest or were worth acquiring for any reason at all. I had been smitten with an insatiable hunger for books and only one thing could cure it: buy, buy, buy!

An unpleasant incident occurred when the Uggly and I chanced to grab the same book simultaneously. We tugged at it for a while, baring our teeth and snarling as we swayed to and fro, until she suddenly lost interest and swooped on another pile of books like a vulture pouncing on a dead sheep.

We were in the throes of book rage! The concertgoers around me shoved and jostled, snatching up armfuls of books as if there would be none left tomorrow. One or two of them came to blows, but most reserved their energy for the task in hand. I staggered across the shop weighed down with books, pausing only to load my basket with still more printed matter.

The first of us made for the cash desk, unable to carry any more, and dramatic scenes ensued when the cost of their intended purchases exceeded their ability to pay. Many wept and rent their clothes when the dealer withheld books to the value of the deficit, and I found their behaviour quite understandable. How could he be so hard-hearted?

At last I myself tottered up to the counter with my basket, which was a dead weight. The bookseller announced his intention of withholding a large proportion of its contents – expensive first editions for the most part – merely because I couldn't pay for them! I wept and wailed, appalled by his mean, small-minded attitude, but he was adamant. Having cursed him violently and stuffed as many books into a huge bag as my purse would stretch to, I departed, broke but blissful.

Back at the hotel I tipped out my haul in the middle of the room and spent a while gazing at the mound of books with a contented grin. Then I slumped down on the bed and lapsed at once into a long, dreamless sleep.

Four Hundred Frog Recipes

My first thought on waking was that I was in the wrong room, or that some lunatic had dumped a mountain of books there during the night. Then it all came back to me: the concert, the Murkholmian trombo-phonists, the primal note, Ilfo Guzzard's Comet Wine, the Shadow King, Moomievillean Ophthalmic Polyphony, the fiery Triadic Circle, my fit of book rage.

Sleepily, I went over to my haul, picked up one of the books and checked the title.

Chimney-Sweeping for Advanced Students by Darko Lum.

I picked up another.

Two Dozen on the Bare Butt – A Flagellator's Manual by Sistomach Owch.

I tossed it aside and picked up another.

A Hundred Hilarious Anecdotes from the Gloomberg Mountains.

What *was* this trash? I picked up one book after another and examined it, shaking my head.

A Little Book of Knots for Left-Handers.

Glass-Blowing with Bellows.

All You Need to Know about Chronic Flatulence.

The Prehistoric Mummification of Insects in Subtropical Peat Bogs (24 volumes).

Applied Cannibalism.

How to Comb a Chicken.

Corrosion Tables for Rust Technicians.

Beard-Washing with Marine Sponges.

An Encyclopaedia of Wood-Planing.

Four Hundred Frog Recipes. Who had bought this load of rubbish? Could *I* have done so?

I continued to rummage through the mound, becoming wider awake and more desperate with every title I came to. I hadn't acquired a single interesting or valuable item, just waste paper and junk. I'd blown all my savings on books fit at best for a bonfire.

In despair, I tottered back to the bed and lay down again. It was only then that I became aware of the throbbing pain in my head. I hoped it wasn't an incurable brain disease. Perhaps the music had triggered a latent psychosis that would shortly land me in a padded cell in Bookholm's lunatic asylum, attired in a straitjacket. It had already ruined me financially, so why shouldn't it drive me insane? Listen! Was I hearing voices? Yes, I could definitely hear voices inside my head – dementia already had me in its icy clutches and was whispering its crazy commands in my ear. But no, it was only the chambermaids dusting the room next door. I strove to calm down.

How could I have come to this? Was trombophone music really so potent? Well, if it could make a Lindworm whimper and roll around on the ground under the impression that he was Colophonius Regenschein, it was bound to be capable of a few other things as well.

I would have no choice but to return to Lindworm Castle hanging my head in shame, a ruined, broken dinosaur. I didn't even have enough money to pay my hotel bill or buy myself some breakfast. Would the bookseller take the books back? No use, I couldn't even remember where his shop was.

Then I thought of Pfistomel Smyke. My manuscript was valuable, he had told me. Perhaps I could sell it to him.

I turned over with a groan. How low I'd sunk! If I was prepared to sell Dancelot's bequest for a bite of breakfast, I might as well go to the Graveyard of Forgotten Writers and move in right away. Shutting my eyes, I saw the fiery Triadic Circle. Not as bright and resplendent as yesterday but in full colour – a beautiful, fascinating sight. I could use a little more trombophone music, I thought.

Then I wrenched my eyes open and jumped out of bed. What had that music done to me? I stared disconsolately at the worthless pile of books. I simply had to get some fresh air, so I washed and made my way downstairs.

Having slunk past the reception desk under the hotel-keeper's suspicious gaze – he had witnessed my return in the small hours, laden with the huge bag of books and uttering triumphant cries – I went outside. It surprised me to see how busy the streets were. I must have slept for an exceptionally long time. To judge by the position of the sun, it was almost midday. This was quite convenient, because it meant that I could take myself off to Pfistomel Smyke's typographical laboratory without delay.

Smyke's Inheritance

Pfistomel Smyke had a sumptuous brunch ready for me – apple juice, poached eggs, bread and honey (sans bees), oven-warm Poet's Ringlets and coffee – as if he'd guessed that I would arrive in a famished condition.

We sat in the literary scholar's small, snug kitchen. He grinned to see the way I fell on my food. I drank several pints of coffee and demolished three slices of bread and honey, four eggs and two Poet's Ringlets. While eating I told him about my experiences of the previous night.

Smyke laughed. 'I ought to have warned you. Those musicians are Murkholmers, after all – one has to be prepared for anything. I once attended a concert after which the entire audience – including yours truly – desecrated Bookholm's Ugglian cemetery. That's Murkholmian humour for you – everything has its price. But tell me, wasn't it worth going?'

'Well, yes,' I said, chewing busily, 'in a way. But now I'm broke.'

'I think not.'

'What do you mean?'

'That manuscript of yours – I've examined it thoroughly and I think it's considerably more valuable than I assumed at first sight.'

'Really?'

My spirits rose abruptly. I took another swig of coffee.

'Certainly, my friend,' said Smyke. 'Its value is immense, especially here in Bookholm. There should be no difficulty in selling it for a substantial sum. I can help you to dispose of it if you like – without charging a commission, of course. If you preferred to hang on to it your credit would be good anywhere in the city.'

'That's wonderful. Were you able to identify the author?'

'I was indeed.'

'Really? Who is it?'

Smyke gave another grin and rose. 'May I keep you on tenterhooks for a bit – and, at the same time, show you one of Bookholm's best-kept secrets? Come with me, please.'

He left the kitchen. I stuffed another Poet's Ringlet into my mouth and followed him. The literary scholar led me into his typographical laboratory and pointed to the shelf with the Leyden Manikins on it. I looked at the bottles, gave a start, and looked more closely. The Manikins were floating in their nutrient fluid – lifeless.

'They're dead,' said Smyke. 'Your mysterious author was responsible.'

'How do you mean?'

'Last night I read them some passages from your manuscript to check the quality of the intonation. At first they broke into song, then they wept. Finally they sank to the bottom of their bottles, one by one, and expired. The quality of the writing killed them. It was too great for such little creatures.'

'Incredible,' I said. 'Has anything like that happened before?'

'No,' said Smyke, 'never.' He went over to the trapdoor, which was wide open. 'Follow me, please.'

The trapdoor gave access to a decrepit wooden ramp that groaned as the corpulent Shark Grub slithered down it. I gingerly climbed down after him. Below ground it was cool and damp – and utterly uninteresting: a typical old cellar with a few dusty shelves on which reposed some bottled fruit, jars of honey and bottles of wine. I could see nothing else apart from cobwebs, firewood and a few broken gadgets from the laboratory.

'Is *this* one of Bookholm's best-kept secrets?' I asked. 'Are you afraid someone will discover your aversion to dusting?'

With a smile, Smyke gave one of the shelves a gentle push. It swung back, together with the wall behind it, and disclosed a long underground passage filled with pulsating light.

'Are you prepared to enter the catacombs of Bookholm?' Smyke asked, pointing along the tunnel with his seven left arms. 'Don't worry, it'll be a guided tour. Return journey guaranteed.'

We entered the passage, which was discreetly lit by jellyfish lamps. The prevailing atmosphere resembled the one in my trombophone vision, except that here there were no shelves and no books. Hanging on the walls at long intervals were some large oil paintings, all of which depicted Shark Grubs in various costumes.

'They're all Smykes,' the literary scholar said with a touch of pride as we made our way past the portraits.

'My ancestors,' he went on. 'There! That's Prosperius Smyke, formerly chief executioner of Florinth. The one with the crafty expression is Harimata Smyke, a notorious spy who died three centuries ago. The ugly fellow beyond her is Halirrhotius Smyke, a pirate who resorted to eating his own children when becalmed in the doldrums. Ah well, we can't choose our relations, can we? The Smyke family is scattered the length and breadth of Zamonia.'

One of the portraits aroused my particular interest. The subject was exceptionally thin for his breed. He displayed none of the obesity typical of Shark Grubs and had piercing eyes in which I seemed to detect a glint of insanity.

'Hagob Salbandian Smyke,' said Pfistomel. 'An immediate forebear of mine. It was he who . . . But more of that later. Hagob was an artist. He produced sculptures. My home is full of them.'

'Really?' I interposed. 'I haven't seen a single sculpture on your premises.'

'No wonder,' Smyke replied. 'They're invisible to the naked eye. Hagob made microsculptures.'

'Microsculptures?'

'Yes. He began with cherry stones and grains of rice, but his works steadily diminished in size. He ended by carving them out of the tip of a single hair.'

'Is that possible?'

'Not really, but Hagob managed it. I'll show you some of them under a microscope when we get back. He carved the whole of the Battle of Nurn Forest on an eyelash.'

'You come of unusual stock,' I said.

'Yes,' Smyke sighed. 'Alas!'

The further we progressed along the steeply sloping passage the older the portraits became. One could tell this from the hairline cracks in their layers of oil paints and glazes, their increasingly primitive technique and their subjects' style of dress.

'We Smykes can trace the roots of our family tree to the edge of the Zamonian Ocean and beyond. They even extend beneath its surface – down, deep down to the ocean floor itself. But I'm not indulging in false modesty, truly not, when I say that my ancestry means little to me. The Smykes have always kept their distance from each other. Love of solitude is another inherited family trait.'

The passage changed direction but remained as featureless as ever. We passed an occasional jellyfish lamp on the ceiling or portrait on the wall, but that was all.

'Habibullah Smyke,' said my companion. 'Also called "The Desert Scorpion". He used to drown his enemies in sand – you can do that, as long as it's quicksand.'

He pointed to another painting.

'Okudato "Godfather" Smyke, once the underworld boss of Ironville. He got a blacksmith to forge him a set of steel dentures and devoured his rivals alive – the only Smyke to have sunk to the level of the Demonocles. And that's Termagenta Smyke, who skewered all her husbands with a red-hot . . . Ugh, it's too distasteful. I'll spare us any further details, we're nearly there in any case.'

The passage had been descending steeply all this time, so we must have been pretty far below ground, but I still hadn't seen a single book. Suddenly it ended and we found ourselves confronted by a dark wooden door with ironwork fittings.

'Here we are,' said Smyke. He bent down, put a hand to his mouth and muttered something unintelligible at the rusty old lock.

'A Bookemistic incantatory lock,' he explained almost apologetically when he straightened up. The door creaked open by itself.

'An alchemistic falderal from the last century,' Smyke went on. 'Nothing

magical about it, just a gravity-operated mechanism activated by sound waves, though they have to be the right sound waves. Saves messing around with a key. After you!'

I walked through the doorway and abruptly found myself standing in the biggest underground chamber I'd ever seen. Devoid of any shape that could have been defined in geometrical terms, it stretched away in all directions, upwards, downwards and sideways. Chasms yawned, stone ceilings soared to an immense height overhead, terraces rose in tiers, caves branched off with other caves branching off them, huge dripstones hung from above or jutted from below, the latter with spiral staircases hewn into them, stone arches spanned ravines – and everywhere jellyfish lamps dispensed their pulsating glow and candelabra were suspended on chains or let into the walls. This was a chamber composed of many chambers – one in which the eye could roam without end until all was engulfed in darkness. I had never felt so disorientated. But the truly astonishing feature of the place was not its shape, size or lighting; it was the fact that it was full of books.

'This is my library,' Smyke said as casually as if he had opened the door of a garden shed.

There must have been hundreds of thousands if not millions of books – more than I'd seen in the whole of Bookholm put together! Every part of the monstrous dripstone cave had been used as a repository for books. Some of the shelves had been hewn out of the living rock, others were made of timber and soared to dizzy heights with long ladders leading to them. Mountainous piles of books stood in rows like endless alpine ranges. There were plain raw deal bookcases, valuable antiquarians' cabinets with glazed doors, baskets, tubs, handcarts and crates full of books.

'I myself have no idea how many there are,' said Smyke, as if he had read my thoughts, '– no idea whatsoever. I only know they all belong to me under the terms of the Bookholmian Constitution.'

'Is this a genuine dripstone cave,' I asked, 'or was it hewn out of the rock?'

'Most of it originated naturally, I believe. Everything here must once have been under water. That's indicated by the fossils embedded in the rock – for which any Zamonian biologist would give his right hand.' Smyke chuckled. 'But all the surfaces look polished, hence the artificial impression. I surmise that some industrious souls gave nature a helping hand – more than that I can't say.'

'And all these books belong to you?' I said stupidly. The idea that such an immense collection could belong to one person struck me as absurd.

'Yes. I inherited them.'

'You mean they're a family heirloom? An heirloom handed down by your – forgive me for citing your own description – degenerate ancestors? They must have been remarkably cultivated and refined for all that.'

'Oh, please don't think that refinement and degeneracy are mutually exclusive.' Smyke heaved a sigh. He took a book from a shelf and regarded it meditatively.

'I should point out that none of this belonged to me at birth,' he went on. 'I grew up in Grailsund, a long way from Bookholm. The business I engaged in there had absolutely no connection with books. It didn't go too well, either, so one day I found myself in dire financial straits. Don't worry, though, I won't bore you with the story of my youthful poverty. I'm just coming to the nice part.'

Smyke replaced the book. My eyes strayed over the incredible subterranean scenery. Some white bats were fluttering among the stalactites high overhead.

'One day I received a letter from a Bookholm solicitor,' Smyke continued. 'I had very little desire to visit this musty old city of books, to be honest, but the letter informed me that I had come into an inheritance, and if I didn't take it up in person it would pass to the municipality. Although it didn't say what the inheritance comprised or what it was worth, I would at that time have welcomed ownership of a public convenience, so I set off for Bookholm. It transpired that my inheritance – the estate of my great-uncle Hagob Salbandian – consisted of the small house that is now some two thousand feet above our heads.'

Two thousand feet of soil and rock between us and the surface? It wasn't a particularly pleasant thought.

'I took up my inheritance with a touch of disappointment, of course, because I'd travelled to Bookholm filled with visions of a considerably more sensational bequest. For all that, a house of my own – a listed building on which I wouldn't have to pay rent – was an improvement on my existing circumstances. As a citizen of Bookholm I was entitled to study at the local university. Since it was obvious how to make money in this city, I enrolled in the courses on Zamonian literature, antiquarianism and typography. I also did a wide variety of menial jobs ranging from book-walking to scissor-washing. A person with fourteen hands can always find work.'

Smyke looked down at his numerous hands and sighed.

'One night, while combing my cellar for something worth selling, I found that its only contents were empty bookcases. Well, bookcases are always in demand in Bookholm, so I thought I'd take one upstairs, spruce it up a little and sell it. When I tried to wrench it off the wall – well, you saw what happened just now: the secret door swung open, revealing the route to Hagob Salbandian's real bequest.'

'Did your uncle collect all these books?'

'Hagob? Certainly not. From what I know of him, he wasn't entirely sane. He used to make those sculptures I mentioned – sculptures carved out of hairs under a microscope with tools of his own invention. He was known

141

throughout the city as a crack-brained eccentric who begged food from bakers and innkeepers. Can you imagine it? There he was, sitting on this immense fortune but engraving scenes from Zamonian history on horsehairs and eating stale loaves and kitchen waste. They didn't even find his body, just his will.'

What a story, dear readers! The last will and testament of a lunatic. The most valuable library in Zamonia far below ground. This was material that cried out to be converted into literature. The outlines of a novel took shape in my mind within seconds. My first promising idea for ages!

Smyke hauled himself up an iron handrail and looked down into a deep chasm whose walls were lined with bookshelves.

'The owner of a house that gives access to a subterranean book cave automatically owns the cave and its contents. That rule has applied for hundreds of years, and this is the biggest cave containing the biggest collection of antiquarian books in the whole of Bookholm. It has belonged to the Smyke family from time immemorial.'

He was still staring into the depths.

'Well, it would be fantastic enough if these books were of average quality, but they're all literary gems: first editions, long-lost libraries, books whose existence has been in doubt for a thousand years. Many a Bookholm antiquarian would be happy to possess even one volume equal in quality to those in my collection. This isn't just the biggest library in Bookholm, it's the city's greatest treasure. Several items on the Golden List are here.'

'Aren't you afraid someone will break in? All that stands in the way is your little house and that ridiculous lock.'

'No, no one will break in. It's impossible.'

'Ah, so you've installed some traps!'

'No, no traps. This cave is entirely unprotected.'

'Isn't that a bit . . . risky?'

'No. And now I'll let you into a secret: no one will break into this cave because no one knows of its existence.'

'I don't understand. You told me the Smykes have owned it from time immemorial.'

'Quite so, and they carefully obliterated all trace and recollection of it over the centuries. They bribed local officials, removed entries from the land

142

register, forged historical works and maps. They're also said to have eliminated one or two people.'

'Good heavens! How do you know?'

'There are countless family papers down here – diaries, letters, documents of all kinds. You wouldn't believe what depths of infamy they reveal. I'm not too proud of my ancestry, as I already told you.' Smyke fixed me with an earnest gaze.

'To all intents and purposes,' he went on, 'this cave doesn't exist. It's known only to me and a few very close associates of mine – people I trust implicitly. Colophonius Regenschein too, of course. And now you.'

I was speechless for a moment.

'What made you confide in me, of all people? A total stranger?'

'I'll explain in due course – it's partly to do with your manuscript – but first let me come to the really interesting part of my story.'

'You mean there's an even *more* interesting part?' I couldn't help laughing.

Smyke let go of the handrail and grinned at me. 'You know, people in the city still regard me as dealer with a specialised stock, a fortunate heir and parvenu with a nose for valuable books and excellent connections with collectors and Bookhunters – one who never keeps more than a crate of books on his premises.'

He suddenly assumed an expression I couldn't interpret.

'But down here I'm a different person. See that bookcase over there, the one filled with first editions from the fourth century? Each of them would buy me a whole urban district, or bribe a politician for life, or get a mayor elected by financing his campaign. I don't do any of those things, of course.'

'Of course not,' I said. I had no idea what he was driving at and hoped he would soon get round to my manuscript.

'No, of course I don't. I get my underlings to do them for me.'

What was he talking about? I was starting to feel uneasy.

Smyke looked at me intently. 'I don't buy books, I buy whole bookshops. I sell vast consignments of books. I flood the market with cheap offers, ruin my competitors and, when they go broke, buy up their businesses for peanuts. I control rentals throughout the city. I own most of the publishing houses and nearly all the paper mills and printing works. All of Bookholm's Master Readers are on my payroll, as are all the residents of Poison Alley. I dictate the price of paper and the size of editions. I determine which books succeed and which don't. I make successful authors and destroy them at will. I'm the ruler of Bookholm. *I'm Zamonian literature personified.'*

Was this a joke? Was this literary scholar submitting me to a test of some kind? Was he giving me a sample of his curious sense of humour?

'And this is just the start. I shall extend my network of antiquarian bookshops from Bookholm to the whole of Zamonia. I've already opened branches in Grailsund, Florinth and Atlantis, and they're all doing splendidly, take it from me. One day in the not too distant future I shall control Zamonia's entire book trade and property market, and from there it's only a short step to political dictatorship. I think on a grand scale, as you see.'

'You're joking,' I said in dismay.

'Not at all. Better take me seriously, because I can assure you of one thing: it's going to be far from funny for people of your kind when I come to power.' Smyke's voice had taken on an edge that made me shiver.

'People of my kind?' I said.

'Artists!' cried Smyke. He uttered the word as if it meant 'Rats!'

'Artists will come off worst under my regime, I fear, because I shall abolish literature. *And* music, *and* painting, *and* theatre, *and* dance – all the arts, the whole decadent, redundant caboodle! I shall have every book in Zamonia burnt, every canvas stripped of paint with acid, every sculpture smashed, every sheet of music torn up. I shall erect bonfires out of musical instruments. Violin strings will be knotted into hangmen's nooses. Then peace will prevail – cosmic peace and good order. We shall be able to breathe freely at last and venture upon a new beginning unencumbered by the scourge of art. It will be a world in which reality alone exists.'

Smyke heaved a voluptuous sigh.

If he wasn't joking, I told myself, he could only be rehearsing for a stage play. Either that, or he'd been smitten with some grave mental disorder. It seemed to run in the family, after all. Hagob Salbandian's eyes, too, had blazed with insanity.

'Can you imagine how lucid our thoughts will be once we've liberated them from the arts?' Smyke demanded. 'Once we've swept our soiled brains clean of senseless dross? Can you imagine how much more time we'll be able to spend on the things that really matter in life? No, of course you can't. You're an *author.*'

He positively spat the word in my face.

'It won't be possible to eliminate the arts without eliminating their exponents. I shall regret that, because many of my acquaintances are artists, and some of them are really nice people – friends, even. However, one has to observe certain priorities.'

Smyke's face hardened.

'Yes, friends will have to die. Doubtless you're wondering why I'm prepared to shoulder such a burden of guilt. Don't I suffer from pangs of conscience? The short answer is: "No!" In my position I simply can't afford pangs of conscience. Fortunately, they fade the more power one acquires. It's an entirely natural process.'

I'd had enough.

'I'd like to go now,' I said. 'Please could you give me back my manuscript?'

Smyke acted as if he hadn't heard the question.

'The only form of art I shall continue to permit is trombophone music. That's because it's a science, not an art at all. You probably suppose that what you heard last night was music. Allow me to correct you: it was acoustic alchemy, hypnosis by means of sound waves. Music is the least resistible of all the arts, so I simply had to make use of it. Try getting an audience to dance by reciting a poem! Try getting them to march! Impossible! Only music can do that. I discovered Doremius Fasolati's scores down here, the Optometric Rondos, and recognised their potential at once. Their circular arrangement made sense to me even before I'd read a single note. Everything goes round in circles, my friend! With the aid of the Murkholm Trombophone Orchestra I've succeeded in converting music into power, notes into commands, instruments into weapons, concertgoers into slaves! You thought you were listening to music, but it was really a series of posthypnotic commands. Yesterday I induced you to buy books, tomorrow I may get you to burn the city to the ground. If I'd instructed you to eat one another you'd have done so with relish.'

Unpleasant though the situation was, I didn't feel threatened. I was physically more than a match for a Shark Grub and I knew the way back.

'Now would you please return my manuscript?' I asked again, as politely and firmly as I could. If he didn't comply I would simply leave and turn his house upside down until I found it.

'Oh, do forgive me,' said Smyke, every inch the kindly host once more. 'The manuscript! I'm afraid my tongue ran away with me.'

He leant towards me and spoke in a conspiratorial tone. 'I'm sure you'll treat my confidences with discretion, won't you? I wouldn't like any of them to become public knowledge.'

He was a screw loose, that was beyond doubt. I nodded to be on the safe side.

'Of course, the manuscript,' he said, undulating over to a bookcase. 'That's why we're here, after all. But first I must show you something.'

He reached into the bookcase and removed a black book with the ominous Triadic Circle blocked in gold on the cover.

'It's an immensely old book, so I had to have it rebound. I designed the Triadic Circle myself. What do you think of it?'

I didn't reply.

'It symbolises the three components of power: power, power and power.' He laughed and handed me the book.

'What am I supposed to do with it?' I asked.

'You have three questions for me. First you'd like to know why I'm telling you all these things, right? Secondly, you're wondering what they've got to do with your manuscript. And, thirdly, you'd like to know if what I've told you is true. All good things come in threes, don't they? You'll find the answer to all three questions in this book bearing the Triadic Circle. On page 333, of course.'

I was loath to open the book.

'How can the answer to today's questions be in such an old book?'

'The answers to almost all of today's questions can be found in old books,' Smyke retorted. 'If you want to find out, look them up. If not, forget it.'

Was this another manifestation of his mental illness? It was thoroughly symptomatic of such cases to cherish a belief in hidden textual signs and commands, numerology and disembodied voices. That would fit. But why in the world shouldn't I simply look up the page? At least that would enable me to satisfy myself that I really was dealing with a lunatic. If the text on page 333 had no bearing on our present situation, my diagnosis would be correct. Then all that remained for me to do would be to get out fast and hope the condition wasn't catching.

I opened the book at random. Page 123. It was blank except for the page number. I looked at Smyke. He was smiling.

146

I turned over some more pages.

Page 245. No text, no illustration. The opposite page was just as blank.

Page 299. Blank.

'There's nothing there at all,' I said.

'You're looking in the wrong place,' Smyke replied, raising three fingers. 'Try page 333.'

I went on turning.

Page 312. Blank.

Page 330. Blank.

Page 333. I was there at last. This time the page really did bear some text in very small type. Resting my paw on the paper, I screwed up my eyes and peered more closely. My fingertips felt strangely cold. Printed on this page and the one facing it was the same short sentence repeated ad infinitum:

You've just been poisoned. You've just been poisoned. You've just been poisoned. You've just been poisoned. You've just been poisoned.
You've just been poisoned. You've just been poisoned. You've just been poisoned. You've just been poisoned. You've just been poisoned.
You've just been poisoned. You've just been poisoned. You've just been poisoned. You've just been poisoned. You've just been poisoned.
You've just been poisoned. You've just been poisoned. You've just been poisoned. You've just been poisoned. You've just been poisoned.
You've just been poisoned. You've just been poisoned. You've just been poisoned. You've just been poisoned. You've just been poisoned.
You've just been poisoned. You've just been poisoned. You've just been poisoned. You've just been poisoned. You've just been poisoned.
You've just been poisoned. You've just been poisoned. You've just been poisoned. You've just been poisoned. You've just been poisoned.
You've just been poisoned. You've just been poisoned. You've just been poisoned. You've just been poisoned. You've just been poisoned.
You've just been poisoned. You've just been poisoned. You've just been poisoned. You've just been poisoned. You've just been poisoned.
You've just been poisoned. You've just been poisoned. You've just been poisoned. You've just been poisoned. You've just been poisoned.
You've just been poisoned. You've just been poisoned. You've just been poisoned. You've just been poisoned. You've just been poisoned.
You've just been poisoned. You've just been poisoned. You've just been poisoned. You've just been poisoned. You've just been poisoned.
You've just been poisoned. You've just been poisoned. You've just been poisoned. You've just been poisoned. You've just been poisoned.
You've just been poisoned. You've just been poisoned. You've just been poisoned. You've just been poisoned. You've just been poisoned.
You've just been poisoned. You've just been poisoned. You've just been poisoned. You've just been poisoned. You've just been poisoned.
You've just been poisoned. You've just been poisoned. You've just been poisoned. You've just been poisoned. You've just been poisoned.
You've just been poisoned. You've just been poisoned. You've just been poisoned. You've just been poisoned. You've just been poisoned.
You've just been poisoned. You've just been poisoned. You've just been poisoned. You've just been poisoned. You've just been poisoned.
You've just been poisoned. You've just been poisoned. You've just been poisoned. You've just been poisoned. You've just been poisoned.
You've just been poisoned. You've just been poisoned. You've just been poisoned. You've just been poisoned. You've just been poisoned.
You've just been poisoned. You've just been poisoned. You've just been poisoned. You've just been poisoned. You've just been poisoned.
You've just been poisoned. You've just been poisoned. You've just been poisoned. You've just been poisoned. You've just been poisoned.
You've just been poisoned. You've just been poisoned. You've just been poisoned. You've just been poisoned. You've just been poisoned.
You've just been poisoned. You've just been poisoned. You've just been poisoned. You've just been poisoned. You've just been poisoned.
You've just been poisoned. You've just been poisoned. You've just been poisoned. You've just been poisoned. You've just been poisoned.
You've just been poisoned. You've just been poisoned. You've just been poisoned. You've just been poisoned. You've just been poisoned.
You've just been poisoned. You've just been poisoned. You've just been poisoned. You've just been poisoned. You've just been poisoned.
You've just been poisoned. You've just been poisoned. You've just been poisoned. You've just been poisoned. You've just been poisoned.
You've just been poisoned. You've just been poisoned. You've just been poisoned. You've just been poisoned. You've just been poisoned.
You've just been poisoned. You've just been poisoned. You've just been poisoned. You've just been poisoned. You've just been poisoned.
You've just been poisoned. You've just been poisoned. You've just been poisoned. You've just been poisoned. You've just been poisoned.
You've just been poisoned. You've just been poisoned. You've just been poisoned. You've just been poisoned. You've just been poisoned.
You've just been poisoned. You've just been poisoned. You've just been poisoned. You've just been poisoned. You've just been poisoned.
You've just been poisoned. You've just been poisoned. You've just been poisoned. You've just been poisoned. You've just been poisoned.
You've just been poisoned. You've just been poisoned. You've just been poisoned. You've just been poisoned. You've just been poisoned.
You've just been poisoned. You've just been poisoned. You've just been poisoned. You've just been poisoned. You've just been poisoned.
You've just been poisoned. You've just been poisoned. You've just been poisoned. You've just been poisoned. You've just been poisoned.
You've just been poisoned. You've just been poisoned. You've just been poisoned. You've just been poisoned. You've just been poisoned.
You've just been poisoned. You've just been poisoned. You've just been poisoned. You've just been poisoned. You've just been poisoned.
You've just been poisoned. You've just been poisoned. You've just been poisoned. You've just been poisoned. You've just been poisoned.
You've just been poisoned. You've just been poisoned. You've just been poisoned. You've just been poisoned. You've just been poisoned.
You've just been poisoned. You've just been poisoned. You've just been poisoned. You've just been poisoned. You've just been poisoned.
You've just been poisoned. You've just been poisoned. You've just been poisoned. You've just been poisoned. You've just been poisoned.
You've just been poisoned. You've just been poisoned. You've just been poisoned. You've just been poisoned. You've just been poisoned.
You've just been poisoned. You've just been poisoned. You've just been poisoned. You've just been poisoned. You've just been poisoned.
You've just been poisoned. You've just been poisoned. You've just been poisoned. You've just been poisoned. You've just been poisoned.
You've just been poisoned. You've just been poisoned. You've just been poisoned. You've just been poisoned. You've just been poisoned.
You've just been poisoned. You've just been poisoned. You've just been poisoned. You've just been poisoned. You've just been poisoned.
You've just been poisoned. You've just been poisoned. You've just been poisoned. You've just been poisoned. You've just been poisoned.
You've just been poisoned. You've just been poisoned. You've just been poisoned. You've just been poisoned. You've just been poisoned.
You've just been poisoned. You've just been poisoned. You've just been poisoned. You've just been poisoned. You've just been poisoned.
You've just been poisoned. You've just been poisoned. You've just been poisoned. You've just been poisoned. You've just been poisoned.
You've just been poisoned. You've just been poisoned. You've just been poisoned. You've just been poisoned. You've just been poisoned.
You've just been poisoned. You've just been poisoned. You've just been poisoned. You've just been poisoned. You've just been poisoned.
You've just been poisoned. You've just been poisoned. You've just been poisoned. You've just been poisoned. You've just been poisoned.
You've just been poisoned. You've just been poisoned. You've just been poisoned. You've just been poisoned. You've just been poisoned.
You've just been poisoned. You've just been poisoned. You've just been poisoned. You've just been poisoned. You've just been poisoned.
You've just been poisoned. You've just been poisoned. You've just been poisoned. You've just been poisoned. You've just been poisoned.
You've just been poisoned. You've just been poisoned. You've just been poisoned. You've just been poisoned. You've just been poisoned.
You've just been poisoned. You've just been poisoned. You've just been poisoned. You've just been poisoned. You've just been poisoned.
You've just been poisoned. You've just been poisoned. You've just been poisoned. You've just been poisoned. You've just been poisoned.
You've just been poisoned. You've just been poisoned. You've just been poisoned. You've just been poisoned. You've just been poisoned.
You've just been poisoned. You've just been poisoned. You've just been poisoned. You've just been poisoned. You've just been poisoned.
You've just been poisoned. You've just been poisoned. You've just been poisoned. You've just been poisoned. You've just been poisoned.
You've just been poisoned. You've just been poisoned. You've just been poisoned. You've just been poisoned. You've just been poisoned.
You've just been poisoned. You've just been poisoned. You've just been poisoned. You've just been poisoned. You've just been poisoned.
You've just been poisoned. You've just been poisoned. You've just been poisoned. You've just been poisoned. You've just been poisoned.
You've just been poisoned. You've just been poisoned. You've just been poisoned. You've just been poisoned. You've just been poisoned.

You've just been poisoned. You've just been poisoned. You've just been poisoned. You've just been poisoned. You've just been poisoned.
You've just been poisoned. You've just been poisoned. You've just been poisoned. You've just been poisoned. You've just been poisoned.
You've just been poisoned. You've just been poisoned. You've just been poisoned. You've just been poisoned. You've just been poisoned.
You've just been poisoned. You've just been poisoned. You've just been poisoned. You've just been poisoned. You've just been poisoned.
You've just been poisoned. You've just been poisoned. You've just been poisoned. You've just been poisoned. You've just been poisoned.
You've just been poisoned. You've just been poisoned. You've just been poisoned. You've just been poisoned. You've just been poisoned.
You've just been poisoned. You've just been poisoned. You've just been poisoned. You've just been poisoned. You've just been poisoned.
You've just been poisoned. You've just been poisoned. You've just been poisoned. You've just been poisoned. You've just been poisoned.
You've just been poisoned. You've just been poisoned. You've just been poisoned. You've just been poisoned. You've just been poisoned.
You've just been poisoned. You've just been poisoned. You've just been poisoned. You've just been poisoned. You've just been poisoned.
You've just been poisoned. You've just been poisoned. You've just been poisoned. You've just been poisoned. You've just been poisoned.
You've just been poisoned. You've just been poisoned. You've just been poisoned. You've just been poisoned. You've just been poisoned.
You've just been poisoned. You've just been poisoned. You've just been poisoned. You've just been poisoned. You've just been poisoned.
You've just been poisoned. You've just been poisoned. You've just been poisoned. You've just been poisoned. You've just been poisoned.
You've just been poisoned. You've just been poisoned. You've just been poisoned. You've just been poisoned. You've just been poisoned.
You've just been poisoned. You've just been poisoned. You've just been poisoned. You've just been poisoned. You've just been poisoned.
You've just been poisoned. You've just been poisoned. You've just been poisoned. You've just been poisoned. You've just been poisoned.
You've just been poisoned. You've just been poisoned. You've just been poisoned. You've just been poisoned. You've just been poisoned.
You've just been poisoned. You've just been poisoned. You've just been poisoned. You've just been poisoned. You've just been poisoned.
You've just been poisoned. You've just been poisoned. You've just been poisoned. You've just been poisoned. You've just been poisoned.
You've just been poisoned. You've just been poisoned. You've just been poisoned. You've just been poisoned. You've just been poisoned.
You've just been poisoned. You've just been poisoned. You've just been poisoned. You've just been poisoned. You've just been poisoned.
You've just been poisoned. You've just been poisoned. You've just been poisoned. You've just been poisoned. You've just been poisoned.
You've just been poisoned. You've just been poisoned. You've just been poisoned. You've just been poisoned. You've just been poisoned.
You've just been poisoned. You've just been poisoned. You've just been poisoned. You've just been poisoned. You've just been poisoned.
You've just been poisoned. You've just been poisoned. You've just been poisoned. You've just been poisoned. You've just been poisoned.
You've just been poisoned. You've just been poisoned. You've just been poisoned. You've just been poisoned. You've just been poisoned.
You've just been poisoned. You've just been poisoned. You've just been poisoned. You've just been poisoned. You've just been poisoned.
You've just been poisoned. You've just been poisoned. You've just been poisoned. You've just been poisoned. You've just been poisoned.
You've just been poisoned. You've just been poisoned. You've just been poisoned. You've just been poisoned. You've just been poisoned.
You've just been poisoned. You've just been poisoned. You've just been poisoned. You've just been poisoned. You've just been poisoned.
You've just been poisoned. You've just been poisoned. You've just been poisoned. You've just been poisoned. You've just been poisoned.
You've just been poisoned. You've just been poisoned. You've just been poisoned. You've just been poisoned. You've just been poisoned.
You've just been poisoned. You've just been poisoned. You've just been poisoned. You've just been poisoned. You've just been poisoned.
You've just been poisoned. You've just been poisoned. You've just been poisoned. You've just been poisoned. You've just been poisoned.
You've just been poisoned. You've just been poisoned. You've just been poisoned. You've just been poisoned. You've just been poisoned.
You've just been poisoned. You've just been poisoned. You've just been poisoned. You've just been poisoned. You've just been poisoned.
You've just been poisoned. You've just been poisoned. You've just been poisoned. You've just been poisoned. You've just been poisoned.
You've just been poisoned. You've just been poisoned. You've just been poisoned. You've just been poisoned. You've just been poisoned.
You've just been poisoned. You've just been poisoned. You've just been poisoned. You've just been poisoned. You've just been poisoned.
You've just been poisoned. You've just been poisoned. You've just been poisoned. You've just been poisoned. You've just been poisoned.
You've just been poisoned. You've just been poisoned. You've just been poisoned. You've just been poisoned. You've just been poisoned.
You've just been poisoned. You've just been poisoned. You've just been poisoned. You've just been poisoned. You've just been poisoned.
You've just been poisoned. You've just been poisoned. You've just been poisoned. You've just been poisoned. You've just been poisoned.
You've just been poisoned. You've just been poisoned. You've just been poisoned. You've just been poisoned. You've just been poisoned.
You've just been poisoned. You've just been poisoned. You've just been poisoned. You've just been poisoned. You've just been poisoned.
You've just been poisoned. You've just been poisoned. You've just been poisoned. You've just been poisoned. You've just been poisoned.
You've just been poisoned. You've just been poisoned. You've just been poisoned. You've just been poisoned. You've just been poisoned.
You've just been poisoned. You've just been poisoned. You've just been poisoned. You've just been poisoned. You've just been poisoned.
You've just been poisoned. You've just been poisoned. You've just been poisoned. You've just been poisoned. You've just been poisoned.
You've just been poisoned. You've just been poisoned. You've just been poisoned. You've just been poisoned. You've just been poisoned.
You've just been poisoned. You've just been poisoned. You've just been poisoned. You've just been poisoned. You've just been poisoned.
You've just been poisoned. You've just been poisoned. You've just been poisoned. You've just been poisoned. You've just been poisoned.
You've just been poisoned. You've just been poisoned. You've just been poisoned. You've just been poisoned. You've just been poisoned.
You've just been poisoned. You've just been poisoned. You've just been poisoned. You've just been poisoned. You've just been poisoned.
You've just been poisoned. You've just been poisoned. You've just been poisoned. You've just been poisoned. You've just been poisoned.
You've just been poisoned. You've just been poisoned. You've just been poisoned. You've just been poisoned. You've just been poisoned.
You've just been poisoned. You've just been poisoned. You've just been poisoned. You've just been poisoned. You've just been poisoned.
You've just been poisoned. You've just been poisoned. You've just been poisoned. You've just been poisoned. You've just been poisoned.
You've just been poisoned. You've just been poisoned. You've just been poisoned. You've just been poisoned. You've just been poisoned.
You've just been poisoned. You've just been poisoned. You've just been poisoned. You've just been poisoned. You've just been poisoned.
You've just been poisoned. You've just been poisoned. You've just been poisoned. You've just been poisoned. You've just been poisoned.
You've just been poisoned. You've just been poisoned. You've just been poisoned. You've just been poisoned. You've just been poisoned.
You've just been poisoned. You've just been poisoned. You've just been poisoned. You've just been poisoned. You've just been poisoned.
You've just been poisoned. You've just been poisoned. You've just been poisoned. You've just been poisoned. You've just been poisoned.

The cold sensation in my fingertips travelled up my arm and permeated my body. My head swam, my eyes went dim and I heard Smyke say: 'You really are one of those dreamers who believe that the answer to any question can be found in a book, aren't you? But the printed word isn't always good or helpful, it can even be thoroughly malign. Haven't you ever heard of the Hazardous Books? Many of them kill at the slightest touch.'

Then everything went black.

Part Two

The Catacombs of Bookholm

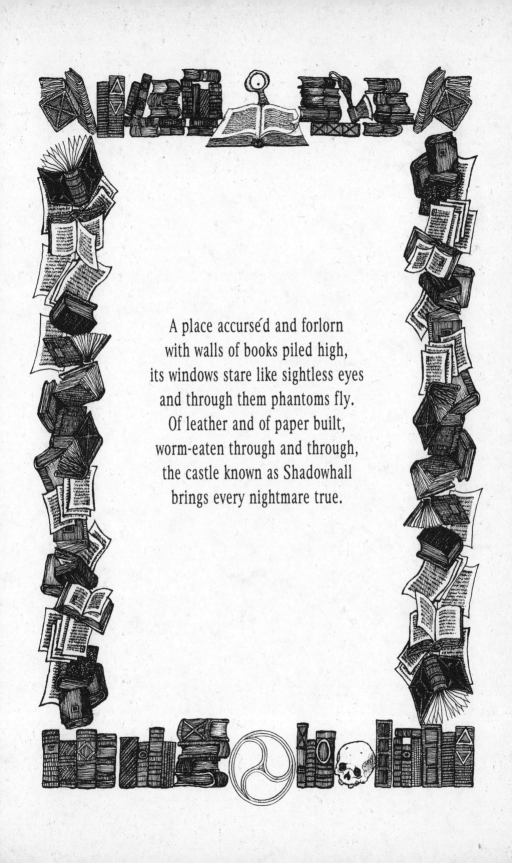

A place accurséd and forlorn
with walls of books piled high,
its windows stare like sightless eyes
and through them phantoms fly.
Of leather and of paper built,
worm-eaten through and through,
the castle known as Shadowhall
brings every nightmare true.

♩♩
The Living Corpse

I had been poisoned, dear readers – poisoned by contact with the envenomed pages of an ancient tome. Now you'll understand what I meant when I said that books are capable of harming and even killing people. I had fallen prey to one of the so-called Hazardous Books.

The poison acted quickly, very quickly. Scarcely had my fingertips touched the pages when an icy sensation surged through my body, a wave of cold that permeated my bloodstream, invading every nerve and freezing every cell until I went numb all over and even my eyesight failed.

You've just been poisoned . . .

Those words were all that remained. In utter darkness, I was bereft of everything save that interminably repeated thought:

You've just been poisoned, you've just been poisoned, you've just been poisoned, you've just been poisoned, you've just been poisoned . . .

Do you know those frightful dreams in which you're imprisoned in an endless cycle that compels you to dream the same thing over and over again? That's how it was with me.

You've just been poisoned, you've just been poisoned, you've just been poisoned, you've just been poisoned, you've just been poisoned . . .

Was this death? Was it death when the last thing you've seen, heard or thought is endlessly repeated until your body finally decomposes?

You've just been poisoned, you've just been poisoned, you've just been poisoned, you've just been poisoned, you've just been poisoned . . .

All at once I saw light again, so suddenly and unexpectedly that I would, if capable of doing so, have uttered a startled cry. What was happening to me?

Then I saw Pfistomel Smyke. All I could make out at first was his vague silhouette, but the image became more and more distinct. He was bending over me and beside him stood . . . Yes, believe it or not, it was Claudio Harpstick, the friendly Hoggling and literary agent! They were regarding me with curiosity.

'He's coming round,' said Harpstick.

'This is the active phase,' said Smyke. 'Amazing how well the poison still works after all these years.'

I tried to say something, but my lips appeared to be sealed. My eyesight was steadily improving, however – indeed, it had never seemed as keen or clear before. The two figures emitted an unnatural radiance. I could make out every hair and pore as distinctly as if I were looking at them through a magnifying glass.

'I'm sure you'd like to give me a piece of your mind,' said Smyke, 'but the poison paralyses the tongue as effectively as it stimulates the eyes and ears. You're temporarily endowed with the eyesight of a Gloomberg eagle and the hearing of a bat, but please don't be alarmed. Your body will remain entirely paralysed and soon you'll relapse into profound unconsciousness. That's all the poison will do to you, however. You won't die of it, you'll simply go to sleep and wake up again. Do you understand?'

I tried to nod but couldn't move a muscle.

'Oh dear, how tactless of me!' Smyke exclaimed and Harpstick gave an asinine laugh.

'How *could* you have answered? Well, I may lack manners but I don't murder people – that I leave to others. Plenty of merciless creatures down here are only too happy to relieve me of that dirty work.'

'Quite,' Harpstick said impatiently, glancing around with an anxious expression. 'Let's get out of here, Pfisto.'

Smyke ignored him. It was incredible how clearly I could see them both. They seemed to glow from within in cold, unreal colours. My pupils must have expanded to an extraordinary extent and my heart was pumping three times as fast as usual, yet my body was as stiff as a board. I was a living corpse.

'Yes, my friend,' said Smyke, and his voice sounded painfully loud and harsh, 'you scratched at the surface of Bookholm a trifle too hard. We've taken you deep into the catacombs beneath the city – so deep that we had to lay a very, very long string to guide us back. Look on this as a form of exile. I could have killed you, but this is far more romantic. Console yourself with the thought that you're going to meet the same end as Colophonius Regenschein. He made the same mistake as you. He confided in the wrong person. Me, in other words.'

Harpstick emitted a nervous laugh. 'We ought to get going now,' he said.

Smyke gave me a friendly smile. 'And please regard it as part of your punishment that I can't explain about the manuscript. It's a long story and I really don't have the time.'

'Come on,' urged Harpstick.

'Look,' said Smyke, 'the passive phase is starting, you can tell by his shrinking pupils.'

I was overcome by profound weariness.

'Pupils . . . pupils . . . pupils . . . pupils . . .' Smyke's voice steadily faded in a series of dwindling echoes. I was being snuffed out like a candle flame in the wind. It went dark again.

'Goodnight, my friend,' said Smyke. 'And give my regards to the Shadow King when you see him.'

I heard Harpstick utter another mirthless laugh. Then I lost consciousness.

ꘖΨ

The Hazardous Books

My first thought on coming to was that I was hallucinating, and that another trombophone concert had deluded me into believing myself in the catacombs of Bookholm. I was looking down an endless passage lined on either side with bookcases and lit by jellyfish lamps.

However, it dawned on me as my anaesthetised body gradually lost its rigidity that I really was in the labyrinth beneath the city. I was half lying, half sitting with my back propped against a bookcase. I felt the warmth seeping back into my feet, legs, torso and head in turn. At length I rose with a groan and patted the dust from my cloak.

I wasn't overcome with panic, strangely enough, perhaps because my nerves were still too benumbed by the poison. What also served to calm me was the venerable company of so many old books. Yes, dear readers, despite this unpleasant and surprising turn of events I felt thoroughly optimistic. I was alive. I had lost my way in one of Bookholm's subterranean bookshops, that was all. This was no dark and savage underworld: it contained passages, lights, bookcases and books. The books themselves were the clearest indication that people had found their way down here and returned to the surface. There were hundreds of exits somewhere overhead. I need only look for long enough – even if it took days – and I would be bound to find one.

Smyke and Harpstick couldn't have dragged me very far, the fat slobs. They looked much too unathletic for that.

So I set off, trying to analyse my predicament as I went. Yes, there was no doubt about it: Pfistomel Smyke and Claudio Harpstick, my supposed friends, were really my most dangerous enemies in Bookholm. Years of seclusion in Lindworm Castle seemed to have done little to educate me in the ways of the world. I was far too trusting.

Precisely what they had against me remained a mystery, however. Or was I just a random victim of theirs? Were they something in the nature of book pirates, an experienced team that preyed on unsuspecting visitors? Harpstick had deliberately lured me into the spider's web at 333 Darkman Street, that much was certain. They were doubtless selling my manuscript to some wealthy collector at this minute. It was probably lost for ever, which meant that my search for its mysterious author was at an end. Reflecting on that sad circumstance, I instinctively felt for the vanished manuscript – and promptly found it in one of the pockets of my cloak!

I came to a halt, took it out and stared at it in disbelief. Smyke must have stuffed it into my pocket – he had banished it to the catacombs in my company. But that didn't make sense; it only made everything more mysterious still!

He was afraid of the manuscript, that must be his motive – afraid it might become public knowledge. He considered it dangerous for some reason, so dangerous that he wasn't content to hide it in his underground library and wanted to get rid of it altogether – it and me both. What perturbed him about it? And why had it thrown such a scare into Kibitzer and the Uggly? Were they in league with Smyke and Harpstick? Had I missed something – had I failed to detect some hidden message decipherable only by experienced antiquarians and literary scholars? No matter how hard I stared at the manuscript, it refused to disclose its secret. I replaced it in my pocket and walked on.

Books, nothing but books. I was careful not to touch any. The more the poison's effect on my system waned, the more suspiciously I eyed them. I would never again open a book without hesitating first. Printed matter had lost its innocence for me. The Hazardous Books! How urgently Regenschein's memoirs had warned me against them! He had devoted a whole chapter to Toxicotomes. It all came back to me now – now that it was too late.

The story of the Hazardous Books had probably originated when one book pirate stove in another's skull with a weighty tome. It had become clear at that historic juncture that books were potentially lethal, and from then on the ways in which they could wreak havoc multiplied and underwent refinement over the centuries.

The Bookhunters' *book traps* were only one variant. Mainly for the purpose of eliminating competitors, they fabricated imitations of especially valuable and sought-after works, which resembled the originals perfectly on the outside but were equipped inside with lethal devices. The hollowed-out interiors contained poisoned darts and firing mechanisms, needle-sharp slivers of glass propelled by tiny catapults, caustic acids in hypodermic syringes or toxic gases in airtight cylinders. One had only to open such a book to be blinded, badly injured or killed. Bookhunters armed themselves against these contrivances with masks, helmets, chain-mail shirts, iron gauntlets and other protective garments – in fact, book traps were the main reason for their fanciful martial attire.

Toxicotomes impregnated with poisons transmissible by touch had been particularly popular in the Zamonian Middle Ages. They were used to remove political opponents and topple kings, but also to eliminate rival authors or persistently hostile reviewers. The wealth of imagination with which the Bookemists of the era had developed a multitude of such poisons was extremely impressive. Contact with a single page could strike you deaf and/or dumb, paralyse or drive you mad, infect you with an incurable disease or send you to your eternal rest. Many toxins induced lethal paroxysms of laughter or loss of memory, delirium or the shakes. Others caused your hair and teeth to fall out or desiccated your tongue. There was even a poison which, if you came into contact with it, filled your ears with a chorus of voices so shrill and piercing that you ended by jumping out of a window of your own accord. The book that had drugged me was innocuous by comparison.

According to Colophonius Regenschein, a certain publisher of this period had not only impregnated one copy of each of his editions with a deadly contact poison but actually advertised the fact. You would have thought that such books would languish on the shelves, but the opposite happened. They sold like hot cakes because they offered a thrill no normal book could provide: a frisson of genuine danger. They were the most exciting books on the market. People read them with hands atremble and foreheads filmed with sweat, no matter how boring their contents. Books of this kind were especially popular with retired soldiers and elderly adventurers who could not afford to expose themselves to undue physical exertion for health reasons.

Toxicotomes had gone out of fashion at the end of the Zamonian Middle Ages because their dissemination was incompatible with modern laws. What now spread fear and consternation were *Analphabetic Terrortomes*, imitations and developments of book traps smuggled into bookshops by a radical sect of bibliophobes. When someone opened an Analphabetic Terrortome the entire bookshop blew up. The sect that manufactured these bombs had no name because its members were opposed to words on principle. They also rejected sentences, paragraphs, chapters, novels, any form of prose, any form of verse and books in general. To them, commercial establishments that sold books constituted an affront to their fanatical illiteracy and were hotbeds of evil that had to be wiped off the face of Zamonia. They smuggled their treacherous explosive volumes into bookshops and libraries, concealed them among popular bestsellers and beat a retreat. It wouldn't be long, they reckoned, before no one dared to open a book at all.

However, they had underestimated the passion for literature common among Zamonians, who were quite prepared to risk getting their heads blown off for the sake of a good read. Explosions became rarer as time went by and the sect eventually broke up because its leader blew off his own head while constructing a bomb that detonated prematurely. For all that, opening books remained a risky business. Analphabetic Terrortomes might still be lurking anywhere, even after centuries, because vast numbers had been put into circulation. Hence the sporadic destruction of antiquarian bookshops in particular, some of which were reduced to little more than deep craters. Fifteen of them had been blown sky-high in Bookholm alone.

There were as many Hazardous Books in Zamonia as there were reasons for wishing someone ill. Among the motives that prompted their manufacture were revenge, greed, envy and resentment – and, when jealousy or unrequited love were involved, infatuation. Poisoned dog-ears with razor-sharp edges, vignettes whose touch arrested the breathing, ex-libris impregnated with olfactory poisons – nothing remained untried. Those who habitually moistened their fingertips with saliva when turning pages were more at risk than most because they might convey tiny amounts of poison from the paper to their tongues and then collapse, gasping for breath, their lips flecked with bloodstained foam. Small cuts sustained from gilt-edged pages infected with bacteria could cause blood poisoning. Encoded posthypnotic commands hidden in Bookemists' books were capable, days later, of causing their readers to jump off a cliff into the sea or drink a pint of mercury.

As time went by, stories about the Hazardous Books proliferated to such an extent that it became almost impossible to distinguish between fact and fiction. The catacombs of Bookholm were reputed to contain books capable of self-propulsion, books that could crawl or even fly, books more ferocious and voracious than many a predator or insect – books that could only be defeated by force of arms.

It was rumoured that some books whispered and groaned in the dark while others strangled people with bookmark ribbons if they nodded off while reading them. It could even happen that a reader was devoured alive by a Hazardous Book and never seen again. All that remained was his empty armchair with the book lying open on it, his sole memorial the fact that it now featured a new protagonist who bore his name.

Such were the ideas and stories that ran through my mind as I roamed the catacombs, dear readers. Although I'm no believer in ghosts or witchcraft or Ugglian curses or hocus-pocus of any description, the existence of the

Hazardous Books was something I knew from personal experience. I resolved never to touch another of the books down here.

So I simply walked on without paying them much attention. My optimism had evaporated by now. All I could see were walls lined with books I dared not touch and the occasional dead jellyfish. I might just as well have been walking through a clump of stinging nettles. Apart from my own footsteps, I heard just about every sinister noise to be found in Zamonian horror stories: rustles and bangs, whimpers and howls, whispers and giggles. It was like listening to a piece of gruesic composed by Octavius Shrooti. The noises undoubtedly emanated from the city's sewers and were of Overworldly origin, but they had been transformed into entirely new sounds on their way through all those layers of soil and along all those tunnels and passages. I was hearing the ghostly music of the catacombs.

At some stage I sank to the ground. How long had I been walking? Half a day? A day? Two days? I was utterly disorientated, temporally, spatially and psychologically. My legs ached, my head rang like a bell. I simply lay there and listened to the unnerving sounds of the catacombs. Then I fell into an exhausted sleep.

⅄⅄

The Sea and the Lighthouses

I awoke unrefreshed, not only hungry and thirsty but in unwelcome company. Crawling and scrabbling around on my face and stomach were dozens of insects and other noisome creatures: transparent maggots, worms, snakes, phosphorescent beetles, long-legged Bookhoppers, earwigs armed with outsize pincers, eyeless white spiders. I leapt to my feet with a horrified scream and lashed out wildly. The creatures flew in all directions as I performed a grotesque dance, flailing away at my cloak in a panic. A gigantic bookworm emitted one last, vicious hiss and rattled its scales at me before disappearing behind a heap of books. It wasn't until I was certain of having put the last of the vermin to flight that I recovered some of my composure.

Then I set off again. What else could I do? By now all my confidence had left me. There was no reason to believe that I was any nearer an exit. I might even have gone deeper still, and those insects had shown how quickly one could become part of the underworld's merciless food chain. Nor was the recurrent sight of half-dead jellyfish calculated to raise my spirits; their futile attempts to escape were all too reminiscent of my own predicament. Like them I would soon be lying dead on some tunnel floor, a desiccated, emaciated cadaver eaten away by vermin. And all because of a manuscript.

The thought of it made me call a brief halt and take it out again. Could I decipher the underlying message that had landed me in this ticklish situation and might possibly help to extricate me from it? It was a foolish, desperate idea, but the only one I could come up with at that moment. So I proceeded to study the manuscript once more. I perused it with the same enthusiasm, the same reactions I'd displayed at first reading, and it afforded me temporary relief. Then I came to the last sentence:

'This is where my story begins.'

It sounded so hopeful, so boundlessly optimistic, that tears of joy welled up in my eyes. No story could have got off to a more confident start. I pocketed the manuscript and set off once more, pondering on the words that had reactivated my brain. I was suddenly overcome by a feeling that the mysterious author had meant to tell me something; that, wherever he might be at this moment, he was speaking to me.

'*This is where my story begins.*'

But what was he implying? That my own story was only just beginning? That would be a very consoling thought. Or ought I to take the sentence even more literally?

Don't ask me why I believed this, my faithful readers, but I felt sure the sentence was a riddle whose solution would help me to regain my freedom. Very well, I would take it literally.

'*This is where my story begins.*'

Where was 'this'? Here in the catacombs? Here where I happened to be at this moment? Agreed! But whose story did the author mean, if not mine? What else was here apart from myself? Insects, of course. And, needless to say, books.

That flash of inspiration almost killed me, it hit me so hard! *Books*, you idiot! It was thoroughly idiotic of me to ignore the books. If I could expect help from any quarter, it was from them. Although surrounded by thousands of wise potential advisers, I had been deterred from enlisting their aid by one unpleasant experience and a handful of legends about the Hazardous Books.

I was involuntarily reminded of the way in which Colophonius Regenschein had found his bearings by means of the books around him. It was mainly the order in which the various libraries and collections in the catacombs were arranged that had led him to his discoveries. That being so, wouldn't it be logical if the books could also guide a person back to the surface?

Although not blessed with Regenschein's great expertise, I did have some knowledge of Zamonian literature, and it required no stroke of genius to determine a book's age from its condition, author, contents and imprint. It was really quite simple: the older the books around me, the deeper in the catacombs I must be. The more recent they became, the closer I would be to an exit. Not invariably, of course, but often enough. Why? Because most libraries reflected the time in which their owners lived. Equipped with this simple compass, I would be able to get my bearings and find my way back to the surface and freedom – *if* I could summon up the courage to examine the books.

What did I have to lose? If a Hazardous Book ripped off my head or drilled me between the eyes with a poisoned arrow I would at least meet a quick and merciful end instead of dying a slow, agonising death from starvation or being eaten alive by insects.

Better to die on my feet than crawling along like a jellyfish! All I had to do now was to overcome my fear and open a book. I came to a halt.

Went over to a shelf.

Took out a book at random.

Weighed it in my hand.

Was it unusually heavy? Could I hear something rattle inside it?

No.

Or was it too light because it contained a cavity filled with lethal gas?

No, it wasn't too light either.

I shut my eyes and averted my head.

And opened it.

Nothing happened.

No explosion.

No poisoned arrow.

No cloud of splintered glass.

Gingerly, I touched the pages.

No cold sensation in my fingers.

Could I detect any signs of incipient madness?

Hard to say.

I glunked my teeth. No, they didn't fall out either. Everything seemed firm enough.

Vertigo? Nausea? Fever?

Nothing of the kind.

I opened my eyes again.

Phew! It was a perfectly normal, harmless book. No explosive device, no cylinder of lethal gas or hypo filled with acid. It was just a book like most other books: paper covered with print and bound in hoggskin. Pah! What else had I been expecting, paranoid simpleton that I was? The odds against encountering a Toxicotome out of all the works down here were probably ten thousand to one.

I looked at the title. Hey, I actually knew this book, though only superficially! It was *Nothing of Importance* by Nemo de Zilch, the founder of Grailsundian Equalitism, a school of philosophy dedicated to total indifference.

'*It is wholly immaterial whether or not you read this book.*' Zilch's opening sentence had always deterred me from reading on, just as it did this time. I replaced the book on the shelf unread – a reaction that would have delighted the Equalitists because it precisely complied with the aim of their sect, which was to be utterly ineffectual.

Nevertheless, the book had supplied me with some important information. It could only have hailed from the Zamonian Early Middle Ages because the Equalitists were active at that period and it was a first impression of the first edition.

I walked on past innumerable bookcases without bestowing any attention on their contents, leaving passage after passage behind me. Then I paused, took out a book at random and opened it.

'"*Life, alas, is all too short," Prince Summerbird remarked, heaving a big sigh.*

"*Well," his friend Navello Fluff rejoined with a smile as he poured himself a glass of wine, "if by that you mean to espouse the view that our span of existence is depressingly limited, I won't take issue with you."*

Madame Fonsecca looked amused. "Ah," she interposed, "I see you gentlemen are once more discussing the regrettable fact that our sojourn on earth is subject to shocking constraints from the temporal aspect."'

No doubt about it: this was a *Plethoric novel*, one of Zamonian literature's more grotesque aberrations, in which variations on a single basic theme were repeated ad nauseam. And when had the Plethorists been active? In the *Late Middle Ages*! I was heading in the right direction, therefore, having progressed from the Early to the Late Middle Ages.

Quick! Go on! Again I passed countless shelves and bookcases without heeding their contents. I saw two variegated jellyfish clinging to each other in their death throes, but the sight no longer dismayed me. I was filled with hope once more. Then I paused.

'*Water cuts no bread*' were the first words I read on opening a book of verse. What was that called? Of course, it was an adynation, a natural impossibility. And what school of poetry had traditionally begun its poems with natural impossibilities? The *Adynationists*, of course! And when was the heyday of the Adynationists? Before or after that of the Plethorists? After, after! I had left the Middle Ages behind and come to Zamonian High Baroque!

From now on I checked at ever shorter intervals, allowed myself more time, examined several books in many bookcases and deployed all the literary knowledge Dancelot Wordwright had instilled in me. Had Horatio Senneker been writing before or after Pistolarius Grenk? When had Platoto de Nedici introduced *Adaptionism* into Zamonian literature? Had Glorian Cucurbit belonged to the Grailsundian Pastellists or the Tralamander Circle? Did Fredda the Hirsute's oxymoronic verses hail from her Blue or her Yellow Period?

I thanked my authorial godfather in retrospect for the relentless way in which he had drummed all these facts into my head. How I had cursed him for it, yet now they might possibly save my life! I felt I was sailing across a dark sea in which countless lighthouses stood on little islands. The lighthouses were writers beaming their lonely messages across the centuries – I was sailing from island to island, guided by those literary beacons. They were the thread that would lead me out of the labyrinth. Hunger and thirst forgotten, I snatched book after book off the shelves, deduced my progress from them and hurried on, then paused once more and took out another.

'*The Universe imploded*' were its opening words. Definitely an *Anticlimacticist* novel, a genre whose exponents began their books at the most exciting and spectacular juncture. Thereafter they allowed the storyline to relapse, becoming steadily duller and more inconsequential until it petered out halfway through a casual remark. The Anticlimacticists were assigned to the Zamonian Romantic era, so I had come a stage further.

'*He desquelched his lips from hers and creakled down in a decrepit old armchair. Holding up the crustling sheet of paper, he examined it peeringly. "Is this really his will?" he surprasked.*

She groansighed.

"You mean he hasn't left us Dunkelstein Manor after all, just an old milking stool?" He cursehurled the document into the fireplace, where it cruspitated to ashes. With a scornlaugh, he gobbocked on the floor.

She sobwept snufflingly.'

Good heavens, *Onomatopoeic Dynaprose*! The authors of the period had presumably lost faith in their readers' powers of imagination and felt they had to beef up their writing with gimmicky neologisms of this kind – which ruined its dramatic impact by modern standards. People like Rolli Fantono and Montanios Trumper had written such stuff in the belief that it was terribly modern, whereas all a modern eye could discern in such fatuities was that their authors were terribly old hat. For all that, these were the beginnings of the Zamonian *nouveau roman*, the first experimental essays in a new form of literature. I was heading briskly for the modern era.

'*Count Elfensenf? May I introduce Professor Phlogisto La Fitti, the inventor of anoxygenic air? Perhaps the three of us could play a hand of rumo together?*'

Ah yes, I had definitely reached modern times, that little snatch of dialogue was proof enough for me. It came from a *Count Elfensenf* novel, the precursor of all Zamonian detective stories, of which Minolo Hack had written dozens just two centuries ago. Although hardly great literature, his books were almost as popular as the *Prince Sangfroid* novels, especially with younger readers. This one was *Count Elfensenf and the Breathless Professor*, which I had read probably half a dozen times in my boyhood. The same shelf held all the other novels in the series from *Count Elfensenf and the Iron Potato* to *Count Elfensenf and the Piratical Zombie*. I wouldn't have minded reading them all again, but this wasn't an appropriate time.

Instead, I took a book from the shelf beside them. It was small, untitled and bound in black leather. Opening it, I read:

THE WAY OF THE BOOKHUNTER
by
RONGKONG KOMA

Bingo! This was a really recent publication. Rongkong Koma . . . Wasn't he the one who had hunted Regenschein so relentlessly? A contemporary, no less! I dipped into the book as I walked on.

RULE NO. 1
The Bookhunter is as lonely in the labyrinth as a Spinxxxx. His home is darkness. His hope is death.

Sombre stuff. Still, it was by a Bookhunter and they couldn't all be as brilliant as Colophonius Regenschein.

RULE NO. 2
All Bookhunters are equal. Equally worthless.

Hm, a really likeable individual, this Rongkong Koma. Not exactly the type of person one wanted to bump into down here in the dark.

RULE NO. 3
Anything alive can be killed.
Anything dead can be eaten.

This, it seemed, was the intellectually limited philosophy of a professional murderer. Hardly my favourite kind of reading but a contemporary work, that was what mattered. I tossed it over my shoulder and pulled out another volume, a particularly striking specimen bound in glittering steel and sumptuously adorned with silver, gold and copper fittings. Imagine my astonishment, dear readers, when I opened it to reveal a complicated mechanism in place of printed pages! At the same time I felt relieved because, had it been a Hazardous Book, I would have been standing there headless or transfixed by an arrow between the eyes. But what was it?

I saw cogwheels revolving, springs tensing, miniature pistons sliding back and forth. And then, at the top of the book's interior, which resembled a peep-show or puppet theatre, a copper curtain rose and some little metal figures appeared on the tiny stage. Although as two-dimensional as the puppets in a shadow theatre, they were impressively lifelike and clearly represented Bookhunters whose martial accoutrements had been reproduced with great skill and accuracy. They proceeded to duel with axes and fire arrows at each other until all sank lifeless to the ground. Despite the bloodthirsty nature of the performance, it had been staged with loving care and considerable artistry. Then the copper curtain fell and, to my great disappointment, the little theatre's show was over.

It was an amazing invention – an intelligent toy for adults! For the first time, in spite of my perilous predicament, I felt the desire to own a book from the catacombs. I had only to take it with me, after all. As things now stood I would be bound to find an exit soon and a rare item like this would surely be worth a fortune up in Bookholm.

But wait! Something was moving in the lower part of the mechanical book! A dozen tiny windows had appeared, a whole row of them with letters of the Zamonian alphabet rotating inside them like the cylinders in a one-armed bandit. Then, with a click-click-click, the letters came to a halt and, when read in succession, formed a sentence. It ran:

GOLDENBEARD THE HAIRSPLITTER WISHES YOU A GOOD TRIP

'Eh?' I said foolishly, as if the book had spoken to me, and in reply I heard a musical box in its mechanical innards strike up a tune. It was the traditional Zamonian funeral march we had played at Dancelot's cremation. I looked again.

GOLDENBEARD THE HAIRSPLITTER WISHES YOU A GOOD TRIP

A disappointingly meaningless message after that brilliant puppet show. Or was it a riddle?

One moment: Goldenbeard the Hairsplitter – wasn't that the Bookhunter claimed by Regenschein to have made a habit of eliminating his competitors with book traps of exceptional subtlety? Yes, Goldenbeard was a former watchmaker who used his knowledge of precision engineering to . . .

It was only then that I noticed a fine silver wire running from the spine of the book to the shelf. It had gone taut and was vibrating violently. I dropped the book in a hurry. It clattered to the floor, still playing the funeral march, but I was far too late. I heard more wires twanging, heard them go taut all along the passage like the strings of a gigantic harp being tuned, followed by a rumble like distant thunder. I glanced over my shoulder in dismay.

At the upper end of the passage the massive wooden bookcases were toppling over one by one. By disturbing this cunning book trap I'd activated a hidden mechanism. The bookcases were felling each other in turn like dominoes. Hundreds and thousands of volumes cascaded on to the steeply inclined floor, and the bookcases came crashing down after them. Wood, paper and leather piled up into a huge wave that bore swiftly down on me like an avalanche of mud speeding along a dried-up river bed.

I sprinted down the passage in the opposite direction, but I didn't get far.

The avalanche overtook me and swept me along in a churning mass of books that battered my head and body and eventually robbed me of sight. I was tossed around, yelling at the top of my voice. Then, all at once, I was falling. As if in the grip of a waterfall, I plummeted into an abyss with the avalanche of books. All I could hear was the air rushing past. I finally came to rest with a sudden, frightful jolt and a hailstorm of books descended on my back. Thousands of them must have piled up on top of me. Total silence and utter darkness engulfed me. I couldn't move, I could scarcely breathe. I had been buried alive in books.

ᘐ

Unholm

If you still harboured any doubts that books can be dangerous, dear readers, they must surely have been dispelled by now. Those books had hurled themselves on top of me in a concerted attempt to squeeze the life out of me. I couldn't see a thing, was unable to move my arms or legs and could breathe only with the utmost difficulty. It was a book that had landed me in this predicament. A Hazardous Book.

GOLDENBEARD THE HAIRSPLITTER WISHES YOU A GOOD TRIP

Now I understood: it was an example of Bookhunter's humour. I had fallen into a trap that wasn't even meant for me. Goldenbeard had laid it for one of his competitors and I, in my new-found faith in printed matter, had blindly stumbled into it. Regenschein had stated that Bookhunters were capable of transforming whole passages and sectors of the catacombs into lethal traps. It seemed that I always remembered the most important things when it was too late.

I was lying spreadeagled beneath a mountain of paper like a botanical specimen pressed between the pages of a book. I tried to move my arms, flex my legs and turn my head, but I could scarcely budge a claw. I was inhaling more book dust than air, so I found it harder and harder to breathe. It would be only a matter of time before I suffocated.

Suffocated by books . . . The songs Dancelot had crooned over my cradle never predicted that I would meet such an end. If destiny really did possess the gift of irony, this was a generous sample of it.

I didn't even know whether I was merely wedged or completely paralysed. Perhaps that headlong fall had broken every bone in my body – it might have, judging by the pain I was in. But that was immaterial now. I was on the verge of bidding this cruel world farewell, and believe me, dear readers, that struck me as a merciful dispensation under the circumstances. Anything would have been preferable to this torment, even death. I prayed that the Grim Reaper would hurry, but my life continued to ebb away agonisingly slowly.

Then something stirred beneath me. I could feel I was being lifted, once, twice, three times, together with the entire mountain of paper on top of me. This hurt even more because it intensified the pressure to which my body was being subjected. Whatever was moving beneath me, it must have been the size of a gigantic whale. It effortlessly lifted me and my burden, my ribcage creaked, and I could hear the mass of books above me start to shift. There was a rumbling sound and the downward pressure lessened perceptibly. Many of the books must have slid off, because I could move at last. It seemed that I hadn't broken every bone in my body after all. The pain was terrible, but I could now move my arms and legs, shovel books sideways and kick them away behind me. I continued to shovel and kick with wild abandon. As the rubble of books loosened, so I could at last breathe more easily. Then I saw light! Dim, multicoloured chinks of light were filtering through some narrow cracks quite near me. I stretched out my paw to them. It went right through and into space! Shoving and kicking like a mad thing, I emerged from the ocean of books in which I'd almost drowned.

I burrowed my way out, panting and coughing, gasping and sneezing, hawking and spitting, vomiting up great gobbets of dust-laden mucus. I sucked in greedy gulps of air again and again. Then I tried to look around, but everything was still too shrouded in dust – all I could see were those multicoloured specks of light. It took me a considerable effort to extricate myself completely from the debris of torn and shredded paper, whole and dismembered books, hard covers and loose pages. I crawled along, then rose to my feet. You couldn't really stand on such an unstable mound of debris – one foot or the other kept sinking into it – but with practice I soon managed to wipe the dirt from my eyes and look about me without falling headlong.

I was in a semicircular cave at least half a mile in diameter. The arching roof high above me was porous, perforated by countless holes of various sizes, and it must have been through one of these that I and the books had fallen. Adhering to the rock between these apertures was the source of the pulsating light: whole colonies of phosphorescent jellyfish of every conceivable size and colour. They must have belonged to a variety of the species in the jellyfish lamps – one that could survive when not immersed in nutrient fluid. Considerably larger and more luminous, they had probably evolved from the inmates of the lamps. I was reminded of the two jellyfish I'd seen clinging to each other in their death throes. Perhaps they'd been engaging in the sex act, not dying at all.

Flocks of snow-white bats flitted around just below the roof, circling endlessly and filling the cave with their shrill squeaks. With a sudden rumbling sound, one of the holes vomited a torrent of dust and paper that showered down on the sea of books, fortunately at a safe distance from me.

All those tattered, mouldering, worm-eaten books – all that torn paper, splintered wood and other debris – really did resemble the surface of a sea in that multicoloured light, the more so because every part of it was ceaselessly stirring, heaving and subsiding. I preferred not to speculate on the nature of the creatures that were causing these upheavals – probably hosts of maggots and rats, worms and beetles busily engaged on the final destruction of literature. Wasn't there a poem on decay by Perla la Gadeon entitled 'The Conqueror Worm'?

Yes, my faithful readers, I had clearly gone down another level and descended even deeper into the bowels of the cave system. I even knew what this place was called: it couldn't be anywhere but Unholm, the rubbish dump of the catacombs. Colophonius Regenschein had visited this ill-famed cave and devoted a whole chapter of his book to it and its environs. He called it the dirtiest and seediest part of the labyrinth. This was where its inhabitants had dumped all their literary rubbish over the centuries. But not that alone. Many of the inhabited caves on the upper levels had shafts leading to the holes in the roof of Unholm and into these were thrown everything of no further value. Book pirates used them to dispose of their murdered victims, decadent book tycoons of their everyday rubbish and excrement, Bookemists of their toxic trash and failed experiments. Regenschein had claimed that some of the shafts led to the surface of the city and came out inside the ancient buildings in Darkman Street.

Centuries of rubbish had accumulated down here, forming a compost conducive to the growth of all kinds of fearsome fauna and flora. Here existed insects and parasites, plants and animals to be found nowhere else in the catacombs. Even Bookhunters gave this place a wide berth because it had nothing to offer but frightful diseases. Unholm was the morbid underside of Bookholm, the putrid, stinking entrails of the catacombs and their merciless digestive system. No one ruled here, neither the Bookhunters nor the Shadow King: decay alone prevailed. Anyone who had made it through the catacombs to Unholm would sooner or later decompose and become part of the restlessly stirring sea of books on which I now stood with legs atremble.

I surveyed the cave. I was roughly in the middle, or half a mile from the edge. Not too far, but picking my way across that heaving mass of paper would not be without its dangers. There were numerous exits on the periphery of the cave, probably gateways through which the inhabitants of the catacombs used to cart their rubbish in ancient times. It didn't matter which exit I chose – they were all potentially hazardous – so I simply made for one at random.

I kept sinking in, sometimes ankle- or knee-deep and sometimes up to my waist, but never so far that I was unable to extricate myself. There were scuttlings and rustlings wherever I trod, and I carefully avoided looking down to see what creatures I'd disturbed.

I was white as a ghost with book dust from head to foot, every muscle in my body ached from my fall and subsequent contusions, and tears of despair were streaming down my cheeks. Nonetheless, dear readers, although this ordeal undoubtedly represented the nadir of my existence to date, I trudged defiantly on. I had survived a book trap and a long fall, I had been buried alive and risen from the grave – never would I have believed myself cut from such hard-wearing cloth. I wasn't destined to die down here, oh no! I had made Dancelot a vow on his deathbed that I would become Zamonia's greatest writer, and I intended to keep that promise despite all the Smykes, Bookhunters and other vermin in the catacombs. I would extricate myself from this living hell even if I had to burrow my way to the surface with tooth and claw.

Hundreds of ideas went whirling through my head – ideas for novels, poems, essays, short stories and stage plays. Born of my rage and defiance, the foundations of a whole oeuvre, a whole shelf filled with Yarnspinners, took shape at this moment – now, when I had absolutely no chance of making any notes. I strove to memorise my ideas, to nail them to the walls of my brain, but they eluded me like slippery eels. I had never been in a more creative state of mind – and I had nothing to write with! It was both tragic and comical. I laughed and cursed by turns, and even the oaths I uttered were of breathtaking originality.

I had completed about half of my laborious trek when the ocean of books emitted a rumbling sound. No, it wasn't just small creatures going about their work in the usual manner. Something more dramatic was in progress – something far bigger was stirring. Not far away the rubbish was heaving and subsiding in a way that reminded me of the movements I'd felt while buried in books. Yes, something was stirring beneath the surface. I could tell from the waves the thing created that it was circling me ever more closely. A roar arose from the depths, a sound so irate and menacing that it not only extinguished my rage and defiance but banished all the ideas that had been running through my mind. My heart and brain turned to ice. This was what it must feel like to be circled by a primeval shark in the sea or a werewolf in a forest at night. Where was the monster now? Immediately beneath me with its jaws gaping?

And then it surfaced. Hundreds of books flew in all directions, paper dust billowed into the air, pages fluttered, startled insects buzzed – and from their midst emerged the biggest creature I'd ever seen.

The Conqueror Worm!

Yes, it might have been a worm, Unholm's biggest bookworm, but it might also have been a serpent or an entirely new life form – at that moment the monster's genealogy was a matter of supreme indifference to me. Its visible portion, which jutted above the sea of books, was as wide and high as a bell tower, its skin was pale yellow and sprinkled with brown warts. Protruding from its whitish belly were hundreds of waving antennae or atrophied arms or legs – I couldn't tell which. The yawning maw at its upper extremity was surrounded by long, curved fangs as sharp, pointed and lethal as scimitars. The huge creature froze for a moment and all I could hear was its whistling intake of breath. It reared up still higher, emitted an earsplitting roar and threw itself flat on the sea of paper with a crash that sounded like a whole forest of trees being felled simultaneously. The megaworm was completely obscured by the dense clouds of grey dust that went whirling into the air. Then they subsided and I saw its huge form heading straight for me.

Those who have never had to make their way across a mass of decaying books can have no idea how difficult this is. I don't know how often I tripped, fell head over heels and tumbled down hillsides of yellowing paper, how often I scrambled to my feet or proceeded on all fours. Again and again I trod on books that fell to dust or disintegrated into colonies of mealworms, on paper that cracked like the thinnest of ice.

The creature's greedy roars filled the cave, drowning the squeaks of the panic-stricken bats and setting the sea of books in violent motion. Believe me, dear readers, I would have preferred not to know exactly what was lurking beneath the surface of Unholm, but alas, that mercy was denied me. The megaworm's paroxysms had alerted every last one of the rubbish dump's inhabitants, and they came to the surface to see who had been impertinent enough to intrude on their digestive slumbers.

It was as if the gates of hell had opened and were spewing out an endless succession of creatures, each of which strove to be more hideous and outlandish than its fellows. Glossy black beetles the size of loaves burrowed their way out

of the rubbish, grinding their mandibles. The cover of one huge tome opened and a spider with a flowing white mane and legs longer than my own emerged, glaring at me with its eight sapphire-blue eyes. I stumbled on, terrified, expecting to feel its hairy limbs on the back of my neck at any moment. Instead, the ground around me rustled and crackled as a long, scaly black tentacle rose from the depths and groped around blindly. A fleshy, bloated sphere swelled up amid the yellowing paper like a bubble of marsh gas, then burst with a disgusting noise and released the clouds of book dust pent up inside it. Colourless crabs, luminous scorpions and ants, transparent snakes and gigantic caterpillars of every hue emerged. Creatures whose names I didn't know – hybrids equipped with scales and wings, horns and pincers – scrambled into the open and fanned out in all directions. I was making my way across a sea of living refuse, the product of centuries of insanitary habits and physical degeneration.

But this was all to the good, dear readers, because the megaworm was blind and reliant on its hearing for a sense of direction, so it lost track of me in the surrounding pandemonium. It hurled itself this way and that, burrowing

through the dusty detritus and cleaving the sea of paper and its denizens asunder with razor-sharp fangs, but I was long since out of range of its sensory perception.

And now a fight broke out between the inhabitants of Unholm, a war in which each did battle against all. I had never witnessed more terrible scenes, not even in my worst nightmares. The white-maned spider was torn to pieces by black tentacles. A huge blind rat was cornered by dozens of beetles and flayed alive by their mandibles. Two luminous red scorpions were dancing round each other, stings poised to strike, when they were suddenly swallowed by a bellowing maw that yawned beneath them. Three giant crabs used their powerful claws to dismember a creature that defied description. And there was I in the midst of this hellish scene, panting and ploughing my way through the rubbish. I expected the ground to open beneath my feet at any moment, expected to be engulfed by a gigantic mouth or seized and strangled by a tentacle, but the monsters were so intent on mutual annihilation that none of them seemed to be interested in me. They sprayed each other with venom, snarling and screeching, they throttled and stung and bit each other with the utmost brutality and savagery – and I threaded my way between them as if wearing a cloak of invisibility. That free-for-all may have been a purificatory ritual performed at regular intervals, a bloodbath from which outsiders were exempt on principle. Perhaps I gave off a scent that rendered me an uninteresting adversary or victim, who knows? The unwholesome nature of that accursed place remains an abiding mystery.

All that mattered was that I eventually reached the edge of the cavern alive and unscathed. I scrambled on to a rock, utterly exhausted, but allowed myself only a few moments' rest. Panting hard, I looked back for the last time. Not far away two millipedes the length of trees were grappling and exchanging spurts of corrosive venom amid a sea of pulverised paper. Elsewhere, however, the fighting was almost at an end. All manner of rending, gulping, chomping sounds filled the air, for the victors' banquet was just beginning. A peculiar emotion, a mixture of revulsion and relief, overcame me at the sight of that terrible scene, a more detailed description of which, dear readers, I should prefer to spare you.

For that, had I been a little less fortunate, could have been my own fate too: to be devoured and digested by Unholm, the gigantic belly of the catacombs. Feeling sickened, I turned away.

♃8
The Kingdom of the Dead

Now that I had cheated death my creative terrors reared their heads once more. What if I had caught some frightful infection on that rubbish dump? I must have inhaled and come into contact with milliards of viruses and bacteria – in fact, many of the creatures had themselves resembled terrible diseases. I shook myself and patted the noxious dust off my cloak.

The cave's numerous exits varied in size. Many were completely choked with books, but marching in through others were whole armies of insects attracted by the sounds of the funeral feast. I chose a tunnel in which I could discern only a few books lying on the dusty floor and no living creatures save a long procession of jellyfish crawling along the roof, bound for who knew where.

The euphoria I'd felt when setting foot on terra firma quickly evaporated. I was far from clear of Unholm, and I knew from Colophonius Regenschein's book that the environs of the rubbish dump were little less dismal and dangerous. The inhabitants of the catacombs had used these tunnels and caves as burial places for centuries, so umpteen thousand corpses lay buried in them. There were even reputed to be secret mausoleums equipped with the most ingenious booby traps. Wealthy book tycoons had been buried in these graves together with their most valuable literary gems. Remarkably enough, even the most rapacious Bookhunters left them alone and avoided the area on principle, many of them being convinced that it was haunted by phantoms and mummies, roaming skeletons and the vengeful ghosts of victims of murder. It was said that the Shadow King himself had been born among the graves of Unholm. This was the cheerless Kingdom of the Dead, into which only underworld insects and vermin had ventured for many a long year.

Although I'm sure I need not emphasise how little I myself believe in such nonsense, dear readers, even the most enlightened soul finds the idea of walking over thousands of anonymous graves distasteful. I shun graveyards even in daylight and attend burials and cremations only when unable to avoid doing so, as in the case of my authorial godfather. I have no morbid propensities and would sooner not look death in the face until the time comes – which is why these surroundings had such a disastrous effect on my state of mind. Beset by memories of reading horror stories in my youth, I couldn't help thinking of skeletal hands that emerged from the ground, seized wayfarers by the ankles and dragged them into the bowels of the earth; of groaning spirits that walked through walls and enfolded one in their chilly embrace; of crazily cackling skulls glowing in the darkness. The further I proceeded from the rubbish dump the quieter it became until, in the end, all I could hear was the sound of my own footsteps.

And each step took me ever deeper, ever further into this Kingdom of the Dead. Not even a beetle scurried across my path. The squeaking of the bats, which had got on my nerves so much, had died away completely. The only living things apart from myself appeared to be the mutated jellyfish, which had evidently seized the chance to conquer and populate a deserted sector of the catacombs. Varying widely in size and colour, they were everywhere. Isolated individuals or whole colonies of them adhered to the walls and roofs of the tunnels, clinging to stalactites and rocky outcrops. The creatures were beginning to nauseate me – there was something sinister and repellent about their silent presence and adaptability. More and more often now, I encountered things that matched Regenschein's descriptions. One tunnel I entered was lined with empty graves and strewn with bones and skulls. Books, on the other hand, were becoming steadily rarer. If there ever had been any in this area, they must long ago have disintegrated into the dust through which I was wading. I rested for a while in a cavern filled with stone pyramids some six feet high – possibly gravestones – but the oppressive silence of the place soon spurred me on.

In one series of interconnecting grottoes I saw vast quantities of bones and skulls, skeletal hands and feet, all of which had been sorted into separate piles. Regenschein had mentioned that many of the catacombs' primeval inhabitants hadn't troubled to bury their dead. They simply piled them up and left them to rot, heedless of the health risks attendant on that method of disposal. Whole stretches of the catacombs owed their depopulation to a frightful plague spread by a particular species of rat. It continued to rage until the Bookemists finally developed an effective poison against the vermin. I passed innumerable mounds of skeletons, repeatedly telling myself that there could be no danger of infection after so many hundreds of years.

From now on there were bones everywhere. Cave dwellers of an artistic bent had used them for decorative purposes, affixing bone ornaments to walls or lining whole tunnels with skulls. Their artistic aspirations and abilities must have developed in the course of time, because I soon saw, all along my route, reconstructed skeletons frozen in everyday poses: standing, walking, leaning against walls, seated on the ground, even dancing in a circle. Shuddering, I traversed a cave full of skeletal sculptures arranged to form scenes typical of the market place: haggling with each other, sauntering along, crying their wares or making purchases – except that their merchandise consisted of skulls instead of cabbages.

In the end, because you become inured to anything you meet in vast numbers, I grew accustomed to the sight of these innumerable skeletons. I ceased to flinch whenever I rounded a bend in a tunnel and was confronted by a skeletal figure with its arm raised in salutation. There was even something comforting about this world of the dead, because the absence of life betokened the absence of danger. All that is evil stems from the living; the dead are a peaceable bunch.

For all that, I wouldn't have minded exchanging their presence for some antiquarian books. Corpses and graves provided no indication of my whereabouts, so I simply had to trudge on, willy-nilly, through this seemingly endless subterranean cemetery. One cave was so full of urns that I inadvertently kicked one over while passing through. It set off a positive chain reaction that caused hundreds more to topple over and spill their dusty contents on the ground. Just then a gust of wind blew through the cave and sent dense clouds of this fine powder whirling into the air. It flew up into my face and down into my lungs, coated my tongue and gummed my eyelids together. I had the dust of the dead in my eyes and mouth, and who could tell what dire diseases had carried them off! Even hours later I felt obliged to spit whenever I thought I'd discovered a grain of dust lodged between my teeth.

On my trek through this dismal world I saw gravestones and evidence of burial methods of all kinds, stone mausoleums and glass coffins, corpses entombed in amber and sarcophagi so huge that they could only have contained the mortal remains of giants. I came across a stalactite cave mentioned by Colophonius Regenschein: the *Hall of Clay Warriors*, in which a tribe of warlike giants had buried their dead in a standing position. After encasing them in clay and covering them with logs, they set them ablaze. All that remained thereafter was a fired clay figure with a baked cadaver inside it.

Five different tunnels led out of the Hall of Clay Warriors. I simply opted for the nearest one, only to realise an instant later that this was a terrible mistake. Although I had never seen a Spinxxxx before, I knew from Regenschein's accurate description that I was immediately beneath one. It lowered three, four, five, six or more long grey insectile legs and hemmed me in on all sides. I was captured, dear readers – imprisoned in a living cage!

ʃƃ
The Twofold Spider

The best way to visualise a Spinxxxx* is to think of it as a twofold spider: a spider with only one body but sixteen legs and sixteen long antennae instead of eyes. A creature that can walk not only on the ground but also on the ceiling and walls – at one and the same time.

Regenschein knew from personal observation that Spinxxxxes are deaf and blind and have no sense of smell. Like many subterranean creatures they rely exclusively on their sense of touch. Above and below mean nothing to a Spinxxxx, nor do ahead and behind. All they know is an endless 'round about' which they ceaselessly explore with the aim of finding food – and food to them is anything that moves. They systematically run their antennae over tunnel walls and eat whatever they catch, whether bookworm, beetle, snake, bat, rat or Bookhunter. The Spinxxxx is immune to the poisons secreted by many life forms in the catacombs. It is also invulnerable. Its small cutaneous scales are composed of granite, and even the sharpest weapons bounce off

---

* Translator's Note: The Zamonian alphabet contains a letter symbolic of polypody, or many-leggedness. It occurs in the name of every life form that possesses more than eight legs. No such letter exists in our own alphabet, so I have had to resort to using the letter X four times, which in my opinion neatly symbolises sixteen-leggedness. This does not, however, mean that the X has to be enunciated four times over. Simply pronounce the word Spinxxxx as if it were spelt with one X only.

186

them. Regenschein surmised that concealed beneath them are muscles of root wood, bones of bronze, intestines of carbon fibre and a diamond heart that pumps resin instead of blood – that the Spinxxxx is, in fact, a genuine creature of the earth's interior, a hybrid mixture of animal, vegetable and mineral. Its feeding equipment, too, is unsurpassed: a mouth filled with stone teeth for chewing, bronze claws for tearing prey apart and a long trunk for sucking it dry. Regenschein considered the Spinxxxxes to be useful creatures because they keep the catacombs free from vermin, but he advised his readers to give them a wide berth.

I had neglected the latter point, unfortunately. But the situation wasn't completely hopeless, dear readers! The first good thing was that the monster hadn't noticed me yet. If Regenschein's observations were correct and the Spinxxxx really was blind, deaf and devoid of a sense of smell, it couldn't possibly have registered my presence because it hadn't touched me so far, either with its antennae or with its legs. It might have lowered its legs by chance, just as I was walking past, and taken me prisoner without knowing it.

The second good thing: the Spinxxxx's attention was distracted. Having detected a phosphorescent jellyfish on the roof of the tunnel, it was busy sucking the creature dry. It had inserted its elephantine trunk in the luckless jellyfish, whose luminosity steadily diminished as the Spinxxxx drained its vital fluids with a repulsive slurping sound.

The third good thing: the gaps between the monster's legs were wide enough to enable me to slip through, given a little care on my part. The wriggling antennae represented the greatest danger, but they were busy palpating the jellyfish. I also had to watch out for the almost invisible cobwebs suspended between the Spinxxxx's legs, which were used to capture aerial prey such as moths and bats, and rendered it an almost perfect hunting machine.

I gathered my cloak round me, drew a deep breath and tucked in my head and stomach to make myself thin and short enough to squeeze through one of the gaps sideways on. The Spinxxxx above me seemed to notice none of this. The greedy slurping sounds were now overlaid by a contented purr that suggested the meal was claiming its full attention.

Off I went, inching sideways with bated breath. I could make out every last granite scale on the Spinxxxx's legs by the pulsating pale pink light of the dying jellyfish. No Lindworm had ever been so close to one of these beasts before. Another few inches and I would be clear of it. Just . . . one . . . more . . . step . . . and . . . I was free! But only for a moment, alas, because the Spinxxxx now changed its stance. Withdrawing its trunk from the jellyfish, it thrust it into the quivering mass at another spot. In so doing it moved a dozen of its sixteen legs, which stabbed and slashed the air above my head before hemming me in once more. It also lowered several antennae, which hit the ground with a smack like sodden ropes. Although it had failed to touch me even now, my prison was more cramped than before.

My heart was pounding, but I strove to remain calm. The gap between two of the legs was wide enough to admit me, but the finely woven spider's web suspended between them came down so low that I would have to crawl beneath it. I tried to banish the thought that the Spinxxxx might have noticed me after all and was only playing a cruel game with me.

Warily, I sank to my knees. Some tiny moths and tunnel flies were caught in the web, already sucked dry. These, coupled with the greedy slurping sounds overhead, confirmed Regenschein's assertion that Spinxxxxes spurned no live food of any kind, however minute.

I crawled between the creature's legs, wrapping my cloak around me as tightly as possible and moving as slowly and deliberately as my nerves would permit. Two antennae came snaking across the floor of the tunnel in front of me. Jellyfish fluid was dripping on the back of my neck, but I resisted the temptation to make any precipitate movements. I glanced up once more to satisfy myself that the Spinxxxx was still preoccupied with its prey. Yes, it was sucking away at the jellyfish and purring contentedly. I peered into the darkness of the tunnel ahead, my escape route. And then I saw it.

The white, one-eyed bat!

As if it had pursued me through my nightmares, all the way from that horrific room at the Golden Quill, Bookholm's hotel from hell, it came fluttering out of the black void of the tunnel, its powerful, purposeful wing-beats carrying it straight towards me and the Spinxxxx.

It wasn't the dead creature from my room, of course, but I'm convinced it was at least a close relation, a brother or sister whom it had commanded from the hereafter to land me in an even worse predicament. Why? Because the stupid creature clearly intended to fly between the Spinxxxx's legs. It had failed to see the gossamer mesh suspended between them.

Get to my feet and run for it – that was all I could do now. But the bat was too quick for me. One more wing-beat and it whooshed into the invisible trap, became hopelessly entangled in the sticky threads, squeaked and struggled – and alerted the Spinxxxx before I'd even half risen from the tunnel floor.

The monster stamped its feet and its antennae thrashed the air like severed cables. I received a blow to the chest, staggered backwards, tripped over an insectile leg and fell to the ground. The Spinxxxx removed its trunk from the jellyfish, exuding long threads of glowing mucus, and brought its grey body down on top of me. Its numerous antennae roamed all over my body and face and palpated the struggling bat at the same time.

This was bound to be a great day in the Spinxxxx's culinary life – one it would doubtless remember fondly. First an hors d'oeuvre of plump jellyfish; next a delicious entrée of furry white bat; and finally, for the main course, this hitherto unknown delicacy with the leathery hide and appetising body odour. I could hear the gastric juices seething in its intestines. Its mandibles clattered together excitedly.

The Spinxxxx's massive body swayed to and fro on eight of its legs while the other eight performed a kind of dance on the roof of the tunnel. It seemed to be debating which of its prey to devour next. The big one or the little one? The little one or the big one? Unable to decide, it continued to clatter its mandibles until a book was thrust between them.

A book?

Had sheer terror caused me to hallucinate? Where had this book come from? Craning my neck, I saw a figure in full armour looming over me. A

Bookhunter! His suit of mail, which was made up of many different metal components, left no part of his body unprotected. His head and face were obscured by a helmet and an iron mask. He had thrust the book in his gauntleted hand between the Spinxxxx's mandibles. Yes, a book.

'Eat that!' he said in a deep voice.

Instinctively, the Spinxxxx's jaws began to close. I just had time to see this before the mail-clad figure hurled itself on top of me and everything went black. I heard a crackling, crunching sound – the Spinxxxx was chewing up the book – followed by a deafening explosion. The Bookhunter's armour jingled and vibrated, and a blast of scorching air surged over me. Then silence fell. Nothing more happened until the Bookhunter rose with a grunt, enabling me to see again. I sat up. My ears were ringing.

The Spinxxxx's body had distributed itself all over the tunnel. Its legs were sticking into the walls like javelins and its stone scales lay strewn across the floor. Resinous fluid was dripping from the roof.

'I'd never have believed it,' the Bookhunter said as he helped me to my feet. 'An Analphabetic Terrortome came in handy for once. They're the confounded things that compel us to go around in all this cumbersome armour.'

'Many thanks,' I said. 'You saved my life.'

'I got rid of a Hazardous Book, that's all,' said the Bookhunter, wiping some Spinxxxx slime from his armour. He walked a few steps down the passage and extracted something from a mound of splintered granite and coal. It was a sparkling diamond the size of his fist.

'Well I'll be damned,' he muttered, 'Spinxxxxes really do have diamond hearts.' He turned to face me again. 'May I introduce myself? My name is Colophonius Regenschein. Will you permit me, after that close shave, to invite you to a modest snack in my humble abode?'

The Giant Skull

Was this the end of my misfortunes, the light at the end of the tunnel? My life had been saved by Colophonius Regenschein himself, dear readers, and he was now conducting me to his subterranean abode to entertain me there. In the circumstances, could anything better have happened to me? If there was one person who could help me to get out of this place alive, it was the greatest Bookhunter of all.

But first came a silent trek through the underworld. Colophonius Regenschein was clearly a person of few words. He simply strode on ahead and the most he ever said was 'This way!' or 'Mind the gap!' or 'Duck your head!'

We soon came to an area of the catacombs in which there were no more jellyfish lamps, just walls of grey rock lit only by Regenschein's jellyfish torch. This was all I saw for a long time: the taciturn Bookhunter marching ahead down narrow granite passages and climbing natural stone stairways like some weird flunkey in a bad horror story. The more cramped our surroundings became the more claustrophobic I felt, because they were an all too forcible reminder of the miles-deep layers of rock overhead.

On one occasion our route was barred by a creature with black fur and a scarlet face. It bared its impressive fangs and emitted a no less impressive screech, looking like a hideously deformed ape, but Regenschein made short work of it without even laying aside his torch. He drew his silver axe and dispatched the beast within seconds. When I squeezed past the spot where the fight had taken place I saw some green fluid trickling down the walls.

'Don't touch that blood,' Regenschein warned me. 'It's poisonous.'

At last the underground chambers grew bigger. We traversed lofty caverns filled with the sound of dripping water and the echoes of our footsteps. At times the luminous Lavaworms adhering to the walls enabled my taciturn guide to extinguish his torch. Nothing here was reminiscent of the catacombs' literary associations. For whatever reason, these bookless caves had remained untouched for thousands of years.

191

We eventually came to a dark cavern full of close-knit stalagmites. Regenschein strode silently on through this forest of stone columns, then came to a sudden halt. He raised his torch and peered up into the darkness as if he had heard something. I listened with bated breath. Did some danger threaten us from above? Before I could say anything, Regenschein produced a big iron key from his armour and inserted it in a stalagmite that jutted high into the blackness overhead. I heard a click followed by a loud metallic rattle, and a monstrous white skull descended out of the gloom. Suspended on stout chains and big enough to have contained Pfistomel Smyke's house, it was the skull of a giant – presumably a Cyclops, since it had only one eye socket.

'What's that?' I asked in amazement.

'It's my home when I'm in the catacombs,' Regenschein replied. 'I found it, so it's mine. It's full of valuable acquisitions, that's why I hoist it up there when I'm away. Wait here, I'll light some candles.'

He climbed in through the eye socket. I remembered that his book had made no mention of where he slept during his long expeditions into the catacombs, but that didn't surprise me: any Bookhunter would be bound to keep the location of his subterranean pied-à-terre a secret. A few moments later the interior of the skull was illuminated by a warm, flickering glow.

'Come in!' called Regenschein.

Hesitantly, I too climbed through the unusual entrance to his abode.

He was just putting his jellyfish torch in a clay vessel filled with nutrient fluid, so that it could recharge itself. The skull's interior was furnished like a living room. There was a crude wooden table, a chair, a heap of furs to sleep on, two shelves of glass jars and some books. Hanging on the walls was a heterogeneous assortment of weapons and pieces of armour, and among them some objects I couldn't identify in the dim light, any more than I could identify the contents of the glass jars. Colophonius Regenschein's living quarters were rather more primitive than I'd imagined, I must confess, but at least there were a few books – extremely valuable ones, I felt sure. The diamond that had once been the Spinxxxx's heart lay sparkling on the table.

'Are there giants down here?' I enquired.

'No reason why not,' he replied, sitting down on the chair. 'I've yet to meet one in the flesh, but there are huge caves and huge worms and huge Spinxxxxes in this place, so why not huge giants?'

I would have dearly liked to sit down too, but there was only one chair.

'Now I can tell you,' the Bookhunter grunted. 'My name isn't Colophonius Regenschein at all.'

'What?' I asked, taken aback.

'I thought you'd be more likely to come with me if I introduced myself as Regenschein. Everyone admires Colophonius Regenschein and no one admires me. My real name is Hunk Hoggno.'

Hunk Hoggno? I didn't care for the name at all. Had I fallen into another Bookhunter's trap? My heart beat wildly, but I tried to disguise my trepidation.

He lit another candle on the table and I could now make out almost every detail of the room's contents. The books on the shelves were adorned with gold and silver clasps. They were immensely valuable, even an amateur like me could see that. They included a copy of Regenschein's book.

The objects hanging on the walls between the weapons were shrunken heads, and reposing in a basket were some well-scraped skulls and bones. I caught sight of various saws and surgical scalpels. Some of the glass containers on the shelf were filled with liquid blood and pickled organs, others with live worms and maggots. I saw hearts and brains preserved in coloured fluids. Severed hands, too. I recalled my encounter with the Bookhunter in the black market. '*Lindworm relics are much in demand here,*' he'd told me. I shivered. I had ended up in the cave of a professional killer, possibly a maniac.

'Hunk Hoggno is a pseudonym,' said my host. 'What's your name?'

'Er, Opt . . . Optimus Yarnspinner,' I said with an effort. My tongue was cleaving to the roof of my mouth, it had gone so dry.

'Is that a pseudonym too?'

'No, it's my real name.'

'Well, it sounds like a pseudonym.'

I refrained from contradicting the Bookhunter a second time. An awkward silence fell.

'Would you care for a little conversation?' asked Hoggno, so abruptly that I gave a violent start.

'What?'

'A little conversation,' he repeated. 'I mean, could we talk for a bit? It's a year since I exchanged a word with anyone.' His voice had sunk to a whisper.

He seemed to be genuinely out of practice where oral communication was concerned.

'Oh,' I said, 'by all means.' I was prepared to do anything that might break the ice.

'Good. Er . . . What's your favourite weapon?'

'Excuse me?'

'Your favourite weapon. Er, look, I'm a bit rusty where talking's concerned. Would *you* prefer to ask the questions?'

'No, no,' I said hastily, 'you're doing fine. My favourite weapon is, er . . . the axe.' That was a lie, of course. If the truth be told, I don't care for weapons of any kind.

'Aha,' said Hoggno. 'Is it possible that you're only saying what I want to hear?'

I thought it better not to reply. I had to weigh my every word like gold dust.

'I'm sorry,' Hoggno said. 'That was rude of me. I'm sure you only meant to be nice. It's a year since . . . but I mentioned that already.'

Another awkward pause.

'Er . . .' said Hoggno.

I leant forward.

'Yes?'

'Now I've gone and forgotten what I meant to ask next.'

'Perhaps you'd like me to tell you something about myself,' I said. 'Background, profession and so on.' I was anxious to steer the conversation in another direction by mentioning that I was a writer. That ought to put him in a friendly frame of mind, I thought – after all, he makes his living out of people like me.

'All right. What's your profession?' Hoggno asked.

'I'm a writer!' I said triumphantly. 'From Lindworm Castle! My authorial godfather was Dancelot Wordwright.'

The Bookhunter gave a grunt. 'I'm not interested in living authors, their books don't make any money. Not for me, anyway. The only good author is a dead author.'

'I haven't published anything yet,' I said apologetically.

'Then you're worth even less. What are you doing down here, unpublished writer?'

'I was brought here against my will.'

'That's the silliest excuse I've heard since I chopped off Goldenbeard the Hairsplitter's legs. He said his compass was broken when I caught him on my territory. At least *he* wasn't lying. His compass really was broken.'

Hoggno pointed to a compass with a splintered glass attached to his trophy belt.

'You killed Goldenbeard the Hairsplitter?'

'I didn't say that, I said I chopped off his legs.' Hoggno pointed to two of the jars on the shelf, in each of which a foot was floating.

'I wasn't lying,' I said. 'I was hijacked and brought here. May I have a drink of water?' I had spotted a jug of water in a corner.

'No, water's scarce down here. Who hijacked you?'

'Someone named Smyke.'

'Pfistomel Smyke?'

'You know him?'

'Of course, every Bookhunter knows Smyke. A good customer of ours. He's universally popular.'

I laughed bitterly. 'Have you read Colophonius Regenschein's book?' I asked to change the subject.

'Naturally,' said Hoggno. 'Every Bookhunter has read it – every literate Bookhunter, at least. I don't like the fellow, but one can learn a lot from him.' He indicated the diamond on the table. 'The fact that there's a diamond inside a Spinxxxx – that one has to find out for oneself.'

'What do you Bookhunters have against Regenschein?' I asked, to keep the ball rolling.

Hoggno acted as if he hadn't heard the question. 'What are you, actually?' he asked. 'A lizard?'

'A, er, Lindworm,' I replied. I could sense him appraising me behind his mask.

'Oh? And how do Lindworms taste?'

I flinched. 'What do you mean?'

'I asked how they taste. Lindworms, I mean.'

'How should I know? I'm not a cannibal.'

'I am.'

'What!'

'I eat anything,' said Hoggno. 'And I haven't tasted any fresh food for ages,

195

just bottled stuff and worms.' He pointed disdainfully to the jars of liquid blood, guts and squirming maggots. 'And phosphorescent jellyfish. I've eaten so many of the confounded things I'm starting to glow in the dark myself.'

I weighed up my chances of escape. They were poor. 'I haven't eaten much lately either,' I replied, hoping to arouse his sympathy.

'You don't look like it. You're nice and plump.'

'You can't eat me!' I protested. 'They poisoned me – my entire bloodstream is awash with poison.'

'So why aren't you dead?'

'Well, er . . . because the poison only paralysed me, I suppose.'

'That's good. It's an age since I did any drugs.' There wasn't a trace of irony in his voice. He meant exactly what he'd said.

I was fast running out of arguments.

'I own a valuable manuscript,' I said. 'I'll give it to you if you guide me to the surface.'

'I'll simply take the manuscript when I've eaten you,' said Hoggno. 'It'll be easier that way.'

Now I really had run out of arguments.

'That's enough conversation,' he said. 'Now I remember why I never missed it. People only try to confuse you with talk.' He stood up and took an axe from the wall, then ran his mailed thumb along the blade with a high-pitched sound like a knife being sharpened.

'I'll make it short and sweet,' he promised. 'Well, I don't know about sweet, but short – that I guarantee you. I'm not a sick bastard like Rongkong Koma. I kill to survive, not just for kicks. I shall process every last bit of you. I'll eat your flesh and pickle your internal organs. Your hands I'll preserve and sell to some dumb tourist. I'll shrink your head and sell it to an Ugglian antique shop. Take off your clothes so they don't get bloodstained!'

I was sweating. How could I gain some time? Resistance would be futile. He was an experienced warrior, armed and in armour.

'May I at least have a drink before you kill me?' I entreated.

Hoggno thought this over. 'No,' he said, 'you'll be dead in no time. It'd be a waste.'

A sudden gust of wind came wafting through the skull. The candles flickered, the shadows on the walls danced. Hoggno turned towards the entrance and gave an exclamation of surprise.

'That's . . .' he said, and broke off in mid sentence. He raised the axe.

The candles went out, the darkness was total except for some little red specks: the tips of the smouldering wicks. I heard something rustle in the gloom like the pages of a big book fluttering in the wind. Then came a savage snarl. Hoggno uttered an oath. His axe whistled through the air. I ducked and went into a crouch. A clatter, a rending sound, another rustle of paper, then silence.

I went on crouching in the darkness for a while, quaking with fear, my heart beating wildly. At length I groped my way to the table, found the matches and lit a candle with trembling fingers. I hardly dared look round.

Hunk Hoggno was lying on the floor – in two pieces. His head had been cut off and placed beside his body complete with helmet. His left hand was holding a few shreds of bloodstained paper. I wasn't cold-blooded enough to remove the helmet and see what species he belonged to. I flopped down on the chair, gasping with horror.

It took me quite a while to regain some of my composure and awaken from a kind of trance. I picked up the jug of water and drained it, took a knife from the wall and stowed it in one of the pockets of my cloak, and removed the jellyfish torch from its clay vessel. Then I left that ghastly place.

ΨΟ

The Bloodstained Trail

I emerged from the huge skull and stood there in two minds. The candle-light in the interior, which flickered restlessly, shone through the gaps in the teeth and made it look alarmingly lifelike. Which way should I go? The way we had come? Back through the cramped stone labyrinth, where Spinxxxxes and other Unholm monsters awaited me? No thanks, not again.

In the other direction, then? Into the darkness, the unknown? Into a world that might be teeming with dangers more terrible still? They were tempting alternatives indeed. It was like being asked to choose between the gallows and the executioner's block. I raised the torch above my head and peered into the darkness. Hey, what was that? Lying at my feet was a scrap of paper.

I picked it up. It resembled one of the bloodstained shreds of paper Hoggno had been holding in his lifeless hand. Closer examination revealed that it was covered with faded writing in a script unfamiliar to me, Bookemist's Runic or something similar. And there, a little further away from the giant skull, lay another. I went over and picked that up too – and sighted yet another a few feet further on! What was this, a trail? A trail left behind by Hoggno's killer? If so, had he left it deliberately or inadvertently? Should I follow it?

Well, that was a third possibility at least. I could now choose between hanging, beheading and quartering. But perhaps a vestige of hope still remained. It was possible that the killer had laid this trail unintentionally. If so, he would eventually, without realising it, guide me back to civilisation. Even if he had laid it on purpose, it didn't necessarily mean that he had done so with evil intent. If he'd wanted to kill me he could easily have done so inside Hoggno's strange pied-à-terre.

So I left the skull and its frightful contents behind in the darkness and followed the trail of bloodstained paper. At first it led me through a stalagmite forest exclusively inhabited by small, timid creatures that fled, squeaking and rustling, from the light of my torch. Water dripped on my head incessantly, wearing me down like a subtle form of torture, until I finally reached a dry, narrow tunnel of granite that zigzagged upwards. Remembering the misshapen ape that had lain in wait for me and Hoggno in a similar passage, I wondered what I would do if I encountered such a creature on my own. I wouldn't even find the knife in my cloak and draw it in time.

At last I came to a broad expanse of loose rubble that might have been the remains of a rockfall from the roof – all I could make out overhead was a pitch-black void in which bats were noisily disporting themselves. The wind whistled round me, a chill, invisible current of air that had long been flowing in my direction. It had clearly found its way down from the surface through ducts of some kind. I envied the wind its knowledge of these, which might have provided me with a way out.

Then the temperature steadily rose and I came to some galleries that ran through solid coal. I picked up one scrap of paper after another, puzzled over the runes and stuffed them into my numerous pockets.

After a while I grew tired of collecting them. I couldn't read the writing anyway, so I simply left them lying where they'd fallen. I'd spent so long staring at the ground for fear of missing one that I'd failed to note the composition of the tunnel walls. Imagine my surprise and delight, therefore, when I suddenly saw that they were lined with rough-hewn stones. These were no natural tunnels; they were passages created by some unknown hand! I was back in civilisation, albeit of a very primitive kind. And I was still finding those scraps of paper. They became steadily rarer and the intervals between them greater until I came at last to the first book I'd seen for a long time!

Lying on the ground in the middle of an otherwise empty passage, it was in such an advanced stage of decay that I knew it would fall to dust if I tried to pick it up, so I left it untouched. On top of the book lay one of the bloodstained scraps of paper, and something told me that this was the last. From now on I would have to find my own way unaided. I sat down with my back against the wall, happy and unhappy, weary but alert. I'd made it, but to where? I had escaped from Unholm and the uncivilised part of the catacombs, but where was I now?

I closed my eyes. Just a short rest, I told myself, but don't go to sleep! That was impossible in any case, because images promptly performed a dance before my inner eye: the frightful insects in the sea of books, the megaworm, the Spinxxxx, Hoggno's headless corpse . . . My eyes snapped open again, and I was horrified to find that my jellyfish torch had gone out. I was in total darkness. Panic-stricken, I felt for the torch but couldn't find it. Had someone taken it? My mysterious guide, perhaps? How had he managed to do that in such a short space of time without my noticing? I went on groping until I encountered the book. It fell to dust at my touch, and I could feel fat white maggots crawling over my paw. Then I heard heavy breathing.

'*Hhhhhhhhhhh...*'

I wasn't alone. Something was there in the dark.

'*Hhhhhhhhhhh...*'

It was coming closer.

'*Hhhhhhhhhhh...*'

And closer. I shrank back against the wall.

'*Hhhhhhhhhhh...*'

The unknown creature was very near my face – I could feel its breath, smell its smell – and it was as if someone had opened the door of a gigantic second-hand bookshop, as if a cloud of pure book dust had arisen and was wafting the musty scent of millions of decaying tomes straight into my face. It was the breath of the Shadow King!

Someone spoke and I woke up. Yes, I woke up and opened my eyes, and there was the torch once more. Neither extinguished nor stolen, it was faithfully illuminating the ancient book and the bloodstained scrap of paper on top of it. I had simply nodded off for a moment. I had nodded off and dreamt of the Shadow King.

⛢♃

Three Distinguished Writers

Yes, dear readers, I'd heard voices. Quite definitely. Or had they merely been the remnants of my dream? Stray echoes, catacomb noises? I took the torch, struggled to my feet, and ... There! I heard it again, coming from the next tunnel! I followed the sound, which was no more than an unintelligible whisper, but it had gone by the time I entered the tunnel.

There were books, though! A whole passage full of books lying strewn across the floor – worm-eaten books, perhaps, but books nonetheless.

Delightedly, I waded through this mass of paper, which seemed more precious to me than a treasure chamber filled with diamonds – and there it was again, that whisper from an adjoining passage. And wasn't that a light I saw too? Shielding my torch, I turned the corner. The phosphorescent jellyfish clinging to the roof shed their usual weird glow, but this time I felt as if I were seeing the light of the sun once more. There were bookcases here as well, ancient ruins of worm-eaten wood enshrouded in dust and cobwebs but containing numerous books. I was gradually returning to civilisation! Civilisation, pah! My requirements had indeed become modest if a few worm-eaten bookcases filled with mouldering tomes struck me as evidence of civilisation. I went over to one and was about to remove a book when . . .

'Well?' said a voice, so loudly and distinctly that I flinched.

'Well? To my eye it's trash!' someone replied. 'Rubbish of the worst sort.'

The voices were coming from the next passage. Two Bookhunters at the same time? I drew the knife from my cloak.

'Ha-ha, listen to this!' said a third voice.

I shrank back against the bookcase. *Three* Bookhunters? I was done for!

'*I arise from dreams of thee,*' the last voice continued,

> '*in the first sweet sleep of night.*
> *When the winds are breathing low,*
> *and the stars are shining bright—*'

'Night . . . bright,' one of the other voices broke in. 'What a tired old rhyme!'

I was so overcome with curiosity, I almost forgot my fear. I could still have slipped away unnoticed, but I simply had to know who these people were. I pocketed my torch, raised my knife and tiptoed over to the mouth of the mysterious passage.

Once there I drew a deep breath and stole a cautious glance round the corner. This passage, too, was lined with bookcases, and in the middle, knee-deep in paper, stood three strange, gnomelike creatures. All I could tell at first sight was that they were certainly not Bookhunters.

They all looked alike to a certain extent, although they differed in stature. One was fat and thickset, one slim but with chubby cheeks, and one thoroughly puny. All they had in common was their diminutive size – even the tallest of them only came up to my waist – and the fact that each had only one eye. The slim one was reading aloud from a book:

> '*I am the eye with which the Universe*
> *beholds itself and knows itself divine;*
> *all harmony of instrument or verse,*
> *all prophecy, all medicine is mine . . .*'

The gnome broke off and tossed the book into the dust. 'To my eye,' he said, 'that's trash too. Al's right.'

'I don't think it's as silly as *all* that,' said the smallest gnome. '*I am the eye with which the Universe beholds itself*' – I find that a telling line.'

'Really?' said the fat one. 'What does it tell you?'

'Well,' said the puny one, 'I can certainly identify with "eye" in the singular.'

The little creatures didn't look as if they presented any danger to me. They were Troglognomes or something similar – just harmless cave dwarfs. What was more, they seemed to be interested in literature. Nothing very bad could happen to me, surely?

I left my hiding place and raised a paw in greeting – quite forgetting that it was holding a knife. What with the raised dagger and my billowing cloak, I must have looked like an assassin as I suddenly emerged from the shadows.

The gnomes gave a terrible start and took to their heels, first blundering into each other and then running in three different directions. They hid themselves behind bookcases and mounds of books and paper.

'A Bookhunter!' cried one.

'He's got a knife!' cried another.

'He means to kill us!' whispered the third.

I stopped short and threw the knife on the floor. 'I'm not a Bookhunter,' I called loudly. 'I've no wish to kill anyone. I need your help.'

'Oh, sure, hence the knife.'

'I've dropped it,' I said. 'I've lost my way, that's all.'

'He looks dangerous,' one of the gnomes exclaimed. 'He's a lizard. He's probably got some other weapons hidden under his cloak. These Bookhunters get up to some very dirty tricks.'

'I'm a Lindworm,' I said. 'I'm from Lindworm Castle.'

This was the second time I'd had to make that clear to someone. These denizens of the catacombs seemed to be pretty ignorant of the outside world.

Slowly, an eye peered round a stack of books and regarded me with curiosity.

'You're from Lindworm Castle?'

'Yes, it's my home.'

A second eye squinted through a crack between two fat tomes on a shelf.

'Ask him something about Lindwormian literature,' said the owner of the second eye.

'Give me the name of a medieval novel by Doylan Cone,' said the one behind the stack of books.

'*Sir Ginel*,' I said, sighing.

The gnomes glunked their teeth.*

'And what's the funniest passage in it?'

'Pfff . . . Hard to say,' I replied. 'Either the bit where Sir Ginel's monocle falls into his breastplate or the lipogrammatical chapter where Doylan Cone dispenses entirely with the letter E.' I gave thanks to providence for my meeting with Kibitzer – and to my own effrontery for the ease with which that lie tripped off my tongue.

The third gnome, whose eye rose from behind a stack of paper like a fast-growing flower, proceeded to recite:

> '*Come, landlord, fill again my glass,*
> *and fill again my dish.*
> *Those things apart . . .*'

I quickly completed the stanza:

> '*. . . a buxom lass*
> *is all that I could wish.*'

'He *must* be a Lindworm,' said one of the gnomes.

---

* Translator's Note: Gnomes can glunk their teeth like Lindworms, it seems, because I assume that Yarnspinner meant they were expressing approval. How he could tell they were doing so with their teeth when their mouths were hidden from his gaze, I do not know. Let us simply put it down to artistic licence.

'You're right,' cried another. 'Nobody else would read that boring old book. Apart from us, of course.'

'*Sir Ginel* isn't bad at all. Once you've ploughed your way through that chapter on the care and maintenance of the medieval lance, it really takes off,' the third gnome objected.

'My name is Optimus Yarnspinner,' I said.

'It doesn't ring a bell.'

'Nor with me.'

'Never heard of you.'

'That's not surprising,' I said sheepishly. 'I haven't published anything yet.'

'What are you doing down here in the catacombs if you aren't hunting for books?'

'I was brought here against my will, then I lost my way. All I'm hunting for is the way out.'

'It's been the same old story for a thousand years,' said the gnome behind the bookcase. 'The catacombs are full of skeletons. The folk up above make a habit of dumping their trash in our habitat.'

I studiously overlooked his allusion to trash.

'You're the first inhabitant of Lindworm Castle I've seen in the flesh,' said the gnome behind the stack of books. 'I've read everything that's ever been written there, but I've never actually set eyes on a Lindworm before.'

I tried to do justice to this historic moment by smoothing my cloak down.

'We're great admirers of Lindwormian literature,' said the gnome behind the stack of paper.

'I'm honoured. Now that you know something about me, may I ask who *you* are?'

The fat gnome emerged a few inches from his refuge and declaimed,

> '*The quality of mercy is not strained,*
> *it droppeth like the drips from stalactites*
> *upon the place beneath: it is twice bless'd;*
> *it blesseth him that gives and him that takes . . .*'

I tried to interpret his meaning. Was he still frightened of me? Was he appealing to my better nature?

'What are you getting at?' I asked. 'Why not simply tell me who you are?' He ventured still further out of his lair.

> *''Tis mightiest in the mightiest; it becomes*
> *the dread Bookhunter better than his axe . . .'*

Why did those lines sound so familiar to me? One moment! They were a quotation! A quotation from . . . from . . .

'You were quoting from Wimpersleake!' I cried. Of course! Aleisha Wimpersleake, the undisputed colossus of Zamonian literature. Much beloved by adults but the scourge of schoolchildren ever since his day. Of course! Those lines came from one of his most famous plays. Dancelot had drummed them into me for decades.

The fat gnome now emerged completely. His skin was the colour of a ripe green olive.

'You've got it. That's my name.'

'*Your* name? *You're* Aleisha Wimpersleake?'

'I most certainly am. You may call me Al, everyone else does.'

I felt bewildered. Wimpersleake had been dead for centuries.

The gnome behind the bookcase left his refuge too. His complexion was pale blue. 'And I'm Wamilli Swordthrow,' he said. 'Wami to my friends.'

Wamilli Swordthrow was one of my favourite poets. He had written 'Imitations of Informality', which was enough by itself to render him immortal in my eyes.

'I see,' I said, humouring him. 'So you're Wamilli Swordthrow.'

'You bet I am!' cried the slender gnome. Clasping his hands together, he declaimed dramatically,

> *'I hovered, lonely as a kite*
> *that floats on high o'er hill and dale,*
> *when all at once I saw a sight*
> *that made my countenance turn pale.'*

That was indeed by Swordthrow. It came from one of his most famous poems, though not his best. Dancelot had made me learn it by heart. Who *were* these strange little creatures?

'And what's your name?' I asked the third and smallest of them, who was pale pink in colour. 'Are you also called after an eminent literary figure?'

'Not as eminent as all that,' he said shyly, coming out from behind his stack of paper. 'My name is Dancelot Wordwright.'

I winced as if he'd slapped me in the face. The name of my authorial godfather went echoing along the passage like the voice of a disembodied spirit.

'**All of us are products of the soil,**' the little gnome quoted. '**Dust we were, and to dust we shall return. We wend our way along in an endless festive procession, a funeral cortège of impermanence.**'

I was dumbfounded. 'Dancelot . . .?' I said, as if he himself were standing there in front of me. It was a passage from his book recited word for word.

'. . .Wordwright,' the little gnome amplified. 'A writer from Lindworm Castle. You may well have heard of him, if you—'

'I knew him personally,' I cut in. 'But how do you come to bear his name?'

'We all bear the names of distinguished writers,' Al said proudly.

'I don't quite understand,' I said.

The three of them looked at each other.

'Shall we?' said Al.

The other two nodded. Then they turned to me and chanted in unison,

> *'Put away your swords and axes,*
> *you cannot us overwhelm,*
> *for your weapons serve no purpose*
> *in the Fearsome Booklings' realm.'*

I took an involuntarily step backwards. The Fearsome Booklings! The all-devouring cyclopean monsters of the catacombs! Their most dangerous life form apart from the Shadow King! Of course! These creatures had only one eye! They were Cyclopses! The three one-eyed gnomes slowly advanced on me.

'Don't be frightened!' Al cried. 'We won't hurt you.'

That was easy to say! They were pretty small for omnivorous Cyclopses, but scorpions could also be small.

'That's just a scary rhyme we made up for the Bookhunters' benefit,' said Wami. 'Down here you have to cultivate an evil reputation or you'd be done for in no time at all.'

'All right,' I said, retreating slowly, 'so you're the Fearsome Booklings. What has that to do with writers' names?'

'I think we'd better begin at the beginning, folks,' said Al. 'He's a bit slow on the uptake.' The others nodded. Then all three came to a halt.

'It's like this . . .' said Wami. 'Every Bookling has to learn the entire work of some great writer by heart. That's our purpose in life and *raison d'être*. Me, I'm currently memorising every last poem in Wamilli Swordthrow's oeuvre.'

'And I', said Al, 'am doing the same with Aleisha Wimpersleake – no mean task, given that he wrote some forty plays and innumerable sonnets. I have to keep refreshing my memory.' He uttered a sigh that would have melted the hardest heart.

'And I can recite the entire works of Dancelot Wordwright, word for word,' Dancelot said timidly.

'Big deal!' Wami scoffed. 'Just one measly book.'

'He may write some more,' Dancelot protested.

I had also come to a halt. 'No,' I said sadly, 'I'm afraid he won't.'

'How do you know?'

'He died quite recently. He was my authorial godfather.'

The three Booklings stared at each other in dismay and Dancelot burst into tears. His friends did their best to console him.

'There, there,' Al said in a low, soothing voice. 'How do you think *I* feel? My writer's been dead for centuries – he'll never produce anything more either.'

'Everyone has to enter the Great Mystery sooner or later,' Wami whispered. 'We're all equal before the Orm.'

Dancelot was sobbing uncontrollably. 'One book!' he whimpered. 'Only *one*!'

Al and Wami looked at me and shook their heads, patting Dancelot tenderly on the back. Their outsize eyes went moist and I myself was just as unable to hold my tears in check. We all broke down and wept with a will.

A Very Short Chapter in Which
Precious Little Happens

Once we had all calmed down the Booklings stepped aside and conferred in whispers. Then they came over to me.

'We've decided to take you to see the rest of our community,' said Al. 'But only, of course, if you agree.'

How could I object? What difference would it make if I were devoured by three Fearsome Booklings or a hundred? Besides, I was beginning to have my doubts about their fearsomeness.

'I'm game,' I said. 'Is it far?'

Instead of answering, the trio opened their eyes as wide as they could and subjected me to a piercing stare. The yellow light in their pupils began to pulsate gently. Then they started humming.

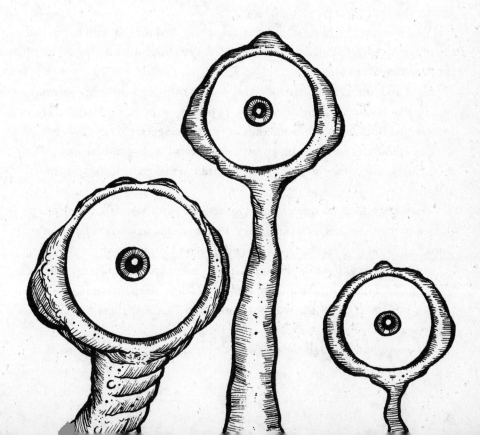

Yes, my good and faithful readers, that's all I have to report in this chapter. I can only tell you that – whoosh! – an instant later we found ourselves somewhere entirely different. I've no idea how the one-eyed gnomes performed this trick, but from one moment to the next we were standing outside a huge stone portal that formed the entrance to a cave.

ΨϚ

The Leather Grotto

'What happened?' I asked. I was feeling drowsy and a trifle unsteady on my legs. 'Where are we?'

'That was a sample of our gift for, er, teleportation,' said Al.

'Teleportation, tee-hee!' Wami tittered. 'Exactly.'

'𝔉rom the stars we come, to the stars we go. 𝔏ife is merely one long journey,' quoted Dancelot.

'You mean you can transport yourselves – and me – from one place to another by the power of thought?'

'You wouldn't be lying if you put it that way,' Al replied with a grin and the other two giggled inanely. 'Come on! We're about to enter the realm of the Fearsome Booklings.'

Al, Wami and Dancelot strode ahead of me through the huge gateway, which was flanked on either side by two enormous stone statues. They represented Booklings, but Booklings of greatly exaggerated size. Awesome-looking monsters with gaping jaws, cyclopean orbs and sharp claws menacingly raised, they were a sight calculated to make any intruder turn tail and run.

'They serve to deter unwelcome visitors,' Al explained, 'should any find their way here. Actually, no one has ever entered our territory who wasn't a Bookling. With two exceptions. You're the second.'

I was still busy digesting his reference to teleportation, quite apart from feeling as if I'd just been abruptly roused from a deep sleep, so neither this last remark nor the sight of the sculptures made any great impression on me. I tottered after the trio in silence.

As we passed through the gateway all my drowsiness left me in a flash.

Ahead of us lay a plateau from which a wide stone staircase led down into a vast stalactite cave. Al paused, threw out his arms and cleared his throat. 'Behold,' he cried,

'This fortress built by Booklings for themselves
against Bookhunters and the hand of war!'

The rest of us paused too. The view was, to put it mildly, remarkable. But the most remarkable thing about it was not that the walls, roof, floor and even the stalactites were dappled with countless shades of brown and gleamed like polished leather. Nor was it the huge machine of weird design that stood in the middle. No, the most fascinating feature of the cave was its occupants: hundreds of little one-eyed creatures that all resembled Al, Wami and Dancelot but differed from them in certain details. Some were fat, others thin, some bigger, others smaller. Some had long, spindly limbs, others were short and sturdy, and each seemed to have a complexion all its own. The cave was teeming with them. They were reading at long tables, toting piles of books to and fro, pushing laden handcarts along or busying themselves with the gigantic machine.

'That's the Rusty Gnomes' book machine,' said Al, as if that explained everything.

The machine, which took the form of a cube some two hundred feet high, wide and deep, appeared to consist of rusty shelving. As far as I could tell at long range, the shelves were filled with books and in constant horizontal or vertical motion. Running round the machine on six levels and connected by numerous flights of steps were walkways on which more of Al's fellow Booklings were bustling to and fro, removing or replacing books and operating various levers and handwheels. Not only the shelves but the whole huge contraption, including the catwalks and stairways, consisted of rusty iron. Its function remained a mystery to me.

At the foot of the machine were some long tables laden with large volumes, also handcarts, crates and more shelves filled with books. There were no phosphorescent jellyfish in the cave. The entire place was illuminated by candles, some in huge iron chandeliers suspended from the roof and others in ornate candelabra with numerous branches. Coal fires were burning in several big fireplaces let into the walls.

'This is the Leather Grotto,' said Wami. 'Our library, academy and community centre. And these are our compatriots, the Fearsome Booklings.'

I was about to ask a question, but Dancelot got there first.

'I'm sure you're wondering about all this leather. It's book covers – the whole cave is lined with them. We'd be happy to claim the credit for that achievement, but I'm afraid we weren't responsible. It was the Rusty Gnomes, who also constructed the book machine. We polish the leather regularly to keep it looking nice and shiny in the candlelight. The atmosphere is ideal for reading. It smells good, too.'

That, at least, was true. The air smelt tolerable for the first time since I'd entered the catacombs. It was a trifle stuffy, perhaps because of the innumerable candles, but laden with pleasant aromas. The cave looked comfortable and elegant despite its size; in fact, it astonished me that a subterranean chamber could make such a cosy impression. I felt an urge to sit down and start reading right away.

'Please note the skill with which the leather was hung,' Al said proudly. 'The most amazing thing is, not a single book cover was trimmed to make it fit. They went to an incredible amount of trouble to find the right cover to fill

each space. It must have taken centuries to line the whole cave. The Rusty Gnomes were obviously very fond of books. They're extinct, alas.'

'Come on,' said Wami, 'we'll show you round.'

We descended the broad staircase. I was still a bit dizzy from the effects of teleportation, but now my legs became really shaky. I don't like walking down long staircases at the best of times, especially with people watching. I always have visions of making an utter fool of myself by tripping and tumbling down them. However, we reached the bottom without incident.

The other Booklings took no apparent notice of me while I was being shown round the cave.

The ones seated at the tables were muttering to themselves as they read. Others strode up and down, gesticulating and soliloquising, and many stood conversing in groups. The cave was filled with voices and their manifold echoes. The little creatures went on with what they were doing, but I could see out of the corner of my eye that they stared after me curiously as soon as I'd gone by. If I turned round, they quickly looked in another direction. Hundreds of them there might be, but I simply couldn't feel scared of them.

'Why do you call yourselves the Fearsome Booklings?' I asked Al. 'You certainly don't strike me as very frightening. I pictured Cyclopses quite differently.'

'It's what the Bookhunters call us,' the fat Bookling replied. 'No idea why.'

'No idea why, tee-hee!' said Wami, smirking for some unknown reason.

'But we don't do anything to salvage our reputation,' Al went on. 'It's wiser not to.'

'Why?'

'Listen, there are over three hundred kinds of Cyclopses in Zamonia. Some are peaceful and others warlike, some carnivorous and others vegetarian. The Demonocles feed exclusively on prey that is still alive and kicking. Other Cyclopses eat nothing but buttercups. There are Cyclopses with the intelligence of a house fly and others of above-average intellectual capacity – my innate modesty forbids me to tell you what *those* are called. The only thing the various Cyclopses have in common is their single eye, but in the public mind they're doltish and dangerous creatures. We decided to take advantage of that prejudice.'

'In what way?'

'How many of us would have survived, do you imagine, if we were called the *Kindly Booklings*?' Al retorted. 'Or the *Nice Booklings*? This subterranean world is a brutal, merciless place. Down here the most highly respected creatures are the most ruthless and dangerous. In the catacombs a good reputation can be more lethal than a Toxicotome.'

Dancelot grinned. 'Most Bookhunters are superstitious, fortunately,' he said. 'They're shockingly uneducated individuals with a barbarous attitude to life. They believe in gods and devils. They love ghost stories and horror stories, and they like swapping Bookhunters' yarns at their get-togethers. They all try to outdo each other with their tales of the Fearsome Booklings; in fact, many of them believe we practise witchcraft.'

'Well,' I said, 'considering how you teleported me, they're not so wide of the mark.'

The three of them nudged each other and giggled.

'Teleportation, huh?' Wami guffawed.

I had no idea why the silly little gnomes kept laughing. Perhaps it was just their own peculiar sense of humour.

'Anyway,' Dancelot resumed, 'we encourage the Fearsome Booklings myth whenever we can. If we go our separate ways some time, it would be

very nice of you to tell everyone you saw us devouring our own kind alive, or something of the sort. Or that we're twenty feet tall with teeth as long as scythes.'

I remembered Regenschein's stories about the Booklings. He had helped to spread the myth of their fearsomeness by including that kind of stuff in his book. I was just about to ask the gnomes if his name meant anything to them when we reached the huge machine.

'When the first of us entered the Leather Grotto,' said Wami, 'this apparatus was too clogged with dust and dead insects to work. The Rusty Gnomes had probably become extinct many centuries before. But then we found the levers and handwheels. We tinkered with them and the machine suddenly started working again. Since then we've kept it in operation by oiling it regularly.'

'But what does it *do*?' I asked.

The three Booklings exchanged conspiratorial glances.

'We'll explain when the time comes,' Al said mysteriously. 'At present we use the machine as a library. It's a bit tiring, the way the shelves never stop moving, but it keeps us in good shape.'

I saw the Booklings on the catwalks hurrying after the shelves as they

removed books or replaced them. The rusty shelves kept superimposing themselves on each other or receding and disappearing into the interior of the machine. It made one dizzy to watch so many books on the move.

'Shelves sometimes vanish for days on end, but they always reappear sooner or later,' said Dancelot. 'The machine never loses a single book we entrust it with. Come on, we'll show you.'

We climbed a rusty staircase to the walkway on the lowest level.

'Kindly note the artistic metalwork on the handrails,' said Al.

I took a closer look. What I'd mistaken in passing for a recurrent pattern was really a series of tiny carvings, all of them different.

'If you study these handrails carefully,' said Wami, 'you'll learn the whole history of the catacombs. Look, here's the battle between the Crimson Book Pirates and Prince Elradodo. And here's the great cave-in at the Glass Pit – four thousand dwarf miners were killed and each of them is shown with a sliver of glass in his head. And this is a representation of the Formic War allegedly waged by two races of ants of monstrous size – no idea if it has any basis in fact. And here are the first Bookhunters entering the catacombs.'

Dancelot pointed to another section of handrail.

'This shows the construction of the Bookway under the supervision of the Rusty Gnomes. It took a century to complete, apparently. And this stretch immortalises a Bookemists' subterranean conference.'

The engravings in the rust were really intricate. I never realised that corroded iron could be engraved so finely.

'The Rusty Gnomes developed a process for preserving rust,' said Wami. 'We're still trying to work out how they did it. Preserving rust is really a contradiction in terms.'

'Is the Shadow King depicted anywhere?' I blurted out, keen to ask a question that would highlight my knowledge of the catacombs.

The three Booklings came to a halt and eyed me gravely.

'No,' Al said after a long pause. 'Nobody knows what the Shadow King looks like, so there can't be any likenesses of him.'

'Are you convinced of his existence?'

'Of course,' said Al. 'We hear him howling sometimes. Down here his howls are so loud they can keep you awake. They break in on our pleasantest dreams and turn them into nightmares.'

'Perhaps he's just an animal of some kind.'

'Only someone who has never heard the Shadow King would say that,' Dancelot said sympathetically. 'No animal has a voice like his.'

'What kind of creature do you think he is?'

'Let's change the subject!' Al enjoined. 'We're here to show you the beauties of the Leather Grotto, not to speculate about the Shadow King. Look at our books instead.'

The Shadow King obviously wasn't one of the Booklings' favourite topics. I obediently turned my attention to the books on the machine's perambulating shelves. It was hard to say how many of them there were because they came and went, rose or fell or glided past us, disappeared into the interior of the machine or emerged from it. I could now see how sumptuous and valuable many of them were: covers of solid gold and silver, clasps set with diamonds, sapphires, pearls and rubies, volumes bound in crystal, jade and ivory.

'Are these on the Golden List?' I asked.

'Forget about the stupid Golden List,' Al said dismissively. 'We've got a list of our own we call the Diamond List. There are books in the Leather Grotto that make the whole of the Golden List look second-rate.'

'We're Bookhunters too, in a way,' said Wami, 'although we naturally don't employ the barbarous methods favoured by those professional killers. Our motive in hunting them is love, not greed. We hunt them with heart and mind, not axe and sword. We aspire to learn, not to enrich ourselves, and we hunt more effectively. Our finds are far more valuable!'

'And the best of it is,' Dancelot added with a grin, 'the Bookhunters believe we eat books! Ha, ha, ha! What fools! They don't have the least idea that we store them here. They think we feed on them when times are hard.'

'Well, yes . . .' said Al, staring at the ground with his single eye. The other two Booklings cleared their throats and for a few moments there was an awkward pause I couldn't interpret. It struck me how smoothly the machine was running. All I could hear were some faint clicks like those made by a clockwork mechanism.

'What books could be more valuable than those on the Golden List?' I asked.

Instead of replying, Wami went over to one of the perambulating shelves. He removed a book with both hands and brought it to me, screwing up his face and grunting as if it were terribly heavy. He was joking, apparently, because it was quite a small, slender volume.

'Here . . . take . . . it,' he gasped.

I took it from him – and was almost flattened by its weight. It was the heaviest book my paws had ever held.

Al and Dancelot grinned.

'Better put it down before you rupture yourself,' said Wami. 'It's the *Tonnotome.*'

I deposited the weighty volume on the iron catwalk.

'We're still wondering how they managed to make it so heavy,' said Wami. 'Each page weighs as much as a complete edition of, say, Aleisha Wimpersleake's plays. You can sprain your wrist just turning the pages. They must have impregnated the paper with some alchemical element with an immense atomic weight. No one has ever manufactured a book less easy to use. It's not only hard to carry around, it's extremely hard to read.'

He opened it at the first page with considerable difficulty. Bending down, I read: '*If one imagines an invisible world that exists within a visible one, but which becomes visible when the visible one becomes invisible, in other words, whenever the sight of the invisible or visible one is focused on it, the invisible one becomes visible and the visible one invisible, always provided that this process is observed by an invisible person situated within a visible world imagined by another invisible person whom a visible person cannot see because the light has gone out.*'

'Phew!' I said. 'That's *really* hard. I don't understand it.'

'No one does,' said Al. 'That's why it was written.'

'I call that downright arrogant,' I said. 'Authors should write to be read.'

Al shrugged. 'I told you, we only collect books of genuine rarity.'

With an effort, Wami and Dancelot picked up the *Tonnotome* between them and placed it on one of the shelves gliding past.

'You didn't put it back where it came from,' I remarked.

'That doesn't matter,' said Al. 'It'll find its way there in the end. The machine handles the sorting.'

'How?' I asked.

'That's what we're still trying to work out,' Al said mysteriously.

'Look at the books on that shelf there!' Wami exclaimed.

We had to hurry to keep up with the shelf in question. All I saw at first glance were a few hundred books in different bindings composed of materials unfamiliar to me.

'That's the private collection formerly owned by a book tycoon named Yogur Yazella the Younger. He had all his favourite volumes bound in the skins of animals of which only one specimen existed – or none, of course, once the bookbinder had done his job. There, that's Ubufant hide . . . And that cover's made of Gogoskin . . . That's Red-Haired Muffon fur . . . Those feathers were taken from a Blue Goldbeak and that's Batcat hide.'

'How barbaric!' I cried indignantly.

'Not only barbaric but decadent,' said Al. 'Especially when you consider that Yogur Yazella couldn't even read. Just think how much these items would fetch in a Bookholm bookstore, allowing for the fact that the pages are made of compressed elfinjade!'

My brain reeled. The books on the Golden List really did pale into insignificance by comparison. I walked past the perambulating shelves open-mouthed.

'But that's nothing,' said Al. 'Here, take a look at this.' He had removed a small, unremarkable-looking book and was holding it out.

'You must open it sideways on, it works better that way.'

Wami and Dancelot cackled stupidly as I opened the book in the desired manner.

Then I dropped the confounded thing in horror. It had stared at me!

Al retrieved it. Wami and Dancelot guffawed with childish glee.

'Pardon my little joke,' Al said with a grin. 'This is an *Animatome*, a live book. All the books on this shelf are alive in their own way. Look closely!'

This time the relevant shelf stopped just in front of us as if the machine knew we wanted to inspect its contents. I went closer.

Just a minute – was I seeing things? These books really did seem to be alive! I blinked, rubbed my eyes and looked again. No, by thunder, it wasn't an illusion, the books were moving! Not a great deal, but I could distinctly see their backs rising and falling as if they were breathing. Something inside me balked at touching them, any more than I would have touched an unfamiliar animal that might or might not be vicious.

'You can safely stroke them,' Al told me. 'They won't do anything to you.'

Gingerly, I ran my paws over the backs. They felt warm and fleshy, and they quivered a little at my touch. Having had my fill of physical contact for the time being, I stepped back.

'We're always finding them in the catacombs,' said Dancelot. 'They must be hundreds of years old. We suspect they're the product of unsuccessful experiments by the Bookemists – early attempts to bring books to life.'

Al sighed. 'We can't understand why they were thrown away – straight on to the Unholm rubbish dump, probably. Perhaps the Bookemists hoped their experiments would have results of a different order.'

Live books – incredible! The Booklings were right, the Golden List was nothing compared to their literary treasures.

'They must be tough little creatures if they managed to extricate themselves from Unholm,' I said.

'You can say that again!' Wami exclaimed. 'It's rumoured that they continued to develop in the catacombs. There are even supposed to be some dangerous specimens among them – ones that have mated with Hazardous Books and learnt to fly and bite.'

'Shadowhall Castle is reputed to be overrun with them,' said Dancelot. 'It's said that—'

'That's enough of your old wives' tales!' Al said sharply. 'We're supposed to be showing our guest round the library, not making his flesh crawl.'

'What do they live on?' I asked. 'What do they eat, I mean?'

'They like bookworms best of all,' said Dancelot. 'I feed them in my spare time.'

As if the machine had decided that we'd devoted enough time to the Animatomes, the shelf moved first upwards and then backwards into the interior. Another shelf took its place and the Animatomes disappeared.

'Well,' said Al, 'we mustn't make you overdo it. You're welcome to stay with us for a while, so there'll be plenty of time to show you some more of our library. Let's leave it at that for today.'

He went over to the staircase and looked down into the Leather Grotto.

'You already know a great deal about us,' he went on, and his voice took on a solemn note. 'It's time for you to make the acquaintance of the rest of our community. This is only the second occasion in the history of the Booklings that a non-Bookling has been accorded such an honour. Wami, Dancelot, tell the others to assemble for Orming!'

ΨႶ

Orming

*O*rming? It sounded like some old-fashioned custom. Was it somehow connected with the outmoded belief in the Orm, or did it perhaps mean 'eating' in the Booklings' language, and were they now assembling for a communal meal of Lindworm? Pfistomel Smyke, Claudio Harpstick, Hunk Hoggno – I'd recently been subjected to too many nasty surprises to trust anyone at all.

Dancelot and Wami were bustling around and transmitting the message from Bookling to Bookling. It spread through the Leather Grotto like wildfire, and within a few minutes the hubbub of voices and echoes combined to form a single cry: 'Orming! Orming! Orming!'

I plucked up all my remaining courage. 'What exactly is it, this, er, Orming of yours?' I asked Al.

'A barbaric old ritual in which you're flayed alive before we devour you,' he replied. 'We're Cyclopses, remember?'

I shrank back, legs trembling.

'I was only joking,' Al said with a grin. 'Are you good at Zamonian literature?'

I struggled to regain my composure. The Booklings' sense of humour frayed my nerves. 'Not bad,' I said. 'I had a good authorial godfather.'

'Then you'll find this entertaining. The thing is, we could introduce you to all the Booklings by their chosen writers' names, one by one, and that would be that. Right?'

'Right,' I said. I hadn't a clue what he was getting at.

'But that wouldn't be any fun and you'd have forgotten the names by tomorrow, or got them all mixed up. Right?'

'Right.'

'So we're now going to introduce each Bookling in turn, and you must *guess* his name.'

'What?'

'You'll memorise the names far better that way, believe me. This is how it works. Every Bookling selects a passage from his writer's works – one he believes him to have written when the Orm was flowing through him with particular intensity. He will then recite the said passage aloud. If you're good at Zamonian literature you'll identify it in most cases, but if you're bad at Zamonian literature you'll make a terrible ass of yourself. Although I said "he" in every case, I should add that our writers can be male or female. That's what we mean by Orming.'

I gulped involuntarily. How good was I really at Zamonian literary history? How high were the standards that applied here?

'But I must warn you,' Al whispered. 'Many of our number select their passages according to very strange criteria. In some cases I suspect they deliberately choose atypical examples to make it harder to guess their names.'

I gave another involuntary gulp. 'Why don't we simply introduce ourselves by name and leave it at that?' I suggested. 'I'm pretty good at remembering names.'

But Al had already turned away. 'Orming time! Orming time!' he called in a thunderous voice. 'Everyone gather round for Orming!'

He led me down from the machine to the floor of the cavern, where the Booklings formed a big circle round me. Escape was impossible. They were now at liberty to stare at me without embarrassment, which they did, fixing me with their glowing, piercing cyclopean gaze. I felt simultaneously naked and like a specimen under a microscope. The hubbub had died away, to be replaced by an expectant hush.

'This, my dear fellow Booklings,' Al cried, puncturing the silence, 'is Optimus Yarnspinner. He's an inhabitant of Lindworm Castle and a budding author.'

A murmur ran round the assembled company.

'He was dumped in the catacombs against his will and lost his way. To save him from certain death, Wami, Dancelot and my humble self' – Al inserted a brief pause, presumably to allow someone to dispute the description 'humble', which no one did – 'and, er, I have decided to grant him temporary membership of our community.'

Polite applause.

'That being so, it will be our pleasure to have a genuine author in our midst for the next few days. He hasn't published anything yet, but we all know that this is only a matter of time. He hails from Lindworm Castle, after all, so it's his destiny to become an author. Indeed, we may even be able to make some small contribution to his literary career.'

'You'll make the grade!' a Bookling yelled at me.

'Sure,' cried another. 'Just write – the rest will come by itself!'

'Practice makes perfect!' shouted someone right at the back.

I was becoming rather embarrassed by the whole situation. Couldn't they at least get on with the confounded Orming?

'Good,' cried Al. 'Now you know his name: Optimus Yarnspinner! May it one day be emblazoned on the backs of scores of books!'

'Scores, scores, scores!' chanted the Booklings.

'But. . .' Al cried dramatically. 'Does he know *our* names?'

'No!' cried his listeners.

'So what shall we do about it?'

'Orm him! Orm him! Orm him!' they bellowed.

Al made an imperious gesture and they all fell silent.

'Let the first one step forward!' Al commanded.

Nervously, I gathered my cloak around me. A tiny, yellowish Bookling came and stood in front of me.

He cleared his throat and, in a voice quivering with emotion, declaimed,

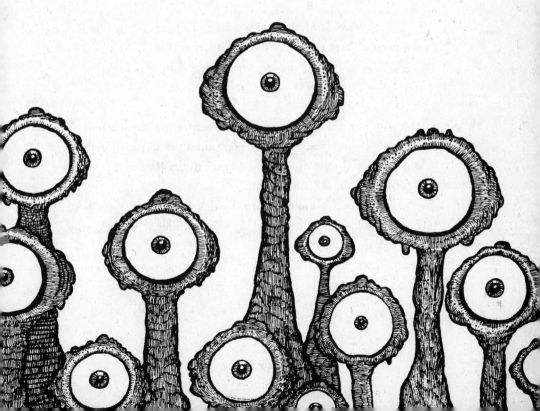

> *'Hear the loud Bookholmian bells –*
> *brazen bells!*
> *What a tale of terror, now, their turbulency tells!*
> *In the startled ear of night*
> *how they screamed out their affright!*
> *Too much horrified to speak,*
> *they can only shriek, shriek . . .'*

Wait a minute, I knew that poem! Its rhythm was unmistakable – it was a unique and masterly example of Zamonian Gloomverse. It was, it was . . .

'You're Perla la Gadeon!' I exclaimed. 'That's "The Burning of Bookholm"! A poetic masterpiece!'

'Damnation,' growled the Bookling, 'I should have chosen something less popular!' But he beamed with pride at having his name guessed so quickly. The other Booklings broke into subdued applause.

'That was easy,' I said.

'Next!' called Al.

A green-skinned Bookling stepped forward and gazed at me sadly with his red-rimmed eye. Then he spoke in a thin, brittle voice:

> *'Bid the last few grapes to fill and ripen;*
> *give them two more days of weather fine,*
> *force them to mature, thereby instilling*
> *all their sweetness in the heady wine.'*

Hm. A wine poem, but not just any old wine poem. One in particular. *The* wine poem to end all wine poems, which recounted the terrible fate of Ilfo Guzzard. And that had been written by . . . 'Inka Almira Rierre!' I cried. 'It's the second strophe from his "Comet Wine"!'

Inka bowed and retired without a word. Deafening applause.

'Next!' I said before Al could do so. My self-confidence was growing. I was beginning to enjoy Orming.

A purple-complexioned Bookling emerged from the crowd with majestic tread. Drawing a deep breath, he flung out his arms and cried:

> *'O!'*

Before he could utter even one more syllable I levelled an accusing finger at him and said, 'You're Dolerich Hirnfiedler!'

Well, Dolerich Hirnfiedler was notorious for beginning every other poem with an 'O!'. It was only an audacious shot in the dark on my part – many poets had done the same – but to my amazement the Bookling gave a shamefaced nod and withdrew. Bingo! I'd guessed his identity on the strength of a single letter! A murmur ran through the Booklings' ranks and several of them glunked their teeth approvingly.

'Next!' Al called.

An albino Bookling with a watery red eye stepped forward.

> *'How do I love thee? Let me count the ways.*
> *I love thee to the depth and breadth and height*
> *my soul can reach. When I behold the sight*
> *of thy bowed head and mournful, careworn face*
> *my spirits sink, beyond all power to raise,*
> *and every day becomes perpetual night.'*

Good heavens, Bethelzia B. Binngrow! My authorial godfather had robbed me of many a night's sleep by compelling me to memorise the lugubrious love poems of that half-demented Florinthian poetess. I still knew that one by heart.

But this time I decided to keep everyone on tenterhooks – to wait before shooting my bolt – so I pretended that this was a particularly tough nut to crack.

'Phew!' I said. 'Gee, that's difficult . . . it might be . . . no . . . or . . . no, he didn't write any poems that rhymed . . . or it's . . . just a moment . . . I can see a name. . . no, two names and an initial . . . they're very faint . . . almost invisible . . .'

The Booklings groaned with suspense.

'I do believe the mist is clearing . . . Yes! Now I've got it! You're Bethelzia B. Binngrow! Barmy Bethelzia!'

The last words just slipped out. The Bookling whose identity I'd guessed emitted a resentful snort, turned on his heel and disappeared into the throng. Everyone broke into relieved applause. I wiped some non-existent sweat from my brow.

'Next!' cried Al.

A thickset Bookling with a pale-blue complexion elbowed his way through the crowd. One or two titters could be heard as he stationed himself in front of me.

> 'A f-f-fish, a s-s-skeletal f-f-fish
> l-l-lay on a r-r-rock.
> How d-d-did it c-c-come
> t-t-to b-b-be there?'

Oh my goodness, a stutterpoem! There had once been a Zamonian literary movement – Gagaism, as it styled itself – that not only sanctioned speech defects but positively cultivated them. They really weren't a special field of mine.

> 'The s-s-sea, the s-s-sea, it
> w-w-washed it up,
> and th-th-there it l-l-lay
> qu-qu-quite c-c-comfortably.'

Wow! Orkle Thunk used to stutter and so did Dorian Borsh. The Waterhead Twins had stuttered whole duets together. There were even stutterpoems written by non-stutterers eager to climb on the Gagaist bandwagon.

> 'Then al-l-long c-came a f-f-f
> a f-f-f-f-f-f-f-f-f-f-f-f-f
> f-f-fisherm-m-man f-f-fishing, f-f-f-fishing
> f-f-for f-f-fresh f-f-fish.
> He t-t-took it aw-w-way, aw-w-way,
> aw-w-way, he t-t-took it aw-w-way.'

T. T. Kreischwurst, whose pseudonym was as asinine as his poetry, had written more stutterpoems than anyone else, but this one might just as easily be by Pankard Murch or Dongo Ghorkhunter. I would have to fall back on guesswork.

> 'The r-r-rock n-n-now l-l-lies there
> b-b-bereft of its s-s-skeletal f-f-fish
> in the m-m-midst of the w-w-wide ocean,
> l-l-looking t-t-terribly b-b-bare.'

The Bookling bowed. At least he'd finished the confounded poem. Gee . . .
No, I really didn't know who'd written that embarrassing drivel, so I simply
settled on the most popular stutterpoet of all.

'You're T. T. Kreischwurst!' I said firmly.

'Y-y-y-y-yes!' the Bookling replied. 'That was entitled "A L-l-l-l-little
P-p-p-poem for B-b-b-b-big S-s-s-stuttuttuttutterers".'

Applause and laughter. Phew! I'd made it again, albeit only by a
whisker.

'Next!' Al called.

More candidates presented themselves in quick succession. Ydro Blorn,
Rashid el Clarebeau, Melvin Hermalle and the rest – I guessed them all, one
after another. Not for the first time since my arrival in the catacombs, I gave
thanks to my authorial godfather for the extensive knowledge of Zamonian
literature he'd drummed into me in my boyhood.

A Bookling the colour of a dark-brown calfskin cover stepped forward
and declaimed,

> *'Away! Old Lindworm Castle, fare thee well!*
> *In freedom will I roam across the plain.*
> *Henceforward all I do shall only serve*
> *to win me the renown I hope to gain.'*

Aha, Lindwormian verse! Couldn't he have made it a bit easier for me?
Although I couldn't identify the poem immediately, I naturally knew every
word that had ever been written in the castle.

> *'Renown! Let that sweet recompense be mine!*
> *May all my dreams of eminence come true,*
> *and may my lonely tombstone bear this line:*
> *"A poet for the many and the few!"'*

Just a minute! I *knew* this poet – he had recited these stanzas to me himself on
some occasion. Of course! They came from Ovidios Versewhetter's farewell
poem on leaving Lindworm Castle. He had recited it to the entire Lindworm
community in the belief that he was destined to become a celebrated literary
figure in Bookholm. I never dreamed that the next time I saw him he would
be languishing in one of the pits in the Graveyard of Forgotten Writers.

'Bookholm, of dreaming books thou city vast,
abode of wealthy poets, I with thee
a bond intend to forge that long will last.
To this may Destiny my witness be!'

There were another seventy-seven stanzas, all of which extolled the joys of a poet's emancipated existence and the fruits of fame that were bound to be awaiting the youthful Lindworm in Bookholm, but I decided to give myself, the Bookling and his confrères a break, so I said, 'You're Ovidios Versewhetter.'

The Bookling grinned. 'Yes, that was too easy. I knew you knew him; in fact, I'm sure you know more about Versewhetter than I do. Perhaps you can tell me why it's been so long since he published anything. Is he engaged on a major work of some kind?'

The poor creature had devoted his life to Ovidios Versewhetter. Should I tell him to his face that all he could now expect from him was extemporised doggerel churned out for the benefit of tourists? I didn't have the heart.

'Yes indeed,' I said. 'He has, er, buried himself away and is working on something really big.'

'I thought as much,' said the Bookling. 'He'll be really big again himself before long.' And he withdrew.

'Next!' Al said impatiently.

A gaunt Bookling with skin the colour of granite stepped forward.

'Where shadows dim with shadows mate
in caverns deep and dark,
where old books dream of bygone days
when they were wood and bark,
where diamonds from coal are born
and no birds ever sing,
that region is the dread domain
ruled by the Shadow King.'

This time I was stumped. It was a poem unfamiliar to me – obviously about the Shadow King, but I knew of no writer who had concerned himself with that figure apart from Colophonius Regenschein, and Regenschein had written no poetry.

It would be pointless to guess. There were hundreds of young poets whose works I didn't know. I admitted defeat.

'Not a clue,' I said. 'I don't know your name. What is it?'

'My name is Colophonius Regenschein,' the Bookling replied.

'That's impossible. He only wrote one book, *The Catacombs of Bookholm*. I read it quite recently and there isn't a single poem in it.'

'Colophonius Regenschein has written another book,' said the Bookling. 'It's called *The Shadow King* and it opens with that poem.'

The crowd was growing restive.

'How can that be?' I demanded. 'Colophonius Regenschein has disappeared.'

The Bookling merely grinned.

'Unfair!' someone shouted.

'Yes, Colo, give him a break!' shouted someone else. 'You can't expect him to know that.'

'Get lost!'

I felt bewildered. A hubbub arose, the crowd started milling around and the Bookling who called himself Colophonius Regenschein disappeared into its midst.

Al claimed the floor.

'That's it!' he cried. 'Orming's over for today! Our guest has acquitted himself well, he deserves a little rest.'

The Booklings murmured in assent.

'We'll go on Orming tomorrow. You'll all get your turn. Dismiss!'

I went over to Al. 'What was all that about just now?' I asked. 'Has Regenschein really written another book?'

'Come on,' he said hastily, ignoring the question. 'I'll show you our living quarters and the place where you'll sleep. You must be tired out.'

ⴲ⅄8

A Cyclopean Lullaby

Al conducted me along one of the passages that led off the Leather Grotto. The Booklings scurrying round us seemed to be taking no more notice of me. I had successfully withstood the initiation ceremony even before it had been completed, apparently, but I still felt like a wasp in an ants' nest. I was twice the height of the average Bookling and had to duck my head to avoid hitting it on the roof of the tunnel.

The passage was lined with book covers like the Leather Grotto. I tried to read some of the titles, but they were all in a script I couldn't decipher.

'Yes,' said Al, who had been watching me, 'it's a shame about all the books that went inside those covers. In their own day they were probably just rubbish, but to us they would now be evidence of an unknown civilisation. Books are perishable.'

'Aren't we all?' I said for want of any more intelligent rejoinder.

'No, not us,' said Al.

'How do you mean?'

'Well, I won't claim that Booklings are immortal, but none of us has ever died a natural death. There have been a few fatal accidents, but disease and decay are unknown here.'

'Really? Where do you come from? I mean, how . . .'

Al's single eye blinked nervously. 'I'm not at liberty to talk about that,' he said. 'Not at present, anyway.'

The passage was flanked by numerous little troglodytic dwellings, I noticed, and each of these miniature caves housed a Bookling. They, too, were lined with book covers, and each contained at least one bookcase as well as a couch thickly padded with furs. Everything was bathed in warm candlelight.

'Jellyfish lamps are no good for reading by,' Al said as if he had read my thoughts. 'They create an unpleasant atmosphere – one that's conducive at best to hunting or murdering things. We abhor jellyfish lamps. They multiply like vermin and one day they'll take over the catacombs. We eject any that dare to crawl into the Leather Grotto. Candlelight is soothing. Did you know that boiled bookworms yield an excellent form of candle grease?'

'No,' I said, 'I didn't.' However, I certainly endorsed his belief in the soothing effect of candlelight. The permanent claustrophobia induced in me by the catacombs had disappeared since I entered the Booklings' domain.

'Every Bookling's cave is individually furnished and appointed – mainly, of course, with books by the writer whose works he's committing to memory.'

We paused and peered into one of the caves. A fat little Bookling was comfortably stretched out on his bed of furs, reading a book. Pinned to the walls were various manuscripts and illustrations. I immediately recognised the writer in question by his picture.

'Hello, Ugor,' said Al. 'I don't think you need take any further part in the Orming. Optimus has already got your number, I suspect.'

'Your name is Ugor Vochti,' I said. 'You wrote *The Midgard Saga*.'

'I wish I had,' said Ugor. 'I'm only learning it by heart. It's a pity, though. I had a passage ready for you that was really hard to identify.'

We walked on. The alleyways here were almost deserted. It seemed that all the Booklings had holed up in their caves and were busy memorising.

'Why do you do it?' I blurted out.

'What?'

'Learn all this stuff by heart.'

Al stared at me uncomprehendingly. 'That's not the question. The question is, why doesn't everyone else do it?'

That needed thinking about. I couldn't come up with a snappy reply.

'These are your quarters,' Al told me, indicating a little cave. There were no books in it, just a couch big enough for someone of my size.

'You're welcome to borrow any books you need from the Leather Grotto. Would you like a few bookworms for supper?'

'No thanks,' I said. 'I'm thirsty, that's all.'

'I'll get you some mountain spring water,' said Al and walked off.

It wasn't until he had gone that I noticed the hum, a pleasant, persistent sound like the purring of countless contented cats. I made up my bed for the night. The night? How could I tell whether it was night or day? No matter, I was dog-tired.

Al returned with a jug of water.

'What's that noise?' I asked. 'That humming sound?'

He grinned. 'That's Booklings learning things by heart. Just before we go to sleep we shut our eyes and run through our favourite passages. We start humming for some reason – and eventually drop off to sleep. You'll get used to it.'

Al said goodnight. I drank some water, blew out the candles and lay down.

My eyelids and limbs were heavy. The humming didn't disturb me; on the contrary, I found it reassuring. It was the Booklings' music – the pleasant, dreamy sound of literature being memorised – that lulled me gently to sleep.

The Chamber of Marvels

It was something of an effort to get my breakfast down when Al brought it to me in the morning – bookworms roasted over an open fire – but I was so overpoweringly hungry by that time, I could have devoured a raw Spinxxxx. Besides, the crisp larvae didn't taste too bad at all.

'Today I'm going to show you some more of our territory,' Al announced as we emerged from my little cave. 'It's not confined to the Leather Grotto, my friend.'

The passages were already filled with Booklings going about their business once more. Books were being transported and candles replaced, voices raised in declamation, conversation or song. There seemed to be a collective aversion to silence – a pleasant change, I found, after the deathly hush prevailing elsewhere in the catacombs. I saw three vituperating Booklings bearing off a phosphorescent jellyfish that had invaded their domain. None of my hosts took any particular notice of me. I seemed to have become one of their number overnight.

'We'll go on with the Orming later,' Al told me. 'First I'll show you our Chamber of Marvels – our archives, in other words. We don't collect books alone, we also hoard anything with literary associations that finds its way down here. Literature is more than just paper, you know – it affects every aspect of existence.'

'You don't say.'

'It pervades life far more thoroughly than people tend to realise. In the case of us Booklings, that's doubly true.'

'In what respect?'

'In every respect. It's like this: sooner or later, every Bookling takes on the character of the author whose work he's memorising. That's inevitable – it's our destiny. By nature we're blank pages crying out to be written on. Not having any personalities of our own, we gradually assume the characteristics of our authors until we become complex individuals. Our Bookling community includes firebrands and cowards, show-offs and manic depressives, sluggards and hotheads, comedians and cry-babies. I, for example, am an exceptionally complex individual – not surprisingly, since Aleisha Wimpersleake's writings range from the thoroughly romantic to the utterly tragic.' Al broke off. 'Hey, look who's coming. That's Slootty.'

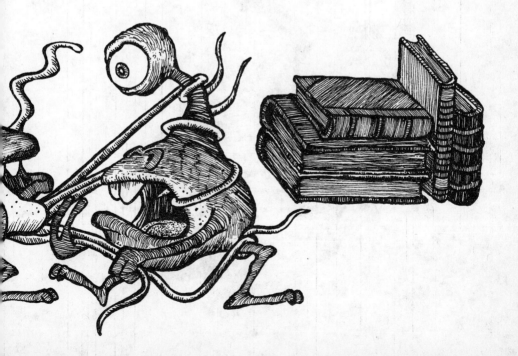

The single eye of the Bookling in question blazed with the cold flame of despair and his lower lip trembled as if he were about to burst into tears at any moment. He strode past us and disappeared into the darkness without a word, even though Al had bidden him a friendly good morning.

'Elo Slootty?' I said. 'The one who wrote that gargantuan novel everyone claims to have read and no one has ever finished?'

'It's a magnificent piece of work,' said Al, 'but it does require staying power. The Bookling who chose to be Elo Slootty definitely overestimated his mental stamina. We have to prevent him from committing suicide at regular intervals.' He broke off again. 'See who's waddling towards us? That's Charvongo.'

'That fat little creature? Navi Charvongo?'

'Yes indeed. See how sluggishly he moves.'

I couldn't help laughing. Charvongo had written a brilliant novel about the Movolob, a primitive creature notorious for its inertia. The fat Bookling ahead of us was lumbering along like an advertisement for indolence.

We passed through a sizeable cave in which thousands of candles were burning. In the centre stood a huge iron cauldron simmering over a coal fire. A number of Booklings had climbed up ladders to the rim of the cauldron and were emptying bucketfuls of maggots into it, others were skimming off the whitish fat with big ladles, and still others were busy moulding the insectile wax into candles in big wooden presses.

'This is our candle factory,' said Al. 'Anyone who wants to read needs light, especially if he lives below ground like us – we abhor jellyfish lamps, as you know.' He sighed. 'How dearly I'd love to read a book by sunlight, seated on a grassy bank in springtime – "*the only pretty ring time*," as Wimpersleake puts it.'

'Why don't you simply go up there and do so?'

'We can't, our little lungs would collapse. We have to live in the stuffiest atmosphere possible.'

'Really? Have you ever tried fresh air?'

'Of course. The higher we went, the harder it was to breathe. Too much oxygen would kill us.'

Beyond the candle factory we made our way along a narrow passage in which only one Bookling was coming towards us. I could tell at a glance that the book beneath his arm was a first edition of *Immoral Tales of Old Florinth*, a work so often banned and burnt that its rare original editions were right at the top of the Golden List.

'What sort of risqué stuff are you reading now?' Al asked as we passed him, wagging his finger in feigned reproach.

'*There is no such thing as a moral or an immoral book. Books are well written or badly written, that's all.*'

So saying, the Bookling disappeared round a bend.

Al grinned. 'I shouldn't tell you this because he hasn't Ormed you yet, but since we're by ourselves. . .' He peered round furtively. 'That was—'

'Rasco Elwid!' I cut in. 'Am I right?'

'Spot on!' Al said admiringly. 'Only Rasco Elwid could be so relentlessly cynical. You've got a really good memory, my friend. You could easily be a Bookling – if you didn't have one eye too many.'

The passages became bigger and bigger, and before long their bare stone walls were no longer lined with book covers. Leading off them and hewn out of the rock were some small chambers in which Booklings were busy operating printing presses, gluing books together by hand or stirring paper pulp in big vats. I also saw some casting lead type.

'This is our book hospital,' Al explained. 'It's where we restore worm-eaten or damaged books. We reconstruct texts and reprint them or repair the bindings. Books can be damaged in many different ways. Some get burnt, torn or eaten away by acid, others are transfixed by arrows or spears. We've even performed cosmetic surgery on some Animatomes before now.'

'Where's that reconstruction of the last chapter of *Knots in a Swan's Neck*?' a little Bookling called down the passage. 'The glue will set if the pages aren't inserted soon.'

'Coming, coming!' called another Bookling, hurrying down the passage with a sheaf of freshly printed pages in his hand.

We passed a pallid, corpulent Bookling who had covered his eye with his hand and was reciting a monotonous list of names and book titles: 'Tarquo Ironbeard – *Pitcher without a Handle.* Albus Karaway – *The Giant's Funny Bone.* Citronia Unkisst – *The Princess with Three Lips . . .*'

These were fictional characters from novels and the relevant titles, all by the same author. What was his name? It was on the tip of my tongue.

This time Al beat me to it. 'Hornac de Bloaze,' he said, lowering his voice to a whisper. 'He was definitely too prolific. The poor fellow who has to remember all his novels keeps getting the principal characters mixed up – and no wonder, considering that de Bloaze wrote seven hundred books populated by umpteen thousand characters. That's why he keeps reciting the names and titles.'

'Februsio Argostine – *Mahogany Soup*. Captain Bloodblister – *Bats in the Campanile*. Erkul Gangwolf – *Death of an Editor* . . . ' The Bookling continued his unceasing recitation of names and titles as we tiptoed out of earshot.

'Hornac de Bloaze was so thoroughly permeated by the Orm that it compelled him to write almost twenty-four hours a day,' said Al. 'He's said to have drunk vast quantities of strong coffee.'

'You honestly believe in the Orm?' I asked with a faint smile. 'In that ancient hocus-pocus?'

Al came to a halt and gave me a long look. 'How old are you?' he asked.

'Seventy-seven,' I replied.

'Seventy-seven?' He laughed. 'Ah, what it is to be young! All right, poke fun at the Orm while you can – that's a tyro's prerogative – but one day it will overwhelm you, and then you'll comprehend its power and beauty. How I envy you! I'm no writer, I'm only a Bookling. I didn't write Aleisha Wimpersleake's works, I only committed them to memory and I'm far from being an admirer of everything that came from his pen. He could write absolute rubbish on occasion and his sense of humour often leaves a modern reader cold. But there are some passages, some lines of verse . . .'

Al's expression became transfigured.

> *'Shall I compare thee to a summer's day?*
> *Thou art more lovely and more temperate:*
> *rough winds do shake the darling buds of May,*
> *and summer's lease hath all too short a date:*
> *sometimes too hot the eye of heaven shines,*
> *and often is his gold complexion dimmed:*
> *and every fair from fair sometimes declines,*
> *by chance or nature's changing course untrimmed . . .'*

I recognised those lovely lines as coming from one of Wimpersleake's sonnets. Al grabbed my cloak and tugged at it wildly. 'That's the Orm for you, understand? You can't write stuff like that unless you're absolutely awash with it! Verse of that quality doesn't just pop into your head – it's *a gift*!'

He let go of me.

'So what exactly do you think the Orm is?' I asked, smoothing my cloak down. His emotional outburst had left me feeling somewhat bemused.

Al looked up at the roof of the passage as if he could see stars there.

'There's a place in the universe where all great artistic concepts accumulate, bouncing off each other and generating new ones,' he said, more quietly now. 'Its creative density must be immense. An invisible planet with seas of music, rivers of pure inspiration and volcanoes that spew out ideas with brainstorms flickering in the sky around them. That's the Orm, a field of force that dispenses its energy in abundance. But not to everyone. Only the elect can receive its emanations.'

Yes, yes, but why was it invisible, like everything you had to take on trust? Because it didn't exist at all? Most older writers believed in the Orm. I decided to refrain from making any more critical remarks for courtesy's sake.

We entered a cave whose dimensions almost equalled those of the Leather Grotto, except that the roof was much lower and displayed no stalactites. Hewn out of the walls were little niches containing all manner of objects – books, letters, writing utensils, cardboard boxes, bones – but I was too far away to identify them all.

'Our archives,' said Al. 'We also call this place *The Chamber of Marvels*. Not because there are any marvels to be seen here, but because we can't stop marvelling at all the stuff we've amassed.' He chuckled. 'This is where we keep any memorabilia we can lay hands on: letters, contemporary documents, devotional objects, manuscripts, contracts bearing authors' signatures, personal ex-libris, hair or toenail clippings, glass eyes, wooden legs – you wouldn't believe the things collectors hoard! We possess numerous authorial skulls and bones, even whole skeletons – even a poet mummified *in toto*. Other items include worn garments and used writing implements, spectacles, magnifying glasses, sheets of blotting paper, any number of empty wine bottles, drawings, sketches, diaries, notebooks, folders containing collected reviews, fan mail – in short, anything that can be proved to have been in the possession of the authors whose works we learn by heart.'

'How does it all get down here?'

'Oh, we have certain contacts that extend as far as the surface of Bookholm – friendly tribes of dwarfs resident in the upper reaches of the catacombs, for instance. Besides, many of these objects used to be stored below ground in the same way as old and valuable books. Then again, there are the Bookhunters, with whom we . . .' Al gave a sudden exclamation and clapped a hand over his mouth as if he'd startled himself.

I looked at him. '*What* do you do with the Bookhunters?'

Al walked on quickly. 'Nothing, nothing. Hic! Pardon my hiccups. I was only going to say that one of Aleisha Wimpersleake's wisdom teeth is worth at least as much as a First Folio in excellent condition.' He cleared his throat noisily.

I refrained from pressing him further. We were now walking in a circle past the niches, in which the writers' memorabilia were arranged in alphabetical order. I saw quills and inkwells, rubber stamps and ink pads, coins, pocket watches, memo slips, letter scales, paperweights, a single glove.

'Do you buy these things with the proceeds of your Diamond List?' I asked.

'No, no, we don't trade in books. We have other sources of income.'

Other sources of income, eh? These Booklings were mysterious little creatures. What did they want with all this junk? A stuffed Gargyll with a glass eye. A bundle of foxed letters held together by a blue ribbon. A pewter urn. Some dried flowers. The sole of a shoe. Some blotting paper. Marvels they certainly weren't.

'Are you interested in any particular author?' asked Al.

I wasn't, to be honest. I'd never been one for personality cults. Did I really want to see one of Melvin Hermalle's toenail clippings? The pen with which Gramerta Climelth wrote *Gone with the Tornado*? A hair from the nose of Asdrel Chickens? Daurdry Pilgink's sun helmet? No thanks, their works were all that mattered. However, courtesy prompted me to cite a name.

'Dancelot Wordwright,' I said.

'Ah, Wordwright, I understand,' said Al. 'Then we'll have to look under W.'

Could one of Dancelot's personal possessions really have found its way so

241

deep into the catacombs? It was unlikely, but I didn't want to rob Al of the pleasure of showing me round his less than marvellous Chamber of Marvels. It was a long way to the letter W and the objects in the niches we passed soon became repetitious: pens, inkwells, pencils, paper, more pens, a letter, two letters, an inkwell – and more pens. I gave an involuntary yawn. Could anything be less fascinating than the personal possessions of an author? Even Atlantean tax inspectors surrounded themselves with objects of greater interest. A toothless comb, a tired old sponge . . . I hoped we would soon get there.

'Trebor Snurb . . . Carmel Stroup . . . Esphalon Teduda . . .' Al muttered the authors' names to himself as he passed their niches. 'Ah, here we are: Wordwright! I *knew* there was something of his.' He took a small cardboard box from the shelf.

I was amazed. 'Is there really?'

'See for yourself,' he said, handing me the little box.

I took it from him, opened the lid and saw a letter lying there – just one handwritten sheet of paper. I removed it and replaced the box in the niche.

'I remember how this letter came to us,' Al said. 'It caused quite a stir. We found it lying just outside one of the entrances to the Leather Grotto. Really alarming, that was. It meant that someone down here – someone who wasn't a Bookling – knew about our greatest secret. We were all very worried for a long time.'

A feeling of excitement surged through me as I examined the letter more closely. It really was in my authorial godfather's handwriting! Dancelot had written this letter, no doubt about it! I read:

My dear young Friend,

Thank you for sending me your manuscript. I can say without a word of exaggeration that I consider it to be the most immaculate piece of prose that has ever come into my hands. It genuinely moved me to the core. I hope you will forgive the following platitude, but I know of no other way to express myself. Your manuscript has changed my life. After reading it, I have resolved to give up writing and confine myself in the future to teaching your principles of literary craftsmanship to others – in particular, to my young authorial godchild, Optimus Yarnspinner.

I experienced another thrill of excitement at the mention of my name. What strange kind of bond – one that transcended time, space and death – was this letter forging between me and Dancelot? Tears sprang to my eyes.

Where you yourself are concerned, however, there is nothing I can teach you. You already know all there is to know, and doubtless far more than that. Though still young in years, you are already a consummate writer more brilliant than any of the classical authors I have ever read. The little I was privileged to assimilate while reading your manuscript reduced the entirety of Zamonian literature to the dimensions of a schoolboy's essay. There is more talent in your little finger than in the whole of Lindworm Castle. The only piece of advice I can give you is this: Go to Bookholm! Nay, hurry there as fast as you can! You have only to show all you have so far written to a competent publisher and your future will be assured. You are a genius. You are the greatest writer of all time. This is where your story begins.

In profound veneration, Dancelot Wordwright

It hit me like a blow in the face, dear readers. The last few sentences banished any remaining doubt that this was the letter Dancelot had written to the author I was trying to find – the one that had sent him off to Bookholm. It had passed from Dancelot's possession into that of the mysterious author, and now I was holding it in my paws. A new bond was being forged, this time between Dancelot, the author and my humble self. I had followed my unknown quarry's trail and lost it. Now, in the depths of the catacombs, I had picked it up again. My head was spinning, my knees started to give way.

'Oh!' I groaned, searching for some means of support.

Al grabbed my arm. 'Are you feeling ill?' he asked.

'No, no,' I gasped, 'I'll be all right.'

'You look as if you'd seen a ghost.'

'I just did,' I replied.

'Our archives contain many ghosts from the past. Would you like to see some more of them?' Al asked.

'No thanks,' I replied. 'This one will do to be going on with.'

The Invisible Gateway

Outside the Chamber of Marvels we bumped into Wami and Dancelot, who had come to assist Al in showing me round the Booklings' territory.

'We're now going to show you those parts of the catacombs that aren't illuminated by candles,' Al told me. 'There aren't any phosphorescent jellyfish either, but Wami and Dancelot are the best flame-throwers we've got.'

Grinning, Dancelot and Wami held up their pitch-pine torches, which were still unlit.

'We'll show you our forests and flower gardens,' said Wami. 'The whole of our untamed natural surroundings.'

Hadn't Al just lamented the fact that he would never sit on a grassy bank? Where could forests and flowers grow down here, and what on earth did 'flame-throwers' mean?

'It's time someone acquainted you with the pleasanter features of the catacombs. Till now you've only seen their sinister, bewildering and unattractive aspects. We'll show you what makes life worth living down here: a part of our gloomy world still untouched by decay and Bookhunters.'

'Does it exist?' I asked. 'And how do we get there?'

Al, Wami and Dancelot gathered round, opened their eyes as wide as they would go and fixed me with a piercing stare. Then they began to hum.

The next thing I knew, I was standing in a stalactite cave on the shores of a lake whose pale-blue waters were as clear as glass. Wami and Dancelot had lit their torches, Al was gazing across the lake with a rapt expression.

I felt dazed.

'My, oh my,' I said. 'Was that another example of teleportation?' My head was ringing like a Bookholm fire alarm.

'Exactly!' said Wami. 'Teleportation, tee-hee!'

'It's much easier than walking,' Dancelot said with a grin.

So why did I feel as if I'd been plodding along for hours? My legs were as heavy as lead.

'We teleported you so you'll never be able to betray the route to our treasures,' said Al. 'We did it for your own good.'

'Where are we?' I asked.

'This is the *Invisible Gateway*. Beyond it lies the *Crystal Forest*. I know it isn't a particularly original name for such a place, but we're no authors. Perhaps you can think of a better one.'

Nothing occurred to me on the spur of the moment. My brain felt like an empty sponge. Well, well, the Crystal Forest. I couldn't see any forest or any crystal, nor could I see an Invisible Gateway – but then, it was invisible by definition.

'Just follow us,' said Al, and the three little Cyclopses strode on ahead – into the blue lake. I followed them reluctantly.

The water was cold, but it only came up to my knees. Inquisitive silvery eels were swimming round us. I worried that I would catch my death and that the eels might give me an electric shock.

We were wading towards a black rock. I was afraid the Booklings would blunder straight into it when I noticed a yawning hole in its midst that was even blacker than the rock itself. The Invisible Gateway was an illusion. It looked like solid rock from a distance, but I now saw that it was a tunnel.

'Ingenious, isn't it?' said Dancelot. 'Nature erected this gateway: a hole disguised as a rock, a rock that's really a gateway. Down here one could be forgiven for believing that rocks can think. We didn't find it for a long time.'

After we had gone perhaps a hundred yards along the narrow, pitch-black tunnel it opened out into a large cavern.

'This is where the Crystal Forest begins,' Al said solemnly, and Wami and Dancelot, as though in response to a word of command, hurled their torches high into the air. On reaching their apogee they rotated several times, hissing loudly, and illuminated a roof of gleaming blue lapis lazuli. Beyond the stretch of shallow water in which we were standing lay what looked like a verdant meadow filmed with sunlit, sparkling dew. Then the torches descended, and Wami and Dancelot deftly caught them before they could land in the water and extinguish themselves. For one glorious moment I felt I was back in the open air again.

'I wouldn't advise anyone who values his feet to walk across that lovely-looking meadow,' said Al. 'The blades of grass are really razor-sharp slivers of green crystal.'

We set off along some stony paths that skirted the deceptive crystal meadow, in which red fire-opals glowed at many points like poppies, almost as if nature were imitating its Overworldly beauties in another medium.

'I know what you're thinking,' Al said, 'but our countryside possesses a beauty all its own. It has no need to imitate the scenery up there. It can even surpass it in splendour.'

He wasn't exaggerating. We traversed an expanse of rock from which projected hundreds of jagged yellow crystals the height of a Lindworm. Partially coated with orange rust, they glowed so brightly in the dark that we could have dispensed with Wami's and Dancelot's torches altogether. Luminous stone trees . . . I had never seen anything as impressive in any forest on the surface.

'They're just condensed sulphuric gas, that's all,' Al explained.

'Show-off,' said Wami. 'No need to act the schoolmaster just because you've learnt a few geology books by heart.'

'You youngsters would do well to take a little more interest in the sciences,' Al retorted. 'Genuine creative writing is founded on a wide and varied education. For instance, if you'd memorised the entire works of Ergor Banco, the so-called Doctor Mirabilis, as I have—'

'No, no!' Wami and Dancelot cried in horror. 'Not him again, we beg you!'

Al lapsed into silence and strode on ahead.

'That's the trouble with Al's plays,' Wami whispered to me. 'He's forever dragging in little bits of arcane knowledge. Don't get him started on Ergor Banco, you'll never hear the end of it.'

Blossoming on every side were minerals of every shape, colour and size: violet amethyst, pale-pink rose quartz, needle-sharp, milk-white crystals bristling like sea urchins, green bloodstone threaded with red streaks that looked like genuine bloodstains – I, with my modest knowledge of geology, could classify only a few of them.

'They're all growing,' Al said. 'See the bush that looks like rusty metal? It was only half as big on my last visit.'

Many of the crystals, which really did resemble plants, formed sinuous tendrils, feathery foliage and prickly stalks. They sprouted from fissures in the grey rock like blossoming flowers, luxuriant weeds or wild vegetables. I saw a lump of quartz that could have been mistaken for one of Dancelot's beloved blue cauliflowers, had it not been ten times the size.

'Thus, the cauliflower is a flower that has come to grief on its own obesity,' Dancelot quoted, 'or, to be more precise, a multiplicity of unsuccessful flowers, a degenerate panicled umbel.'

'The few buds that have proved durable turn blue and swell up, then flower and produce seeds,' I chimed in.

'Honest and true to nature, these gallant little survivors are the saviours of the cauliflower fraternity,' Dancelot wound up.

We sighed in unison. I was sure my authorial godfather would have been mightily pleased with this subterranean garden.

Wami and Dancelot were truly outstanding flame-throwers. They hurled their torches into the air again and again, and everything the whirling flames carved out of the gloom was breathtaking in its beauty. Flowers of multicoloured glass grew upside down on the roof of the cave, which consisted of transparent crystal, sparkling red manganese oxide or metallically glinting iron pyrites. Long spears of black crystal jutted from the smooth, rounded slabs of milky quartz beneath our feet. It was like walking across the snow-mantled remains of a forest fire.

'All the minerals in Zamonia have congregated in the Crystal Forest so as to display the full spectrum of their beauty in a single spot,' said Al. 'One could almost credit them with artistic aspirations.'

We walked along a narrow passage suffused with a fitful red glow. The air had become so warm, we might have been passing close to a huge furnace. I could hear a sinister bubbling, gurgling sound.

'We're now entering the *Devil's Kitchen*,' Al announced. 'Watch your step. If you trip and fall into that boiling soup, no one can save you.'

Although the Devil's Kitchen wasn't an especially large cave, its contents were all the more impressive. The volcanic crater in the centre, which was the size of a village pond, continuously spewed forth red-hot skeins of molten lava that almost hit the roof.

We paused on the lip of this miniature subterranean volcano. Dozens of heavily perspiring Booklings were seated all round the crater, gasping and grunting in the heat as they feasted their eyes on this natural spectacle.

'Why do they do it?' I asked in amusement. 'Why do they sit so close to the lava?'

'We come here to unwind,' said Al. 'The heat relaxes your body and staring at the lava for a while transforms your brain into a porridgy mass – you cease to think of anything at all. We find it helps us to recuperate from our mental exertions.'

'Not that *you* need to stare at the lava,' Wami muttered behind his hand, so quietly that Al couldn't catch what he said. '*Your* brain has always been a porridgy—'

'What was that?' Al demanded.

'Nothing,' Wami said quickly.

We left the Devil's Kitchen by another route, one that took us across a lake of solid amber. Preserved in its depths were thousands of primeval insects, many of them larger than me and so horrific in appearance that even a Spinxxxx would have turned tail at the sight of them. I felt a trifle uneasy for the first time.

'Yes,' said Al, 'this part of the forest *is* a bit unnerving. A whole river of boiling resin must have flowed through here at one time, probably the result of some volcanic upheaval. Do you see the stone trees over there?'

Beyond the amber lake stood a forest of grey stone tree trunks that seemed to disappear into a black sky. They looked menacing, like stone giants only waiting for a secret word of command to release them from their rigid state.

'We haven't set foot in this part of the forest for quite some time,' Wami said. 'It isn't safe. Booklings have entered it and never returned. You can sometimes hear noises coming from it – noises like singing, but not pleasant singing. Huge, hideous, foul-smelling mushrooms with pointed caps grow there. We avoid this place.'

I tiptoed on. I now regarded this subterranean splendour with mixed feelings. Beneath me a host of imprisoned primeval insects, behind me that dark, menacing stone forest . . . For a few blissful minutes I had forgotten that I was still in the perilous catacombs of Bookholm, but now I was uneasy again. Anything down here might conceal some lethal threat. The Booklings had come to terms with this environment because they had no choice, but I would never get used to it. They conducted me along a ravine and into another cave. Wami and Dancelot hurled their torches into the air, enabling me to see that it was grey, high and not particularly large.

'This is the part of the forest we wanted to show you,' Al said.

'I don't see anything special about it,' I replied.

'Just be quiet!' Wami said softly.

'Be quiet and wait!' whispered Dancelot.

'Ssh!' Al hissed.

So I waited in silence. Nothing happened for a long time, we simply stood there in the fitful torchlight. I had just begun to suspect I'd once more fallen prey to the Booklings' peculiar sense of humour when I heard a voice.

'**Hello!**' someone called.

I reacted instinctively. 'Hello!' I called back. It was only then that I wondered who had spoken.

'No one,' whispered Wami, who seemed to read my thoughts like an open book. 'This is the *Chamber of Captive Echoes.*'

'**Hello!**' someone called again, and a steadily fading echo replied: '**Hello...** hello ... hello...!'

'**Ah!**' sighed a new voice. '**Ah ...** Ah ... Ah...!'

'**Help!**' shouted someone, so loudly that I gave a jump. '**Help ...** Help ... Help...!'

'We can't explain it exactly,' Al said in a subued voice, 'but the echoes found their way into this cave by some means and now they can't get out.'

'They're trapped,' said Wami.

'For ever and a day,' Dancelot put in. 'Sad, isn't it?'

'It's been like this ever since we discovered the place,' said Al. 'Always the same voices, the same words and sighs, though from time to time they're joined by new ones. We think they've all been uttered by people who have got lost in the catacombs. They find their way in through fissures in the rock, never to escape.'

'**Is anyone there?**' called another voice. '**Is anyone there ... ?** Is anyone there ... ? Is anyone there ... ?'

'**Where am I?** Where am I ... ? Where am I ... ?'

'**I don't want to die!** I don't want to die ... ! I don't want to die...!'

'**Why doesn't someone help me?** Why doesn't someone help me ... ? Why doesn't someone help me ... ?'

'**I'm dying!** I'm dying ... ! I'm dying...!'

I was growing more and more uneasy. The despair in those voices was too intense, too reminiscent of my own despair as I roamed the catacombs in search of a way out. They were the voices of the lost and dying, of people who might long be dead.

'Is anyone there? Is anyone there . . . ? Is anyone there . . . ?'

'Where am I? Where am I . . . ? Where am I . . . ?'

'I don't want to die! I don't want to die . . . ! I don't want to die . . . !'

More and more voices joined in, their cries of lamentation becoming ever more insistent. The echoes intermingled. They rose to a shout and faded to a whisper – to the whispers uttered by invisible ghosts that circled me, forcing their way through my auditory canals and into my brain.

'Why won't somebody help me? Why won't somebody help me . . . ?' 'Where am I? Where am I . . . ?' 'I don't want to die! I don't want to die . . . !' 'Ah! Ah . . . ! Ah . . . ! Ah . . . !' 'Why won't somebody help me?' 'Help! Help . . . ! Help . . . !' 'Where am I? Where am I . . . ? Where am I . . . ? Where am I . . . ?' 'Why won't somebody help me? Why won't somebody help me . . . ?' 'Ah! Ah . . . ! Ah . . . !'

And suddenly a new voice joined in the chorus of echoes. It uttered a scream, a cry of horror more desperate than all the rest and consisting of only three words:

'The Shadow King! The Shadow King. . . ! The Shadow King. . . ! The Shadow King. . . !'

There was such a note of fear in the voice that I almost cried out myself. It went echoing through the cave again and again, to mingle at last with the others and take its place in the grisly vocal corps de ballet whirling around me.

'The Shadow King! The Shadow King . . . ! The Shadow King . . . ! The Shadow King . . . !' 'Why won't somebody help me? Why won't somebody help me?' 'Where am I? Where am I?' 'The Shadow King!' 'Ah!' 'I don't want to die! I don't want to die. . . !' 'Why won't somebody help me? Why won't somebody help me . . . help me . . . help me . . . ?' 'The Shadow King!' 'Where am I? Where am I . . . ? Where am I . . . ? Where am I . . . ?' 'Is anyone there? Is anyone there?' 'The Shadow King!'

The echoes pierced my brain like ice-cold needles, ever deeper, ever more painfully, until I shielded my head with my arms and fled from the cave in panic. Al, Wami and Dancelot hurried after me.

Although the voices ceased as soon as I'd made my exit from the cave, I ran on, lashing out with my arms like someone fending off an invisible swarm of bees. The three Booklings caught up with me, held me tight and did their best to calm me down.

'Those echoes don't belong in our world, they just became trapped here,' Al said apologetically. 'We listen to them from time to time, but only to reassure ourselves of how well off we are.'

'We only wanted to make it clear to you, yet again, what awaits you outside our territory,' said Wami.

'Sooner or later,' Dancelot said softly, 'you'll be overcome by an urge to leave us. When that happens you may remember the despairing voices in the Chamber of Captive Echoes.'

'Many thanks,' I said, still breathing heavily. 'I certainly won't forget them in a hurry.'

'You can take it easy now,' said Al. 'Next comes a pleasant part of our tour.'

'Would you like to see a treasure?' Wami asked. 'The greatest treasure in the catacombs?'

The Star of the Catacombs

What had begun like an excursion to the world above seemed now to be taking us into ever deeper, ever gloomier subterranean regions. We had descended into a part of the forest where there were very few beautiful crystals, just walls of black, coal-bearing rock. Every bend revealed yet another low gallery lit by chandeliers suspended from the roof. We passed a number of Booklings so caked with grime that one could hardly tell the colour of their skin. They were carrying pickaxes and other miners' implements or pushing wheelbarrows filled with lumps of coal. A coal mine? The Booklings were naturally bound to regard coal, their source of warmth and light, as a substance of inestimable value. Then a Bookling came towards us with a wheelbarrow that contained, in addition to some coal, an uncut diamond the size of a pumpkin.

Al, Wami and Dancelot took no notice of this apparition. I alone stared at the Bookling and his priceless cargo until they disappeared round the next bend.

I might have been mistaken, of course. Perhaps it hadn't been a diamond at all, just a piece of worthless crystal, a lump of quartz – I wasn't too well up on mineralogy. But then another Bookling came towards us, and *his* wheelbarrow really *did* contain a diamond. This one was perfectly cut, and I could certainly tell a cut diamond from a lump of rock crystal. It was quite as big as the previous one, if not bigger.

'Did you see that?' I asked. 'That diamond, I mean?'

'Hm,' said Wami. 'Of course.'

'But . . . it was the size of a pumpkin.'

'Yes,' said Al, 'a pretty measly specimen.'

I was too disconcerted to pursue the matter. More Booklings came towards us carrying baskets filled to the brim with diamonds as big as my fist, but Al, Wami and Dancelot ignored them too.

It became lighter as we neared the next bend, presumably because of the candles burning beyond it. I could hear a host of people humming and murmuring, wielding hammers and operating grindstones. When we rounded the bend the sight that met our eyes took my breath away. Hewn out of the coal-bearing rock, it was a long, fairly low gallery in which thousands or even millions of diamonds were sparkling. A hundred or more Booklings were bustling around, engaged in a wide variety of activities, and all were humming a lively tune.

'This is our diamond garden,' Al said. 'It isn't as varied as the Crystal Forest, but the vegetation we harvest here is considerably more valuable.'

I was at a loss for words. I had always considered myself relatively indifferent to earthly riches, but the sight of the Booklings' treasure chamber left me speechless.

'We discovered this cave a long time ago,' Al went on. 'It was much smaller in those days. The Rusty Gnomes must have started it. We've been enlarging it continuously ever since, and we keep on finding larger and larger diamond deposits. Let's take a look.'

We made our way down into the cave by a flight of steps hewn out of coal. Still speechless, I surveyed the scene with marvelling eyes. There were diamonds of every size and state: rough stones, stones only half or completely cut, stones the size of peas, apples or pumpkins – the ones Wami had dismissed as 'measly'. Then there were the really large ones. Hundreds of these lay around like boulders, as tall as me and as big round the middle as wine casks. The ones that had already been cut and polished flashed and sparkled in the flickering light of countless candles, their facets dappling the walls of the cave with all the reflected colours of the rainbow. Glittering right at the back was one specimen easily the size of a house.

The Booklings were hard at work among these precious stones. They hacked away with their pickaxes, dug out diamonds or bore them off by the basketful. Some were seated at workbenches, splitting the stones with tiny hammers or cutting them with the aid of grindstones, others checked their purity with large magnifying glasses. Still others were unloading rough diamonds into heaps or trundling them around in wheelbarrows.

'Actually,' said Wami, as we strolled through this hive of activity, 'coal is worth considerably more to us than diamonds – at least we can burn the stuff. These rocks are merely hard work.'

'All we can do is hoard them,' said Dancelot, who had picked up a cut stone the size of a grapefruit and was holding it up to the light. 'However, we've fallen in love with diamonds. There something so . . . so irresistible about them. Processing them is fun. They bring light into our dark world. It's a cold, useless light, and candles are needed to extract it from them, but it's beautiful for all that.' He slowly rotated the stone in front of a candle and was instantly deluged with tiny, multicoloured specks of light.

'We cut and polish them to perfection, then hide them in the catacombs,' said Wami, happily plunging his fingers into a basket filled with tiny diamond slivers. 'We've installed hundreds of secret treasure chambers. Each of them would be the envy of the most powerful king on earth.'

'We're like hens trying to hatch stones,' Al said with a laugh. 'The diamonds are of no practical use to us. We're the wealthiest creatures in the catacombs, but we don't get anything out of it.'

Although I had regained my composure and power of speech by now, I couldn't think of any questions to ask. I only just resisted an impulse to fall on the mounds of diamonds and wallow in them like a pig in mud.

'We're rather extravagant with our diamonds, I must admit,' said Wami. 'We can afford to be, we've got so many. We cut them into shapes of all kinds.'

The Booklings seemed to engage in diamond mining without any commercial ambitions. They regarded it more as a game. Many of the huge precious stones were only half exposed and cut, others had been completely unearthed and split in two or reduced to little splinters. Heaps of fine diamond dust lay all over the place. It was less a diamond mine than a sculptor's studio.

Standing everywhere were sculptures the Booklings had fashioned out of diamonds. Many had been cut from one big stone, others were composed of numerous small ones. Some were representations of underworld fauna and flora – an impressively lifelike Crystalloscorpion, for instance, or plants such as I had earlier seen in the Crystal Forest. Other sculptures were more abstract and strictly geometrical. The Booklings had clearly developed a certain amount of skill as diamond cutters. I couldn't help laughing when I sighted a lifesize portrayal of one of their number.

'That's the so-called *Diamond Bookling*,' said Wami. 'As a rule we fight shy of self-portraiture except for purposes of deterrence, but in this case we simply couldn't resist. Come on, we'll show you our pièce de résistance.'

We now went over to the mammoth diamond I had already spotted from the other end of the cave. The closer we got to it, the more fantastic and unreal it looked. A Bookling stationed behind the colossal gem was whirling a torch in a circle – I could see him and the rotating flames reflected a hundredfold in all its polished facets. The precious stone radiated an incredible spectrum of colours and sprinkled its surroundings with variegated pools of light. Dazzled by the diamond's scintillations, I eventually had to shut my eyes.

'That's the biggest one of all,' said Al, 'the *Star of the Catacombs.*'

I had grown up with the legend of the Lindworm Castle Diamond, which was said to lie hidden in the heart of the fortress. Reputedly the size of a house, this ill-famed and mythical gem was responsible for the sieges Lindworm Castle had undergone at regular intervals because sundry brain-dead barbarians clung stubbornly to the belief that such a huge diamond existed. Although no Lindworm believed in its existence, I had been obsessed as a youngster with visions of the Lindworm Castle Diamond slumbering

away inside the castle rock – and in my childish imagination it had looked just like this Star of the Catacombs. I felt I was revisiting a scene from my childhood.

'Well,' said Al, 'now you've seen everything: the Crystal Forest, the Devil's Kitchen, the Chamber of Captive Echoes, the Diamond Garden and the Star of the Catacombs. It's time to get back to the Leather Grotto.'

I rubbed my eyes like someone awaking from a dream.

'More teleportation?' I asked.

'We must insist, I'm afraid,' said Al. 'No one who isn't a Bookling can be allowed to know how to get here, and in your case it's doubly important.

You're an author. Some day you'll write about the Crystal Forest and the Diamond Garden. That's perfectly all right, it's your duty to do so, in fact we'd be pleased if our scenic beauties were at last accorded their rightful place in Zamonian literature – as long as you don't include a description of the route.'

'I'd never do that.'

'Of course you wouldn't,' Al said with a smile, 'but it's better to be safe than sorry.'

He, Wami and Dancelot gathered round me and started to hum.

ʓʃ

One Breakfast and Two Confessions

Once I had regained consciousness after being teleported back to the Leather Grotto we spent the rest of the day Orming. I guessed the identity of, among others, Honj Steak ('A thing of beauty is a joy for ever'), Auselm T. Edgecroil ('Water, water everywhere, nor any drop to drink'), Samoth Yarg ('The curfew tolls the knell of parting day') and Selwi Rollcar* ("Twas brillig, and the slithy toves did gyre and gimble in the wabe').

The next morning I was brought my breakfast (toasted bookworms and root tea) by Al, Wami and Dancelot. They watched me intently, almost furtively, while I was consuming it. This prompted a question on my part.

'Tell me something: when do *you* eat? I haven't seen a single Bookling take any nourishment since I've been here.'

All three cleared their throats in a sheepish manner.

'What's the matter, my friends?' I demanded. 'Why always so secretive?

---

* Translator's Note: Selwi Rollcar and Weddar Rale were founder members of a Dullsgardian school of poetry notorious for its deliberate cultivation of unintelligibility. To this end they larded their verse with bizarre neologisms designed to reduce their readers to a state of mental confusion as profound as the one from which they themselves suffered. The school broke up when Rollcar, muttering incomprehensible gibberish, was carted off to a lunatic asylum in Atlantis, there to end his days embroidering pocket handkerchiefs with endless repetitions of the same word, *Bandersnatch*, whose exact meaning has never been elucidated.

What's the meaning of all this giggling and throat-clearing? You're concealing something from me! Is there something in those stories after all? Are you only fattening me up with a view to eating me?'

I had asked the last question half jokingly, but once uttered it hung in the air like a Damoclean sword.

Al, Wami and Dancelot stared hard in three different directions.

'Come on, what do you feed on?'

'Feed, read, feed, read, what's the difference?' Al replied cryptically. 'They sound almost the same.'

'Meaning what?'

Dancelot nudged Al. 'Go on, tell him.'

Al lowered his single eye and looked embarrassed. 'This is a bit awkward,' he said in a low voice, 'but there really is some truth in the Bookhunters' stories about our eating habits.'

'You mean you devour anything that comes your way?' I put down my bowl of bookworms.

'No,' said Al. 'The other rumour.'

I thought for a moment. 'You eat books?'

'Exactly.'

'You actually eat them?'

'No. Yes. In a way. Not really, though. How can I put it?' Al struggled for words.

'We don't really eat them,' said Wami, coming to his rescue. 'Not in the sense of gobbling paper like a bookworm. It's just that reading assuages our hunger.'

'Come again?'

'We find it rather embarrassing', said Al, 'that an activity as sublimely intellectual as reading should be associated in our case with a process as vulgar as digestion, but that's how it is. We feed on reading.'

'I don't believe it,' I said, laughing. 'This is another of your jokes, isn't it?'

'We never make jokes about reading,' Al said gravely.

'This is the craziest thing I've ever heard, and I've heard plenty of crazy stories in the last few days. How does it work?'

'We can't tell you that ourselves,' said Al. 'We're Booklings, not scientists, but it *does* work, I can assure you. In my own case, rather too well.' He kneaded his rolls of fat with a worried air.

'*I* can read anything I like,' said Dancelot. 'I simply never put on weight.'

Al glared at him. 'How I detest these leptosomatic types who can stuff themselves to their heart's content without gaining a single ounce! Yesterday he read three Baroque blockbuters on the trot – three of them! – and look at him! Thin as a beanpole! If I did that I'd have to go on a reading diet for weeks.'

'So books differ in nutritional value?' I asked.

'Of course. You have to be very careful what you eat. Novels are substantial fare – you have to watch yourself. At present I'm on a strict poetry diet. Three poems a day, no more.' Al sighed.

'A strict poetry diet?' scoffed Wami. 'You only started it today.'

'All we need is water and stale air,' Dancelot put in. 'Apart from that, reading is sufficient to sustain us. We're always trying to discover which books contain the most nourishment.'

'The classics, of course!' Al said sternly.

'That remains to be proved!' Wami objected. 'I spent years feeding exclusively on avant-garde verse from the Impic Alps and I was in first-class shape.'

'It's almost too good to be true,' said Dancelot. 'We're the only creatures in the catacombs exempt from the merciless cycle of eat and be eaten, hunt and be hunted. There's always plenty to read.'

'Too much, if anything,' sighed Al. 'Far too much!'

'I sometimes think we're the only people who really get something out of literature,' Wami said with a grin. 'Books mean nothing but hard work to everyone else. They have to write them, edit them, print them, publish them, sell them, remainder them, study them, review them. Work, work, work, whereas we only have to read, browse and enjoy. We really can devour books and we never grow tired of it. I wouldn't swap places with an author.'

Al's eye glowed. 'You start your meal with a few light aphorisms, perhaps by Rasco Elwid, and move on to a sonnet – one of Wimpersleake's, let's say, they're all equally tasty. Next, a fat-free novella or a few short stories. Finally, the main course: a novel by . . . well, Hornac de Bloaze, for instance – you know, a really fat India-paper edition of three thousand pages, complete with some delicious footnotes! Last of all, for pudding—'

'Get a grip on yourself!' Dancelot broke in. 'You only started dieting this morning and you're cracking up already.'

Al fell silent. A thread of saliva was trickling from the corner of his mouth.

All kinds of questions occurred to me. 'Can you reread a book?'

'Yes, if you digested it thoroughly the first time. You can devour the same book again and again.'

'Which tastes better, poetry or prose?'

'That's a matter of opinion.'

'Are some books indigestible?'

'Horror stories give you nightmares. Light reading doesn't provide any long-term sustenance. Thrillers are supposed to be bad for the nerves.'

'Are authors with big vocabularies more satisfying than others?'

'Definitely.'

'What about non-fiction?'

'It makes a change occasionally.'

'And cookbooks?'

'Now you're pulling our leg!'

'How about reviews?'

'They leave a nasty aftertaste.'

I could have gone on questioning the Booklings for hours, but they were eager to get going. Another Orming session had been scheduled for this morning. That was fine with me because I was already growing bored with the business and wanted to get it over as soon as possible.

On the way to the Leather Grotto I remembered something that had occurred to me just before I went to sleep. I hesitated for a moment before broaching the subject to Al, then plucked up courage.

'I say, Al, I've been wondering . . .'

'Yes?'

'It's about your talent for teleportation. Would it be possible for you to teleport me back to the surface of Bookholm?'

'Er, no,' Al replied. 'Impossible, I'm afraid.'

'But why? Is it because you couldn't breathe up there?'

'Yes,' Al said rather uncertainly. 'Among other things.'

'What if you deposited me a little way below the surface? Somewhere you could still breathe?

'Er . . .' Al said helplessly.

'We ought to tell him,' Dancelot chimed in. 'We may as well, while we're on the subject.'

'Yes,' Wami said, 'why not? Go on, tell him.'

'All right,' said Al. 'The thing is, we played a little trick on you. We can't teleport at all.'

'You can't?'

'Afraid not.'

'So how did I get to the Leather Grotto? How did I get to the Crystal Forest and back?'

'Like the rest of us: on foot.'

That would at least account for my muscular fatigue. Each bout of teleportation had made my legs ache as if I'd walked for miles.

'Why can't I remember anything?'

'Because we hypnotised you. That's all we *can* do, but we're really good at it.'

'The best,' said Dancelot.

Wami fixed me with a piercing cyclopean gaze. 'Look into my eye . . . look into my eye . . . !' he whispered.

Al elbowed him aside. 'Stop that nonsense!' he said, and to me: 'Yes, we're genuine experts at mental manipulation. That's the real reason why Bookhunters never dare to come here.'

'I don't see the connection.'

'We lure one of them into the catacombs from time to time,' Wami said with a grin, 'and then we hypnotise him good and proper. Believe me, he wakes up believing that he's just managed to escape from some Booklings ten feet tall and equipped with razor-sharp fangs. Then he passes the story on to his colleagues – very plausibly, too. That's how most of the myths about us got started: we invented them ourselves.'

'And each of you can do it?'

'Hypnotise people? No, not individually,' said Dancelot. 'It's a collective accomplishment. There must be at least three of us and the more we are the better. The entire Bookling community could hypnotise a whole army.'

'And you can do it to anyone?'

'Anything or anyone capable of dreaming,' said Al. 'We once hypnotised a Lavaworm. No idea what Lavaworms dream about, but that proves they *do*.'

'We aren't talking about a cheap fairground trick,' Wami put in. 'Our hypnosis is mental manipulation of the highest order. We could transform you into any living creature we liked – or at least, you'd *think* you were that creature. The same goes for plants. Or crystals. If we chose to, we could transform you into the Star of the Catacombs.'

'Really and truly?'

'Like to try it?' Al asked with a smile. 'Eh?'

Murch and Maggot

We were back in the Leather Grotto soon afterwards. Al had assembled all the Booklings and informed them that Orming was to be postponed in favour of a demonstration of collective hypnosis.

I couldn't help feeling a little uneasy when I saw the expectant Booklings gather round, but it was too late to back out now. The announcement had bred a mood of excitement and eager anticipation, and they were all jabbering away at once. It seemed that they were trying to decide what creature to transform me into, because the air was thick with the names of animals.

'What will I imagine I am?' I asked Al nervously.

'That I can't tell you,' he replied, 'or it won't work. You'd tense up and block the hypnotic message. Knowing *that* we're going to hypnotise you will make it hard enough for us. Just wait and see.'

Wonderful, I thought, cursing myself for agreeing so rashly. I felt more apprehensive than ever. At that moment, Orming seemed infinitely preferable!

'On my command!' cried Al. The Booklings fell silent. They all gazed at me and started to hum.

I waited.

They went on humming.

I waited some more.

More humming.

Nothing happened. Trombophone music was far more effective! I felt nothing. Nothing at all. I wasn't even tired. Perhaps there were too many of them. Either that, or they couldn't hypnotise me because this time I was concentrating. That was it: I couldn't be hypnotised because I didn't *want* to be! I was resistant to hypnosis. I was a strong-willed, unhypnotisable Murch.*

Yes, I was a proud Murch, a Murch in the rutting season. I at once proceeded to blow out my cheeks and murch loudly, thereby asserting my territorial rights and attracting the attention of any female Murches in the vicinity. I waddled around and displayed my majestically inflated cheeks to warn the Booklings off: this was Murch territory, they proclaimed! I ruffled up my feathers and murched with a will, totally imbued with murchdom.

I did my best to ignore the Booklings' hysterical laughter – Booklings were of no interest to me. But where had the female Murches got to? I was murching with such heart-rending fervour, I couldn't believe they were deliberately ignoring my irresistible mating calls.

The Booklings' humming changed pitch, becoming considerably lower, and it occurred to me that I was really a maggot, not a Murch. Of course, I was a bookworm! Why was I, a bookworm, murching around like this? I at once got down on my stomach and crawled along in the dust at the Booklings' feet. Some of them guffawed and giggled, but I didn't care. I was engaged on a mission, so I couldn't allow myself to be distracted by the irrational behaviour of other life forms. I was in quest of a book.

Crawl, crawl, that was my destiny: to crawl until I'd found a book. The

---

*Translator's Note: Everyone in Zamonia has known what a Murch is since the publication of Gofid Letterkerl's novel *Zanilla and the Murch*, so Yarnspinner dispenses with a description of that quaint little animal. Resident mainly in marshy areas, the Murch is a very rare creature best described as a cross between a duck and a frog. It gets its beak and downy plumage from the duck, its powerful hind legs and inflatable cheeks from the frog. The impressive sound a Murch can produce, known as 'murching', resembles the quacking of a duck and the croaking of a frog in equal measure.

silly Booklings could guffaw and slap their thighs all they liked, I simply ignored them. Crawl, keep crawling along through the dust until . . . there, a book at last! I had found a book, the bookworm's natural foe and, at the same time, its chief source of nourishment! It must be destroyed at once: that was my mission! I fell hungrily upon the rather tattered old tome. It tasted a trifle mouldy, but I tore it to shreds with my pitiless larval jaws and chewed up every scrap until I'd digested the whole book.

I was feeling thoroughly replete and contented. My mission had been accomplished. What could I do next? It didn't take me long to decide: I would lay a few eggs. Yes, that's what I'd do.

⸨⸩

A Pike in a Shoal of Trout

That, dear readers, was when my new life began. The Booklings had admitted me to their community and seemed to have resolved to make me forget about my previous existence. In order to dispel my dream of regaining the surface of Bookholm, they involved me in their many and various activities. Although I still felt like a pike in a shoal of trout because of our physical dissimilarities, that feeling of strangeness steadily wore off as the days and weeks went by. The absence of fear: that was what I relished most. In here I was protected, surrounded by a rampart of friends in a comfortable environment abounding in books and marvellous natural phenomena awaiting thorough investigation on my part. I hadn't altogether suppressed my desire to return to the surface, of course, but I temporarily shelved my plans in that regard. I looked upon my sojourn with the Booklings as an expedition to an alien tribe, an extended research trip for a book I would some day write.

I was surrounded by a living library. By that I don't mean the weird Bookemistic volumes inside the machine in the Leather Grotto, the ones with eyes and ears; I mean the Booklings themselves, who were round me at all times, continuously reciting passages from the books they had learnt by heart.

I was encompassed by literature wherever I went. One or more Booklings were forever bombarding me with poetry or prose, essays or novellas, aphorisms or sonnets. What may sound like a never-ending burden on the ears and nerves seemed to me like a wonderful dream, because the technical expertise with which the Booklings delivered their recitations was of the highest quality – even better, probably, than that displayed by Bookholm's Master Readers at their timber-time readings, for the little Cyclopses were more than just professional reciters: they *lived* their literature. They had an immense range of gestures and expressions despite their physical limitations, and their voices sounded as well trained as those of experienced stage actors. I doubt if anyone who has not actually experienced it can grasp how closely you can study literature when confronted by it in such a vital and uninterrupted manner.

I now got to know several Booklings apart from Al, Wami and Dancelot, and I made a special point of consorting with those whose work I found of abiding interest.

Perla la Gadeon, for example, turned out to be a sociable if sometimes moody individual. He taught me all manner of things about poetic craftsmanship and even more about the composition of horrific short stories. Hornac de Bloaze had the epic stamina you need in order to write vast novels and the strong constitution without which no one can assimilate the vast quantities of coffee required to keep you awake for long periods at a stretch. He initiated me into the mental technique with which he kept the plots and characters of dozens of novels in his head without going mad.

Rasco Elwid was a witty raconteur who always kept me hugely entertained. He was simply incapable of saying anything commonplace or banal, and each of his utterances was a polished aphorism or brilliant *aperçu*. I hardly dared open my mouth in his company because anything I had to say seemed so stupid and boring.

I developed a special relationship with Dancelot, whose occasional recitations from the work of my authorial godfather not only moved me but made me feel I was back home. For his part, he sought my company in order to pump me about Lindworm Castle and details of my godfather's life. To distinguish between the two of them, I secretly took to calling them Dancelot One (my godfather) and Dancelot Two (the Bookling). Having now come to terms with the regrettable certainty that he could not expect

264

any more publications from Dancelot One, Dancelot Two wanted at least to learn as much about him as possible – even about the episode in which my godfather had believed himself to be a cupboard full of dirty spectacles. For Dancelot Two's benefit I recited the little poem that had come into my hands. He absorbed it like a sponge and would declaim it at the drop of a hat:

For ever shut and made of wood,
that's what I am. My head's no good
now that it by a stone was struck.
Old spectacles besmirched with muck
repose within me by the score.
I'm just a cupboard, nothing more.

One morning I told Dancelot Two about the manuscript I was still carrying on my person but had almost forgotten in the last few eventful weeks.

'My authorial godfather was so impressed by this, he gave up writing,' I said, handing him the manuscript. 'I think you ought to read it.'

'It might be better if I didn't,' said Dancelot Two. 'If it's really responsible for the fact that I've only got one book to memorise, I'm bound to take a poor view of it.'

'At least take a look.'

With a sigh, Dancelot Two reluctantly started reading. I watched his every sign of emotion. Within seconds I had ceased to exist for him. His single eye scanned the text at a gallop, his breathing quickened, his lips mouthed the words. Then he began to read aloud. At some stage he started to laugh, softly at first, then ever more heartily until he was bellowing with hysterical mirth and pounding his knee with his fist.

When he had calmed down a little his eye filled with tears and he fell to sobbing gently. At length, having come to the end of the manuscript, he stared into space for minutes on end.

'Well,' I asked, breaking the silence, 'what do you think of it?'

'It's awesome. Now I understand why your godfather gave up writing. It's the finest thing I've ever read.'

'Any idea who could have written it?'

'No. If I'd ever read anything by someone capable of writing like that, I would remember it.'

'Dancelot sent the author to Bookholm.'

'Then he never got there. If he'd reached the city he would now be famous. He'd be the greatest author in Zamonia.'

'My sentiments entirely. For all that, the letter in which my godfather urged him to come here found its way into your Chamber of Marvels.'

'I realise that. I know the letter by heart. It's a thorough mystery.'

'One I'll probably never solve,' I said with a sigh. 'May I have the manuscript back?'

Dancelot Two clasped it to his chest.

'May I memorise it first?' he entreated.

'Of course.'

'Then please give me a day's grace. I couldn't possibly read it again right away.'

'Why not?'

'Because I'd go pop, I'm afraid.' Dancelot Two smiled. 'I've never felt so full after reading anything.'

The Apprentice Bookling

I subsequently showed the manuscript to several other Booklings with very similar results. They were all fascinated by it, but none of them had any idea who the author could be. Many wanted to learn the text by heart because – being less overtaxed by their authors than Al, for instance – they were interested in absorbing other literature as well.

I began to like the Booklings in the same way as I liked my own kind in Lindworm Castle. I may even have liked them a little better because of the touching way in which they made me the focus of their existence. They sought my company because they regarded me as a genuine author, or even as someone far more interesting: an author in the making. Being acquainted with plenty of accomplished writers, they saw in me an opportunity to help to mould an artist's character and exert a personal influence on his development.

I had suddenly acquired hundreds of little one-eyed authorial godfathers, all unselfishly devoted to my welfare. Like my former teacher, Dancelot One, they tirelessly offered me advice about my future work – advice as varied as the Booklings themselves:

Never write a novel from the perspective of a door handle!
Foreign words are foreign to most readers.
Never put more words in a sentence than genuinely belong in it.
If a full stop is a wall, a colon is a door.
If you write something while drunk, read it through sober before you submit it to a publisher.
Never write with anything but quicksilver; it guarantees narrative flow.
Footnotes are like books on the bottom shelf. No one likes looking at them because they have to bend down.
A single sentence should never contain more than a million ants unless it's in a scientific work on ants.
Sonnets are best written on deckle-edged paper, novellas on vellum.
Take a deep breath after every third sentence.
It's best to write horror stories with a wet flannel round your neck.
If one of your sentences puts you in mind of an elephant trying to pick up a coconut with its trunk, better give it some more thought.
Stealing from one author is plagiarism; from many authors, research.
Big books are big because the author didn't have the time to express himself succinctly.

Even though I hadn't really become a Bookling, I'd at least become an apprentice Bookling. I was subjected to an incessant barrage of well-meant advice and technical tips. Although I tried to make a note of them all, I retained only the most obvious. It often happened that two pieces of advice were mutually contradictory, and I frequently became the centre of an altercation between two or more Booklings who exchanged volleys of quotations like arrows.

I had become the gnomes' new *raison d'être*, a living, breathing vindication of all their activities, especially their cult of learning texts by heart. I was their chance to unload all that was pent up inside them. In me, so they believed, their texts would finally fall on fertile soil, destined one day to yield a bumper crop in the shape of novels, poems and anything else I committed to paper. I imbued the Booklings' anonymous existence with a meaning for which they may always have yearned.

A typical day in the Booklings' domain went roughly like this. In the morning, when I emerged, yawning, from my sleeping quarters, a Bookling would promptly latch on to me and put my brain into gear with a few inspiring lines of verse: '*Grey dawn, dost thou portend my final breath? The trombophones will soon announce my death . . .*'

At breakfast, which I now prepared myself, several of the little Cyclopses would keep me company, reading in turn from their letters: '*My dear Gofid Letterkerl, many thanks for the dedicated copy of* Zanilla and the Murch. *How daring of you to make a Murch the protagonist of a tragic novel! I was greatly moved, especially by the passage where your lovesick hero murches for days on end before throwing himself into Demon's Gulch. Your bold initiative will probably launch a whole genre of Zamonian literature teeming with Murches – in fact, I myself am already toying with the idea of writing a Murch novel. With renewed thanks and best regards, Ertrob Limus.*'

After breakfast I usually went off to the Leather Grotto, where I liked to clamber around on the book machine, pick out a book or two and browse for a bit. I was usually joined by Al, who spent a lot of time in the machine's vicinity because he had made it his job to fathom its secrets. He believed he had detected certain patterns in its movements and was now tinkering with an extremely complicated mathematical table designed to elucidate every last mystery in the catacombs.

As soon as I left the Leather Grotto I would again be pounced on by several Booklings who accompanied me on my walks through the tunnels and showered me with erudite essays or aphorisms. These they declaimed with a self-important air as they strutted along beside, behind or ahead of me. We must have been a strange sight, rather like a family of ducks that communicated, not by quacking at each other, but by loudly reciting maxims and bons mots:

'*Reading is an intelligent way of not having to think.*'
'*The light at the end of the tunnel is often no more than a dying jellyfish.*'

*'Writing is a desperate attempt to extract some dignity – and a modi-
cum of money – from solitude.'*

I also enjoyed watching the Booklings at work in their book hospital. This
taught me a bit about the manufacture and restoration of books, as well as
printing and the chemical processing of a wide range of papers. Most of the
books fortunate enough to be admitted to the hospital emerged from it
looking as good as new. The one-eyed gnomes knew all the tricks of the trade
when it came to repairing damaged paper or leather, and even when stumped
they reprinted and rebound their patients more handsomely and sumptuously
than before.

My afternoons were devoted to fiction. Hornac de Bloaze, Asdrel
Chickens and other Booklings with a rich repertoire of narrative prose recited
their novels to me. A single step would transport me from Zamonian Baroque
to modern times. If I heaved a sigh, a dozen worried Booklings would tug at
my cloak and enquire how I was. I had never before been treated with such
solicitude.

In the evenings we met in the Leather Grotto to exchange ideas. Seated
round the fireplaces there, the Booklings chatted and laughed, recited and
argued about literature. This was where they relaxed after their daily
exertions. They showed me rare books, maps of the catacombs and finds from
the Chamber of Marvels, told me all about forgotten authors I'd never heard
of and recounted horrific anecdotes about the Bookhunters in the same way
as the Bookhunters recounted horrific anecdotes about them.

Usually exhausted by the end of the day, I would flop down on my couch
and fall asleep at once. And dream. Of books, naturally.

⟨8

Zack hitti zopp

'Did I actually eat a book?' I asked Al one day when we were once more standing on the book machine together, watching the shelves glide past. 'Under hypnosis that time, I mean?'

'You turned up your nose at the cover,' Al replied with a grin. 'But real bookworms do that too. You had the right idea, biologically speaking.'

This finally solved a question that had been preying on my mind for quite a while. Another one occurred to me: 'Where do Booklings come from?'

Al hesitated. 'We don't exactly know. We surmise that we develop inside books like chickens in eggs – in very old, brittle volumes of indecipherable runes slumbering deep down in the catacombs. Sooner or later a book of that kind cracks open like an egg and a Bookling as small as a salamander hatches out. Then it finds its way to the Leather Grotto. By instinct, probably.'

'Is that really so?'

'A few new Booklings turn up in the Leather Grotto every year. Either that, or we discover them somewhere nearby. They're still tiny, little bigger than a thumb, unable to speak and without a memory. Then we give them some books to eat – we read automatically, you know, it's probably innate – and they learn to talk in no time. That's why the Bookling community continues to grow. Very slowly, but grow it does. Hey, watch: that shelf is just about to slide back and disappear into the machine, like to bet?'

A moment later the rusty machine's entrails emitted a series of loud clicks and the shelf behaved precisely as Al had predicted. He grinned contentedly and made a mysterious mark on his mathematical table.

'But you could have come from somewhere else, couldn't you?' I said. 'You don't know for sure.'

'True, we may also have sprung from the stinking rubbish in Unholm or the laboratories of evil and demented Bookemists, but hatching out of old books is the story we like best.'

By now I had learnt not to dispute the pseudo-scientific theories with which Al explained all manner of things, nor did I cast doubt on his outmoded belief in the Orm, it only involved me in endless arguments. Besides, I myself found the idea that Booklings hatched out of books very appealing, so I left it at that.

I had stopped keeping a tally of the days I'd spent among the Booklings. Mathematics had never been my strong point and there weren't any days down there, let alone clocks. I don't think I'm boasting, dear readers, when I say that I'd learnt quite a lot in the interim. The very fact that I listened to the Booklings with unflagging attention had greatly expanded my vocabulary, and I was now acquainted with vast numbers of novels and short stories, poems and stage plays, essays and letters. I could spout aphorisms until everyone round me dozed off, and my familiarity with descriptions of landscapes was so extensive that I could have equipped a whole continent with them. Characters, plots, cliffhangers, twists in the tail, gradual build-ups, dramatic climaxes – the Booklings had imparted more literary material and techniques than I could have acquired by reading for a lifetime. They were all stored away in my brain like the props of a well-equipped theatre. I now knew how good dialogue should sound, how to lend the opening pages of a book a momentum that would instantly carry the reader along, and how a novel of epic dimensions could systematically send its thousand characters to their inexorable doom. I had heard so many poems that I sometimes unwittingly spoke in rhyme and my vocabulary was at least as extensive as Aleisha Wimpersleake's.

The Booklings were no literary snobs, fortunately. Far from confining themselves to the classics, they also memorised a lot of so-called light fiction. One of them knew the entire *Prince Sangfroid* series by heart, another had learnt all my favourite *Count Elfensenf* novels and could recite them to order. I was now familiar with every cheap literary device, every banal cliché, every escapist flight of fancy that ought, in my opinion, to form part of every author's repertoire. The Booklings had provided me with all I needed to become a decent writer. The only trouble was, I still hadn't committed a single sentence to paper.

I may have conveyed the impression that life with the Booklings was a bed of roses, but alas, it wasn't quite as idyllic as that. Fond though I was of the little Cyclopses, many of them were more than capable of getting on my nerves. It was a regrettable fact that I didn't share the literary tastes of each and every one, and that some of the Booklings had devoted themselves to authors I found positively insufferable. I tried to avoid those individuals whenever possible. The more tactful among them accepted this and troubled me no further, but there were a few insensitive specimens who mercilessly strove to foist their stuff on me and those cussed little fellows sometimes made my life a misery.

Foremost among them was Dolerich Hirnfiedler, who had never got over the fact that I'd unmasked him on the strength of a single exclamation ('O!'). He had been taunted by his fellow Booklings ever since, and a number of 'O!' jokes were circulating in the Leather Grotto. To pay me back he dogged my footsteps with a persistence comparable only to that which Rongkong Koma had displayed when hunting Colophonius Regenschein. One day I rounded a bend in a tunnel, all unsuspecting, to find Dolerich barring my path. His single eye blazed as he addressed me in a hoarse bellow:

> *'O greet thy father from me if thou wilt!*
> *I know him well, and my name, too, he knows.*
> *Friend of his friends am I. That he was here*
> *I knew not, since we did not meet till now,*
> *and I was long in ignorance of it!'*

I almost had a heart attack, not only then but on other occasions as well – for instance when he crept up behind me while I was seated in an armchair in the Leather Grotto, drowsily reading in peace, and bellowed some *Oedipus* in my ear with all his might:

> *'O Light! This last time do I see thee now!*
> *They say I am of wrongful parentage;*
> *that I illicit intercourse enjoy*
> *and slew him whom I had no right to kill.'*

Not vengeful like Dolerich, just plain crazy, was a Bookling who had devoted his life to the works of Lugo Blah. Lugo Blah was a prominent exponent of Zamonian Gagaism, and the deliberate insanity of that literary genre had rubbed off on his Bookling namesake a trifle too effectively for my taste. I'd always found Zamonian Gagaism suspect because I had a hunch that its primary aim was not so much concentrated creative endeavour as the consumption of hallucinogenic mushrooms and strong liquor. At their functions and readings the Gagaists liked to dress up as sausages or brass instruments, play music on Oxenfrogs and spray their audiences with saliva. I always found it suspicious when writers got together in groups because it was obvious that they did so, not with any serious work in mind, but for social reasons.

The Gagaists, and Lugo Blah above all, tended to write in languages of their own invention (a practice that makes it rather too easy for the writer, in my opinion). Thus it often happened that Blah's demented devotee would jump out of a crack in the rock and bombard me with poetic gibberish.

'tressli bessli nebogen leila
flusch kata
ballubasch
zack hitti zopp

zack hitti zopp
hitzli betzli betzli
prusch kata
ballubasch
fasch kitti bimm'

he would yell, prancing round me and gesticulating in an idiotic way. More than anything else, it was the ingenuity with which he chose the most unlikely hiding places that rendered his unheralded appearances so nerve-shattering.

I learnt many other interesting facts about the Booklings during my stay with them, I can assure you, dear readers. It would exceed the scope of the present book to enumerate them in detail, but I intend to do so in a future publication.*

I began to suffer from occasional fits of depression and a feeling of homelessness as the weeks went by. Whenever this happened I got the Booklings to hypnotise me into the Crystal Forest, where I often roamed for hours with Dancelot Two until the beauties of the underworld had made me forget all else. Then we would sit beside the bubbling magma in the Devil's Kitchen, sweating as we chatted of this and that. It was Dancelot Two who broached the subject one day.

'You miss Overworld, don't you?'

I would never have said so myself. The Booklings treated me with such touching solicitude that I couldn't possibly have mentioned my longing for sunlight and fresh air – it would have seemed ungrateful. I was relieved that Dancelot Two had raised the subject on his own initiative.

'Of course I do. I almost managed to forget it for a long time, but recently I've found it harder and harder.'

'We can't take you up there, you know.'

---

*Translator's Note: Optimus Yarnspinner subsequently kept this undertaking in a work on the Booklings' secret subterranean world.

'I realise that, but Al once told me you're in contact with other inhabitants of the catacombs.'

'We are – with Demidwarfs and Troglotrolls, but they can't be trusted. They supply us with certain commodities from the surface – at a price – but I couldn't guarantee your safety if we placed you in their care. They might hand you straight over to the Bookhunters or do something nasty to you.'

'What about maps? I've seen some in the Leather Grotto with routes through the catacombs marked on them.'

'We could provide you with maps, of course, but the catacombs are always changing. One cave-in and all the maps in the world wouldn't help you. As for maps that show where dangers are lurking, they just don't exist. There's no reasonably safe route to the surface, believe me.'

'If I want to survive I'll have to stay with you for ever, is that what you mean?'

Dancelot Two heaved a sigh, gazing mournfully into the lava.

'I knew this moment would come sooner or later. For selfish reasons I'm tempted to say that you're right, that there's no hope. But . . .'

'But what?'

'I know of another possibility.'

'You mean there *is* one?' I asked, suddenly wide awake.

'Yes. There are a few secrets we haven't confided, even in you.'

'What, for instance?'

'I could introduce you to someone who knows his way around the catacombs even better than we do.'

'You're joking.'

'Would you like to meet Colophonius Regenschein?' asked Dancelot Two. 'Bookholm's greatest hero?'

Bookholm's Greatest Hero

Dancelot Two guided me to an area I had never set foot in before, one where there were only numerous small cave dwellings and no sub-terranean chambers in communal use. On and on he went, even when all the little caves we passed were unoccupied: vacant quarters for future Booklings. There was no one around but us.

'Are you really taking me to see Colophonius Regenschein?' I asked. 'Or do you just mean the Bookling who knows his book by heart?'

'We discovered him a few years ago,' said Dancelot Two, hurrying on ahead. 'Deep down in the catacombs. He was badly wounded – half dead, in fact – after a duel with Rongkong Koma. We brought him here and nursed him back to health. He regained his strength – well, more or less, but he's never really recovered from that fight. He wrote his second book while here. We've learnt a great deal from him, just as he has from us. He advised us where to find rare books for the Leather Grotto and we told him all we knew about the catacombs. His health has been deteriorating lately and we spent a long time debating whether or not to take you to him. We didn't want to put him at risk – it's for his own protection that everyone thinks he's dead; on the other hand, he's the only person really capable of helping you. Anyway, he recently took a turn for the worse, so we decided, with his consent, to . . . Ah, here we are.'

Dancelot Two had paused outside the mouth of a cave covered by a heavy chain curtain. 'I must get back to the Leather Grotto,' he whispered. 'The Animatomes need feeding. Al is inside with Colophonius, he'll introduce you.' He hurried off and I parted the jingling curtain.

The chamber, which was at least ten times the size of the other cave dwellings, was lit by numerous candles. The bookshelves lining the walls were filled with sumptuously bound books whose gold and silver covers were studded with diamonds, rubies and sapphires.

The celebrated Bookhunter was lying on a big mound of furs beneath a blanket of some dark, heavy material that covered all of him except his head and paws. Al was seated on a stool beside him, looking worried. I was appalled by the sight of Regenschein's face when I got near enough to make it out in the flickering candlelight, but I tried not to show anything.

The Vulphead was clearly on his last legs. I needed no telling that this was the last resting place of someone at death's door, and that all three of us were aware of the fact.

'I'm not what you were expecting, am I?' Regenschein said in a hoarse voice. 'You had visions of an intrepid daredevil bursting with vitality, didn't you? Well, I worked hard to cultivate that image in my first book: Bookling's greatest hero and so on. It exhausted my stock of superlatives.'

He gave a faint chuckle.

'My name', I began, 'is—'

'Optimus Yarnspinner – yes, I know. The Booklings have told me about you. You come from Lindworm Castle. Pfistomel Smyke knocked you out with a Toxicotome, just as he did me. We must get down to business without wasting time, because time is what I've got least of.'

'What happened?' I asked. 'How could Smyke exile you to the catacombs when you're the person who knows them best?'

Regenschein sat up a little. 'He anaesthetised me with a Toxicotome just to get me into the catacombs. The Bookhunters were supposed to do the rest, but they didn't do a thorough job. I escaped. Deeper and deeper into the catacombs I went, until only Rongkong Koma dared to follow me. Then I turned and confronted him – too soon, alas, being still under the effect of the poison. I was too weak to finish him off. We fought the longest duel in our long and checkered relationship. Neither of us really won, and I wouldn't describe the condition in which Rongkong eventually hobbled off as healthy.'

He smiled. 'If my little friends hadn't found me I would have died without a doubt. They gave me the opportunity to write my second book down here. I entered the catacombs in search of the Shadow King and I've become a Shadow King myself. A living legend. A disembodied spirit.'

'Why did Smyke treat you this way?'

'Shouldn't you ask yourself the same question?' Regenschein demanded. 'I've no idea. To be honest, I was hoping that *you* could supply me with the answer.'

'I can't, I'm afraid.'

'It makes no sense,' Regenschein said. 'If he hadn't told me about his megalomaniac plans, I would never have heard of them. Until then I knew nothing about Smyke that could have harmed him.'

'It was exactly the same with me,' I said. 'May I show you something? I believe this to be the reason for my banishment to the catacombs.' I took the manuscript from my cloak and handed it to him. He held it up and studied it, narrowing his eyes.

'Ah yes,' he murmured. 'The paper is high-grade Grailsundian wove, 200 grammes. Unevenly trimmed, probably with an obsolete guillotine—'

'I don't think Smyke exiled me to the catacombs because the edges are ragged,' I ventured to interrupt. 'It's the text that matters.'

Regenschein began to read in silence. His present condition made it impossible for him to react like me and the others – that I realised – but he was unmistakably enthralled. He laughed from time to time, breathing heavily for minutes on end, and once I saw a little tear trickle down his furry cheek. He had sat up as straight as he could, and the paw that held the manuscript was trembling violently.

Al gave me an anxious look and it occurred to me, too, that reading the manuscript might be too much for him. At length the Vulphead lowered the sheaf of paper and just sat there for a while, breathing stertorously.

'Thank you,' he said at last. 'It's the finest piece of writing I've ever been privileged to read.'

'Have you any idea who the author could be?'

'No, but I can understand why Smyke banished you to the underworld. It's too good for the world above.'

Regenschein handed back the manuscript and I pocketed it again.

'May I ask you a question?' I said.

He nodded.

'Forgive me, but I simply can't restrain my curiosity. Your quest for the Shadow King – was it successful in any way? Did you see him?'

A faraway look came into Regenschein's eyes.

'See him? No, but I've often heard him. Once I even touched him.'

'You touched him but didn't see him?'

'Yes, in the dark, when he saved me from being crushed to death by a bookcase Rongkong Koma had overturned on top of me. I managed to catch hold of him for a moment, and . . . Aleisha, kindly pass me that little casket beside the bed.'

Al handed him a small black box. Regenschein opened the lid and held it out. 'I tore those off his clothing.'

I looked into the box. Lying inside were some little scraps of paper covered with indecipherable symbols.

'One moment,' I said. I felt in my pockets and pulled out a few of the pieces of paper that had shown me the way to Bookling territory. I held them alongside the ones in the casket. They were identical.

'These scraps of paper guided me to the Booklings,' I said. 'They formed a trail through the labyrinth.'

'In that case,' Regenschein said excitedly, 'you, too, have encountered the Shadow King!'

'Yes,' I said. 'It must have been he who saved me from Hunk Hoggno.'

Regenschein looked amazed. 'You fell into Hoggno's hands and lived to tell the tale?'

'Somebody cut off his head in the dark.'

'Typical of the Shadow King. It seems we both owe him our lives.'

'That's all very nice for you two,' Al put in. 'Personally, I'm alarmed that he knows the location of our secret headquarters.'

'I don't think you need worry about that,' said Regenschein.

'Have you any idea what his big secret is?' I asked.

'His frightful appearance, perhaps,' Regenschein replied quietly. 'On the other hand, he may wish to conceal the fact that he doesn't look as frightful as we suspect.'

'Like us,' said Al. 'Our fearsome reputation is a tremendous asset.'

Regenschein sat up even straighter. 'But we aren't here to chat about the Shadow King. You want to know how to get out of here, don't you, Yarnspinner?'

'Well,' I said cautiously, 'it would be very helpful.'

'Good, then I may be able to assist you. But let me say something first, and please listen closely.'

I leant forwards and pricked my ears.

'You'll only be safe – *really* safe, I mean – if you stay down here with the Booklings. No route through the catacombs is without its dangers and even if you make it to the surface you could be killed the instant you see daylight. Is that clear?'

'Because of Smyke, you mean?'

'You wouldn't get two streets from the exit. Judging by what Smyke told me before he banished me to the underworld, the situation looks like this: you and I are in the most closely guarded prison in Zamonia and Smyke has slammed the lid on us. And woe betide you if you lift it. The whole of Bookholm is swarming with spies, all of whom work for him.'

'Perhaps I'll be lucky.'

'Yes, perhaps. Perhaps you'll be lucky and Smyke's accomplices will all be smitten with blindness just as you crawl out of a sewer.'

'I could disguise myself and slip away under cover of darkness.'

'Look at it this way. You're a lucky devil: you're alive! You could have been killed by Bookhunters or devoured by Spinxxxxes. There are a thousand different ways of meeting a horrible end in the catacombs. Instead, you've landed up in a snug, safe place whose inhabitants revere literature. You're an author and authors can write anywhere. You'll get used to the food and the poor atmospheric conditions. You'll forget about sunlight and fresh air. Well, not altogether, but you'll think about them less and less often as time goes by.'

'Is there or isn't there a way out?' I demanded impatiently. After all, Regenschein himself had said that his time was short.

'Very well, since you seem genuinely determined. But I'll say it one more time: this route isn't safe either – nothing in the catacombs of Bookholm is really safe – but no Bookhunter knows of it. It's too cramped to accommodate any large and dangerous creatures. There are no intersections, so you can't get lost, and it leads straight to the surface.'

'Where does it come out?'

'It doesn't go all the way to the surface, but near enough. The city is already audible from there.'

'That sounds like a genuine possibility.'

'It's a long climb, but you'll get out in the end if you stay the course.'

'Why haven't you used this route?'

'Do I look as if I'm capable of a long climb?'

I made no response.

'The real problem will arise if you try to leave the city. Bookhunters will be after you. There's bound to be a price on your head, just as there is on mine. You'll yearn to be back in the catacombs – you'll wish you'd remained here with the Booklings.' Regenschein heaved a sigh. 'Well, that's what I wanted to tell you. There's still time to reconsider your decision. Personally, I wouldn't stake a dog-eared paperback on your chances of survival once you've left Bookling territory.'

I gazed into his bloodshot eyes.

'Would *you* risk it if you could make the climb?' I asked.

The Bookhunter sat up straighter still and grabbed my arm, eyes shining. 'You can bet your Lindworm's life on it!' he gasped. 'I certainly would, with my last ounce of strength! It would be worth it just to feel sunlight on my fur again, to fill my lungs with a single breath of fresh air.'

'Then please tell me how to find this route.'

'Aleisha,' said Regenschein, 'you'd have to guide him to the mouth of the shaft. It's outside your territory. Would you do that?'

'Of course,' Al replied, 'as long as it's not too far up. I don't like the idea, but if that's what you both want . . .'

'Then listen closely,' said Regenschein. 'It's a natural shaft of volcanic origin. Not too far off, just a day's walk.'

I leant towards him with my authorial godfather's admonition ringing in my head:

'The last words of a dying man on the point of imparting a sensational revelation – make a note of that literary device, it's a guaranteed cliffhanger! No reader can resist it!'

He was about to go on when the chain curtain over the mouth of the cave jangled and a Bookling dashed in. We all turned to look. It was Lugo Blah, the demented Gagaist who kept pursuing me with his eccentric poems.

'The Leather Grotto's on fire!' he gasped. 'It's the Bookhunters – they're killing anyone that gets in their way!'

'Push off, Lugo,' Al said brusquely. 'This isn't the time for one of your jokes.'

Instead of complying, Lugo tottered over to the bed and raised his arms. I was afraid he was about to unleash one of his crazy poems on me when he collapsed at our feet. There was an iron crossbow bolt protruding from his back. Al hurriedly bent over him, then looked up at us with tears in his single eye.

'He's dead,' he said.

Regenschein stiffened. 'Run for it!' he cried. 'Don't wait, save yourselves! It's me they've come for. They'll go away as soon as they've got me.'

'We're not leaving you,' said Al.

'But I'm as good as dead anyway!' Regenschein said hoarsely. 'Get going!'

'Out of the question,' Al told him. 'You'll outlive us all.'

'You're a cussed devil, Aleisha,' Regenschein growled. He smoothed the covers down and seemed to deliberate for a moment. Then he said, in a surprisingly firm voice, 'Very well, you leave me no choice. I shall have to die.' And he sank back against the pillows with a sigh.

'What are you doing?' Al demanded anxiously.

'I just told you,' said Regenschein. 'I'm dying.'

'No you don't!' cried Al. 'You can't simply die of your own free will, no one can!'

'*I* can,' the Bookhunter said defiantly. 'I'm Colophonius Regenschein,

Bookholm's greatest hero. I've done plenty of things no one thought I could do.'

He shut his eyes, uttered a final sigh and stopped breathing.

'Colophonius!' cried Al. 'Don't be silly!'

For a while, total silence reigned. I rested a hesitant paw on the Bookhunter's heart.

'It's stopped beating,' I said. 'Colophonius Regenschein has died for our sake.'

ℜℂ

The Book Machine

Colophonius Regenschein had taken his knowledge of an escape route from the catacombs to the hereafter with him, but there was no time for me to lament that fact. The Booklings' domain was in dire peril – the Bookhunters had invaded it! We set off at once for the Leather Grotto.

'Do you have any weapons?' I asked Al as we hurried back along the tunnels.

'No.'

'None at all?'

'Not unless you include paperknives,' he said. 'The most we've got are a few pickaxes and shovels.'

'I . . . smell . . .' a deep voice boomed at us from round the next bend. We stopped short and froze.

'I . . . smell . . .' the voice boomed again. 'I . . . smell . . . Vulphead flesh!'

Without a word, Al pulled me into the nearest unoccupied cave dwelling. We cowered down in its darkest corner and watched the entrance, which was lit only by a single candle in the passage outside. Something was approaching with ponderous tread – something that cast a big, bulky shadow. Then we saw a terrifying figure slink past. It was of immense size and had a green face in which, to my horror, three eyes could be seen. Bizarre pieces of jewellery consisting of dozens of shrunken death's-heads adorned its lank hair and dangled from its neck. The monster came to a halt and sniffed the air, then slowly turned its head in our direction. I felt sure it could smell us in the darkness, but instead of pouncing on us it grinned for an instant and continued on its way.

'I . . . smell . . . Vulphead flesh!' the figure growled again. 'Are you there, Colophonius? I've come to settle some unfinished business!'

The shadow disappeared and the footsteps receded, but we remained in the cave until we were absolutely sure the sinister intruder had turned down one of the side passages.

'Was that a Bookhunter?' I asked softly.

'Far worse,' Al whispered. 'That was Rongkong Koma himself.'

'Why doesn't he wear a mask?'

'Rongkong Koma is the only Bookhunter who doesn't need one. His real face is more horrific than any mask.'

The Bookling slipped out of the cave without waiting for my reaction. I sighed, rose to my feet and followed him.

I hardly recognised the Leather Grotto, which was bathed in a wildly flicke-ring glow and filled with clouds of smoke. Flames were burning every-where. Glowing embers had been raked off the hearths and lay strewn all over the cave, tables and bookcases were ablaze. The book machine was enveloped in a dense pall of smoke, the furniture and candlesticks had been overturned. Turmoil reigned on all sides. Screams, words of command and peals of malevolent laughter rang out, arrows whistled through the air, swords and chains clattered. The fragrance of waxed leather had been com-pletely supplanted by an overpowering stench of burning paper. The Leather Grotto was a battleground.

Al and I concealed ourselves in a rocky niche from which we could survey the course of events. I saw dozens of heavily armed figures attacking the Booklings with axes and swords, clubs and crossbows. Some of the little creatures were already stretched out on the ground, a few were still defending themselves or pushing bookcases over on top of the invaders, and others were milling around in helpless confusion, but most were sprinting for the various exits. I looked for Dancelot Two but couldn't see him anywhere. 'What can we do?' I asked.

Al was speechless. He clung to my arm, sobbing and trembling.

Mailed figures were stalking along the upper walkways of the book machine and discharging their crossbows at the fleeing Booklings. The battle of the Leather Grotto was over bar the shouting. The Booklings had been defeated and put to flight, the Bookhunters had assumed control. I might just as well have answered my own question: we could do absolutely nothing.

'There are so many of them,' Al whispered.

Yes, I myself had never seen so many Bookhunters. There were several dozen inside the cave alone, and who knew how many more had fanned out in the neighbouring tunnels? They all wore different kinds of armour and concealed their faces behind fearsome masks, some in the form of death's-heads, others representing mythical beasts or dangerous predators. The Bookhunters were armoured all over, many sheathed in metal, many in leather or other materials, and their every movement produced a terrifying rattle and clatter. Some had attached fluttering pennants to their armour and helmets, others were draped in shrunken heads or bones. They didn't look like living creatures, more like fighting machines activated by some baneful magic spell. One of them was brandishing a long whip studded with razor-sharp blades and chain links that whistled through the air, another had silver pincers instead of hands. I caught sight of one Bookhunter who had kindled a coal fire in a brazier welded to his helmet and was trailing long plumes of smoke behind him. I had never seen a more terrifying sight.

'We must get up on the book machine,' said Al, who had suddenly found his voice again.

I bent down and hissed in his ear. 'What?! There are Bookhunters up there. Anyway, what would we do on that rusty contraption?'

'I can't explain now,' he said. 'I know what I'm doing, trust me.'

'How do we get there? Those devils are everywhere.'

'The smoke is very thick over there, where those bookcases are burning. We can sneak through it and reach the machine unobserved. All you have to do is follow me!'

'But what do we do when we get there?'

'You'll see when the time comes.'

Al seemed to have a plan of some kind. That was fine with me – anything was better than simply waiting to be slaughtered by the Bookhunters. He crept out of our niche first and I followed, bending low. We sprinted for a few yards, then plunged into the acrid smoke.

I could see nothing now. I had to shut my eyes and follow Al's voice blindly, stumbling over unseen pieces of debris.

'Come on!' he whispered. 'Come on, we're nearly there!'

He was right. A moment later I blundered into the book machine's iron framework. Cautiously, I opened my eyes. Whorls of grey smoke were enshrouding the machine like dense fog. I could hear it clicking and whirring away as I clung to a rusty handrail. 'We must get to the second floor,' said Al. 'Come on!'

On we went, this time over some iron gratings, up one flight of steps, then another. Suddenly the smoke parted. I rubbed my streaming eyes and surveyed the whole scene. We were standing on the second floor of the book machine, which was still in operation. Shelves were gliding past us, both horizontally and vertically. Al seemed to be the only Bookling left alive in the Leather Grotto, all the rest having fled. The Bookhunters, who obviously felt they'd won and need fear no further opposition, behaved accordingly. They were rampaging around, knocking over bookcases and rummaging in their precious contents. A few of them were loudly quarrelling over their booty.

Four heavily armoured Bookhunters were stalking up and down two floors above us, their footsteps clattering on the iron catwalk. Why had Al got us into such a hazardous position? It could be only a matter of moments before one of them spotted us. Had fear or desperation robbed the Bookling of his wits?

'Al!' I hissed. 'What are we doing here? What's this plan of yours?'

'I've worked something out,' he replied.

'What?'

'Here! With the aid of my table!' Al held out his mysterious list, which he'd left up here on the machine. 'This is it!' He pointed to one of the shelves that were slowly gliding past. It drew level with us and came to a stop.

The Bookhunters down below started cheering: Rongkong Koma had just emerged from one of the tunnels and entered the Leather Grotto. To my horror, I saw that he was carrying Regenschein's severed head.

'Colophonius Regenschein is dead!' he cried, tossing the head into the cave. It rolled past a few dead Booklings and came to rest in front of a heap of burning books. Al averted his gaze.

The Bookhunters roared with laughter.

'The Leather Grotto is ours!' Rongkong Koma cried. 'Kill anyone else you find. And destroy that damned machine.' He pointed straight in our direction – and stopped short. Then, with a sharp intake of breath, he took several rapid steps towards the book machine. Finally he grinned: he had spotted us.

'I smell . . .' he said, 'I smell . . . lizard flesh!'

All the other Bookhunters turned to look. Axes and spears were brandished.

'It's time,' said Al. 'Climb on!'

'What?'

'Climb on that shelf, I've got it all worked out.'

'But they'll kill us anyway!'

'You must trust me. I can't explain now.'

'That nice, plump lizard there!' yelled Rongkong Koma. 'Pfistomel Smyke has put a big fat price on its head. Bring it to me!'

The four Bookhunters above us had already sprung to life and set off down the stairs. They had just reached our own floor.

I mounted the shelf and Al climbed up beside me.

'Hang on tight!' he commanded. 'Hang on tight!'

The Bookhunters came pounding along the catwalk, heading straight for us. One of them raised a huge spear and levelled it at me. I shut my eyes and prepared to die. There was a whirr and a click behind me and I suddenly felt a breath of air on my cheek: we were moving! Opening my eyes again, I saw the Bookhunters staring up at us in bewilderment. The shelf had risen into the air.

'I've got it all worked out,' Al repeated.

The Bookhunters ran back up the stairs. The shelf had stopped on the fifth floor.

'What now?' I asked.

'Stay on the shelf,' Al said. 'Just do as I say. Above all, hang on tight.'

'Get them!' Rongkong Koma called from below. 'Hurry up!'

The Bookhunters had already reached our floor.

'Damnation,' Al muttered. 'They're too quick.'

'What?'

'I'll have to hold them off. It's a shame, I'd sooner have come with you.'

He jumped off the shelf and barred the Bookhunters' path.

'Al!' I shouted. 'What are you doing?'

The Bookhunters were so flummoxed, they actually came to a halt. Al raised one hand and addressed them in such a thunderous voice that they retreated a step. They probably shared the widespread and deep-rooted belief in the Booklings' magical powers.

> 'Stop up the access and passage to remorse,
> that no compunctious visitings of nature
> shake your fell purpose, nor make peace between
> Bookhunter and Bookling. So do your worst!'

The Bookhunters looked at each other and exchanged grunting sounds. Al turned to me once more and cried,

> 'Had I but died an instant before this chance,
> I had liv'd a blessed time; for from this instant,
> there's nothing serious in mortality;
> all is but toys; renown and grace is dead,
> the wine of life is drawn, and the mere lees
> is left for Bookhunters to brag of . . .'

I heard a loud, metallic click behind me. Chains rattled, rusty cogwheels ground together. The next moment the shelf retreated into the book machine's dark interior. In front of me, two sliding panels converged like curtains, blotting out my view of Al, the Bookhunters and the Leather Grotto. Then the shelf keeled over backwards. I clung on tight, nonsensically calling out Al's name. There was a loud noise like an iron bolt being drawn and the shelf abruptly plummeted into the depths.

The Rusty Gnomes' Bookway

Imagine, dear readers, that you are lying on your back on a toboggan travelling at breakneck speed down a snowy slope on a dark night. That conveys a pretty accurate idea of the situation in which I now found myself.

I would never have thought it possible for a bookshelf to propel itself at such a rate. It was mounted on rails, as the screech of metal and the showers of sparks to left and right of me indicated, but the light of the glowing splinters revealed no sign of a steering device, let alone a brake. So I clung on tight and shut my eyes. This did not, however, dispel the physical sensation of falling. It scrambled my brain and turned my stomach until I felt so queasy I thought I would have to vomit. Striving to pull myself together, I opened my eyes and craned my neck to see where this wild ride was taking me. It was while speeding downwards in this unnatural position that I saw it for the first time: the *Rusty Gnomes' Bookway.*

Its supporting columns, rails and cross-ties – every iron girder, every nut and bolt in this amazing structure – was coated with a film of rust that emitted a phosphorescent green glow in the darkness. Seen from my viewpoint, the Bookway resembled a huge, luminous millipede winding its way through an endless dark void.

Colophonius Regenschein's book had given a detailed account of this miracle of the catacombs and also of its legendary builders. The Rusty Gnomes were a race of dwarfs who derived their name from their rust-coloured beards and their passion for anything to do with metal and corrosion. They were the first inhabitants of the catacombs to have given any thought to the transportation of large numbers of books.

In ancient times it had been a laborious business to convey large numbers of weighty old tomes from one part of the labyrinth to another, and dangerous as well. Wild animals, huge insects and book pirates lurked everywhere, as did the threat of yawning chasms, cave-ins and flash floods. The transportation of books, especially valuable ones, was immensely hazardous. The Rusty Gnomes, as Regenschein reported, had snow-white skin, rust-red hair and beards, and eyes with scarlet irises. They were better acquainted with the layout of the catacombs than any race before them. Inspired by love of scientific research, they fearlessly explored every last corner of the subterranean labyrinth and compiled a detailed atlas of it. They were also exceptionally skilful craftsmen and inventive mechanical engineers. They mined and smelted iron ore, canalised underground rivers, guided streams of molten lava along artificial channels and used it for heating purposes. They linked huge caverns by means of shafts, installed iron stairways and ladders throughout the catacombs, and greatly improved their stability with an ingenious system of buttresses.

The Rusty Gnomes bred a special type of rust and crossed it with luminous algae and phosphorescent fungi, thereby producing something that could not be assigned exclusively to the mineral or the vegetable kingdom. They used this substance, which emitted a subdued glow and continuously reproduced itself, to light large parts of their territory, and they eventually coated their Bookway with it. The other inhabitants of the catacombs referred to this rust mutation as *shimmermould.*

In addition, the Rusty Gnomes left behind vast libraries of books devoted exclusively to problems of mechanics, chemistry and physics, as could be inferred from their drawings of mysterious contrivances, machinery and tools. These books cannot be read to this day, since the Rusty Gnomes' script has still to be deciphered. It is said that they communicated with other life forms solely by means of sign language in order to preserve the secrecy of their own language and, thus, of their scientific expertise.

There were many abiding legends about these dwarfs: for instance, that they had installed a flywheel at the centre of the earth to keep our planet rotating and that they possessed diamond teeth capable of masticating iron.

But one thing was proved beyond doubt: they had built the Bookway, a sort of railroad of which ancient vestiges still existed at several places in the catacombs – Regenschein himself had seen stretches of it. The Rusty Gnomes' greatest achievement, it had originally been intended to connect the entire labyrinth. This vast technological scheme was never completed, however, because the Rusty Gnomes were carried off by a mysterious epidemic allegedly caused by – of all things – iron deficiency. Their shimmermould, on the other hand, had withstood the passage of time.

So the book machine in the Leather Grotto was nothing more nor less than a set of sidings forming part of the Rusty Gnomes' railroad system. To be honest, though, dear readers, this meant precious little to me at the time. What interested me far more was where my adventurous, breakneck ride was taking me and whether I would survive it. I thought for one moment that it would soon be at an end, because the gradient steadily decreased until I was travelling almost horizontally and had even started to climb.

I took advantage of this deceleration to turn over on my stomach. Not only was this a more comfortable position, but I could at least see where I was going. The track continued to ascend at first, ever more steeply, until it reached the top of the rise. Then it fell away sharply and I resumed my rapid descent.

My cloak fluttered like a flag in a gale. The luminous green cross-ties flashed past beneath me, one after another, as the wheels screeched down the track spewing a long trail of white sparks. One more descending curve, then up I went, higher and higher. I braced myself for another wild plunge but continued on my way at a relatively moderate speed – descending, it was true, but at nothing like the previous rate. Then came a long, steep bend. I didn't dare speculate on the chasms that yawned beneath the two thin strips of luminous metal along which I was travelling. The track supports were only partly visible – their green glow was swallowed up by the darkness some fifty or sixty feet below me – so I had no idea how big the drop might be.

At length my self-propelled bookshelf came to a long, straight stretch of track. It slowed down and proceeded at a steady tempo. I felt that I could now afford to relax my grip slightly and take a short breather.

One thing was certain: none of the Bookhunters had followed me this far. I was using an ancient system of transportation whose layout and function had been known only to the members of an extinct race of dwarfs, and a Bookling had entrusted me to it.

Reassured by such considerations, I eventually entered even larger caves in which other tracks loomed out of the darkness at various points. They too were coated with shimmermould, but here it glowed pink, blue and orange as well as green. I saw the tracks ascend, descend and describe long, steep curves, many of them beside or beneath my own. It was strangely impressive to see those intricate structures hovering in the gloom like ghostly edifices. By now my conveyance was trundling through this bizarre scenery at a walking pace. And then I saw something that made my blood run cold.

I was travelling parallel to a stretch of track coated with phosphorescent blue rust and gazing in wonderment at the dead straight rails atop their spindly piers, which were reinforced by a spider's web of wire mesh, when the rails abruptly ended: the piers had collapsed and the wire mesh hung in shreds. Although the track continued on its way after fifty feet or so, a black chasm yawned where the missing section should have been.

The Rusty Gnomes' Bookway was a ruin – I'd been suppressing that thought all the time. My 'toboggan' was traversing a structure hundreds of years old and long deprived of maintenance. It was inevitable that there would be a gap somewhere on my own route and that a chasm would suddenly open up in front of me.

My mobile bookshelf now seemed like a flying carpet that might lose its magical powers at any moment.

I debated whether to get off and proceed on foot. That would have been quite possible, now that I was moving so slowly, but the cross-ties were over a yard apart, and one false step . . . No, I preferred not to think of it. I could only hope that I was travelling along an exceptionally well-preserved section of the Bookway and would soon reach my destination.

Unfortunately, what I now saw was hardly calculated to reinforce my confidence. I kept passing breached stretches of track, snapped rails and buckled piers. The Bookway's skeleton was being eroded not only by time but by living rust. In another hundred years there would probably be nothing left but gigantic colonies of shimmermould proliferating on the floor of the cave like a luminous sea of every conceivable colour.

So on I went, staring apprehensively in the direction I was going – not that I could see very far in the dim light. I kept fancying that I'd sighted a gap in the rails not far ahead, but they always proved to be intact when I got there.

And then, quite suddenly, a mountain loomed up in front of me. No, mountain would be an exaggeration: a grey, conical monolith some eight or ten feet high, right in the middle of the track and only a stone's throw ahead. Where had it come from? Perhaps it was a stalactite that had snapped off the roof of the cave. But why, if it was as massive as it looked, hadn't it smashed the flimsy rails?

I gauged my speed. The bookshelf was now travelling so slowly that it would probably collide with the rock quite gently and come to a stop. There was no need for me to jump off, but I shuddered to think how hard it would be to clear the track. I clung on tight for safety's sake, so as not to be pitched off by the impact. By now, only a few yards separated me from the obstacle.

Which suddenly stirred.

Puckered up.

Stretched, expanded, changed shape.

Emitted a peculiar gurgling sound.

And finally, only inches from a collision, dived off the track into space.

The bookshelf trundled on. Dumbfounded, I turned to stare after the apparition but could see nothing, hear nothing. I rubbed my eyes and peered into the depths as the scene of this strange encounter steadily receded.

All at once I heard another unpleasant gurgle below me! There followed a fluttering sound like a vast flock of pigeons taking wing. And then the thing came soaring back out of the darkness. It had turned into a birdlike creature, unfurled two huge wings and was vigorously propelling itself upwards.

The head was narrow, almost spindle-shaped, with a beak like a pair of pincers, the skin grey and leathery. The ears were remarkably big and upstanding, the feet and wing joints tipped with sharp talons, but the most salient feature of this life form was that it had no eyes, just two deep, dark cavities that made its head look like a skull. Neither a bird nor a bat, it was a very special creature to be found only in the catacombs of Bookholm. I even knew its name. It was a Harpyr!

ℜℑ
The Song of the Harpyrs

Colophonius Regenschein had written that there is only one kind of creature capable of inflicting a fate worse than death: the Harpyr, whose screams can drive its prey insane.

Resident only in the catacombs of Bookholm, this cross between a harpy and a vampire can utter screams of a frequency that induces dementia in anyone exposed to its frightful song for a certain length of time by disrupting the rhythm of the brainwaves. Not until its prey has been rendered absolutely helpless does the Harpyr pounce on it and drink its blood.

The thing that had dived off the track was one of these legendary creatures. I had roused it from its slumbers and now it was clearly eager to pay me back. Like most eyeless life forms, the Harpyr relies for guidance mainly on its sense of hearing. While soaring upwards on its powerful wings, the creature abruptly turned its head in all directions and swivelled its ears until, with a sudden click, it homed in and pointed the tip of its beak straight at me. It must have detected the faint rattle of the bookshelf's wheels, or even, perhaps, my heartbeat.

I would have given anything for my conveyance to have picked up speed again, but it continued to trundle along as leisurely as before. I waited for the Harpyr to pounce on me, but for some unaccountable reason it hovered on the spot, uttering more strangled screams. Although piercing and far from pleasant, they did not strike me as loud enough to drive a person insane and were evidently just another aid to orientation. Their echoes reverberated round the cave, filling the air with the sound waves the Harpyr needed to navigate by. Surprisingly, however, the echoes rebounding off the walls grew steadily louder, not fainter. Surely that was a total impossibility?

I had little time to ponder the problem because it resolved itself a moment later. The echoes weren't echoes at all; they were the cries of other Harpyrs that now came fluttering out of the darkness: one, two, four, seven – a full dozen of them converged from from all sides. The first creature's screams had been intended to summon others of its kind. Harpyrs hunted in packs, it seemed. Why hadn't Regenschein mentioned *that* in his book?

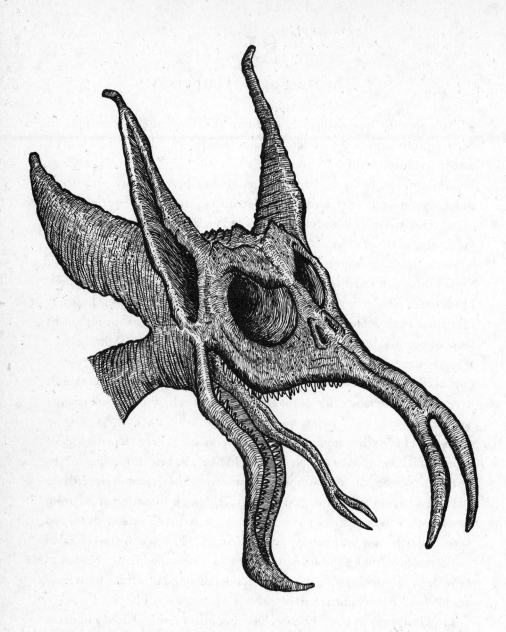

The aerial monsters assembled above the track, fluttering and screeching at one another, while my laggardly bookshelf continued to dawdle along at a snail's pace. Then the heads of the twelve Harpyrs clicked to and fro until all their beaks were pointing in my direction. Having jointly decided on their route through the air, they pricked their ears and emitted a collective screech. The hunt was on: vigorously flapping their wings, they headed straight for me.

Just then my conveyance plunged into space. Or so I thought at first, because the motion was so abrupt and unexpected, I felt convinced that the rails had come to a sudden end. In fact, the track had merely resumed its descent and renewed the bookshelf's momentum. The Rusty Gnomes had evidently gauged the physics and dynamics of their Bookway with the utmost accuracy.

I was lucky not to fall off the shelf because I wasn't holding on to anything at that moment, being too preoccupied with the sight of the swiftly approaching Harpyrs. Although I fell over backwards, I just managed to hang on as the downward plunge began. The sparks were flying again at last!

The Harpyrs detected the rattle of the wheels and dived in pursuit, screeching loudly. A self-propelled bookshelf scattering sparks as it sped down a ghostly, glowing green track like a meteor plunging into a pitch-black void, and perched on it a desperate inhabitant of Lindworm Castle, his purple cloak streaming out behind, pursued by a dozen eyeless Harpyrs screeching with bloodlust . . . It was a pity there were no witnesses to be duly awestruck by such a unique spectacle.

Little by little the Harpyrs' strangled cries changed pitch, giving way to a mixture of screams and croaks, but I felt, even now, that they couldn't rob me of my sanity. The bookshelf was travelling even faster than before. Swift as an arrow, it rounded precipitous bends, veered left and right, swooped and soared. I slithered and rolled around but hung on doggedly by my claws.

I was now speeding into a truly gigantic cave. It might once have been the Bookway's central station, because it was criss-crossed by vast numbers of tracks mounted on piers. Many of the latter had collapsed, snapping the rails and cross-ties. Here and there huge stalactites projected from the gloom overhead, but I saw as I drew nearer that they were really towering bookcases filled with books and thickly coated with dust: the ruined remnants of an ancient library system. Monstrous cogwheels coated with orange rust loomed out of the darkness, and I saw no fewer than three book machines mounted on tall iron frames like the one in the Leather Grotto. Linked by stretches of track, they were all out of commission, draped in cobwebs and thick with dust. This was the defunct nerve centre of a mechanical system by means of which the Rusty Gnomes had conveyed their store of knowledge from place to place: the Bookway's inanimate brain.

What impressed me most of all, however, were the fauna that populated this central station. I had read accounts of them in Regenschein's book but come to the conclusion that they were merely figments of his imagination, an elaborate joke indulged in at his readers' expense, because the creatures he described were too bizarre and improbable even for the catacombs. Now I knew better: everything, down to the most unlikely-seeming detail, accorded with reality.

To pass through the Bookway's central station was like being immersed in an aerial sea, a world where the ocean's natural laws prevailed in the absence of water. All the denizens of this vast cavern resembled marine creatures. I saw flying fish with dragonfly's wings that glowed in the dark. Shoals of them wound endlessly in and out of the Bookway's buckled girders, possibly in search of insects, and they all underwent a simultaneous change of colour every time they altered course. White jellyfish the size of captive balloons floated up and down, their transparent bodies throbbing gracefully. The pinpoints of light that twinkled inside some of these jellyfish danced like coloured snowflakes. Black octopuses with luminous violet suckers clung tightly to the track supports and book machines, discharging dark clouds of vapour that dispersed in the air like ink in water. Translucent manta rays with the wingspan of Harpyrs and long, luminous, hectically pulsating tails glided gracefully around. Colourless sea spiders scuttled over the ruins of the Bookway and cocooned them in gossamer threads.

Regenschein surmised that this colossal cave had once, in very ancient times, been completely filled with water and connected to the Zamonian Ocean, which would have accounted for the genesis and development of its unique fauna.

I felt sure that gigantic crabs were even now crawling across the floor of the cave, and that the pearls in the oysters lying there were the size of houses. One day, when the ocean returned and repossessed the cave, it would find its inhabitants ready to turn back into the marine creatures their ancestors had been so long ago.

But, dear readers, these amazing sights had almost made me forget what a predicament I was in! Screaming incessantly, the Harpyrs threaded their way skilfully through the glowing ruins and the creatures hovering around them. However, every time they got almost to within arm's length and were greedily snapping at me with their sharp beaks, the track went into a nosedive or

298

banked, almost as if the Rusty Gnomes had constructed it solely for my benefit many centuries ago.

I was becoming drunk with speed. A feeling of elation and power overcame me. I felt invincible – beyond the Harpyrs' ability to catch me. Was I starting to go mad? No, I was still unaffected by the monsters' screams. It was simply that extreme danger had filled me with a kind of exuberance, a mental defence against the paralysis of fear. I no longer gave any thought to the risks, to the possibility of gaps in the track and the uncertain outcome of this chase. It was the moment that counted, the little triumphs I scored over my pursuers, the abrupt twists and turns and dives that kept foiling them and made them more and more furious. I was a hare zigzagging in flight from a pack of hounds, a swallow evading a flock of eagles.

And then the Harpyrs *really* gave tongue. They proceeded to emit a new, third kind of sound, and I realised only now why I hadn't heard their true song before. The gurgles and screeches had been only an overture, a mere rehearsal for the demented chorus to follow. At the very moment when I had ceased to expect it, the Harpyrs broke into their hunting song.

It was a mixture of trills and hisses that swelled and faded, rose to a shrill coloratura and sank to a menacing snarl – just the right musical accompaniment for the crazy route the Bookway now followed. Ascents alternated at almost one-second intervals with descents, rises with falls, left-hand with right-hand bends, but the Harpyrs remained hot on my heels like greyhounds steadfastly matching their quarry's every twist and turn. Their cries made my eyeballs boil and my tongue smoulder. I felt the convolutions of my brain become contorted, felt my vital fluids come frothing up to poison it. I was gripped by an ever more irresistible urge to end it all by leaping into space before the Harpyrs finally triumphed. One jump and it would all be over. One jump, then peace for evermore.

'Yoo-hoo!' said a voice in my head.

Of course, that's how madness usually starts, isn't it, dear readers? You hear voices in your head. All the same, I couldn't help feeling offended by the fact that this particular voice had hailed me with an exclamation as banal as 'Yoo-hoo!'

'Yoo-hoo!' it called again. It sounded familiar somehow.

'Hello?' I called back in my head.

'Hello there, my boy! How goes it?'

'Who are you?'

'**I'm a cupboard full of dirty spectacles,**' the voice replied.

'Dancelot?'

'Are you acquainted with another cupboard full of dirty spectacles?'

The insane often heard the voices of the dear departed, didn't they?

'I only wanted to say that the mentally deranged condition into which you're now lapsing is common enough. A large stone hit me on the head during one of the sieges of Lindworm Castle and from then on—'

'I know, Dancelot.' Conversing with a disembodied voice while in mortal danger? Of course I was losing my mind!

'Yes, my boy, for a while I was mentally deranged – completely cracked, in fact. I genuinely believed myself to be—'

'A cupboard full of dirty spectacles – I'm aware of that, Dancelot. Listen: I'm tearing along on a ghost train pursued by a flock of ravening Harpyrs bent on sucking my blood, and I'm in the process of losing my mind. Would you please tell me, briefly and concisely, what you want?'

'I thought you'd be happy to hear from me.' Dancelot sounded half sad, half piqued.

'I *am* happy – or as happy as can be expected under the circumstances. It's just that I'm rather . . . stressed at the moment, Dancelot.'

'I understand. I only want to give you some advice, then I'll go.'

'Some advice?'

'I regained my sanity, as you know. Have you ever wondered how I managed it?'

I'd never thought about it, to be honest.

'It was like this. One day I heard the voice of my great-grandfather, Hilarius Wordwright, who also suffered from strange hallucinations – there's a very long history of mental illness in our family, and—'

'Dancelot! Would you kindly come to the point!'

'Yes, well, Hilarius advised me to climb to the very top of Lindworm Castle hill and shout as loudly as I could.'

'Shout?'

'Exactly. I did as he had said: I climbed up there and shouted, and that shout expelled my dementia. It disappeared into thin air like an exorcised demon. I'm not joking! That shout changed my life at least as much as the manuscript which you—'

'What do you mean, Dancelot? You want me to shout? Now, this instant?'
No answer.
'Dancelot?'
The voice had gone.

Well, there were precisely three explanations for that incident, dear readers. The first and least likely was that the voice really had belonged to my late authorial godfather. The second and somewhat more likely: it was a symptom of madness induced in me by the Harpyrs' strident song. The third: it was simply a manifestation of fear, and it was my own psyche that had borrowed Dancelot's voice in order to convince me how frightened I was. Or it could have been a combination of all three – I shall probably never know. All I do know is that I took Dancelot's advice regardless of its source – the hereafter, a sick mind or common sense – and proceeded to shout.

℞Ψ

A Shout and a Sigh

If there were such a thing as a Golden List for vocal feats, it would inevitably be headed by the shout I uttered in the Rusty Gnomes' railroad station.

Simply imagine all the sounds in the world you associate with extreme danger, dear readers: the muttering of a volcano on the verge of an eruption; the growl of a werewolf about to pounce; the rumble that precedes a major earthquake; the roar of an approaching tsunami; the hiss and crackle of a forest fire; the howl of a hurricane; peals of thunder in the Gloomberg Mountains. You will then have the basic ingredients of my shout to end all shouts.

Now add sorrow at the loss of my authorial godfather, despair at my steadily worsening lot and the dire effects of incipient dementia. Mix all these together with the primeval forces that still slumber in my savage, dinosaurian blood, and then imagine the roar that emerged from my throat. But be careful! Stop up your ears before you do, because the mere idea of such a sound is capable of bursting a person's eardrums and eyeballs!

I let it out, that shout which effortlessly drowned the Harpyrs' shrill chorus and filled the huge cave with an ear-splitting din. The flying fish fled in shoals, feverishly changing colour, an immense jellyfish shot upwards, pulsating in panic, and took refuge amid the girders of a book machine, sea spiders toppled off the ruined Bookway.

I was aware that Lindworms possessed robust vocal cords, but I had no idea that my lungs were so powerful. I'm convinced that everyone in the catacombs must have heard that shout, that it carried to every corner of the labyrinth, to every Bookhunter's ears and up to the surface of Bookholm – indeed, that it may be roaming the Chamber of Captive Echoes to this day and will do so for evermore. My dismay and apprehension left me, and for one long, wonderful moment I felt afraid of nothing at all, neither the Harpyrs nor insanity. Still shouting, I glanced in the direction I was going – and saw that the track ended not far off. The rails simply stopped short in mid air.

So that was it, the end of the line – my own end too, in all probability. But, dear readers, at that moment I feared nothing, not even death. I allowed my shout to fade away and prepared to fall, to plunge into the darkness and smash myself to smithereens on the floor of the cave. The Rusty Gnomes' railroad station was a grandiose place in which to die, a colossal monument to the futility of all endeavour. Here in the heart of the catacombs my bones would bleach and decay amid those iron skeletons. Death could have chosen no better moment, no better place, to make an end of me.

But then came a surprise. No, that's an understatement: several surprises at once. Six of them, to be precise.

Surprise No. 1: When I got to the end of the track it didn't end after all. Instead of plunging into space I continued my descent. No fall, no downward plunge – no, there were still rails beneath my wheels and showers of sparks trailing behind me. I was still bowling along at high speed.

Surprise No. 2: I heard a series of splattering sounds. Around a dozen of them, and they sounded like chunks of meat being hurled at a brick wall.

Surprise No. 3: The song of the Harpyrs ceased abruptly.

Surprise No. 4: My brain unknotted itself.

Surprise No. 5: The sounds around me took on an entirely different quality from one moment to the next. All at once they sounded dull and muffled, devoid of spatial depth and resonance.

Surprise No. 6: The Harpyrs, together with the entire station and its fauna, had suddenly vanished.

It took me a few startled seconds to grasp what had happened: the track had simply dived into a narrow tunnel.

My infernal bellowing had disrupted the Harpyrs' guidance system to such an extent that their acoustic coordination had failed. Unable to detect the massive rock face ahead of them, they had flown towards it as fast as their powerful wings would carry them. While I was entering the tunnel, all twelve had run smack into the rock. It was probably safe to assume that none of them had survived the impact.

If the gradient hadn't been so steep I might now have been able to relax a little. After all, I had escaped the Harpyrs, avoided going insane and remained on the track – a threefold triumph.

Cramped surroundings add greatly to the sensation of speed. Here in the tunnel the wheels rattled and screeched more loudly and the sparks rebounded off the walls like ricochets. And then my blood ran cold: something had gripped my ankle like a vice.

For the first time since entering the tunnel I looked back. There, crouching on the bookshelf behind me and visible in the flashes generated by the flying sparks, was a Harpyr. I couldn't have sworn it was the one whose slumbers I'd disturbed, but that, curiously enough, was the thought that ran through my mind at the sight of it – I say 'curiously' because it was a matter of supreme indifference which of the twelve monsters had clung to the bookshelf in the nick of time and been carried into the tunnel with me. Whichever it was, it opened its beak and snarled.

I snarled back, surprisingly unimpressed by this new threat. If the Harpyr wanted a fight, here of all places and now of all times, it could have one.

Evidently unaccustomed to defiance, the creature released my ankle. It might have a brain the size of a pea, but instinct seemed to tell it that this was an extremely inopportune moment for a fight. We were both too busy trying not to fall off the bookshelf.

The walls enclosing us suddenly receded. We had left the tunnel and were entering a long cavern whose floor was largely covered with pools of water. Luminous green droplets rained down from the roof and there was a smell of rotting vegetation.

The blind Harpyr had also detected the change in our surroundings. It jerked its head to and fro and swivelled its ears in all directions. At length it uttered one of its strangled cries. Was it summoning others of its kind? Fortunately not: the only response was an echo that rebounded off the rocky walls and faded away to nothing.

The track was now dead straight, the gradient almost imperceptible. Our speed steadily decreased. The Harpyr rose to its full height, uttered some more strangled cries, and spread its leathery wings. Then it started groping for me with its talons.

I shrank back as far as the shelf allowed and looked down to gauge how big the drop was. Big enough! I also saw that the track supports were in a far more decrepit condition here than elsewhere. Many of the trestles and tie-bars had snapped or buckled, with the result that the rails were cripples on crutches, so to speak. I couldn't help noticing that one or two cross-ties became detached and fell off into space as we passed over them. The straining metal creaked and groaned, the rails shed nuts and bolts, and fine clouds of luminous rust showered down.

Quite suddenly the Harpyr went over to the attack, and it did so in a way I would never have dreamt of. I had been expecting it to go for me with its talons or beak – to try to punch a hole in my head or sweep me off the bookshelf with its wings – but not to assail me with its tongue!

The tongue came darting out of its mouth, and I could scarcely believe how long it was. Two or three yards of it emerged from the creature's jaws, encircled my body in an elliptical orbit and wound itself round my neck. Then, with a slurping sound, the Harpyr retracted it a little, brutally squeezing the air from my lungs.

At that moment the mobile bookshelf tilted once more and sped downhill. The Harpyr hung on tight with its talons, still maintaining its stranglehold. The tips of its forked tongue appeared in my field of vision disclosing that they were equipped with pairs of needle-sharp teeth.

We had already come to another uphill bend. I could no longer breathe, my eyelids were fluttering and the Harpyr was preparing to sink its teeth in my neck. A sudden silence ensued. No rattle of wheels, no trail of sparks, no metallic squealing or screeching, just the faint whistle of air rushing past my ears.

I knew that something crucial had happened. The Harpyr seemed to sense this too, because it relaxed its stranglehold and retracted its whiplike tongue at lightning speed. I clutched my throat, gasping for breath – and spotted the reason for the sudden hush: I saw the track receding behind the Harpyr's back. That, of course, was an optical illusion, because we were receding from the track, not it from us. The rails had stopped short in the middle of the uphill bend: we were soaring into space complete with the bookshelf.

We soon reached the apogee of our flight and hovered there absolutely weightless for a moment, the Harpyr, the bookshelf and I. Then several things happened at once.

First, the bookshelf took leave of us. It followed a route of its own, a long, descending trajectory destined to end on the cave's rocky floor and reduce it to splinters.

Secondly, the Harpyr spread its powerful wings and proceeded to flap them.

And I? What did I do? Well, I possessed wings too. However, those stunted appendages inherited from my ancestors might have been sufficient to impress the Ugglian owner of an antiquarian bookshop, but they were no use for flying. My only recourse was to cling to the Harpyr – which is precisely what I did: I grabbed its ankles and hung on tight. It uttered a startled squawk and flapped its wings violently to remain airborne. Fortunately, the laws of anatomy precluded it from slashing at me with its beak at the same time.

I heard a crash as the bookshelf landed on the rocks far below. The Harpyr now seemed to grasp that the quickest way of getting rid of its irksome passenger would be to jettison it, because the creature went into a nosedive. The closer we got to the ground, the greater my hopes of surviving this involuntary trip aboard what was probably the most singular form of transportation any passenger has ever used.

But the Harpyr's only motive in diving was to smash me against the stalagmites protruding from the floor of the cave. I just managed to avoid colliding with the tip of one of these, which was as tall as a church spire, by drawing up my legs – only to crash into another moments later. The impact was so violent that the tip snapped off and hurtled into space, but I felt no pain and continued to hang on like grim death. The Harpyr was at last showing signs of fatigue. Our contest was sapping its strength, just as it was mine, and it may have dawned on the monster that my dogged determination to survive was the equal of its own. Its wing-beats became slower and more feeble, and when only a few feet separated us from the floor of the cave I plucked up courage and let go.

I scarcely felt myself hit the ground, although the impact was considerable and I turned several somersaults on landing; the pain didn't filter through until later. Quickly, I scrambled to my feet and looked up. The Harpyr was hovering in the air only a few feet overhead, flapping its wings and screeching in an attempt to determine my location. Its pea-sized brain was obviously debating whether to launch another attack or simply fly away.

Having decided on the former course of action, it landed on the rocky ground not far from me, then opened its hideous jaws and extended its long, toothed tongue once more. I bent down and reached for a lump of rock, intending to hurl it at the creature's head, only to discover how weak I was after all my exertions. Although I managed to grab hold of the rock, I hadn't the strength to pick it up and throw it. It slipped through my paws and fell to the ground.

The Harpyr circled me with outspread wings and talons extended, its tongue lashing the air like a bullwhip. I clasped my throat with both paws, which was all I could think of to do in self-defence. Our aerial struggle had left me utterly exhausted.

At that moment the cave was pervaded by a sound that put me in mind of a ghostly sigh whistling down a chimney on a stormy night. It seemed to jolt the Harpyr like an electric shock. The monster retracted its tongue and wrapped its wings round its talons and beak as if to conceal those deadly weapons from the gaze of someone who had given it a hard time in the past.

It preserved this submissive pose a few moments. Then, with another vicious snarl in my direction, it uttered a piercing cry, spread its wings and took off. It disappeared into the darkness with a protracted screech that seemed to me to convey relief as well as fear and rage.

Like the Harpyr, I recognised the author of that terrifying sound because I'd heard it once before: in Hunk Hoggno's pied-à-terre. It was the sigh of the Shadow King.

Denizens of the Darkness

I headed in the direction from which I thought the sigh had come – not that I really felt it was a good idea. Most of the decisions I'd made down there had landed me in even bigger trouble, so it seemed fairly certain that this one would also have disastrous results.

I stumbled over uneven, rocky ground through gloomy, lofty caverns in which ubiquitous pools of fluorescent blue water emitted little domes of light that helped me to find my way. Although I heard occasional rustles and squeaks in the darkness, I was pretty inured to such sounds by now. Not long ago they would have scared me to death. Doubtless it was only some harmless catacomb creature fleeing in panic from me and the noises I was making.

For all that, I couldn't rid myself of the uneasy feeling that I was being watched. Are you familiar with that sensation, dear readers? You're lying in bed late at night, having just blown out the candle and settled down to sleep, when you suddenly feel that there's *something there in the dark*! That, however improbable it may seem, you aren't alone in the room! The door hasn't opened, the window is firmly shut, you can see nothing and hear nothing, but you can sense it, can't you, that menacing presence? You light the candle again and there's no one there – naturally not. Out goes the candle, the uneasy feeling subsides, you chide yourself for your childish fears – and there it is again, the sinister certainty that there's something lurking in the dark. Now you can even hear it breathing. You hear it coming nearer, slinking round the bed . . . And then you feel an icy breath on your neck. With a shrill cry you sit bolt upright, panic-stricken, and light the candle yet again – and yet again there's no one there.

What lingers with you is the dismaying suspicion that darkness conjures up things that shouldn't really exist. That extinguishing the light creates a magical realm in which invisible beings can run riot – beings that need darkness the way we need air to breathe. And you spend the rest of the night fitfully dozing by candlelight, don't you?

Hardened though I was, such were the sensations and premonitions that continually stole over me down there. The expanse of darkness surrounding

307

me was too immense for there to be nothing, absolutely nothing, lurking in it. I saw long shadows loitering among the stalagmites, tall dark figures that dissolved into thin air as I drew nearer. I saw rocks that swayed like poplars in the wind. I heard the rustle of paper and heavy breathing, echoing footsteps, unintelligible murmurs, giggles. Were those my own footsteps? Was I talking to myself, was I giggling to myself in a half-demented fashion without realising it? Or was something really stalking me? If so, was it the Shadow King? Why was he taking the trouble to spy on me, why didn't he simply show himself and make short work of me? A creature that struck terror into Harpyrs and Bookhunters need hardly be frightened of a would-be author from Lindworm Castle.

I stopped to rest beside one of the pools. I resisted the temptation to drink some of its luminous water, but I was glad at least to be able to see my own paws. I noticed to my surprise that they were clutching the manuscript. I must have taken it out instinctively and was clasping it to my chest with both paws as if it could protect me. At first I was shocked by my childish behaviour, but then I breathed a sigh of relief. Of course, all those noises – the rustle of paper, the breathing, the footsteps, the giggling – had been made by me. I alone had produced them and scared myself stiff. There was no one here but me.

It became steadily lighter as I went on. The rocks, too, were now coated with luminous blue algae. I felt I was walking at night under a full moon, in that strange blend of frigid light and darkness. And then I saw a scrap of paper floating on the surface of a small blue puddle. I stooped and picked it up, stared at it for a long time. Feeling dizzy, I leant against a rock to preserve my balance.

It resembled one of the pieces of paper I had found in the vicinity of Hunk Hoggno's grisly abode, the trail that had guided me to the Booklings. This piece, too, had a bloodstained edge and bore the same indecipherable characters. Peering into the gloom, I caught sight of another scrap of paper lying just beside another puddle. I tottered over and picked that one up too. Further on I saw a puddle with yet another snippet of paper floating on it. The Shadow King had laid another trail.

But how could he have followed me throughout that breakneck ride on the Bookway? Not even a phantom could have done that. I wiped the cold sweat from my brow, pocketed the manuscript and gathered my cloak around me. Then I drew a deep breath and continued to follow the bloodstained trail.

The Symbols

Sulphur and phosphorus fumes drifted about me as I made my way through the next few caves, obediently following the snippets of paper I never failed to find lying on the ground every few yards. The unpleasant smells came from volcanic springs. Pools of magma and boiling water were bubbling on all sides, but more violently than the contents of the modest crater the Booklings called their Devil's Kitchen. These pools seethed and hissed, and I had to take care where I trod because even the water in an innocuous-looking puddle could be unbearably hot.

The temperature and humidity had risen considerably, and the heat was comparable to that prevailing in the vicinity of a smelting furnace. It had grown appreciably lighter thanks to the golden-yellow glow of the molten lava, which lit the lofty caverns from floor to vaulted roof. I inferred from the volcanic conditions that I had penetrated even deeper into the catacombs. I couldn't be absolutely sure of this, however, because my knowledge of geology was too limited.

The further I progressed through these caves the less natural they seemed. The walls and floors looked as if they had been artificially buffed and polished, and I soon began to notice ornamental designs and symbols that could only have been handmade. Someone equipped with tools had carved, engraved or milled patterns into the rock, but none of them reminded me of any well-known civilisation or art form. Nowhere could I discern a familiar shape. These were abstract symbols, and even they looked alien because they did not embody conventional geometrical shapes and dispensed entirely with squares, circles, triangles and the like.

I was now making my way through caves of which every square inch was occupied by these symbols. Covering the floor, walls, roofs, stalagmites and boulders, many of them had been carefully painted in shades of red, yellow and blue. Seen from a distance they made a strangely, beautifully ornamental impression. If I stared at these coloured patterns for any length of time they seemed to move, to revolve and dance around. They rose and fell like the ribcage of some huge, sleeping beast, together with the walls on which they were inscribed.

Could the walls be my own cerebral cortex? Was my demented psyche roaming among them and were the symbols my own insane ideas, which I myself was past deciphering?

I couldn't help rubbing my eyes again and again. This, I thought, was what it must be like to discover the remains of an alien civilisation on some distant planet. I pictured the former inhabitants of these caverns as a race of intelligent giant ants able to climb all over the walls and roofs and carve or etch their symbols into the rock with endogenous tools and acids. There seemed no other explanation for how they had managed to reach so many inaccessible places.

The caves became steadily wider and higher, and I felt smaller and more insignificant at every step. Nature alone had never had that effect on me – I had never been overly impressed by lofty mountains or broad expanses of desert. It was artistry on such a vast scale that induced this feeling of humility in me. Was this the manifestation of a very early literature? Of writing that was still ignorant of paper or printing? Were these not ornaments at all but a form of script? If so, I might be making my way through a very primitive type of book, a colossal subterranean tome in which each cave represented a chapter.

I ascended a flight of steps hewn out of the rock. Completely covered with symbols, they led to a lofty, richly decorated portal. I was suddenly overcome by a notion that the purpose of all these symbols was merely to prepare me for another, even greater work of art – that they were an immense salutation carved in stone, or possibly a warning designed to attune me to what awaited me beyond the portal. I trembled, almost riven with suspense. Was it really wise to go on? My knees were knocking, my body was streaming with sweat. The symbols danced around me like snowflakes in a blizzard. They might be calling to me to turn back at once, for all I knew, but I didn't understand their language.

And then, after another three or four steps, the symbols disappeared from view. I was through the gateway and standing on the threshold of the next cave – in another world. Although it certainly wasn't the biggest cave I had seen so far – the Rusty Gnomes' railroad station was somewhat bigger – it contained what had to be the most astonishing edifice in the catacombs. While searching for words to describe it, I was reminded of Colophonius Regenschein's lines of verse:

A place accursèd and forlorn
with walls of books piled high,
its windows stare like sightless eyes
and through them phantoms fly.
Of leather and of paper built,
worm-eaten through and through,
the castle known as Shadowhall
brings every nightmare true.

A long, winding flight of steps led some way down into the cave, then up in a series of serpentine bends until it reached the building that seemed to jut from the opposite rock face like the bow of an enormous ship. A ship, whether of the future or dating from very ancient times, it might have been built by giants who had sailed the seven seas in it before sinking to the bottom of the Zamonian Ocean.

Its windows stare like sightless eyes . . . Shadowhall Castle had a multitude of windows and doorways of various sizes, all of which had been bricked up except for one big open portal situated at its central point and approached by the winding flight of steps. At the foot of the castle, on either side of the steps, molten lava bubbling in hundreds of little craters bathed the building in a golden glow. The acrid vapours rising into the superheated atmosphere almost took my breath away. From time to time there was an audible gurgle followed by a dull plop, and a thin jet of liquefied rock soared into the air in front of the castle. It shot upwards like a rocket, then fell back in a shower of incandescent droplets.

There was another remarkable feature, to my eyes perhaps the most remarkable of all: on every fourth or fifth step lay a scrap of paper. The trail that had been laid for me was intended to lure me straight into Shadowhall Castle.

At this stage, dear readers, I naturally had no idea that this really was Shadowhall Castle, nor did I know what awaited me within its walls. I knew only that, if this was a trap, it was the biggest and most impressive trap the catacombs of Bookholm had to offer. Feeling duly flattered, I set off up the steps to the castle.

ஃ
Shadowhall Castle

As I drew near Shadowhall Castle I noticed to my great surprise that it was a literary structure. What I had taken from a distance to be bricks were really close-knit layers of books. Having reached the top of the steps and, thus, the entrance to the castle, I was at last able to examine them at close quarters.

With walls of books piled high . . . I now understood this line from Regenschein's poem as well. Yes, the books were fossilised and seemed to have been laid without mortar, but it was hard to tell whether they were fossilised when used as bricks or had become so subsequently. I couldn't help thinking of Pfistomel Smyke's house and its ingenious dry-stone building technique. I was also reminded of my giant ant theory. I could readily imagine the creatures fetching books from the surrounding labyrinth, then gluing them together with an endogenous secretion at the behest of their monstrous queen, who had flown here from some distant planet and was now waiting for me inside, ready to join me in breeding a super-race of dinosaurs and giant ants that would . . .

My imagination had run away with me, a sign of extreme tension. I had reached the threshold of the castle; now I would have to decide whether to enter it or beat a retreat. I could still turn back.

I ran my eyes over the façade once more. Was this really an entire castle deeply embedded in the rock, or was it just a dummy, a gigantic half-relief? I couldn't make up my mind whether it was forbidding or inviting. It was certainly fascinating.

Its windows stare like sightless eyes, and through them phantoms fly . . . I didn't find those lines particularly inviting, any more than *of leather and of paper built* or *worm-eaten through and through.* Whatever they were meant to convey, they didn't conjure up visions of an agreeable stay at a luxury hotel.

There are several Zamonian horror stories in which the hero finds himself in a similar situation – one that makes you feel like shouting, 'No, don't! For heaven's sake don't go in there, you fool! It's a trap!'

But then you lower the book and sit back. 'Well, why not?' you tell yourself. 'Let him go in! Ten to one there's a gigantic, hundred-legged spider lurking inside, poised to spin a cocoon around him or something. It's bound to be entertaining. He's the hero of a Zamonian horror story, after all. He's got to be able to take it.'

And so, being the hero of a Zamonian horror story, he ignores all the dictates of common sense and does go inside, to be promptly imprisoned in a cocoon by a gigantic hundred-legged spider – or something of the kind.

Not me, though! *I* wouldn't go inside. Once bitten twice shy: I'd been inured to traps by bitter experience. I wasn't some asinine hero who risks his neck to satisfy the vulgar requirements of a lowbrow readership. No, I wouldn't go *right* inside, I would only go *a little way* inside. Where was the harm in that, after all? Just a couple of steps and a quick peek with one eye on the doorway. I would gain an idea of the place and turn back at once if anything looked fishy.

The fact was, dear readers, I simply couldn't bring myself to leave without taking a look inside Shadowhall Castle. Curiosity is the most powerful incentive in the world. Why? Because it's capable of overcoming the two most powerful *dis*incentives in the world: common sense and fear. Curiosity accounts for why children hold their hands over candle flames, why soldiers go to war or scientists venture into the Cogitating Quicksand of Nairland. Curiosity is the reason why all the heroes of Zamonian horror stories 'go inside' sooner or later.

So I went inside – but only a little way inside. Therein lay the small but important difference between me and the reckless heroes of Zamonian horror stories: I went inside but promptly came to a halt and looked around with a mixture of relief and disappointment.

No gigantic hundred-legged spider. No Shadow King. No phantoms. No creatures of leather or paper. Just a relatively modest entrance hall, a circular chamber with a low, domed ceiling softly illuminated by the glow of the molten lava coming through the open doorway. Like the outer walls, the entrance hall was built of fossilised books. Twelve passages led off it, but that was all. No furniture or anything of that kind.

So why had I made such a fuss about taking a look at what was probably the most unspectacular part of what was probably the most spectacular building in the catacombs? There had to be more to the castle than this.

Why not venture a little further? Along one of those passages, perhaps? It wouldn't be risky provided I could still see the glow of the lava. Even the faintest reflection of it would guide me back to the exit. I would keep going until the light ran out.

So I set off down one of the twelve passages, which was long and dark and as bare as the entrance hall. Another passage branched off it after only twenty paces, as far as I could see in the steadily dwindling light. Why not take a quick look down that one and then turn back? The interior of this building might contain nothing spectacular whatsoever.

When I reached the intersection I saw that the next passage was dimly illuminated by a candle in an iron candlestick, which was standing on top of a book on the ground. There was nothing else in the passage. Nothing *else*? Candles and books were triumphs of art and technology, signs of civilisation! A *burning* candle, what was more! Someone must have lit it only a short time before!

My heart leapt. Yes, someone must be here – some animate creature must live here, whether good or evil it remained to be seen. I was well on the way to being lured ever deeper into Shadowhall Castle, propelled by my own curiosity like a puppet on a string. However, those two greatest disincentives in the world, common sense and fear, were still potent enough to prompt me to consider my future course of action.

Somebody lived there, that was enough to be going on with. I decided to go back outside and work out a plan. Perhaps I should lay a trail, pluck a thread from my cloak and attach it to the doorpost – something like that. Think first, I told myself! Look before you leap!

So I retraced my steps. But, when I came to the place where the passage debouched into the entrance hall, the doorway had disappeared! There was nothing there, just bare wall. I was thunderstruck. Was this really the place? If not, how could I have gone astray in such a short distance? The candle would help me to find the exit, so I went back to fetch it. I also wanted to take a look at the book, which might provide some helpful clue. But the intersection had also disappeared, like the whole of the passage with the candle in it! This was a sheer impossibility. Then I had an idea born of desperation: unlikely as it seemed, perhaps somebody was cutting me off by erecting walls at lightning speed. So I returned once more to the spot where the door to the entrance hall had been. If the wall was newly built I might be able to knock it down.

This time, however, the doorway had staged a bewildering reappearance and so had the glow from the lava! I hurried back into the entrance hall – only to discover, to my horror, that it wasn't the entrance hall but a far larger chamber with twice as many passages leading off it. Nor was it lit by lava, but by torches burning in rusty iron sconces that jutted from the walls like gnarled branches.

I tottered round the empty chamber for a while, bemused and utterly at a loss. How could one whole chamber vanish and be replaced by another? Had I headed in the wrong direction? There was only one thing for it, I would have to go back. But the thought of setting foot in one of those passages filled me with dread. Would it lead me still further astray? Eventually I screwed up my courage and set off down a long corridor lit by candles standing at intervals on the floor. I walked on until I suddenly noticed something alarming out of the corner of my eye. Were the walls closing in on me? Horrified, I came to a halt. No, it was just an optical illusion. For all that, I got the impression that the passage had become somewhat narrower. I hurried on, only to be overcome once more by a claustrophobic sensation that the walls were closing in on me. If I halted the sensation disappeared; if I walked on the walls seemed to converge. One thing was certain, however: the passage was steadily narrowing. The walls had been considerably further apart at first. My claustrophobia intensified at every step. And then, at last, the mystery solved itself: the walls eventually met and the passage came to an end. Anyone walking along it fast had the illusion that the walls were closing in. It was the most deceptive dead end I had ever encountered.

So Shadowhall Castle was a maze. A maze inside a labyrinth. Despite all the care I'd taken, I was in an even worse predicament than before. Even the walls were conspiring against me now. All I needed was for the ceiling of the passage to descend and crush me. But it never came to that: the floor descended instead.

I thought at first that the ceiling had risen, but that too was an optical illusion. I could tell from the faint vibrations beneath my feet that the floor was sinking – all along the passage, as far as I could tell. Then, when the ceiling was some thirty feet above my head, the vibration ceased. Dozens of dark doorways yawned in the walls on either side of me.

Feeling dizzy, I sat down on the ground. Shadowhall Castle was not only a maze. It was a maze capable of changing shape, with floors that sank and walls that appeared out of nowhere. Those who had built the castle might be long dead, but their handiwork was only too alive.

೫6

The Hair-Raisers

On recovering from this latest shock I struggled to my feet, groaning as if I'd been beaten black and blue, and tottered along the passage on trembling legs. Seemingly endless, it zigzagged to and fro and was flanked by countless dark doorways. The candles were few and far between.

The claustrophobic nature of my architectural surroundings was now compounded by noises: I could hear the creak of distant hinges and a disembodied humming that might have been caused by a current of air. The interior of the castle was agreeably cool compared to the almost tropical heat of the magma cave – that much, at least, could be said in its favour. Sometimes I even thought I heard water dripping, which kindled my hopes of finding something to drink somewhere.

But it was odd: I had an instinctive dread of entering one of those dark apertures. The gloom beyond them had a menacing quality, as if one step could send me hurtling into an abyss, so I preferred to stick to my ill-lit route.

All at once I caught sight of another scrap of paper on the ground. I must have presented a ridiculous spectacle, a big, strong Lindworm wincing at the sight of a tiny snippet of paper like an elephant shying at a mouse, but it was simply too much of a surprise. I had no need to pick it up to satisfy myself that it was one of the ones that had guided me to the castle. A whole trail of them had been laid along the passage and ended in front of one of the doorways leading off it.

I stared into the adjoining darkness until it almost rang in my ears, so dense and alive did it seem, but I eventually overcame my fear and walked through the dark opening. I didn't step into a void or plunge into an abyss, I merely found myself in a pitch-black chamber. What happened then was something I'd experienced before, but in reverse order. I refer to the moment when

316

something entered Hunk Hoggno's abode and extinguished the candle. This time it was as if something had left the room and *lit* a candle instead of extinguishing it. The match and wick flared up so quickly that their light briefly dazzled me and made me blink. I heard a rustle of paper. Then I thought I saw a shadow – a colossal shadow! – flit through the doorway and disappear from view.

My limbs were still tingling from the shock when I saw something that had a reassuring effect on me: books. The octagonal chamber's walls were lined with shelves full of books. Not fossilised books misused as bricks, but a regular library of them. It wasn't one of those huge, outsize libraries to which I'd become almost accustomed down here, but a modest private collection of a few hundred volumes at most. In the middle of the chamber was a leather armchair, and beside it a small iron table bearing a glass, a jug of water and a bowl of desiccated bookworms. Food and drink! I subsided into the armchair, poured myself a glass of water, gulped it down and tossed a handful of bookworms into my mouth. Mm, delicious, they were even salted! I chewed them as I looked round the room, feeling thoroughly restored. A drink of water and a handful of smoked maggots had sufficed to turn a despairing wreck into a cheerful optimist. It isn't the brain that governs our state of mind, it's the stomach.

I got up and went over to the shelves, removed a book and opened it. The script was Old Zamonian, the title *Screams from a Sarcophagus* by Bamuel Courgette. I gave an involuntary sob.

The very fact that I could read the script was enough to prompt that involuntary display of emotion. The gulf between me and the civilised world had been bridged once more. I could not only decipher the script, I even knew what the book was about! I had read it in my youth, and it had given me the most terrible nightmares. It was a so-called *Hair-Raiser*, a subsection of Zamonian horror literature.

I took another book from the shelf. Entitled *Clammy Hands*, it was by Nector Nemu and was another Hair-Raiser. Nemu had been one of the most eminent writers of horror stories. I put my head on one side and ran my eyes over the titles. They included:

Skeletons in the Reeds by Hallucinea Krewel;
On a Gibbet at Midnight by Macabrius Sinistro;

Frozen Phantoms by Murko de Murkholm;
Laughter in the Cellar by Norsius Yukk;
A Handful of Staring Eyes by the Weirdwater sisters;
Where the Mummy Sings by Omar ben Shokka

and so on and so forth. The authors' pseudonyms alone left me in no doubt that these books were Hair-Raisers, one and all. I went from shelf to shelf, checking one title after another, and ended by being convinced that this was a choice collection of Hair-Raisers, probably the most comprehensive and valuable I'd ever set eyes on.

I couldn't help laughing suddenly.

Because some of you, dear readers, may not be too familiar with the Hair-Raiser genre of Zamonian horror literature, permit me to indulge in a brief digression. It really won't take long and will help you to understand my amusement.

There was a time when people believed that Zamonian horror literature had reached the end of the line. Authors had used up every goose-flesh- and nightmare-inducing character and plot in existence, from headless phantoms to roaming Marsh Zombies to foot-eating Polterkins resident under cellar stairs. They continued to populate their books with the same old Semimummies, Gulch Ghosts and Hazelwitches until even schoolchildren ceased to be frightened of them. Sales slumped dramatically. In desperation, the publishers of Zamonian horror literature invited all the authors of the genre and one or two celebrated Bookemists to attend a conference at which measures designed to tackle the crisis would be discussed and implemented.

The conference took place behind the yards-thick walls of Ignis Fatuus Castle in Demon's Gulch. No members of the public were admitted, so secrecy long surrounded the measures discussed there and eventually put into effect. It is a fact, however, that the first of the so-called Hair-Raisers came on the market only six months later, and that they ended the crisis affecting Zamonian horror literature at a stroke.

These books were so effective, so gruesome and terrifying, that their readers' only recourse was to fling them into a corner halfway through and hide behind the nearest piece of furniture. Many fans of Hair-Raiser literature were said to have been driven mad with fear by over-indulging in it. Subsequently locked up in mental institutions, they went into paroxysms of hysteria at the very sight of a book in the distance, be it only a cookbook.

Even respected literary critics and scholars believed that the powerful impact of Hair-Raisers was based on some subtle new form of literary technique. They surmised that the foremost exponents of Zamonian horror literature had mutually disclosed their most closely guarded writer's tricks during the conference at Ignis Fatuus Castle. All these literary devices had then been skilfully combined to produce a new, more potent and considerably more effective type of horror literature – one that was even capable of generating supernatural phenomena which assailed its readers while reading and turned even the most hardened of them into whimpering bundles of nerves. This, incidentally, was also the beginning of the Gruesome Period, during which the Hair-Raiser genre and Octavius Shrooti's 'gruesic' scored their greatest triumphs.

It was said that Hair-Raiser books could be heard whispering and sobbing in the dark. Their covers creaked open like the rusty doors of long-forgotten dungeons in which unspeakable horrors were lurking. Turn their pages and one would often hear a ghostly cry or a peal of horrific laughter. They could emit chill exhalations, whispering breezes like those that fill the faded curtains in ancient enchanted castles reputed to be haunted by the restless presence of souls in torment.

These books could dissolve into thin air while being read, only to reappear, giggling, elsewhere in the room. A severed, hairy, ten-fingered hand could leap from the page and scuttle up the reader's arm, then hurl itself into the fire and scream until it was burnt to death.

The language in which Hair-Raisers were written consisted almost entirely of words that conjured up highly unpleasant images – words like *clammy*, *bony*, *eerie*, *gloomy*, *chilly*, *scary*, *spooky* and *deathly*. Hair-Raiser literature also introduced a vogue for neologisms in which those words were combined for greater effect, for instance *speathly*, *gleerie* or *clooky*. Even one of them could make a reader's hair stand on end, and it was this characteristic from which the new literary genre derived its name.

Reading a Hair-Raiser was like walking through a subterranean chamber discovered on the stroke of midnight behind a secret door in a deserted lunatic asylum haunted by the sleepless spirits of deceased mass murderers – a musty,

cobwebby chamber which you explored with a guttering candle in your trembling fist while red-eyed rats snarled in the gloom and icy tentacles grabbed your ankles.

Every sentence, page and chapter of a Hair-Raiser could conceal some lurking horror in the shape of a gruesome phrase that made its readers' blood run cold. Taut as a bowstring, their nerves would cause them to stop reading again and again. There! they would think. Is that a hand silhouetted against the window-pane? The hand of an unscrupulous body-snatcher, perhaps, who has run out of corpses from the outcasts' graveyard from which he usually obtains his supplies for the demented Ugglian alchemists' laboratory nearby – the one from which those terrible screams keep issuing at dead of night? No, it's just a five-pointed leaf plastered against the pane by the wind – but a leaf that bears a chilling resemblance to the hand of the imbecilic village idiot who, when the moon is full, peers through lighted windows in search of new specimens for his collection of severed heads. Eek! Are those his fingers closing round your throat? No, it's just the shawl you've put on to ward off the autumnal chill creeping into your living room.

Unnerved, the reader lowers the book and chews his fingernails. Wouldn't it be better to lay it aside? Bury it? Burn it? Wall it up? But it was so exciting! There! A distant chime like a death knell tolled by the black-clad Grim Reaper, who has come to . . . No, it was just your empty wineglass, which you jogged with your elbow. Ice-cold sweat beads your brow, your hair stands on end, your pulses race – and then there's a rustling sound: the Hair-Raiser on your lap has just turned a page by itself, a startling and unexpected phenomenon that almost gives you a heart attack . . .

I myself, dear readers, would have preferred to believe that such effects were achieved by literary skill alone, but it wasn't so, of course. The astonishing truth did not come out until decades later, when one of the authors who had attended the conference at Ignis Fatuus Castle made a deathbed confession.

For it wasn't the authors of the Hair-Raisers who had invested them with such suggestive power; it was the Bookemists. They had exchanged their professional secrets, especially where the manufacture of hypnotic perfumes was concerned. They had created an elixir with which book paper could be scented, thereby producing all the symptoms of fear described above, from goose pimples to heart failure. The horror stories the books contained were not one whit better or more effective than their predecessors – in fact, it didn't matter if they were worse. All the authors had to do was ensure that they embodied as many instances as possible of words such as *clammy*, *bony*, *eerie*, *gloomy*, *chilly*, *scary*, *spooky*, *deathly*, *gleerie*, *speathly* and *clooky*. This had sufficed to convince reviewers that literary magic was at work.

It was not only common or garden alchemy but illegal into the bargain, so Hair-Raisers were eventually banned. However, they enjoyed great popularity with collectors and continued to be read beneath the bedclothes, particularly by the young. I myself must have read Bamuel Courgette's *Screams from a Sarcophagus* at least twenty times, shuddering with undiminished pleasure as I inhaled its fear-inducing aroma again and again.

But none of this would be any reason to laugh, would it, dear readers? Nor was it grounds for hilarity that my mysterious host had lured me into a room full of volumes which the Zamonian public health authorities had classified as Hazardous Books, and which were bound, even now, to be exuding their hypnotic perfume.

Nor, above all, was it funny that the Hair-Raisers' dangerous aroma was already having an effect on me. I could hear the creak of coffin lids slowly opening, the demented laughter of Marsh Mummies, the sobbing of poor souls walled up alive. I could see severed hands scuttling across the library ceiling and the shadows of horned creatures flitting across the backs of the books. No, it wasn't funny.

The funny thing was, I found these things profoundly reassuring.

The funny thing was that, even in a library entirely devoted to horror stories – even in the midst of a nightmare come true: a subterranean castle with no exit – I didn't get the creeps and was imbued with a feeling of security by the very sight of some books I could actually read. That, dear readers, was why I couldn't help laughing long and loud.

Then I pulled myself together, partly because there's something rather pathetic about a person laughing to himself in solitary state. I took out a couple of Hair-Raisers, sat down in the armchair, drank the rest of the water, nibbled some bookworms and browsed for a while. And then, just as the Booklings' murmured recitations had lulled me to sleep, so I was swiftly but gently wafted into the arms of Morpheus by the wailing of Zombies, the giggling of Hazelwitches and the screams of ghostly Sirens. Hairy hands scampered across the floor and transparent bats fluttered round my head, but I couldn't have cared less. The last thing that went through my head was a quotation from Regenschein's poem, which I now understood somewhat better:

Of leather and of paper built,
worm-eaten through and through,
the castle known as Shadowhall
brings every nightmare true.

80

The Melancholy Ghost

By now it no longer worried me unduly that the walls moved and the floor rose and fell wherever I went. The whole of Shadowhall Castle seemed to be a gigantic mechanism in constant motion, not that I could discover any purpose behind it all. However, the purpose of the Rusty Gnomes' book machine in the Leather Grotto had also escaped me at first. Perhaps this castle was another of their megalomaniac structures.

I awoke in the Hair-Raiser library feeling rested and refreshed. No matter what appalling nightmares had made me toss and turn, I must have slept for hours on end. So I set off once more along the endless passages. Although I was still beset by spectral, transparent bats fluttering round my head, severed white hands crawling about on my cloak, shrill voices urging me to drown myself in the moat and other such phenomena, the hallucinogenic effects of the Bookemistic perfume wore off after a while and my head eventually cleared.

I was a guest at Shadowhall Castle, that much was certain. I had been provided with board and lodging. Meagre board and strange lodging, it was true, but all the same: someone not only tolerated my presence but might even be appreciating it. Although the fact that he had chosen Hair-Raisers, of all things, to be my goodnight reading matter might be symptomatic of an eccentric nature or a peculiar sense of humour, it did not necessarily imply evil intent. But what was I really, guest or prisoner? How long was my stay to be? Why was my mysterious host putting me up? I decided to construe the latest developments as an improvement in my general situation. Better to be put up by a phantom than pursued by Harpyrs, Spinxxxxes or Bookhunters.

Aeolian music came drifting along the passages. The longer and more attentively I listened, the less I could believe that it was generated by random currents of air. As in the case of the symbol-adorned caves leading to Shadowhall Castle, I detected certain recurrent patterns and themes. Given that these were far too strange be described as melodies or harmonies, a contradictory term – *melodious dissonances* – was the most apt description I could find for them. Sometimes I thought I heard voices or familiar musical instruments, but no life form known to me was capable of producing such ghostly, otherworldly sounds. No violin ever built could have brought forth those thin, crystalline notes and no brass instrument on earth those infinitely deep bass notes. If Shadowhall Castle was a gigantic machine, why shouldn't it also be a gigantic musical instrument? Why shouldn't its constantly shifting walls and rising and falling floors be simply a means of channelling currents of air like the complex pneumatic system of a trombophone? Just as the symbols outside had seemed to me to be the writing of some extraterrestrial race, so Shadowhall Castle's music seemed to have been composed on an alien planet.

Now and then I heard something rustle in the shadowy, more dimly lit reaches of the castle. The sound came sometimes from the floor, sometimes from the ceiling, and I occasionally thought I saw flitting shadows roughly the size of a cat. The disconcerting thing was, I could detect nothing animal or even insectile about their shape. If my eyes didn't deceive me in the subdued light, they appeared to be *rectangular*. I sometimes sensed that several of the things were in my vicinity, because the rustling sounds came from several dark corners at once and created a claustrophobic sensation of encirclement. As soon as I came to a lighter part of the castle I would hear the patter of many feet and glimpse those angular shadows disappearing into crevices in the walls. Once, in a particularly dark spot, I heard and felt something whoosh over my head like a bat with a hundred wings.

I explored lofty halls with fireplaces of monstrous size, chambers containing long refectory tables and petrified chairs. There were also benches, smaller tables and huge thrones, but all the furniture consisted of fossilised books. One gained the impression that the builders of Shadowhall Castle had subscribed to the architectural principle that everything must remain in its accustomed place, even if a tidal wave surged through the building.

Once, when I entered a small, square chamber, it was as if my weight had activated a mechanism of some kind, because the walls to left and right of me sank into the floor, disclosing other walls beyond them. These, too, sank into the floor, disclosing still other walls – and so on until the small, square room had transmuted itself into a long corridor whose extremities were lost in darkness.

On another occasion the contrary happened. I entered a long corridor from whose floor a series of walls suddenly rose until I was cooped up in a small room whose floor suddenly descended, taking me down a level. It was as if Shadowhall Castle were thoroughly capricious and permanently dissatisfied with my location, which was why it restlessly conveyed me from place to place. At other times nothing moved for hours on end and I was able to roam its subterranean chambers in peace.

I must have been wandering around for an entire day when I suddenly came across another paper trail on the floor of a passage. It led to a large dining room furnished with long stone tables and benches. Awaiting me on one of the tables, which had a throne built of books at one end, was a jug of water and a bowl of roots.

Dinner time! I accepted my mysterious host's invitation with a courteous bow to thin air and sat down on the fossilised throne. The water was fresh and ice-cold. The roots tasted, well, like roots, but they took the edge off my hunger. While eating I tried to imagine who had dined at these tables in ancient times, but my giant ant fantasy took over again. In my mind's eye I was surrounded by fellow diners with faceted eyes and scissorlike mandibles who cracked millipedes open and sucked out their guts with relish, simultaneously conversing in an insect language composed of clicks. Banishing this unpleasant vision, I finished off my frugal repast.

I got up from the table refreshed and reinvigorated, and I'm still glad in retrospect that what happened shortly afterwards did not overtake me at a moment when I was feeling weary and depressed. My sensitive authorial heart might not have withstood the shock.

I heard someone coming. Yes, I could distinctly hear someone approaching the dining room. I heard no footsteps, just the regular, stertorous breathing of some creature approaching the door. Was it my phantom host at last? Was the Shadow King on his way? I stood rooted to the spot, almost unable to move a muscle, as the asthmatic breathing drew steadily nearer.

The something entered the room. I say 'something' because I know of no word adequate to describe that indefinable apparition. It frightened me more, dear readers, than anything I'd so far encountered on my travels, which had abounded in frightening creatures. It was just a shadow, a transparent, faceless, indistinct, two-dimensional figure – just a grey silhouette. If anything approximated to my own idea of a disembodied spirit, it was this panting shadow that glided slowly across the room towards me. All I saw was a grey mist forever changing shape like a cloud of smoke being blown in my direction by the wind. Hundreds of voices seemed to whisper inside it, together with that hoarse, laboured breathing which moved me so strangely and made me feel so infinitely sad.

And then the shadow enveloped me too, from head to foot, and I felt it *pass right through me.* For one brief, crazy moment our two forms merged and a tidal wave of strange ideas, images, landscapes and creatures surged suddenly through my brain. Then it was over. The shadow had gone past, had flowed through me like water through a sieve. I turned, shivering, to stare after it. It simply glided on across the room as if it hadn't even noticed me. I now saw that it was leaving a trail, a thin trail of moisture such as snails leave behind them, and I bent to touch it before it evaporated. Everything I did at that moment was unconscious and instinctive. My brain was uninvolved, for under reasonably normal circumstances I would never have acted as I did. Never! I touched the damp trail, put my paw to my lips and licked it.

The moisture was tears.

I realised only then that the shadow wasn't panting; it was sobbing. Having reached the end of the room, it melted into the darkness of the passage beyond.

89

The Animatomes

I was still standing on the spot where the shadow had passed through me, trying to collect my thoughts and analyse my feelings like someone abruptly roused from a violent nightmare.

Was that really the Shadow King? If so, he bore no relation to all the stories about him. He hadn't impressed me as a creature that could harm someone, still less cut off Hunk Hoggno's head or strike terror into a Harpyr. Or had that been only one of many forms he could assume? What were those curious images and unintelligible ideas he had sluiced through my brain and borne away with him? I couldn't remember a thing about them.

I hurried in pursuit, fervently hoping that he hadn't vanished into Shadowhall's labyrinthine recesses. Fortunately, there was the trail of tears he had left behind. It led along the passage, across a big, dark, empty chamber, into a narrow, torchlit corridor, and finally up a flight of stairs. They were the first stairs I'd seen in Shadowhall. I certainly hadn't been in this part of the castle before.

The stairs ended in a lofty passage lit by candles in sconces on one side of it. On the other side were some tall, narrow windows with nothing visible beyond them but a dark void. Shadowhall's weird, persistent music continued to whisper in my ears. I hurried on, faithfully following the trail of moisture, which now led through a big archway filled with dancing light. I could once more hear the stertorous breathing, the sobs and whispering voices, but they now seemed to issue from more than one throat. Beyond the archway I found myself looking down into a torchlit chamber more spacious than any I had seen hitherto. It was laid out like an amphitheatre. I was standing at its highest point, looking down over the tiers of seats at a large stage in the centre. And that, dear readers, was where I saw a spectacle that genuinely moved me to tears.

Hundreds of the shadowy creatures were restlessly passing through each other, whispering and sobbing. I saw them melt and merge, glide through each other and draw apart. Others came in through the numerous entrances round about and descended the steps to mingle with the throng on the stage. Here in the amphitheatre the music of Shadowhall Castle had greatly increased in volume. It sounded like a discordant funeral march accompanied by a chorus of sighs and sobs, and the weeping shadows seemed to be dancing to it.

Tears welled up in my eyes. I too began to weep, strangely moved by this ineffably sad and fantastic scene – until another wave of thoughts and images surged through me quite as suddenly and surprisingly as in the dining room. One of the shadowy creatures, which had entered behind my back, had simply passed straight through me. It now glided down the steps to join its own kind on the stage. This was too much. I turned and fled back through the gateway.

I continued to weep outside in the passage, why and for how long I've no idea, but my tears had a soothing and reassuring effect. When they finally ceased to flow I felt strong enough to return to the amphitheatre – even, perhaps, to mingle with the dancing shadows and fathom this latest addition to the castle's mysteries.

When I turned round, however, the gateway was shut – bricked up by a wall of fossilised books that had silently erected itself behind me. The music, too, had fallen silent as though walled up inside. I strained my ears but could hear nothing, not a sound. The foregoing episode might never have occurred. And to be honest, dear readers, I wished it hadn't, because my poor brain was now beset by a host of unanswered questions.

There was a sudden rustle behind me. I spun round, and this time I really did see something: a dark, rectangular object disappearing into one of the passages that led off my own. Being now in the right frame of mind to wrest every last secret from this accursed place, I boldly dashed in pursuit.

The passage was only dimly lit by a few isolated candles, so I was never able to get a really clear view of the little object zigzagging ahead of me from one pool of shadow to the next.

We rounded numerous corners, turned left and right, raced up one flight of stairs and down another, but I remained hot on the diminutive creature's heels. We sped up a spiral staircase that stopped short at a rusty iron grating. The shadowy little thing slipped through it with ease; I could only stand there cursing.

I was about to turn back when the grating creaked open and I continued to climb. The staircase spiralled upwards for a couple more turns and came out in a large room.

It reminded me of the Hair-Raiser library: the same octagonal shape, the walls lined with bookcases, the armchair, the central table with the candlestick on it – for a moment I thought I'd found my way back there.

But there was something different about the place. Perhaps I missed the hallucinogenic perfume, or perhaps the books were differently arranged. This certainly wasn't the same library and I couldn't see the little creature anywhere.

The books were real enough, though, and I thought they might assist me in some way. I went over to one of the shelves, took out an ancient leather-bound tome and opened it.

And froze.

In the central margin between the pages was a single, blinking eye. The book was staring at me in alarm, just like the Animatome Al had shown me in the Leather Grotto. My reaction was just as horrified as it had been then: I dropped it.

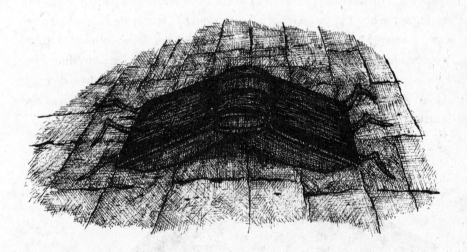

It hit the floor with a crash and rustled indignantly. Then half a dozen little legs sprouted from the fore-edge and bore it away. It scuttled off and made straight for the opposite wall, where it crawled up the shelves and disappeared into a crack between two big leather-bound volumes.

I turned on the spot. There were rustles all round me, and the backs of one or two books began to move almost imperceptibly. No, these were no Hair-

Raisers, even if their behaviour was enough to make a person's hair stand on end. This whole library was alive! All those little rectangular shadows were books, of course. Live books, *Animatomes*!

> *Of leather and of paper built,*
> *worm-eaten through and through . . .*

Were Animatomes something in the nature of rats? Were they Shadowhall Castle's vermin? Had they originated in the Bookemists' laboratories and found their way here via the rubbish dump of Unholm? Had they actually bred here? A fascinating notion: books capable of reproducing themselves and banding together into a library on their own initiative. I wondered what the little creatures found to eat within these barren walls, but then, I had probably explored only a small proportion of the castle.

I scanned the room again. If all these books were really Animatomes, the collection must be worth a fortune. I took another volume from a shelf and opened it. The interior resembled a mouthful of needle-sharp teeth. I was still staring at the book in amazement when it emitted a menacing snarl and bit my paw. I uttered a yell – 'Ouch! That hurts!' – but the confounded thing wouldn't let go. Still snarling, it sank its teeth yet deeper in my bleeding paw. I yelled again, this time with rage, and pounded the cover with my other fist. At last it relaxed its grip and fell to the floor. It sprouted eight little legs and scuttled off into a corner, whence it growled at me viciously.

The shelves around me were stirring. Leather squeaked against leather, paper rustled and crackled, little piping voices could be heard. The Animatomes were waking up, roused by their colleague's growls or the scent of my blood. For after that vicious bite, dear readers, I felt certain that these were not only Animatomes but Hazardous Books as well – a savage, bloodthirsty subspecies of the domesticated Animatomes in the Leather Grotto. And I could guess what they fed on. It was time to get out of there fast!

I took a couple of swift steps towards the head of the stairs that had brought me to the library, but there was nothing there, just a wall.

I looked around, trying to estimate my chances. How many books were there? A few hundred? All right, they weren't Spinxxxxes or Harpyrs, they were vermin, nothing more. Vermin are cowardly. If I disposed of a few of them quickly enough the rest would come to heel. I was a dinosaur, after all. I possessed claws and teeth. Having survived Unholm's rubbish dump and a ride on the Rusty Gnomes' Bookway, I should be able to deal with a few shelves of mutated books.

I heard a rumble beneath me and the floor began to vibrate. Then it descended, taking me with it. Well, that was fine with me. Perhaps this unexpected development would put some distance between me and the Animatomes.

But all that happened was that the walls grew. The further the floor descended, the more books it revealed, all of them in the process of waking up. When it finally came to rest the bookcases were at least four times higher than before. I would now have to contend with thousands of vermin, not hundreds.

The first of them were already descending on me. It surprised me that they came from the topmost shelves, but I realised why when they opened their covers in free fall and proceeded to flap their pages: they were *flying* Animatomes – the bat variety. A whole flock of them swooped down and soared round my head, screeching savagely. Where normal books were cut off flush at the head, these possessed little mouths armed with tiny teeth that gnashed at me avidly.

Other Animatomes behaved like snakes. They emerged from the bookcases very slowly, their leathery bodies stretching and contracting in an elastic, rhythmical manner, and they hissed like venomous Midgard cobras.

The most unpleasant specimens walked on eight legs, spider fashion. More agile and aggressive than the snakelike variety, they struck me as being capable of committing the worst atrocities. I couldn't tell which way up they were. They could change direction at lightning speed, confronting me with their leather backs and rustling pages alternately, and they kept rotating on the spot. I had no idea what they would use to bite or sting me with, but doubtless I would find out soon enough.

So the Animatomes hemmed me in on all sides. The circle round me drew ever tighter as more and more of them came creeping, crawling or fluttering out of the bookcases. If I didn't very soon shake off the paralysis that had gripped me, they would bury me beneath them and tear me to pieces.

I'm rather embarrassed to admit this, dear readers, but I was suddenly, to my shame, reminded of a maxim in *The Way of the Bookhunter*, Rongkong Koma's awful, shoddily written autobiography. To be precise, I was reminded of his Rule No. 3:

Anything alive can be killed.

Yes, a book that was alive and moving could be killed – that sounded logical, didn't it? This merciless underworld had taught me a lesson or two and the time had come at last to put them into effect.

I dealt one of the flying books a swingeing blow with my paw in mid air. The pages went flying everywhere, whole swaths of them, before its remains tumbled to the floor, where I crushed them underfoot. Its innards gurgled and blood as black as printer's ink went spurting in all directions. I took advantage of the universal consternation this caused to stamp on two snakelike specimens in my immediate vicinity. They emitted a startled hiss and lay still.

Another two swipes of the paw, and the airborne books I'd hit

disintegrated into a blizzard of fluttering
pages. The rest of the squadron went into
a steep climb that took them out of range.

Meanwhile, I readdressed myself to
the Animatomes' ground forces. I stamped
on another book snake, strode over its
remains to one of the bookcases and
wrenched at it. The heavy piece of furniture
toppled over and crashed to the floor, burying
dozens of spiderlike specimens beneath it. A cloud of
dust went up as it disintegrated into countless splinters and
fragments of wood. Having selected the longest and sharpest of these, I went
hunting the Animatomes, which fled in all directions. They crawled up the
walls and bookcases, and the flying specimens hovered as near the ceiling as
possible. The crawling specimens came off worst, being too slow. I transfixed
them with my makeshift spear, one after another. When I'd skewered at least
a dozen I brandished the weapon triumphantly, threw back my head and gave
a bestial roar like the one I'd uttered in the Rusty Gnomes' railroad station.
All the bookcases shook, together with the Animatomes still on the shelves.

Then absolute silence fell.

The surviving Animatomes had fled to the upper reaches of the library and
were keeping as still as mice. I hurled my shish kebab of kicking, writhing
books into the dust and surveyed the battlefield, breathing heavily. Isolated
pages were floating through the air and the floor was awash with inky, black
blood. I had conformed to the barbarous ways of the catacombs.

I had become a Bookhunter.

85

Homuncolossus

The Animatomes lingered a while in the upper reaches of the library, apparently conferring in whispers. Then I noticed that their numbers were steadily diminishing. I could hear them rustling and scuttling around behind the bookcases, so I overturned each bookcase in turn until I exposed a big hole in the wall, their secret exit and entrance. Squeezing through this, I made my way along the passage beyond it but failed to encounter a single Animatome. After roaming unfamiliar parts of the castle for another few hours, I simply stretched out on the ground and fell into a deep, exhausted sleep.

I had a wonderful dream in which I could fly. Without any effort on my part, my body rose from the cold floor and floated along the castle's interminable passages, light as thistledown carried on the breeze. I floated up and down long flights of stairs, through lofty chambers in which big wood fires were burning, and across rooms lit by hundreds of candles.

I awoke at last to find that I really was in a different part of the castle. Had I been sleepwalking? Had Shadowhall's mysterious mechanisms transported me there, or had someone carried me there in my swoonlike slumbers?

Then I smelt smoke. A fire? A conflagration? Alarmed, I got up and set off in the direction from which the smoke was coming. Before long I could hear the hiss and crackle of burning wood. Ahead of me was a tall, narrow doorway that emitted a flickering glow. Cautiously, I drew nearer and, after a moment's hesitation, peered in.

And there he was, the Shadow King himself! Believe me, dear readers, I have never seen a lovelier, wilder, more awe-inspiring sight than the monarch of the shadows dancing amid the fires burning round him. Nor had I ever seen a sadder sight, for his dance was an antidote to loneliness. The leaping flames multiplied his shadow many times, projecting it this way and that, so that it looked as if he was in the best of company.

At the same time I felt frightened. He was big and strong, at least twice my height, and he vaulted the flames with a series of prodigious leaps. All that I could see of him, even now, was his dark figure silhouetted against them, but

I recognised his beauty, the beauty of a wild, untamed beast. He had to be the most remarkable creature in the catacombs of Bookholm.

And then he laughed. Pausing with his back to me, he lowered his arms and gave a full-throated laugh. Now I really did feel frightened, because his voice had a rustling, rattling quality that made it sound as if it came from another world, a world of darkness and death.

'Come with me!' he said.

I flinched at the words, which hit me like a whiplash, just as the Harpyr had flinched at the sound of his sigh. He had spotted me long ago. I now saw that his silhouette looked curiously angular, as if he were wearing a bizarre suit of armour and a many-pointed crown. He threaded his way between the fires and disappeared through a dark doorway. I followed him obediently.

The adjacent chamber was a throne room, the throne room of the loneliest king on earth. It contained only one piece of furniture, the throne itself, a massive winged armchair constructed of fossilised books. He was already seated in it by the time I entered.

I still couldn't see him clearly because the room was only sparsely lit by a few candles and the Shadow King had withdrawn into the throne's recesses.

The floor was strewn with books. As I hesitantly approached, many of them rose on their little legs and scuttled off or crawled out of my way. My reputation had evidently preceded me.

'Are you a Bookhunter?' asked the Shadow King. His hoarse, unearthly voice pierced me to the marrow. I came to an involuntary halt.

'No,' I replied. 'I merely defended myself. My interest in books is of another kind. I'm a writer.'

'Really?' said the Shadow King. 'What books have you written?'

I broke out in a sweat. 'None as yet,' I replied. 'I mean, none that have been published.'

'So you still can't write books,' the Shadow King said, 'but you can already kill them. Are you sure you wouldn't prefer to be a literary critic?'

Unable to think of a witty reply, I said nothing.

'What is your name?'

'Optimus Yarnspinner.'

A long silence.

'You come from Lindworm Castle?'

'Yes. That's obvious, I'm afraid.'

335

'What are you doing in the catacombs of Bookholm?'

'I was brought here against my will,' I replied. 'A literary scholar and antiquarian named Pfistomel Smyke drugged me with a poisoned book and hauled me off to the catacombs. I've been roaming around here ever since.'

An even longer silence.

'And who are *you*?' I ventured to ask, if only to relieve the tension a little. 'If I may make so bold.'

An even longer and more awkward silence ensued.

'I have many names,' he murmured at length. 'Mephistas. Soter. Eevel. Existion. Tetragrammaton. The Demidwarfs in the upper caves call me Keron Kenken. The Dark Folk in the lower labyrinths refer to me as Ningo Spora Doodung Mgo Gyuli Thorchugg – I can hardly remember it all myself.'

'Are you . . . the Shadow King?' I asked.

'That's the silliest name of all,' he said. 'It's what they call me on the surface, isn't it? Yes, if you like, I'm the Shadow King too, but the name I like best is the one I was given by my direst foe. He christened me Homuncolossus. It's the most appropriate name of all.'

'Was it you that killed Hunk Hoggno?'

'No. Hoggno killed himself with his own axe. I merely guided his hand,'

I nodded. 'Then you also laid the trail?'

'I did.'

'But why? Why don't you kill me? Why are you helping me?'

Homuncolossus sighed and sank back even deeper into the throne's shadowy recesses. 'I could tell you a story,' he said. 'Would you like to hear it?'

'I like stories,' I replied.

'It's a rather weird story, mark you.'

I shooed away a few Animatomes that had ventured nearer again and sat down on the floor.

'Weird stories are the best,' I said.

336

♂♀

The Shadow King's Story

I had been hoping that the Shadow King would show me his face at last, but he preferred to conceal his true exterior in the dim recesses of his throne.

'To some degree,' he began, 'this is the story of someone I used to know – an old friend whom I remember sometimes gladly and sometimes far less so, because the recollection saddens me so much. Isn't it absurd that tears should spring to your eyes far more readily at the memory of good times than bad?'

He didn't seem to expect an answer to this question, because he went on at once. 'This friend was a man, a member of the human species, one of the few that still dared to go on living in Zamonia and hadn't yet emigrated to other continents. He lived with his parents in one of the small human colonies in the Midgard Range, where a few survivors are said to be hiding to this day.

'This friend was a writer when he came into the world. I don't mean that he could write at birth – no, he learnt to do so later on, like everyone else – but he was already brimming with ideas and stories when he first saw the light of day. His little head was filled to bursting with them, and they frightened him, especially at night, when it was dark. His one desire was to get rid of these stories, but he didn't know how. Talking wasn't his forte and he hadn't yet learnt to write, so new ideas kept flowing into his brain from all quarters. They weighed it down to such an extent that he spent his entire childhood going around with his head bowed.'

A puff of wind caressed my cheek and extinguished a nearby candle. As if to order, Shadowhall's weird music had started up again.

'At last he learnt to write and was able to unload all that ballast,' the Shadow King went on. 'It flowed out of him like the ink from his pen, which covered square miles of paper. He simply couldn't stop writing, nor had he any wish to, because that was what made him feel best of all: putting stories down on paper.'

The Shadow King paused for a moment. 'Is this a story that might interest you?' he asked. 'Or am I boring you?'

So it was to be a story about a writer. Without meaning to be unkind, dear readers, I'd had something more exciting in mind. His promise of a weird story had summoned up visions of Spinxxxxes and Harpyrs, Bookhunters and masses of gore. I certainly hadn't been expecting a story about a writer. Stories about writers were about as exciting as a peek at the dusty shelves in the Booklings' Chamber of Marvels. Nonetheless, I shook my head.

'In that case,' the Shadow King said with a laugh, 'I suppose I shall have to make a bigger effort to bore you. My friend had had little experience of life when he wrote his earliest stories, so they were pretty nonsensical. On the other hand, he was knowledgeable in a strange, dark, primordial way. He knew things that could only have happened in alien, far-off worlds or other dimensions. He described creatures that existed in the voids between the stars, and he knew their strange thoughts, dreams and desires. He described a place on the bed of an ocean composed of gas and inhabited by venomous creatures that fought, loved and killed each other in its depths. Nobody knew where he got all these preposterous ideas, and some people thought he wasn't quite right in the head.'

The Shadow King's breathing sounded like paper bags being slowly inflated and deflated.

'My friend couldn't watch clouds scudding past without visualising an epic tale about a race of Cloud Folk. To him, no rushing stream was without its colony of water sprites, no meadow without its army of blades of grass on the march. Insects flitting round his head recounted their little life stories. Ants from rival nests waged war so that he could chronicle their sanguinary battles.

'Because his parents and playmates poked fun at his stories, he felt misunderstood and started to write for a readership of disembodied spirits. For them he devised, constructed, moulded, polished and portrayed a world in which every word and emotion, every creature and event, every letter and incident was in its proper place. Once that world was complete – once it had been fully committed to paper and purged of spelling mistakes and errors of style – he felt sure that his readers would come and live in it with him. It would be a world of the mind constructed by his own mind and inhabited by many others.

'So he erected it word by word, sentence by sentence, chapter by chapter. He carefully superimposed syllable on syllable, linked words together, piled paragraph on paragraph. They were curious edifices, the tales he invented, many woven entirely out of dreams and others built of fears and premonitions.

'He constructed an abode for those who had frozen to death, a palace of snow and ice, and peopled it with snow crystals that floated along its frozen passages and filled them with their tinkling song.

'He created a lake for victims of drowning, one on which drowned children could drift peacefully aboard waterlily leaves and make friends with frogs and lotus blossoms.

'He kindled a blaze for those who had been burnt to death – an immense conflagration that roared like a forest fire and billowed like a storm-tossed sea – in which their ghosts could dance for ever in the form of leaping flames, oblivious of their terrible agony.

'He built a home for those who had done away with themselves, the *Teardrop Hotel*, with walls of eternal rain.

'Last of all, he built a refuge for those who had died insane. The biggest and most magnificent edifice of all, it was painted in iridescent colours that did not exist in reality. It also conformed to laws of its own: you could walk on its ceilings and time went backwards.

'One day, while studying his reflection in a mirror, my friend saw how perfectly it reproduced his grimaces and facial contortions. "I want to become like this being in the mirror," he thought. "I want to be able to imitate life just as perfectly. I want to be just as lonely."'

There was a brief pause.

'It sounds as if your friend was losing his mind,' I blurted out. 'As if he needed to consult a psychiatrist.'

The Shadow King gave a terrible laugh.

'Yes, that's what he himself thought at times. But his illness never attained the merciful degree of severity that would have entitled him to a spell in a lunatic asylum and absolved him from further work. It wasn't quite severe enough for a lunatic; only for a writer.'

I couldn't help laughing myself. It seemed that the Shadow King possessed something akin to a sense of humour, albeit of a rather black kind.

'My friend saw that things couldn't go on this way, or he would wind up in a straitjacket. He realised that he must address himself more to earthly matters, so he quit his illusory edifice, left it to crumble into wonderful ruins which he seldom revisited, and concentrated on his surroundings.'

The Shadow King inserted another brief pause, breathing heavily as if all this talking were something of a strain. I seized the opportunity to survey my own surroundings. I'm sure they were not so unlike the conditions that may have prevailed inside the mysterious writer's castles in the air. Ghostly music came wafting across the throne room and the Animatomes, which had formed a circle round the Shadow King at a respectful distance, seemed to be listening to him attentively. Then again, perhaps they were only listening to the strange modulations in his voice.

'My friend the writer now described the simplest things he could find,' he went on, 'and discovered that it was the hardest thing in the world. It was easy enough to describe a palace built of ice and snow but incredibly difficult to write about a single hair. Or a spoon. Or a nail. Or a grain of salt. Or a splinter. Or a candle flame. Or a drop of water. He became a chronicler of the most mundane, everyday events and jotted down the most trivial conversations in his vicinity with such perseverance and self-discipline that he turned into a walking notebook that automatically converted all he saw and heard into literature. And, as before, he realised just in time that this was leading him down a blind alley.'

'If he hadn't,' I ventured to remark, 'he would probably have become a clerk or a stenographer in some government office in Atlantis.'

'Precisely,' said the Shadow King. 'My friend was close to despair. The more he wrote the less his words seemed to convey. He ended by being unable to write at all. For days, weeks and months he sat in front of a blank sheet of paper and failed to produce a single sentence. He was already toying with the idea of checking into the Teardrop Hotel and hanging himself with an imaginary rope. And then, out of the blue, he underwent what was probably the most crucial and gratifying experience of a lifetime.'

'He found a publisher?' I interjected.

The Shadow King remained silent long enough for me to feel thoroughly ashamed of my inane remark.

'He was pervaded by the Orm,' he said at length. 'So suddenly and intensely, he thought at first that he wouldn't survive.'

Did the Shadow King really believe in the Orm? No matter how deeply one delved into this continent, it seemed impossible to find a place where no one believed in that hoary old myth. However, I refrained from making another flippant remark.

'The Orm flowed through him quite suddenly. It liberated his spirit and sent it soaring up to a place in the universe where all the artistic ideas in existence intersected and merged. It was a planet devoid of substance and life, devoid of a single atom of matter, but endowed with such concentrated creativity that it made the stars around it dance. There one could plunge into pure imagination and become charged with more energy than most people are granted in a lifetime. One brief second in that field of force sufficed to give birth to a novel. It was a preposterous place where all the laws of nature seemed to be in abeyance, where dimensions lay in untidy stacks like rejected manuscripts, where death was merely a stupid joke and eternity a bat of an eyelid. My friend returned from there filled to bursting with words, sentences and ideas, all so thoroughly polished and prefabricated that he had only to write them down. He was half delighted, half dismayed by the excellence of what flowed from his pen and by how little he himself had contributed to it.'

No wonder so many would-be authors fantasised about the Orm, I thought. The Shadow King had just defined the dream of every lazy writer: simply pick up a pen and the whole thing will write itself. Some hope!

'It was only now, after my friend had written this story under the influence of the Orm and read it again and again, that he truly felt like a writer. He eventually summoned up the courage to send it to Lindworm Castle with a covering letter.'

'Lindworm Castle?' I said, dumbfounded. The sudden mention of my home had hit me like a punch in the solar plexus.

'Well, that's what young Zamonian writers do when they think they've written something worth submitting. They send it to one of their idols in Lindworm Castle.'

True, the castle was positively inundated with manuscripts from youthful writers.

'In my friend's case the idol's name was Dancelot Wordwright,' said the Shadow King.

Whoomph! A second punch in the solar plexus. I was sitting down, fortunately, or my knees would have given way.

'Dancelot Wordwright?' I repeated in a daze.

'Yes. Do you know him?'

'He's . . . he was my authorial godfather.'

'Well, well, what a coincidence.' The Shadow King cleared his throat.

'Just a minute,' I said. 'Your friend wrote Dancelot a letter? Sent him a manuscript? Sought his opinion and advice?'

'Yes, but you're welcome to finish the story yourself if you like. *You're* the author here, after all.'

'So sorry,' I said.

'Very well. To cut a long story short, Dancelot was delighted with my friend's story. He advised him to go to Bookholm at once and look for a publisher there, which he did. My friend spent the first few days roaming the streets. Then, one day, he was accosted by a literary agent on the lookout for talented young writers and showed him a few of his literary efforts. The agent's name was Claudio Harpstick.'

'Harpstick?!' I almost shouted the name.

'You know him too?'

'Yes,' I said dully.

'Another coincidence, eh?' said the Shadow King. 'Life is full of surprises, isn't it? Well, Harpstick could make precious little of my friend's writings, but he stood him a bee-bread and gave him the address of a literary expert named—'

'Pfistomel Smyke!'

'Exactly, Pfistomel Smyke. The kindly benefactor who consigned you to the catacombs. My friend called on Smyke and showed him some of his stuff. Poems, short stories, a copy of the story he'd sent to Lindworm Castle and so on. Smyke asked for twenty-four hours in which to assess his work. When my friend returned the next day, Smyke was completely beside himself with enthusiasm. He predicted that my friend had a great future and described him as the greatest talent he'd ever discovered. Smyke had already worked out a sophisticated strategy for launching my friend's literary career and drawn up some complicated contracts – he'd even chosen the typeface that would suit his work best, or so he said. Before all these things could be put into effect, however, Smyke said he wanted to show my friend something important: a passage in a book.'

'No!' I cried, almost as if I could still prevent an accomplished fact.

'No?' the Shadow King repeated indignantly. 'You want me to stop?'

I shook my head.

'Forgive me,' I said.

'Smyke got out a book adorned with the symbol of the Triadic Circle. At his bidding, my friend leafed through it until he came to page 333. Then he lost consciousness, because the book was a so-called Hazardous Book impregnated with a poison that anaesthetised him on contact.'

There was another long pause.

'And this,' the Shadow King said at length, '– *this is where my story really begins.*'

That was too much. I flung up my arms to stop him in his tracks. If I didn't blurt out my suspicion now, I would explode.

'Please,' I exclaimed, '– please answer me one question: are . . . are you the writer who sent that manuscript to Dancelot? Are you yourself the friend you keep talking about? You simply must tell me!'

The Shadow King uttered an even more terrible, embittered laugh than before.

'Do I look like it?' he demanded. 'Do I look like a *human being*?'

No, he really didn't, I had to admit. Or at least, what I had so far seen of him did not. From the little I knew of the human species, he was almost twice the height of an average man. I was stumped for a reply that wouldn't offend him.

'Tell me,' he repeated in a cold, peremptory tone. 'Do I look like a human being?'

'No,' I replied meekly.

'Very well,' he said. 'In that case, perhaps I may be permitted to finish my story. I propose to do so without any further interruptions – unless I myself consider it appropriate to insert a pause for dramatic effect. Are we agreed?'

'Yes,' I muttered.

The Shadow King drew several deep, soothing breaths.

'When my friend regained consciousness,' he went on quietly, 'he thought he was under water. But the fluid surrounding him had curious properties that ordinary water doesn't possess. It was warm and slimy, and he could breathe it! Through the glass side of the aquarium in which he was imprisoned he could see Smyke tinkering with some alchemistic laboratory equipment. The fluid was not only around him, it was everywhere: it filled his throat, his respiratory tracts, his auditory canals, his lungs. Still paralysed and unable to lift a finger, he was floating in an upright position. His body neither rose nor fell.

'Smyke came over to the aquarium. He grinned, tapped the glass with his numerous knuckles and spoke to my friend, who could hear his voice just as someone buried alive might hear the voices of mourners round the grave through his coffin and the layers of earth on top of it.

'"You're awake at last," said Smyke. "You slept so well, so soundly and for so long. Long enough for me to get everything ready for the grand transubstantiation. Yes, my human friend, I'm going to transform you. Then you won't be human any more, oh no! You'll be a superior being, understand?" He tapped the glass again. "I'm going to help you to acquire a new body, one that will suit your authorial brain far better. What's more, I'm going to help you to acquire a new existence. No need to thank me. It'll be a pleasure."

'My friend was panic-stricken. The fluid became steadily warmer, then hot – unbearably hot. Big bubbles rose slowly, sluggishly before his eyes and it dawned on him that the fluid was beginning to seethe. He was being boiled alive.

'Smyke gave another tap on the glass. "Now you know how a lobster feels," he called. "Chefs claim a lobster feels nothing, but I think that's a lie. I can't say I envy you your unique experience."

'My friend lapsed into merciful unconsciousness. He dreamt that Bookholm was being consumed by a vast conflagration. Then he perceived that he himself was the fire-raiser – that he was striding through the city like a human torch, setting house after house ablaze. In his dream he was the Darkman of Bookholm, whom legend credits with having caused the city's first great fire.

'Then he came to again. Smyke seemed to be standing right in front of him, because all he could see was the Shark Grub's face. But he still couldn't move a muscle, even now. To his astonishment, Smyke was cupping his head in two of his little hands, almost as if he were about to kiss him. My friend was relieved to find that the fluid had disappeared and that he was once more surrounded by air.

'"Oh dear," said Smyke, sounding genuinely regretful, "you've woken up at an inopportune moment. Please don't think I've done this to you on purpose. It's just a stupid mischance, but the anaesthetic in your brain can be capricious. Well, now that this has happened I'm going to show you a unique sight – one that is seldom granted to any living creature."

'Smyke turned my friend's head in another direction. He could now see a laboratory table with a silver bowl on it. Floating in the bowl, which was filled with milky liquid, was a human arm.

'"Yes," said Smyke, "that's *your* arm. The one you write with!"

'Then he turned my friend's head in another direction. Standing on a pedestal was a tall, thin jar of some clear fluid, and immersed in it was a neatly severed leg.

'"And that's one of your legs," said Smyke. "The left one, I think." He laughed.

'Again he altered the direction of my friend's gaze. Lying on a dissecting table was a torso from which the arms, legs and head had been removed. The raw stumps had been discreetly draped with muslin cloths.

'"That's your torso. I'm in the process of disinfecting the incisions with an alchemical solution. Yes, you really have woken up at an awkward moment. We're just at the dissection phase. It's essential to aesthymise the separate body parts carefully. But don't worry, I shall sew them together again in the correct order. I'm quite skilled with a needle."

'A figure came into view beyond the torso. It was Claudio Harpstick, the literary agent, holding a saw and wearing a white apron liberally bespattered with blood. He gave my friend an amiable smile and brandished the saw, which was also smeared with blood.

'That was when my friend grasped the truth at last. This was no nightmare. He really was in Smyke's laboratory, but he wasn't standing in front of him, as he'd thought, because his body was scattered around the laboratory in several pieces. Smyke was holding up his severed head and turning it to and fro.

'And then Smyke tossed the head into the air like a ball. For one ghastly moment my friend had an aerial view of the whole laboratory complete with its mysterious appliances, glass vessels and powerful alchemical batteries. He caught another glimpse of his separate body parts and saw Harpstick and the Shark Grub staring up at him in amusement. Then gravity reasserted itself and his head fell back into Smyke's hands.

'"The next time you wake up," said Smyke, "you'll be a different person."

'My friend relapsed into profound unconsciousness.

'The next time he awoke he really was standing upright, because he could feel his body beneath him and was all too conscious of the pain that racked his limbs. Looking down at himself, he discovered that he was firmly secured to a vertical wooden board. His entire body was swathed in sheets of ancient paper covered with unfamiliar symbols. He tried to free himself but was utterly immobilised by iron clamps round his wrists and ankles, neck and thighs. He was still in the laboratory. Then Pfistomel Smyke and Claudio Harpstick swam into his field of vision.

'"Ah, he's awake again," Smyke exclaimed delightedly. "Look, Claudio!"'

'"Did you fasten those clamps securely?" Harpstick asked in an anxious tone.

'"See how big he is," said Smyke. "A regular colossus!"'

'They had come right up to my friend, and he wondered why he was looking down at them. He seemed to have grown overnight.

'"You must be wondering about all that paper," Smyke went on. "You probably think it's part of some silly Bookemistic ritual and will soon be removed, but it isn't and it won't. Far from it!"'

Something about the Shadow King's tone rang an alarm bell in my head, dear readers. I had been spellbound by his vivid account of this exciting horror story, but now his narrative flow dried up. He seemed to be in the grip of some powerful emotion, and the frightening quality in his voice was gaining the upper hand.

'"No, far from it!" cried the Shadow King, still in the role of Smyke. "That integument of yours is far more than a sheet of Bookemistic wrapping paper. It's your new skin! I made you a promise and I've kept it: I've transformed you into a new creature!"'

I jumped to my feet in a single movement, for the Shadow King had suddenly begun to rise from his throne. Leaning on the arms, he slowly heaved himself erect. His voice became as thunderous and awe-inspiring as the roar of a wounded lion.

'And Pfistomel Smyke said to my friend, "You used to be a human being and now you're a monster! You used to be small and now you're a giant. I am your creator and you are my creation. 'Homunculus' is the alchemists' name for the little manikins they try to create. *You* I shall call . . . *Homuncolossus!*"'

As he uttered that name, dear readers, the Shadow King emerged into the candlelight and I saw his true stature for the first time. A shrill cry escaped my lips and I retreated several steps like the Animatomes, which recoiled at the horrific sight.

The creature confronting me was swathed from head to foot in paper. All that still recalled a human being was the shape of its body. It had arms, legs, a torso, a head – even a face. Everything was there, but made up of countless layers of ancient, yellowing paper – thousands of snippets covered with the same strange runes that had adorned the paper trail I'd followed through the catacombs. What I had mistaken in the gloom for the points of a crown were the jagged scraps of paper from which the creature had been fabricated. If a stone or bronze statue had suddenly sprung to life, it could not have terrified me more than this gigantic artificial being made of paper, which was slowly advancing on me.

'No,' said the Shadow King, and his tone became more menacing with every word he uttered and every step he took, 'I have ceased to be human. No longer am I the writer you have been seeking all this time. I used to be him. Now I am something new and different – something far greater. I am a monster. A murderer. A hunter. I am the king of Shadowhall Castle. I am . . . Homuncolossus!'

8 ⟩

Exiled to Darkness

I stood there without moving and got ready to die. There was no point in trying to escape from such a monster, it would only have prolonged my agony to no avail. Homuncolossus had lured me into his murky kingdom with revenge in mind: I was to die on behalf of all who had done him an injustice. He bore down on me with the calm self-assurance of a mighty predator that knows how futile it would be for its quarry to run away. His face had a certain bizarre beauty, even if it was the mask of a monster. His nose, lips and ears were composed of skilfully assembled layers of paper, and I could well imagine how patiently and lovingly Pfistomel Smyke had modelled them with his abundance of little hands. Even Homuncolossus's teeth consisted of jagged pieces of parchment, possibly stiffened with resin, judging by the way their golden tips glinted in the candlelight. Most terrible of all, however, were his eyes: just two black cavities where the eyeballs should have been.

I now saw, too, that he did not consist entirely of paper. His shoulder joints, elbows, knees, hips and neck were coated with a brownish, elastic substance resembling leather. Of course! It was leather that held the pages of

347

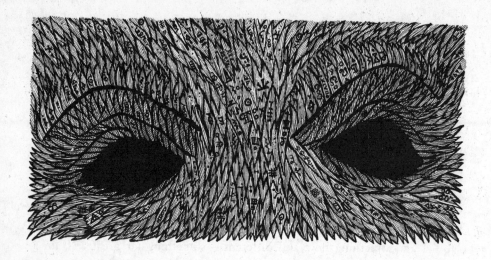

a book together, so it was only natural that the same should apply to this creature. Being a stickler for quality, Smyke was bound to have used the finest bookbinder's leather.

When he was only an arm's length from me, Homuncolossus bent down. He was now so close that his breath, which was laden with a strangely agreeable smell of old books, fanned my cheeks.

'Well,' he said, 'how about it? Do you want to hear the rest of my story?'

I nodded, although I thought he was merely indulging in a last, sinister jest before slitting my throat with his paper talons.

But all he said was 'Very well. You're doubtless wondering about this paper body of mine. Why am I a prisoner down here, although a big, strong creature like me need fear no one? Why don't I simply go up and rip Smyke's heart out of his fat body? If he thought so highly of my literary ability, why did he banish me to the catacombs?'

I responded to each of his questions with a nod. The power of speech seemed to have deserted me permanently. If I had tried to speak at that moment, all that would have emerged was a croak.

The Shadow King resumed his seat. The Animatomes, seeing that their lord and master had regained his composure, sidled a little closer to the throne.

'Pfistomel Smyke explained everything to me while I was still immobilised in his laboratory,' Homuncolossus went on. 'First, the business of the paper. He came right up to me and ran his many hands over the yellowing scraps of paper that covered me.'

'"Do you know what sort of paper this is?" he asked. "It's a secret, very ancient Bookemistic paper. The Bookemists who lived and worked beneath Bookholm many centuries ago were always terrified that their arcane knowledge, their precious notes and records, might be stolen and misused by scientists from the world above. So they devised a secret script so cunning and sophisticated that no one has deciphered it to this day – even I have failed to crack it. But that wasn't enough for the over-anxious Bookemists, oh no! They invented a kind of paper so sensitive to light that it would instantly burst into flames if exposed to a single sunbeam – indeed, even to a single moonbeam. A paper that could exist only in the darkness of the catacombs." Smyke removed his hands from my body and grinned at me.

'"This secret paper bearing the secret cipher is your new skin," he said. "We have steeped it in various animistic and Bookemistic oils and essences and glued it to your flesh with a unique adhesive that resists any form of solvent. If you tried to tear off your new skin, you would rip yourself to shreds." Smyke held up numerous fingers in an admonitory way.

'"It was far from easy to get hold of this rarest of all papers," he went on, "but thanks to my manifold connections I finally managed to do so. You've no idea how valuable that makes you. We used vast quantities of the said paper, tore up hundreds of Bookemistic notebooks and carefully glued them to your body parts, layer upon layer, before reconstructing you. That's why you're so big: a third of you now consists of paper. Discounting its combustible nature, this material is extremely tough and durable. The Bookemists manufactured it to preserve their notes for thousands of years. But, as I said, a single sunbeam or moonbeam would suffice to envelop you in flames from head to foot. As an exile in the dark depths of the catacombs you will be able to live for a very, very long time. On the surface of Bookholm you would burn to death within seconds."

'"So be a good boy and stay put!" Claudio Harpstick put in from behind Smyke's back.

'"I also took the liberty", Smyke went on, "of implanting a few new organs in your body. I'm sure you've heard of the experiments the Bookemists conducted on Animatomes. They made immense strides in the field of artificial organ manufacture – a process sadly prohibited by the laws of Zamonia. I have given you a new heart powered by an alchemical battery.

Your liver was constructed out of five ox livers and should last you for centuries. Your brain now contains an anger-management gland that once belonged to a mountain gorilla. As for your muscles, we persuaded an exceptionally well-built Bookhunter to donate a few of his – after giving him one of my Toxicotomes to read. Then there's the organ which few people realise *is* an organ: the blood."

'Smyke went over to a cupboard and took out a large, empty glass bottle.

'"We took the liberty of pepping up your blood a little. For this we used a precious fluid – the most precious fluid of all, in fact: a whole bottle of Comet Wine, the rarest wine in Zamonia. We spared no expense, as you see."

'Smyke tossed the empty bottle heedlessly over his shoulder, smashing it.

'"It's said that the admixture of blood in Comet Wine is imperishable and imparts eternal strength, so there's a kind of fountain of youth flowing inside you. What I find far more interesting about Comet Wine, however, is the fact that it's accursed, so you'll always carry a curse inside you. That renders you a tragic figure, so to speak. Romantic, no?"

'Smyke looked at me with feigned regret.

'"We've also changed one or two other things inside you, some organic, others mechanical – I won't bore you with the details, you'll notice this from your increased energy and new faculties once you've recuperated properly. Lead a healthy life in the catacombs and you'll be able to survive there for centuries."

'Smyke went over to a laboratory table and proceeded to fill a large hypodermic syringe with yellow fluid.

'"There's something else that must be puzzling you," he said. "Why on earth have we gone to so much trouble? Why don't we simply kill you? There's a very simple and valid reason for that too. It's like this: on the surface of Bookholm I've got everything under control, but what goes on in the catacombs is an entirely different matter. It's quite impossible for me to intervene and regulate things down there. The Bookhunters have been running amok lately. There are too many of them and they've grown too greedy, too stupid. Some of them, especially that demented butcher Rongkong Koma, have become too powerful and arrogant for my taste. In short, I'd like you to restore a little order down there. That's why I've made you so strong, so big and dangerous. I'd like you to effect something of a clearance among the Bookhunters – to prune their numbers a trifle, let's say. Would you do that for me?"

'Smyke grinned.

'"I know what you're thinking," he went on. "Why the devil should I do Pfistomel Smyke's dirty work? Well, I've taken care of that too. I've put a big fat price on your head and I've promised Rongkong Koma the biggest bounty of all. If you don't go after the Bookhunters, they'll come after you. They've no idea how strong you are. You'll have sent half of them into retirement before the word gets around. There's nothing you can do about it. The moment you appear down there they'll be hot on your heels, and I'll make sure your arrival is signalled by a few fanfares, take it from me."

'Smyke looked at the fluid in the syringe.

'"So now you're a walking book – the rarest, most valuable, most dangerous and sought-after book in the catacombs. You're the stuff of which legends are made. Which brings us to your last and probably most pressing question: Why am I using you for this purpose? You haven't done me any harm. You showed me a sheaf of manuscript, that's all, so what is it that makes you so dangerous to me?"

'Smyke heightened the suspense by leaving the question in the air for a moment.'

Homuncolossus, too, fell silent and left Smyke's question in the air for one agonisingly long moment. It was all I could do to refrain from making some interjection. Even the Animatomes rustled and squeaked impatiently. At last Homuncolossus went on.

'"I'll tell you the real reason for all these measures," said Smyke. "You write too well."

'He gave a hoarse laugh and approached me with the syringe.

'"Unlike our obtuse friend Claudio Harpstick here," he said, "I'm quite capable of telling the difference between a piece of good writing and a hole in the ground. I've read everything you've written, including the story about your writer's block, and I have to admit that nothing as good has ever come my way. Not ever! It made me laugh, it made me cry, it drove me to despair one moment and banished all my cares the next – in short, it had everything really good writing ought to have. That plus a bit more. All right, much more

– very much more! There's more meat in a single sentence of yours than many a whole book contains. Your writing is pervaded by the Orm with an intensity I've encountered in no other form of literature. I attached your poems to my Bookemistic ormometer and it burnt out all the alchemical batteries! You're hot, my friend. Far too hot!"

'Smyke expelled the last remaining bubbles from his syringe.

'"To put it simply: if you published even one title here in Bookholm, the Zamonian book market would be up the spout, and the Zamonian book market is me, Pfistomel Smyke. Your kind of writing is so perfect, so pure, so utterly satisfying, that nobody who sampled it would want to read anything else. It provides a shameful demonstration of the banality of our usual reading matter. Why browse on that rubbish when *your* books can be read again and again? Have you any idea how much time and trouble it has taken me to reduce Zamonian literature to the carefully controlled mediocrity it now displays? Worse still, you might set an example. You might inspire other writers to produce finer books and aspire to the Orm – to write less but better."

'Smyke gave me a look of entreaty. "The problem is this: in order to make money – lots of money – we don't need flawless literary masterpieces. What we need is mediocre rubbish, trash suitable for mass consumption. More and more, bigger and bigger blockbusters of less and less significance. What counts is the paper we sell, not the words that are printed on it."

'Smyke found a spot in my thigh, inserted the needle between two shreds of paper and thrust it into my flesh.

'"To sum up," he said, "you were an endangered species at birth. You're the first and last of your kind, the greatest writer in Zamonia and, thus, my direst foe. I wish you a new life in the catacombs and better luck there than in your former existence, which is now at an end."

'So saying, he injected the fluid into my bloodstream and rendered me unconscious.

'When I awoke I was deep in the catacombs. Beside me lay a bundle containing all the manuscripts and other possessions I'd brought with me to Bookholm. I had been exiled here, complete with my life to date. And in the labyrinth of passages around me, which were lined with ancient volumes, I could already hear Bookhunters in full cry.'

8ℛ

The Bookhunter Hunter

Homuncolossus gave a mirthless laugh. 'Believe me,' he said, 'it wasn't long before I started to enjoy hunting Bookhunters. I killed the first one purely in self-defence. Still completely bemused by Smyke's toxic injection, I had no idea where and who I was when he turned up in his crazy armour, equipped with an arsenal of weapons. He probably thought I was easy meat for his spears and his two-edged sword when he saw me staggering around in a daze.'

Homuncolossus raised his right hand and regarded it thoughtfully. Outlined against the candlelight, his talons looked as sharp as a set of carving knives.

'Paper shouldn't be underestimated,' he said. 'Have you ever cut yourself on a sheet of ordinary writing paper?'

Yes, I had, more than once, when hurriedly sorting out manuscripts or opening letters. The cuts had always hurt a lot and bled profusely.

'Then perhaps you can imagine the damage inflicted by sheets of sharp-edged, carefully laminated and neatly glued parchment, especially when they're wielded by a colossus with the muscles and reflexes of a gorilla. Believe me, I was even more astonished than the Bookhunter when he sank to the ground at my feet, streaming with blood. And that concluded the Bookhunters' hunting of me. From then on, I hunted *them*.'

Homuncolossus lowered his hand.

'I felt at home in the catacombs from the very first. I mean, I was naturally bewildered and angry, at a loss and in despair, but my new environment never for a moment struck me as alien or menacing. I liked the scent of the Dreaming Books, the chilly gloom, the silence and solitude. I had been reborn into a world for which Smyke had literally made me to measure. I had no need to create an imaginary world in order to come to terms with the real one. The catacombs of Bookholm appealed to me on sight; they were like a vast palace in which every room belonged to me. I wasn't even angry with Smyke, not at first. Once the drug wore off I experienced an immense accretion of physical strength. Energy surged through me like a tidal wave of unadulterated Orm. I had been relieved of all my fears and cares. I was as wild and free and unconstrained as a predator in a primeval forest.

'My new body held some new surprise for me every day: greater strength and speed, unlimited stamina and amazing reflexes, the toughness of my new skin and the ease with which I could see in the dark. I could hear the inaudible squeak of a bat and locate an insect by smell in utter darkness.

'I liked the shadows in the catacombs and they liked me. They concealed me from Bookhunters and allowed me to become one with them, so that I could suddenly emerge and fall on my enemies like a ghost. They enshrouded me and kept watch over my slumbers. It's not surprising that people in many parts of the world call me the Shadow King, although no name could be less appropriate. No one rules the shadows of the catacombs.'

Homuncolossus gave a little bark of laughter and fell silent.

'Are you referring to the shadows that flit through this castle?' I asked.

He looked up. 'So you've seen them too? Yes, they're the ones I mean, but first things first. All in good time. I still haven't got to Shadowhall Castle in my story, not by a long chalk.'

I was afraid he might give me another harsh reprimand, but he simply picked up where he'd left off.

'All Bookhunters have a style of their own, their identifying marks, their own types of armour, their special weapons, methods of hunting and killing and so on. These are dictated by their personal vanity and code of honour. They may band together to carry out joint military operations, but they always go their own way afterwards. Most of them are inveterate loners. That was my great advantage from the start, and they still haven't grasped that they'll never deal with me unless they cooperate. But then they'd have to split the bounty and they're too avaricious for that. So I picked them off one by one, and it gave me particular pleasure to employ their own techniques against them. For instance, Hokum Bogus used to hound his adversaries until they went mad with fear. I drove him insane by whispering to him out of the darkness for a whole year without ever showing my face.

'The Krood brothers, Aggro and Glubb, were among the few Bookhunters who operated as a team and attacked their victims from two directions at once. I managed to trick them into slitting each other's throats.

'Yonti Yooble, known as "The Sexton" because he liked to bury his opponents beneath piles of books, I buried beneath a pile of books.

'But what I enjoyed most was using my own body as a weapon in one-to-one confrontations. I sensed that I was growing stronger every day. If paper is compressed tightly enough it turns back into timber. My arms are as robust as tree trunks, my fingers as sharp as spears, my teeth as keen as razor blades.

'I hounded many Bookhunters to death, pursuing them with my inexhaustible reserves of energy until their heart or their whole organism failed and they simply dropped dead. I led them astray, luring them over precipices or into their own traps. I ambushed them in the most unlikely places – even in their own secret haunts. That frightened them most of all, because they now knew that nowhere was safe. Some I knocked unconscious and dragged off to remote parts of the catacombs they'd never dared to set foot in before. They may still be roaming around there, if the Spinxxxxes haven't devoured them. Either way, their cries of despair will be audible for ever in the Chamber of Captive Echoes.'

Homuncolossus rose and proceeded to circle his throne as he spoke.

'I became the secret ruler of the catacombs, it's true, but nobody knew what I really looked like, because anyone who did was dead shortly afterwards. That was how the legends began, and soon there were a hundred different notions and descriptions of who or what I was. To some I was an animal, to others a ghost, a demon, an insect, or a combination of all three. That made me proud and gave me an unfamiliar feeling of omnipotence that intoxicated me more and more.

'One sigh or cry of mine was enough to depopulate whole areas of the catacombs and drive out their inhabitants for ever. I had only to kill one Bookhunter for rumour to transform him into a dozen and for two dozen Bookhunters to abandon their profession. Many believed me to be a whole host of shadows, an army of darkness, a legion of ghostly, invincible warriors that marched through the catacombs and devoured their victims alive.'

Homuncolossus came to a halt and fixed me with his dark, empty eye sockets.

'How do you think I felt with all that blood on my hands? When everyone or everything I met, even the vilest and most vicious denizen of the catacombs, shrank away from me in terror? Did I feel guilty? Remorseful? What do you think?'

He laughed.

'No, anything but! I felt wonderful! It was a sensation of absolute freedom. I was free at last from all moral constraints, from feelings of guilt, responsibility, compassion and other such pointless ballast. That's the greatest freedom of all, take it from me. Artistic licence is a joke in comparison.'

Homuncolossus returned to his throne. He had uttered the last few words in a loud, resonant tone, as if drunk on the sound of his own voice. Now his voice sank almost to a whisper.

'All the mental energy I used to devote to my literary work I now invested in the art of killing. I was always trying to think of even more ingenious ways of sending Bookhunters to kingdom come and, believe me, I thought of one or two. I hardly noticed that the shadows of the catacombs had turned away from me. I lay down to sleep, but they no longer tucked me up. I registered their absence but I didn't miss them, nor did I need them any longer. What protection could they afford to someone like me? Me, Homuncolossus, whom no one dared to approach? Whom everyone feared more than death itself?'

Homuncolossus paused and stiffened for a moment. The candlelight flickered over his rune-covered body and I tried to imagine the horror felt by any Bookhunter taken unawares by such an apparition.

'On one of my restless subterranean reconnaissance patrols I came to a cave in the upper reaches of the catacombs which a megalomaniac book prince had converted into his secret palace. It contained a hall of mirrors that must have been abandoned centuries before – the cobwebs were thick as fishing nets and the mirrors milky with dust. I must have activated some secret mechanism as I walked in, because the whole room slowly started to revolve. The dust and the cobwebs began to dance to a gentle melody that sounded like a melancholy children's song played by a mechanical piano in need of tuning. The walls of the circular room were lined with a hundred-odd mirrors, each in a gold frame and big enough to reflect a figure as bulky as mine. Many were cracked and others too thickly coated with dust, but a few were clear enough for me to see myself in. It was ages since I'd seen my own reflection. I had quickly averted my eyes on the few occasions when I glimpsed my new face and body in an enemy's shield or a pool of water, but this time I gazed at my reflection with a strange blend of pleasure and disgust. I perceived for the first time the strength and majesty that emanated from my massive form and – also for the first time – the full extent of the terror it inspired. Simultaneous thrills of happiness and fear ran down my spine. I remembered admiring my reflection as a child and hoping to become just like this figure in the mirror. Just as solitary.

'And then I started to weep. I shed no tears, for no tears have been available to me since Smyke did heaven knows what to my eyes, but my emotions were the same as those of a weeping child who feels that everyone has abandoned him. Why? Because I realised what I had become: Pfistomel Smyke's tool and accomplice, who got drunk on the blood he shed to no purpose, merely so as not to have to remember the person he used to be. I saw the monster into which I had transformed myself. Not the one fabricated by Smyke, but the real monster deep inside this paper shell, for which I myself bore responsibility. I smashed the mirrors – smashed them all in a towering rage.'

Homuncolossus hid his face in his hands. Several Animatomes had sidled right up to him and were emitting thin, piping sounds as if trying to console him. He straightened up again.

'For some considerable time,' he went on in a firmer tone of voice, 'one Bookhunter had been dogging my footsteps with exceptional tenacity. Not only did he venture into areas no normal Bookhunter would have dared to enter, but he was forever surprising me with his tricks, his intelligence and staying power. He never set eyes on me, of course, but he aroused my curiosity to such an extent that I began to study him.'

'Colophonius Regenschein,' I put in quietly.

'Correct. I learnt his name from a dying Bookhunter who also told me that Regenschein was no ordinary hunter. He hunted books. Far from lying in wait for other Bookhunters, he tried to avoid them, and the most impressive thing about him was that, although the others kept trying to kill him, he succeeded again and again in escaping or even eliminating them. I actually helped him once, when Rongkong Koma tried to bury him alive beneath a bookcase.'

'He went looking for you because he wanted to be your friend,' I was bold enough to interject in a low voice.

'Really?' said Homuncolossus.

I wondered whether to inform him of Regenschein's death. It seemed an inopportune moment, however, so I decided not to do so until later.

'That was when I began to think about myself,' Homuncolossus went on. 'Regenschein demonstrated that an inhabitant of the catacombs could do something other than hunt and be hunted, kill and eat and die. He tried to steer clear of confrontations instead of seeking them as I did. This vast subterranean realm, which contained a store of invaluable knowledge, was in the hands of murderers and bandits, wild beasts, rats and insects whose senseless ravages were rendering it uninhabitable and would one day destroy it completely. Regenschein, it seemed, had different aspirations. I watched him making notes and read them in secret while he slept. He wanted to salvage the catacombs' greatest treasures, not in order to possess them himself, but to conserve them and make them accessible to the general public. That earned my respect. I watched and followed him more closely still. When he visited the surface, as he did from time to time, I trailed him ever higher into the upper reaches of the catacombs and the vicinity of the world I had avoided until then – the world I was trying to forget. The result was just what I'd been dreading: overcome with curiosity about life and freedom in the real world above, I began to spy on the inhabitants of Bookholm through the chinks and cracks in their floors. So near to them again, yet so far, I was separated by a magical frontier I was not at liberty to cross. Only a few feet above my head was an immense stage, a vast theatre presenting an endless tragicomedy, a spectacle I never tired of observing with envy and nostalgia. It was the life Smyke had wrested from me, real life lived in the light of the two heavenly bodies that illumine our planet; the diametrical opposite of my own ratlike existence in subterranean gloom. I attended timber-time readings, seated beneath the cellar steps like an old ghost, and listened to lousy poems being recited by tipsy jobbing poets as if they were the music of the spheres.

'I also watched writers at work in their shabby basements. There's nothing more tedious than the sight of an author writing, believe me, but I never tired of watching some pale, careworn novice scratching away at a pad of cheap paper. That was how I myself had looked in a state of supreme happiness during the finest hours of my former existence.

'The hatred I felt for Smyke became steadily more ferocious and preoccupied me more and more. I conceived a plan to break into his library and lie in wait for him there. Sooner or later he would visit it; then I could kill him.

'But whenever I tried to get to the library I wound up in a cunning maze of passages that made it impossible for me to reach my destination. The Smykes must have developed and perfected this defensive system for centuries, because it's genuinely impenetrable – the most sophisticated labyrinth in the catacombs. It took me days, sometimes weeks, to find my way out again, and once I almost died there of thirst. I was eventually forced to accept that Smyke was beyond my reach.'

Homuncolossus sank back on his throne and sighed.

'That was when I resolved to descend as far as possible into the catacombs, never to return. I renounced my existence as a hunter of Bookhunters and plunged ever deeper into the bowels of Bookholm.

'Not even the rubbish dump of Unholm and its surrounding graveyards or the Rusty Gnomes' railroad station seemed secluded and deserted enough for my taste, so I went deeper and deeper. That was how I discovered Shadowhall Castle. It reminded me of my childhood castles in the air, as if my imagination had built it for me a long time ago. I made Shadowhall my home. This was where I wanted to live and some day die. This was where I rediscovered the beloved shadows that had fled from me and my rampages. At Shadowhall we finally made peace.'

I ventured to ask Humuncolossus a question that had been plaguing me: 'Do you know who or what those Weeping Shadows are?'

'I can't say for sure, I must admit,' he replied. 'After much thought, I've come to the conclusion that they're the restless souls of old books. Buried and forgotten down here, they now lament their sad fate in perpetuity. All I can say for certain about the Weeping Shadows is that they mean no harm. If you have the good fortune to be tucked up by one when you go to sleep, let it happen and don't be afraid. You'll be rewarded with dreams of exceptional beauty.'

He rose from his throne.

'I've talked a great deal,' he said. 'More than I have in a very long time. Now I'm weary.' And he prepared to leave the throne room.

'Thank you,' I called after him. 'Thank you for your trust and hospitality. Please answer me one last question.'

He paused.

'Am I your guest or your prisoner?' I asked.

'You are free to leave Shadowhall Castle at any time,' he replied. 'If you can do so unaided.'

Then, with scores of Animatomes trailing after him, he strode out.

88

The Plan

I didn't see Homuncolossus again for the next three days. At sporadic intervals I came across food and water, which had obviously been left out for me, and I sometimes heard rustles in the darkness while vainly reconnoitring Shadowhall Castle's nightmarish architecture, but this was all that enabled me to infer his presence.

I had reached a tacit understanding with the Animatomes: we left each other in peace. They no longer fled in panic when I entered a room, though they respectfully stood aside when I crossed it. I sometimes threw them a few of the desiccated bookworms of which my meals consisted and, although hesitant at first, they didn't spurn them.

As for the Weeping Shadows, I was never sure if they registered my presence at all, or if *their* presence occupied another dimension that happened to coincide with ours at the point where Shadowhall Castle was located. From time to time I would glimpse one gliding through the eternal twilight, sobbing. Then my heart became heavy and I welcomed its disappearance.

Once, when I was lying sleepless in the semi-darkness, one of them entered the room and enshrouded me in its shadowy self with a sigh. Paralysed with fear at first, I soon became weary and dozed off. I dreamt of a city whose curious buildings were composed of the most unusual materials – cloud or flame, ice or rain – until it occurred to me that these were the imaginary edifices of which the Shadow King had dreamt in his childhood. Then I awoke to find the shadow gone.

Whether a guest or a prisoner, I was quite uninterested in leaving Shadowhall Castle 'unaided'. Once outside, where would I have gone? Back into the domain of the Harpyrs and Bookhunters, or still deeper – if that were possible – into the catacombs?

If anyone could show me the way back to Bookholm, it was Homuncolossus himself, so I racked my brains on those endless, lonely excursions for some way of persuading him to guide me back to the surface. I was in an extremely weak negotiating position, admittedly, because I had nothing to offer in return but gratitude. What good would that be to him? It would only reopen old wounds and rekindle his hatred of Pfistomel Smyke.

He would watch me ascending to freedom, whereas he himself would have to return to the darkness below. From the Shadow King's point of view, not a good bargain.

I kept wondering what he really wanted of me. Why did he tolerate me, of all living creatures endowed with speech, in his palace populated by Animatomes and Weeping Shadows? Why had he told me his story?

One thing was certain: I would never succeed in leaving Shadowhall Castle, that place of windowless exile, without his help.

Windowless exile...

What did that remind me of? Of course, a passage in Colophonius Regenschein's book. All at once, I perceived a thoroughly realistic way of helping Homuncolossus to resume life on the surface of Bookholm. Regenschein had devised the solution a long time ago. Yes, that could be the answer, the incentive Homuncolossus needed. But first he would have to reappear so that I could submit my plan.

86

Conversation with a Dead Man

Towards the end of the fourth day (if one could speak of days in the catacombs; I simply counted the periods during which I was awake as days and the hours I spent asleep as nights) I found Homuncolossus in the dining hall where my frugal repasts were customarily left out for me. The spacious room was lit by only a few candles, the way he liked it. He was seated at one of the tables with a key, a jug and a glass in front of him. One or two Animatomes were scurrying around at his feet.

'Good evening,' I said.

He gave me a long, silent stare.

'I'm sorry,' he said at length. 'Good evening. It's an age since I heard anyone say that. I never know for sure if it's morning, noon or night. Time means little down here. Nothing at all, in fact. Here, this food is for you. Sit down.'

He pushed a bowl of root vegetables towards me, also the water jug and glass.

'Tell me,' he said when I was seated, 'in your opinion, how many days have elapsed since our last meeting?'

'About four,' I replied.

'Four?' he exclaimed in astonishment. 'And I thought it was only one! I really have lost all sense of time.'

He reached beneath the table and produced a bottle. 'Would you care for a glass of wine with your meal?'

'Wine?' I repeated, rather embarrassed by the tremor of excitement in my tone. I pulled myself together. 'Yes, some wine would be nice,' I said, doing my best to speak in a calm, steady voice.

He poured me a glass of red wine, and only iron self-control prevented me from draining it at a gulp. I took a sip. The wine tasted more delicious than any I'd ever drunk.

'Excellent!' I said, smacking my lips. I took another sip – a bigger one.

'Forgive me if I don't join you,' said Homuncolossus, 'but I seldom touch alcohol. The fact is, I've been a trifle tipsy ever since that bottle of Comet Wine started flowing through my veins. Even another two or three glasses might send me into a state fit only for the company of Bookhunters.'

'A state of bloodlust, you mean?' I quipped inanely, already emboldened by the few drops of wine I'd drunk.

'That's one way of putting it. Your health!'

'Thank you.' I took another sip and relaxed still more. 'How does one get hold of wine down here?' I asked.

'You can obtain anything in the catacombs if you know how. This wine comes from Rongkong Koma's personal cellar.'

I nearly choked. 'The Bookhunter? You know his hideaway?'

'Of course. I pay his cave a visit now and then. I turn the place upside down, steal a few books and some wine, bend his iron arrows, block up his source of drinking water and so on. It drives him crazy.'

'Why have you spared his life?'

'I don't know. Perhaps because Smyke was so insistent on my killing him. If Smyke is afraid of him, I told myself, he may come in handy some day.'

'Rongkong Koma cut off Regenschein's head,' I said.

Homuncolossus sprang to his feet. I recoiled at the sudden movement.

'Koma killed Regenschein?' His voice reverberated round the dining hall, so loudly that the Animatomes scuttled off and hid beneath the other tables.

'No, he cut off his head when he was already dead. Regenschein killed himself. He simply stopped living.'

'He did that?' Homuncolossus sat down again.

'Yes. It was the most remarkable feat of will-power I've ever witnessed.'

Homuncolossus brooded in silence for a while. 'What happened? How did Rongkong Koma get into the Leather Grotto?'

'I've no idea. He raided it with a lot of other Bookhunters. They slaughtered some of the Booklings and drove the rest away. The Leather Grotto is now in their hands, I'm afraid.'

Homuncolossus fidgeted impatiently. 'That's bad,' he said. 'The Leather Grotto was one of the last bastions of civilisation in the catacombs. The Booklings took good care of it.'

'I know. You guided me to them. Why?'

'I've been observing them for a long time. They're the only folk in the catacombs who don't do business with the Bookhunters. I'm surprised the Bookhunters found the Leather Grotto. Still, I suppose it had to happen one day.'

'What drew your attention to me, of all people?' I enquired.

Homuncolossus laughed. 'I'm surprised you ask. You've been behaving like a bull in a china shop ever since you entered the catacombs. I was on one of my reconnaissance trips when you fell into Goldenbeard's clumsy trap and brought down half the labyrinth with you. They must have heard it up in Bookholm.'

I hung my head.

'Then you landed with a crash in the rubbish dump and woke up all its inhabitants including that megaworm. I've been watching you ever since you crawled out of Unholm. I thought you were done for when the Spinxxxx captured you, but then Hoggno rescued you.'

'You wouldn't have?'

'Probably not. I didn't find you sufficiently interesting at the time.'

'So why did you save me from Hoggno?'

'I'd been eavesdropping on your conversation. You'd suddenly gone up in my estimation.'

'Why?'

'What is this, an interrogation?'

'Forgive me.'

'The next time I heard you I was on patrol near Shadowhall. It was that diabolical cry you gave on the Rusty Gnomes' Bookway. Everyone in the catacombs must have heard it. That's how I knew you were in trouble again.'

I felt thoroughly ashamed. From his point of view, I really had behaved like a total idiot since entering the catacombs.

'May I ask *you* a question for a change?' he demanded.

I nodded.

'What brought you to Bookholm?'

I felt in my pockets for the manuscript and put it on the table. I had really wanted to save it for a more dramatic moment. 'This,' I said.

'I thought as much,' said Homuncolossus.

'You knew I had it on me?'

'I searched you while you were asleep, just before you encountered the Booklings.'

'I remember. I dreamt of you that time.'

'No wonder.' He grinned. 'I'd never been so close to you before. You must have been able to smell me.'

'Did you really write this?' I asked. 'If so, you're the greatest writer of all time.'

'No,' said Homuncolossus. 'It was written by someone I ceased to be a long time ago.'

'But I left Lindworm Castle in search of the person who could write like this.'

'That's really sad, my friend,' said Homuncolossus. 'You set off on a long and perilous journey, only to find that the person you sought has long been dead.'

On that note he got up from the table and left the room. The Animatomes gathered at my feet, squeaking expectantly. With a sigh, I tossed them the remains of my meal and proceeded to finish off the delicious wine. I had forgotten to tell Homuncolossus about my splendid plan. My courage had simply failed me.

ʆ◖

The Inebriated Gorilla

I awoke the next day with a curious buzzing in my head. The Aeolian music, the rising and falling walls, the scurrying Animatomes – all these things were starting to grate on my nerves. My one desire was to get away from this godforsaken castle and its lord and master, a demented phantom who had probably left his wits behind with his former existence. But I, too, seemed to have checked my brain on entering Shadowhall Castle. I was beginning to develop an affection for this paper monster, this serial murderer and universally anathematised ghost. I was becoming inured to self-propelled walls, Weeping Shadows and scurrying Animatomes! It was high time for me to leave.

I no longer wandered aimlessly through the castle's halls and chambers but deliberately looked for an exit, tried to memorise the rooms' special features, the number of tables and chairs, the location of the fireplaces, the nature of the ceilings, the height of the doors. I spent the entire day roaming around to no avail, only to totter back to the dining hall, where Homuncolossus and my supper were awaiting me.

Tonight, in addition to the usual eating utensils, the table was piled high with books. The candle that reposed on them lit up the Shadow King's paper mask more brightly than usual. There was no wine this time; I could tell from the two empty bottles at my host's feet that he had already polished it off.

'You're late,' he said thickly. He was drunk and in a sombre, possibly even dangerous mood.

'I've been looking for something,' I replied.

'I know. You didn't find it, though.' He gave an unpleasant laugh.

'Very funny,' I said, tucking into my bowl of insipid underworld vegetables.

There was a long silence broken only by the rustling sound of the Animatomes scurrying around beneath the table. At length Homuncolossus asked, 'Do you believe that some literature lives on for ever?'

I didn't have to think for long. 'Yes, of course,' I replied with my mouth full.

'Yes, of course!' Homuncolossus mimicked. He glared at me. 'Well, I don't!' he said, taking a book from the table.

'Does *this* look eternal?' He hurled it into the air. Even before it reached the top of its trajectory the pages fell apart, disintegrated into fragments as they came fluttering down and eventually dissolved into a fine dust that sank slowly to the floor. Only the cover landed intact, but the impact smashed it to

pieces. The few maggots that crawled out of the debris were promptly devoured by the Animatomes, which converged from all directions.

'And that was a classic,' Homuncolossus said with a laugh. 'The story of *Vaddi Flopperdice* by Asdrel Chickens.'

He had never behaved as strangely before. The restless way he shuffled around on his chair reminded me of some animal, I couldn't think which.

'No, literature isn't eternal,' he cried. 'It's a thing of the moment. Even if you made books with pages of steel and diamond letters, they would some day crash into the sun and melt, together with our planet. Nothing is eternal, least of all in art. It doesn't matter how long an author's work continues to glimmer after his death. What matters is how brightly it burns while he's still alive.'

'That could be the motto of a successful novelist,' I put in. 'An author whose sole concern is how much money he can earn during his lifetime.'

'I'm not talking about material success,' said Homuncolossus. 'It doesn't matter how well or how badly a book sells or how many people take notice of an author. That's unimportant – it's dependent on far too many coincidences and injustices to be a valid criterion. *What matters is how brightly the Orm burns inside you while you're writing.*'

'You believe in the Orm?' I hazarded.

'I *believe* in nothing whatsoever,' he said darkly. 'I *know* the Orm exists, that's all.'

I felt in my pocket. 'When you wrote this,' I said, producing the manuscript and holding it up, 'the Orm must have been burning inside you like a bonfire. It's the most immaculate piece of writing I've ever read. It *is* eternal.'

The Shadow King leant towards me. So near that I could smell his musty breath, he gazed at me with infinite sadness and held his hand over the candle flame. The tip of his forefinger turned black and started to sizzle.

'You've no idea how quickly something can be over,' he whispered. Tiny flames began to dance on his fingertip and a tendril of smoke spiralled into the air.

I seized my glass of water and tipped it over his hand. The flames expired with a hiss.

Homuncolossus sprang to his feet as if about to pounce on me, but he only gave me a menacing glare. Then he began to laugh. It was a louder and

more terrible laugh than he had ever uttered before. Finally, to my utter astonishment, he went down on all fours and scampered out of the room like a gorilla, albeit at a rate that would have made any gorilla's fur stand on end.

⚇ Thirst

This much was certain: I was at the mercy of the most dangerous and demented creature in the catacombs of Bookholm. Homuncolossus, the Shadow King, Mephistas, Keron Kenken, or whatever he was called, had lost his mind, either when transmogrified by Smyke or in the course of his exile. I was now convinced that he intended to keep me a prisoner here for ever. Why? So that I could share his sufferings in lieu of his real tormentors.

I roamed the passages in despair. He hadn't shown his face for several days and I had forgotten at some stage to go on counting them. Although I could happily have dispensed with the company of the Shadow King as I had last seen him, the alarming aspect of the situation was that he had stopped providing me with food and drink. Deprivation of solid food was tolerable for a certain length of time, but I would die of thirst unless I got something to drink before long.

Was it a test? A punishment? Or had he gone off on one of his excursions through the catacombs and fallen prey to the Bookhunters? Anything was possible. Perhaps it was just a crazy whim of his to leave me to die. I cursed myself for not having had the courage to tell him of my plan in good time.

Meanwhile, I hardly dared leave the dining hall for fear of missing the moment of his return – if it ever came. I was finding it increasingly difficult to think. If someone is deprived of food and drink for a considerable period, his cerebral activity soon becomes reduced to devising succulent recipes and envisioning thirst-quenching beverages.

I had even reached the stage where I considered breaking my truce with the Animatomes. The little creatures continued to scurry around between my feet, as before. They had become more and more trusting, and they made a lively, healthy impression which suggested that, unlike me, they were being amply supplied with food and drink – either that, or they knew where to forage for themselves. They aroused my envy, then my mounting anger. In the end my feelings for them became transmuted into sheer hatred. The useless, well-fed creatures swarmed all over the castle, filling almost every room with their squeaks and rustles.

Of leather and of paper built,
worm-eaten through and through . . .

Those lines from Colophonius Regenschein's poem came back to me. Had he really found his way into Shadowhall Castle? How else could he have known about the Animatomes? If he had, he must also have found his way out of this labyrinth. Perhaps it was possible after all.

370

I had to act soon if I didn't want to die of thirst while waiting in vain for the Shadow King's return, but I was now too weak to leave the dining hall and look for an exit. That being so, I decided to hunt, kill and devour an Animatome and drink its blood.

I settled on a particularly plump, leather-bound volume that was slowly crawling past me. Throbbing within it must be juicy organs suffused with black fluid. My mouth watered at the very thought of tearing that unwitting

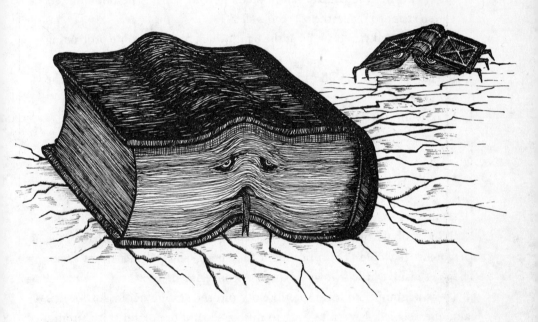

little creature to pieces. I shook off my lethargy, went down on all fours and proceeded to crawl towards my prey.

As though they instinctively sensed what was in the wind, the other Animatomes took fright. They scattered in all directions, rustling and squeaking.

I focused my gaze on the fat volume and prepared to pounce on it from a crouching position.

'Would you care for a glass of Gargyllian Bollogg's Skull with your Animatome?' a familiar voice enquired. 'Or would you, in your dehydrated condition, prefer some ice-cold spring water?'

I looked up. The Shadow King was seated in his customary place, smiling at me. On the table in front of him were an opened bottle of wine, a jug of water, two glasses and a whole smoked ham on a platter.

I stared at him stupidly for several seconds.

'Where have you been?' I croaked, getting to my feet.

'In the Leather Grotto,' he replied. 'I went there to gain an idea of the current situation.'

He poured me a glass of water. I staggered over to him and gulped it down.

'It was awful to see that library looted,' he said sadly. 'The Bookhunters have even stripped the leather off the walls.'

I sat down and stared avidly at the ham, which had a big knife protruding from it.

'Help yourself,' said Homuncolossus. 'I filched it from the Bookhunters.'

I carved myself a thick slice and started to eat.

'Did you do anything to them?' I asked with my mouth full.

'No, there were too many. However, I got the impression that most of them will soon be leaving the Grotto. There's hardly anything left to loot.'

'Did you see any Booklings?'

'Not a single one. They must have retreated into the depths of the catacombs. It wouldn't surprise me if they never showed their faces again. They're sensitive little fellows – experts at concealment, too.'

I was beginning to feel more like my old self. Homuncolossus looked calm and relaxed. I wasn't going to miss a second opportunity to submit my plan.

'Listen,' I said, 'I've had an idea – a way of getting us both out of the catacombs.'

'Thirst must have desiccated your brain,' said Homuncolossus. 'Better replenish your reservoirs before you start thinking again.'

'I've never been more clear-headed. The idea isn't even mine.'

'Whose is it, then?'

'Colophonius Regenschein's.'

'Regenschein is dead, my friend. You're delirious.'

'No one who writes a good book is really dead. I got the idea from *The Catacombs of Bookholm.*'

'Regenschein wrote a book about the catacombs?'

'A very good one, too. Among other things, it describes how he built a sort of, er, compound on his large estate in Bookholm.'

'What kind of compound?'

'A compound for the Shadow King.'

'What? For me?'

'Yes. It was to be your new home on the surface in the event that he captured you. Not a prison, don't get me wrong! It reproduced conditions in the catacombs. No windows and lots of old books. You could survive in it just as well as you do down here.'

Homuncolossus gave me a lingering look.

'He actually had this thing built?'

'So it says in his book.'

A longish silence ensued. I cut myself another slice of ham.

Homuncolossus cleared his throat.

'And you'd come to feed me once a day, the way I feed you?'

'Well, yes – I can imagine some such arrangement.'

'You can, can you? How many rooms does it have, this compound of yours?'

'It isn't *my* compound. I've no idea how many. Several, certainly.'

'Several, eh? Well, well! And the public could come to see me there? For a small charge, I mean? Hey, we could go fifty-fifty!'

'That wasn't the intention. You were to–'

'No, no, it's a fantastic idea! After all, I'd have to earn my keep. I could do a bit of scribbling for the spectators on demand, like those poor devils in the Graveyard of Forgotten Writers. Or I could pull frightful faces for the children. We'll hang up a sign outside: *"Visit the paper monster! See the terrible Homuncolossus being fed!"* I could set fire to myself, then you could put me out. We'd naturally have to give Pfistomel Smyke a piece of the action. He created me, after all.'

The conversation was taking an alarming turn. Homuncolossus put the wine bottle to his paper lips and drained it in one, then rose to his feet. The Animatomes fled in all directions as if warned by instinct of what was to come.

'A *compound*?' Homuncolossus bellowed. He gave the table such a thump with his fist, the top cracked like crazy paving.

Then he hurled the wine bottle into a dark corner, smashing it. 'I'm the master of Shadowhall!' he yelled. 'I rule the whole labyrinth! The catacombs of Bookholm are under my control! I can go wherever I please in my immense domain! I'm free! Free to live and to kill! Freer than any other living creature!'

Homuncolossus vaulted across the table and landed beside me. I was scared stiff – I prepared to get up and make a run for it, but he was too close. Seizing me by the cloak, he hauled me to my feet. Again I smelt his mildew-laden breath and this time I also detected a glint in his dark eye sockets. I had never seen him so angry.

'I'm a king!' he snarled. 'A king with a castle of my own, and you propose to put me in a *zoo*?!'

'It was just a suggestion,' I mumbled. 'I only wanted to help.'

Homuncolossus was breathing heavily. 'Listen, there's something we must straighten out once and for all.' His voice was quieter now but no less menacing. 'We must lay our cards on the table and settle matters. You know it and I know it.'

What did I know? What 'matters' did he mean? What was going on in his wine-fuddled head? I hadn't the first idea what he was talking about. I only knew that I was cursing myself for being a blabbermouth. One incautious word would be enough to turn him into a wild, unpredictable beast.

Homuncolossus reached inside my cloak. I felt sure he was about to rip out my heart, but he merely removed the manuscript and held it under my nose.

'You want to know how to write like this,' he said hoarsely. 'Am I right?'

I nodded.

'You want to know how to acquire the Orm?'

I still didn't believe in the Orm, but I nodded again.

'Most of all, you want to know how to become the greatest writer in Zamonia?'

I nodded even harder.

'Say them, then! Say the magic words!'

I was tongue-tied.

'Say them this minute,' he roared, 'or I'll tear you to shreds even smaller than the ones I'm composed of.'

'Teach me!' I whispered.

'What? Louder! I can't hear you!'

'Teach . . . me . . . to . . . write!' I shouted at the top of my voice. 'Please, I beg of you! Teach me to write the way you can!'

Homuncolossus let go of me.

'At last,' he said, smiling for the very first time. 'I thought you'd never ask.'

65

The Alphabet of the Stars

That was the whole secret, dear readers: Homuncolossus's immense self-esteem. That was why he had lured me into his castle, to pass on the secrets of his craft. That had been his aim ever since eavesdropping on my conversation with Hunk Hoggno and learning that I was Dancelot's authorial godson. Only his grotesque vanity had prevented him from simply offering to help me. I had to be tested. I had to suffer. I had to beg and implore him to accept me as his pupil.

'Show me your paws!' he commanded.

He had conducted me to the Animatomes' library, sat me down on the chair and stationed himself in front of me. The Animatomes were thronging the shelves like the audience in a rather bizarre theatre about to present a play entitled *Optimus Yarnspinner's first lesson in writing from Homuncolossus of Shadowhall*. No inhabitant of the castle wanted to miss this première, it seemed. They kept changing places and clambering over each other, squeaking with excitement. A few were fluttering in the air.

Obediently, I showed Homuncolossus my paws. He took hold of them and gazed at the palms as if he could read the future in them.

'Which paw do you write with?' he asked.

'The right.'

'And you still haven't produced anything you consider worth publishing?'

'Not really.'

'Then you're writing with the wrong paw.'

'What?'

'You've been misrouting the flow of poetic inspiration from your brain. Your right paw isn't your writing paw. You must write with the left.'

'But I can't. I learnt to write with my right paw.'

'Then you must start again from scratch.'

'Do I really have to?'

'If you don't write with the correct paw you'll never amount to anything. It's like writing with your feet.'

I sighed. Great! I had to learn to write before I could learn to write.

Homuncolossus released my paws and proceeded to circle the table.

'Anyone can write,' he said. 'Some people can write a bit better than others; they're called authors. Then there are some who can write better than authors; they're called artists. Finally, there are some artists who can write better than other artists. No name has yet been devised for them. They're the ones who have attained the Orm.'

Oh no, not the Orm again, per*lease*! Because I still hadn't attained it, the Orm pursued me with infinite tenacity. It ran me to earth in the remotest places, even miles below ground in the Animatomes' library.

'The creative density of the Orm is immeasurable. It's a source of inspiration that never runs dry – as long as you know how to get there.' Homuncolossus was speaking of the Orm as if it were a place he regularly frequented as a matter of course.

'But, even if you're fortunate enough to attain the Orm,' he went on, 'you'll be a stranger there unless you've mastered the Alphabet of the Stars.'

'The Alphabet of the Stars? Is that a script?'

'Yes and no. It's an alphabet, but it's also a rhythm. A form of music. An emotion.'

'Can't you be a bit vaguer?' I sighed. 'Are you sure it isn't a plum pudding as well?'

Homuncolossus ignored this gibe.

'Only a handful of true artists attain the Orm. That's a great privilege in itself, but very few of them know the Alphabet of the Stars. They're the élite. Master it, and you can, if you've attained the Orm, communicate there with all the artistic forces in the universe. You can learn things whose existence you would never have suspected in your wildest dreams.'

'This Alphabet of the Stars – you yourself have mastered it, of course?'

'Of course.'

Homuncolossus stared at me as if I were an imbecile. How could I have doubted it, even for a moment?

'Will you teach me it?' I asked boldly.

'No.'

'Why not?'

'Because it isn't transmissible. I can't teach you how to attain the Orm, either. Either you'll manage it some day or you won't. Many do so once but never again. Some attain it repeatedly, but they don't know the Alphabet of the Stars. Others attain the Orm with ease and communicate there by means of the Alphabet.'

'For instance?'

Homuncolossus thought for a moment.

'Hm . . . Aleisha Wimpersleake attained the Orm. Many times, in fact, but if he hadn't known the Alphabet of the Stars as well he might have remained a humble thespian all his life.' Homuncolossus chuckled.

I couldn't help grinning at the memory of Al declaiming blank verse.

'Then there's Inka Almira Rierre. He was a regular visitor to the Orm, and no one could have written a poem like 'Comet Wine' unless he'd memorised the Alphabet of the Stars.'

Homuncolossus kneaded his brow.

'Perla la Gadeon too, of course! He bathed daily in the Orm, and he was born with the Alphabet in his blood. He was so talented, he died of it.'

'And how did *you* learn it?' I asked.

He stared at the ceiling.

'It was when I was a little child – I didn't even know the Zamonian alphabet,' he said quietly. 'I could neither read nor write nor speak. One night when I was lying in my cradle, gazing up in wonder at the cloudless sky, I suddenly saw some thin threads of light appear among the stars and link them up into wonderful shapes. One symbol after another appeared until the whole sky was covered with them. I laughed and gurgled, being only a baby, because the symbols shimmered so beautifully and made such glorious music. That was the first and last time I saw the Alphabet of the Stars, but I never forgot it.'

Homuncolossus was being serious, it seemed – so serious that my scepticism wavered a little. Perhaps I could coax him out on to thin ice with a question or two.

'So you believe that – what did you call them? – "artistic forces" exist on other planets? Are you talking about extraterrestrial writers?'

'I don't just believe so, I know so.'

'Yes, of course, you always *know* everything.'

'Writers exist on billions of planets. You can't imagine what they look like. I know of one who lives on a planet not *so* far removed from our own solar system. A microscopically small fish, he lives at the bottom of a dark sea, beside the crater of a continuously erupting submarine volcano, and composes magmatic poems of breathtaking beauty.'

'How does he write them down?'

Homuncolossus gave me a pitying look.

'You won't believe it, but there are a few methods of recording ideas in this universe other than scratching them on paper with a goose quill.'

'You don't say.'

'I know of a living sandstorm on Mars that engraves its ideas on stone while racing across the surface of the planet. The whole of Mars is covered with sandstone literature.'

I grinned and Homuncolossus grinned back.

'I realise you don't believe a word I say,' he said. 'I can only hope for your sake that the Orm sets you right some day, or you'll remain a pathetic prisoner of your own limited imagination. You'll probably wind up as a greetings-card poet employed by some Bookholmian printer.'

The Animatomes rustled their pages with a sound like applause. Was I imagining it, or did I really detect a malicious undertone in their chorus of squeaks? Surely not – or so I hoped.

'But that's enough theory,' said Homuncolossus. 'Let's get down to some practice. You're going to spend the night in this room.'

'In here with the Animatomes? Why?'

'As a punishment. You were going to eat one of them.'

'But I was almost dying of hunger and thirst! It was your fault for leaving me alone.'

'There's no excuse for eating my loyal subjects, even in your imagination! You're going to learn to live in peace with them. You're to remain here. I'll bring you some paper and writing things, then you can start to practise writing with your left paw.'

I groaned. 'But what shall I write about?'

'That's quite immaterial,' said Homuncolossus. 'It'll be unreadable in any case.'

The Dancing Lesson

I hardly need emphasise, dear readers, that I didn't sleep a wink that night. First I spent hours practising writing with my left paw – something that seemed a near impossibility to a person who had written with his right paw for upwards of seventy years.

Next, I tossed and turned on the hard floor for a considerable time, vainly trying to sleep. I couldn't stop thinking about my recent tutorial. What had I let myself in for? I had been told to learn to write from scratch like a youngster in nursery school and subjected to a load of drivel about the Orm, the Alphabet of the Stars, and literary fish and sandstorms on distant planets. Was that how to become the finest writer of all time? I would probably have received better tuition in the high security wing of a Zamonian lunatic asylum.

Then there were the Animatomes. I now felt certain that they had divined my evil designs on them in the dining hall and were taking their revenge by special permission of the Shadow King. They continued to whisper for hours after the candles had burnt down. Every time I was drifting off into merciful oblivion, something tugged at my cloak, which I had draped over myself, or I would hear the rustling wings of an airborne Animatome circling overhead. Or, worse still, an arachnoid Animatome would scuttle over my face like a spider.

The next day, as I was tottering wearily through the castle, wondering what bizarre place would be the venue for my next tutorial and what form it would take, I heard some Weeping Shadows sobbing.

I was walking along a gloomy passage when several of them, half a dozen or so, came towards me. I turned on my heel, anxious to rid myself of their depressing presence, but more of them were advancing on me from the opposite direction. I hurried off down a side passage, only to find that it, too, was teeming with the creatures. Turning round once more, I went back to the original passage, but it was now jam-packed with shadows in both directions. I ought to have walked straight through them, but the thought of doing so gave me the creeps.

Just then the floor gave way beneath my feet, conveying me and the shadows into the depths. Down and down we went, until the walls on either side of us receded and opened out. We were descending into the great ballroom, the amphitheatre in which I had watched the Weeping Shadows dancing. We landed on the enormous dance floor and came to rest.

The floor was thronged with hundreds more shadows. They advanced on me, sobbing. The melancholy music of Shadowhall Castle struck up and the grey silhouettes began to circle me slowly.

I caught sight of Homuncolossus's motionless figure seated in one of the upper tiers. He was watching the strange scene intently, and I realised that his presence was not fortuitous: this was another tutorial. For whatever reason, he meant me to dance with the shadows.

They now proceeded to pass through me one by one. Images, words, voices, landscapes and sensations raced through my brain. I trembled as I strove to capture those impressions, but they glided through me too swiftly. Again and again the shadows traversed me. For brief instants they flooded my mind with billowing images and soaring choirs of voices, then they were gone. It was like being repeatedly dunked in a tub of ice-cold water filled with sights and sounds.

The dance became wilder still. I spun round and round as more and more shadows glided through me at one and the same time. I felt ever colder – felt that the onset of so many outlandish thoughts was driving me out of my mind.

Then, all at once, it was over: the shadows had disappeared. I collapsed in a heap, surprised that I didn't disintegrate into a thousand little slivers of ice when I hit the ground.

I lay there for a while, panting and shivering. Then I saw that Homuncolossus was bending over me.

'What was all that about?' I asked, still completely drained of energy. 'Wouldn't you prefer to kill me and get it over?'

'You've just read the whole of the Weeping Shadows' library,' he said. 'It was a dancing lesson of a very special kind.'

'But what was the point?' I demanded, sitting up with a groan. 'I nearly went mad, I didn't understand any of it, and I've as good as forgotten it all again.'

'It's always the same with demanding literature,' Homuncolossus replied as he helped me to my feet.

The Vocabulary Chamber

One's memory functions like a spider's web. Unimportant things – the wind, for example – a web lets through, whereas captured flies become lodged in it and are stored there until the spider needs and devours them.

I've read and long forgotten many books in my life, but their important features have lodged in my mental net, ready to be rediscovered years or decades later. The incorporeal books of the Weeping Shadows were another matter. They had passed through me like water trickling through a sieve. I thought I'd forgotten them within seconds, but I noticed the next day that some of them had lodged in my mind after all.

I suddenly knew words I'd never heard or read before. I knew, for example, that *plumose* was an archaic synonym for *feathered*. Although this knowledge may at first sight seem useless, whenever I visualise a young chick the word *plumose* strikes me as far more appropriate, somehow, than the humdrum word *feathered*. To my amusement, whole hosts of cute and exceedingly plumose chicks had suddenly begun to strut and cheep in my mind's eye.

What had happened? How did I suddenly know what *spinking* meant? Everyone is familiar with the penetrating mouth odour given off by a garlic eater, but few people know that there used to be a word, *spinking*, that combined the notions of speaking and stinking. Read the words '*"Oh, those lamb cutlets were absolutely delicious!" he spinked*' and you instantly know – without the word 'garlic' having been mentioned even once – that the character in question will leave an olfactory trail behind him throughout the novel in question.

Bolmigant, grandiferous, disconstutive . . . Knowing those words gave me a feeling of *superiosity* – a hybrid term, now sadly obsolete, formed by the amalgamation of superiority and seriousness. I also knew the meaning of *mesomorphic, leptogamic, ectogilic, yogudromic, spheralic* and *indigabluntic* – all of them derogatory epithets with which one could insult a person to one's total *contentification* (another word regrettably out of fashion).

It gradually dawned on me that the Weeping Shadows were in possession of a store of knowledge dating from a long forgotten epoch when language was considerably more precise and discriminating than it is today. When describing a person we are apt to content ourselves with such woolly adjectives as *pretty* or *ugly*, but my dance with the Shadows had taught me, for example, that a *nasodiscrepant* was a person with nostrils of markedly different sizes, a *puncheonist* someone with a figure like a barrel, and a *neplusultra* someone more than averagely good-looking. Those words were far more subtle.

The Weeping Shadows' love of exactitude embraced every field. Instead of lumping noises together under such banal headings as *bang*, *rustle* or *clatter*, they assigned them onomatopoeic designations appropriate to their special characteristics. The gentle sound of a fluffy feather landing on the floor was a *bfft*. The noise that results when you involuntarily burst out laughing halfway through a glass of beer and squirt the liquid through your nose was known as a *splurph*. The appetising sound of a square of chocolate being broken off a candy bar was a *thnukk*. The terrible noise made by a stick of chalk grating on a blackboard was a *skreek*. As for the awe-inspiring sound of a volcanic eruption, that was aptly termed a *rumbumblion*.

That day, instead of wandering around Shadowhall Castle, I quickly roamed the convolutions of my own brain in search of all the words the Weeping Shadows had so generously deposited there.

Ambivaliguous described a problem you can't make up your mind about.

An *ooff* was the moment when you go to pick something up and find it's too heavy for you, a *whaaa* the sensation you get when you slip on a bar of soap.

The sensual pleasure you derive from squeezing an orange until it goes all soft and squidgy was *fructodism*.

Someone with an obsession for arranging things in alphabetical order was an *abcedist*, whereas someone with an obsession for arranging them in reverse alphabetical order was a *zyxedist*.

Humodont, gnadophile, moptobulism, cryptococcid, blintic, interbodal, phnerkish, insubordious, gnavesome, hoppification, contraptive, bibilogue, omnigorm – there were hundreds and thousands of forgotten words. I snapped them up one by one and bore them off to the cerebral ventricle in which I kept my vocabulary. By the end of the day it had almost doubled in size.

I lingered in my vocabulary chamber for a long time, examining each of my new acquisitions with gratitude and loving pride like a pirate appraising the doubloons and diamonds in a captured treasure chest.

68
Theerio and Practice

I was making rapid strides where writing with my left paw was concerned. It really was my natural way of writing, I suppose, and I had suppressed it for decades. The words now flowed straight from my brain to the paper without drying up repeatedly, as they so often had in the old days. I realised that a writer's writing arm can be likened to the sword arm of a fencer or the leading arm of a boxer. I really could write better with the correct paw. The rhythm of my thoughts now matched the physical movements necessary to transfer those thoughts to paper. There are times when a writer's ideas start flowing and must continue to flow, and that is impossible unless he uses the correct arm.

The Shadow King's tutorials bore little relation to what is customarily taught in the course of a normal artistic training such as I had already received from Dancelot. The curriculum was extremely unconventional – indeed, I might almost call it questionable – and comprised subjects which he alone may have been capable of mastering and transmitting.

'Today I'd like to tell you something about gaseous verse,' Homuncolossus would say. He would then lecture me for hours about poets on a distant planet who consisted of luminous, animate vapour and employed chemically complex methods of writing extremely volatile gaseous poems. According to him, he was in constant touch via the Orm with all the writers who had ever lived at any point in the universe, even those long dead, and exchanged ideas with them regarding their technique and subject matter.

This was nonsense, of course, but he lectured so brilliantly and plausibly that I could only marvel at his inexhaustible ingenuity. His unorthodox didactic method of imparting his monumental store of knowledge was a curious mixture of megalomania and modesty, because he claimed to have picked it up from others. The truth was, he had invented it all himself and never tired, day after day and lesson after lesson, of devising new absurdities that would fire my imagination.

Although lacking any discernible system or serious foundation, the Shadow King's curriculum was singularly well suited to setting my thoughts and my writing arm in motion. It reminded me of the light fiction I'd read in my youth and my inability to stop thinking about a book after laying it aside. Incidentally, the Weeping Shadows had a fitting word for this form of easygoing literary theory – one that sounded far more cheerful and less scholarly, almost like a drinker's toast: *theerio*.

But despite the increasing mobility of my writing paw, and despite my expanded vocabulary and the unusual methods Homuncolossus employed to boost my creativity, I had still written nothing of note. Yet I wrote unceasingly. My spelling and style were flawless, but *what* I wrote was so insignificant that I usually threw my efforts into the fire. Wasn't it all a case of love's labour's lost? Wasn't it possible that I was one of those relatively untalented writers who would never rise above the mediocre? I felt so tired and depressed one day that I shared these dismal thoughts with Homuncolossus.

He deliberated for a while, and I could tell that the decision he seemed to be turning over in his mind was not unimportant to him.

'It's time we addressed the practical side of your training,' he said firmly. 'The Orm cannot be attained by force, but anyone with literary aspirations must also have undergone certain experiences. In that respect, Shadowhall Castle presents opportunities afforded by no other building in the whole of Zamonia.'

'That hadn't escaped me,' I said.

'You don't know the half of it!'

'I thought I knew most of the premises by now.'

Homuncolossus gave a scornful laugh. 'Don't you ever wonder what Shadowhall Castle really is?'

'Of course, all the time.'

'And what conclusion have you come to?'

I shrugged.

'Is it a building?' he asked. 'A trap? A machine? A living creature? Would you like to come with me and find out?'

'Of course.'

'The trip won't be devoid of danger. However, I think I can guarantee that it will provide you with the first great story you'll commit to paper with your new writing paw and your new vocabulary.'

'Let's go, then!'

'To repeat, it could be dangerous. Very dangerous.'

'What can go wrong? I've got the Shadow King as a bodyguard.'

'There are creatures in the catacombs more dangerous than the Shadow King.'

'Even in Shadowhall Castle?'

'In the part of the castle we're going to, yes.'

'Ooh, now you've really whetted my curiosity. Where *are* we going?'

'To the cellar.'

'Shadowhall Castle has a cellar?'

'Of course,' said Homuncolossus. 'Every creepy castle has one.'

68

In the Cellar

It's hard to say how long we took to descend the stairs that led to the cellar of Shadowhall Castle, but it must have been several hours. Besides, the term 'stairs' is rather too simple for the context. In the Weeping Shadows' long-forgotten vocabulary, the kind of route we took was called a *chasmogloom*, which combined the notions of depth and darkness.

We began by descending a flight of stone steps cut into the rock, then climbed down some ornate cast-iron ladders covered with luminous rust (probably installed by the Rusty Gnomes), and in places we even had to abseil or slide down chutes. Eventually we came to a stalactite cave. I expressed disbelief that it really formed part of the castle.

'Of course it does,' Homuncolossus retorted sharply. 'These caves are situated beneath Shadowhall; ergo, they're the castle cellars.' The jellyfish torch he was carrying shed only a meagre light over the spacious cavern, which was cold and damp and smelt of mould and dead fish. I was already beginning to wish myself back in the bizarre but reasonably temperate environment of the castle itself.

Homuncolossus went on ahead with the torch held high. Its light was reflected by amber-coloured crystals that sprouted from the ground on every side like mushrooms. I could no longer detect any signs of civilisation, no carved rocks, no petrified books, no symbols engraved on the walls. I was once more in a part of the catacombs seldom frequented, or so it seemed, by creatures endowed with the power of thought.

'I'm sure you've heard of the *Gigantotomes* found down here,' said Homuncolossus, striding briskly on ahead. 'Books the size of barn doors and so heavy that ten Bookhunters couldn't carry them.'

'Yes, there's something about them in Regenschein's book. He called them old wives' tales spread by the Bookhunters to glamorise their work – and, I suspect, to deter people from following them into the catacombs, because giant books imply the presence of giants.'

'There were legends about giants in the catacombs long before any Bookhunters arrived on the scene. They were known as *Ultrabigs* or *Megabods*. They're believed to have been the earliest inhabitants of this underworld. A long extinct race too bulky for such a cramped environment.'

'The huge skull Hunk Hoggno lived in could have belonged to a giant.'

'It belonged to an animal. An exceptionally large animal, but not a giant.'

Homuncolossus climbed down a shaft and I followed him willy-nilly. It came out in a dark cave so vast that his jellyfish torch illuminated only part of the floor, whose smooth, even surface made an artificial impression. The scent of old books was almost powerful enough to be called a stench.

'Where are we?' I asked. 'Are there some books around here?'

'Pay attention,' said Homuncolossus. 'I'm now going to do something I learnt from the Booklings while observing them in secret.'

'You spied on them? I suppose you do that to everyone, don't you? Haven't you ever heard of the right to privacy?'

Homuncolossus grinned. 'For instance, I left Dancelot's letter outside the entrance to the Leather Grotto. That's how they led me to their Chamber of Marvels. I know ways through the rocks unknown to anyone else. I also know where the Booklings hide their Star of the Catacombs.'

'*You* took them Dancelot's letter?'

'Who else?' Homuncolossus demanded with some justification. 'You read it, I gather.'

I nodded.

'I suppose you always read other people's letters. Haven't you ever heard of the right to privacy?'

I hung my head in shame, only to look up quickly because Homuncolossus had hurled his torch high in the air.

'The Booklings call this flame-throwing,' he said.

'I know.'

387

The blue light of the whirling torch revealed that the cavern was huge – at least a hundred feet high and lined from floor to ceiling with bookcases. This wasn't so remarkable in itself, because I had seen even taller bookcases in the catacombs. The astonishing thing was, the books in them were the size of barn doors.

Having deftly caught the torch, Homuncolossus grinned at me and hurled it into the air once more.

At the sight of those long rows of gigantic volumes standing side by side, I was overcome by an emotion for which 'respect' would be an inadequate definition. The Weeping Shadows had a word for it, namely *chillspine*, a feeling of awe verging on stark terror – a state of mind in which you can barely restrain the urge to fling yourself face down in the dust and beg for mercy.

Homuncolossus caught the torch again.

'Some of the books in here are as big as a house,' he said.

'But surely,' I croaked, 'the folk they belonged to must have been dead for ages?'

'Oh yes,' said Homuncolossus, 'they're long dead and gone.'

I breathed again. These books were merely the artefacts of an extinct race of giants.

'All except for one.'

I gave a start. 'You mean there's something alive down here?'

'Yes, I'm afraid so.'

'What is it?'

'Hard to say. Something very big. A monster.'

'There's a monster living in this cellar?'

'There's a monster in every cellar.'

'So it's a giant *and* a monster?' I was growing uneasy.

'Yes. I don't know how else to put this,' said Homuncolossus. 'It isn't just its size that makes it so monstrous. There's worse to come: I suspect the creature of being a cannibal.'

A monster, a giant and a cannibal – better and better. I could only hope that Homuncolossus was making another attempt to stimulate my imagination with the figments of his own.

'And now', he said, I'll tell you something you certainly won't believe. This giant is a scientist – a sort of alchemist. He can read. He reads all these huge books you see here. He conducts experiments in a gigantic laboratory not far from here. He has stacked the corpses of his ancestors in a vast ice cave. I think he owes his survival to having devoured them one by one. It's their frozen blood that keeps him going.'

Yes, yes, that was the kind of tale you told your playmates as a child, to give them the creeps. Perhaps the Shadow King intended to train me to be a thriller writer.

'Do you know what else I think?' he asked.

'I can hardly wait to hear.'

Homuncolossus bent down and addressed me in a hoarse, conspiratorial whisper. 'I think this giant is insane – completely off his head.' He tapped his brow. 'Except that he doesn't have a head.'

'He doesn't?'

'No, not what *we* would call a head. He doesn't have a mouth either, but I once saw him devouring one of those corpses. Believe me, it was the most unappetising sight I've ever—'

'That's enough!' I exclaimed. 'You don't scare me. Come on, it's time you told me what we're really looking for down here.'

'I already did. We're looking for the secret of Shadowhall Castle, the ultimate mystery of the catacombs.'

'There isn't any giant here. You're simply trying it on.'

'Take the lead, then, if you're so unafraid.'

'I will.'

'In that case, carry on.'

I brushed past the Shadow King and took a few hesitant steps into the gloom.

'If this really is the haunt of a dangerous monster,' I said, 'why would you be crazy enough to set foot in it?'

'I'm not,' Homuncolossus retorted. '*You* are.'

'What do you mean?' I asked, turning round. But he wasn't there any more. His jellyfish torch was lying on the ground, but that was all.

66

Dinosaur Sweat

I was reminded of the pranks we used to play in my boyhood. At Lindworm Castle we would lure younger playmates into dark, eerie caves and then run off. We thought it was terribly funny to leave them there, blubbing helplessly as they stumbled around in the dark while we laughed ourselves sick in some secret hiding place. But I was thirty or forty years old at the time – a mere child. The Shadow King's practical jokes were equally infantile.

'Homuncolossus!' I called. 'What is all this nonsense?'

No answer.

I went over to the torch and picked it up.

'Homuncolossus!' I called again.

'*Coloss . . . loss . . . loss . . . us . . . us . . .*' the echoes replied.

He was bound to be lurking in the darkness somewhere. However, I wasn't going to gratify him by showing any sign of fear or weakness, so I simply raised the torch above my head and strode further into the enormous library. He could slink after me if he was enjoying himself so much.

The sight of those monstrous great books in the blue light of the torch was theatrical, like the backdrop for a play about ogres. They must have been thousands of years old, judging by the smell, so it was remarkable that they hadn't disintegrated. Perhaps the giants who produced them knew of a special method of preserving paper – *if* the pages were made of paper and not of metal or the hide of some primeval beast. I could only see their massive, sometimes scaly backs, which were adorned with little studs. These, too, may have been a form of writing. What stories did the books contain? Or were they scientific works devoted to crazy giganto-alchemism? I would have needed a dozen pairs of sturdy arms to topple such a volume off a shelf and examine it.

Lying at the bottom of one of the bookcases was a metal gadget resembling a pair of compasses, except that it had three points and was twice my size. The legs were of silver, now almost black with oxidation, whereas the pivot, screws and points were made of brass. Unfamiliar symbols were engraved on the metal. Units of measurement, perhaps? An archaeological find of this nature would have caused a sensation in Bookholm, except that I would have needed a horse and cart to shift it.

So I really was in the domain of a race of giants and this had been their library. It gradually dawned on me what Homuncolossus was up to. He had brought me here and left me on my own so as to kindle my imagination with these fascinating sights. Perhaps he meant me to write a story about giants when we got back to Shadowhall. Anyone intending to write on a monumental scale needed monumental material to work with. And what wonderful material this was! No legend, no fairy tale, no chimera, but the true story of a vanished race of titans to be researched with the aid of their artefacts. Perhaps I might, after all, be able to heave one of these enormous volumes off a shelf and leaf through it.

I really wasn't scared any more, just burning with curiosity. In search of more details, I got as close to the shelves as I could. They also held objects other than books: a gold needle as long as a spear; a heap of dried skins covered with indecipherable symbols and so big that they could only have been elephant hides; a crystal the size of a boulder, possibly a paperweight.

What had these things looked like from a giant's perspective? If I had encountered one of these ancient behemoths, would he have trampled me like a bug, perhaps without even noticing me?

It had been an excellent idea to bring me here. I was grateful to Homuncolossus for granting me this experience. He was welcome to giggle to himself in the dark like a schoolboy if it injected a little variety into his dreary existence.

Overcome with exuberance, I felt an urge to prove to him how unafraid I was: I would climb the nearest bookcase and try to extract a book. I might be able to cope with one of the smaller specimens.

So I hoisted myself on to the bottom shelf and, like a general inspecting a guard of honour, strolled along the row of books in search of a particularly slender volume. I found one no thicker than myself and barely a head taller – a mere shrimp compared to the others. That one I felt I could cope with. Putting my torch down, I climbed over the book into the space behind it and proceeded to push.

I felt a trifle uneasy all of a sudden. The cavity was so dark and smelt so musty, an outsize spider or giant earwig might easily be lurking in there! Galvanised by this unpleasant idea, I pushed the book out with little difficulty. It landed on the floor with a loud crash whose echoes reverberated round the dark library for several seconds.

Success! I patted the book dust from my cloak and looked around, but Homuncolossus still didn't show himself, the cussed devil. He was probably skulking in the dark somewhere, marvelling at my nerve. I climbed down off the bookcase and examined the book.

I opened it eagerly. The cover creaked open like the lid of an ancient sarcophagus. The pages were as thick as my thumb and composed of some leathery grey material that bore little or no resemblance to paper. They were covered with the same little pyramidal knobs that adorned most of the books' spines – the giants' alphabet, probably. They afforded no clue to what the book was about.

I was proud of myself for all that. I had to be one of the very few people who had ever leafed through a Gigantotome. I was a pioneer in the field of gigantological research!

Suddenly I pricked up my ears – I thought I'd heard something. Was that me trembling with curiosity, or was the ground vibrating? Yes, the ground was definitely vibrating and so was the book. The tremor became more and more pronounced.

Rather uneasy now, I peered around anxiously in search of Homuncolossus. Perhaps it was an earthquake. Or a subterranean volcanic eruption. Perhaps a huge mud slide was speeding through the catacombs towards me.

The rumbling sound became more alarming still. Big grains of dust started to dance on the shelves. Pneumatic sounds like the squeal of a dozen bagpipes and the thunder of an organ were issuing from the darkness. The high-pitched, agitated trills were underlaid by a deep, persistent diapason.

And then, out of the darkness and into the blue light of my torch, came . . . the giant!

At first sight he looked like a mighty wave. Grey and tapering to a point, he was at least twenty or thirty times my height. Then I realised that the substance billowing towards me – and giving off an infernal stench – was living flesh. In some strange way, the giant's conical shape reminded me of the hill on which my home, Lindworm Castle, was situated.

He was covered all over with trunklike excrescences, many of which hung limp while others flailed the air in an agitated fashion. Between these trunks were membranes the size of windows. There must have been dozens of these perforated filters of flaccid grey flesh, which expanded and contracted like gills. I could discern no eyes, nor were there any arms or legs to be seen. The gigantic, animate mass seemed to propel itself along like a snail.

The giant came to a halt. His trunks sniffed the air in all directions, his membranes pulsated with a steady rhythm. I wondered why he didn't come straight for me and the torch, the only light source in the cave. Surely he had seen me?

And then I understood: he was blind! Like so many creatures in the catacombs, he found his way around by touch, hearing and smell, hence all those trunks and membranes. He had a hundred noses but no eyes at all. The noise of the book hitting the ground had attracted his attention. For the moment, however, I didn't exist for him because I wasn't making a sound.

So why all the books, I wondered. What did a blind creature want with them? Could he see after all, possibly with those curious membranes or an eye concealed in one of his trunks? Should I simply run off in the opposite direction? If he really was blind, that might be a bad idea. He might hear my footsteps, my cloak flapping, my laboured breathing.

Better to stay put, then? Better not to make a sound, to hold my breath and wait till the danger passed? That seemed the wisest course of action. Perhaps he had only paused to listen and would soon retire again. Yes, I would stay put and keep quite still, that was the best idea. Wasn't that the thing to do when confronted by any large and dangerous creature?

Suddenly, I broke out in a sweat. I had always found it odd that I hardly perspired at all while engaged in physical exertion, whereas the sweat streamed down me as soon as I stopped. That was what happened now: I was bathed in sweat within seconds.

And believe me, dear readers, dinosaur sweat has a very special aroma. It smells considerably stronger than the sweat of any other life form because its original function was to signal our *presence*. This property of dinosaur sweat dates back to primeval times, when we were the most dangerous, most feared creatures far and wide. Our body odour was designed to paralyse our prey with fright. Other life forms camouflage themselves or assume a deterrent appearance, whereas we dinosaurs give off a stench like a compost heap in August. I might just as well have operated a fire alarm or struck a gong to attract the giant's attention.

The colossal creature gave a contented whistle and pointed all its mobile trunks in my direction. It had discovered me! Its membranes began to throb violently and emitted a series of frightful slurping sounds. Then the mountain of flesh got under way again, heading straight for me.

I did what I would probably have done had a tidal wave been bearing down on me: nothing at all. There was no point in running away from such an elemental force, quite apart from the fact that my legs wouldn't have obeyed me. The monster performed two or three huge, squelching undulations and came to a halt just in front of me with its numerous trunks trumpeting simultaneously. I was seized by several of these yards-long excrescences and passed from one to another until I was almost at the summit of the conical monster, where one of its pulsating membranes was situated. Still paralysed with fear, I was convulsively gripping the jellyfish torch, which bathed the giant's upper extremity in a ghostly blue glow. Two of its trunks supported me under the arms and held me just in front of the membrane, which now expelled a blast of warm air through its numerous perforations. The smell was so appalling, dear readers, that my sole recourse was to lapse into profound unconsciousness.

The Giant's Zoo

I came round to find myself at the bottom of a glass jar as tall as a house complete with chimney. The sides were so smooth, I could never have scaled them and climbed out. I saw through the glass that the jar was standing on a shelf quite high up in a rectangular room whose walls were lined with more shelves. These were laden with gigantic books and at least a hundred more glass jars. I also saw some bizarre metal instruments whose function eluded me.

My jellyfish torch, which was lying on a shelf opposite, bathed the room in dim blue luminescence. The giant appeared to have taken it from me for further examination.

What alarmed me most about my predicament was not just the fact of my captivity but the contents of the other jars. Living creatures of the most repulsive kind, they were all denizens of the catacombs known to me either from descriptions or from personal experience. One jar contained a Spinxxxx, another a huge gold millipede with massive pincers. A white-haired spider the size of a horse was scuttling around in the jar immediately beside my own. On the shelf opposite, a captive Harpyr was clawing at the sides of its glass prison. I also saw a scaly green Tunnel Python of immense length, a plumed Catamorph, a black-eyed rat with red fur and chisel teeth as big as sabres, a Crystalloscorpion and a Wolfbat with a wingspan of at least ten feet.

In short, the room seemed to contain one specimen of every dangerous species in the catacombs, the only reassuring circumstance being that each was a prisoner like me. Sporadic clicks could be heard whenever the creatures strove to escape from their glass containers and scrabbled at the smooth sides in vain. Many of the jars were open at the top, but others had grilles over them because their inmates possessed suckers or wings that would have enabled them to escape. It was a zoo of a very special kind. I now knew what Homuncolossus had meant when he told me the giant was a scientist.

I could already hear him piping and trumpeting in the distance. My fellow prisoners became so agitated on hearing those noises that I could only fear the worst. He was coming to experiment on us.

The pneumatic sounds grew rapidly louder. Moments later the giant appeared in the doorway, which was pyramidal in shape like his body. The overpowering stench emitted by his membranes assailed my nostrils, even inside the jar, and made me feel sick again. He greeted us on entering with a deep bass note that sounded like a tuba. Then, having undulated to the middle of the room, he turned on the spot several times with all his trunks extended and sniffing audibly – a blind creature's method of surveying its surroundings. At length he emitted another contented blast on the tuba and went over to a shelf from which he removed a jar containing an insect.

I'm not much of an expert on entomology because most insects fill me with a revulsion proportionate to the number of legs they possess. Being regrettably ignorant of the precise scientific designation of the creature in question, therefore, I christened it the *Flying Tailor*.

Its scorpionlike body was as big as that of a calf and its six long arms and legs terminated in pincers that gleamed metallically like scissors. It also had a long, thin tail – just as shiny and metallic – resembling an outsize bodkin. This 'tailor' could not only cut and sew, it could fly as well, because it was equipped with two pairs of big, whirring dragonfly's wings.

The giant thrust one of his trunks through the grille over the jar and blew into it briefly, whereupon the Flying Tailor collapsed. Having opened the jar, he removed the unconscious insect, replaced the jar on the shelf and came straight towards me, trumpeting happily.

I shrank back against the glass in terror, but I wasn't his intended destination. That privilege was reserved for the white-haired spider in the jar beside mine. He uncorked the jar and dropped the insect in. The white spider reacted promptly: it proceeded to cocoon its visitor in long, sticky threads of its own secretion. At that, the Flying Tailor woke up.

I will spare you an overly detailed description of what happened in the neighbouring jar, dear readers, and confine myself to the bare essentials. The Flying Tailor, which was vastly superior to the white spider, eventually transfixed it with its bodkinlike tail, then systematically dissected it with its razor-sharp pincers.

More revolting still, however, was the behaviour of the giant scientist. He listened delightedly to the gruesome noises issuing from the glass vessel and accompanied them with a veritable symphony of notes of varying pitch. From the relish and artistry with which he did this, he might almost have been improvising a musical accompaniment to the insects' duel to the death.

Once the white-haired spider had been completely dismembered and spitted on the Flying Tailor's bodkin, the terrible giant lost interest and turned away. He propelled his enormous stone-grey bulk over to another shelf, took down one of the huge books and opened it. Then whistling to himself, he systematically ran several of his trunks over the pages.

I was still so dismayed by recent developments that it took me a while to grasp the truth: the giant was reading. I should have been quicker on the uptake: the pyramidal studs on the pages were a form of Braille and he was deciphering it by touch. He was probably consulting some bizarre scientific manual for advice on which dangerous insects to pit against each other next.

At length, having emitted another booming bass note that made every jar in the room vibrate, he replaced the book and went over to a mysterious apparatus mounted on the wall between two bookshelves. It was an intricate system of gold tubing fitted with numerous valves and controls.

Using some of his trunks simultaneously, he manipulated several gold stopcocks and handwheels. There was a loud bubbling and gurgling from inside the pipes. Then, quite suddenly and to my utter amazement, the ghostly music of Shadowhall Castle rang out.

It was only now that I noticed some inconspicuous triangular apertures in the walls just above the bookcases. They were the source not only of the music, but also of an audible current of air that quickly dispersed the giant's stench and at last made breathing less unpleasant.

Fresh air . . . So that was Shadowhall's secret! The entire building was a ventilation system installed by a primeval race of huge scientists and designed to channel the air of the catacombs into the nether regions where they lived. The weird music was probably just a side effect of the controlled airflow, but the giant seemed to enjoy it, for he joined in with a series of high-pitched whistles and his monstrous body swayed in time to the melody.

He went over to a shelf and removed a jar with an insect rampaging around inside it, then undulated over to me and deposited the jar beside my own. Inserting one of his trunks in our glass prisons, he sniffed us in turn, first the insect, then me. To judge by his ensuing fanfares, he found the scent of my dinosaur sweat delightful in the extreme. It wasn't hard to guess what he had in mind: I and the creature in the adjacent jar had been selected to fight the next duel.

That creature, dear readers, probably an outcast from the nethermost regions of the underworld, was without doubt the most repulsive and disgusting thing I had ever set eyes on. Imagine a full-grown pig from which the skin has just been flayed to reveal its raw flesh and sinews. Supporting this torso were five milk-white, unarticulated tubes equipped with suckers. Dozens of black, faceted eyes were distributed all over its body, together with the same number of beaklike feeding orifices. Most unreal of all, however, was the fact that its suckers enabled it to walk up the jar's glass sides like a fly. What would this monster do to me? The white spider's ghastly fate would doubtless seem positively merciful in comparison.

All at once there was a distant sound that made even the giant stop short. It came from outside the room, and I was probably the only living creature present in whom it aroused hope instead of trepidation: it was the sigh of the Shadow King.

The giant turned away, drew himself up to his full height and trumpeted with annoyance. At length, after seeming to deliberate for a moment, he started to whistle cheerfully and shut off the music and airflow by spinning the handwheels on his ventilation system. Then he swiftly undulated out of the laboratory. He had probably decided to capture the Shadow King for his menagerie before staging some more gladiatorial contests.

Peculiar noises were issuing from the jars – all expressive of relief, no doubt, that the evil giant had gone. At least that granted me a brief respite in which to assess my chances of escaping.

My assessment didn't take long, however. I could see absolutely no possibility of escaping from my glass container unaided, dear readers. The repulsive creature in the adjacent jar was regarding me greedily with its numerous eyes as it squelched round the glass sides on sucker-equipped feet. Had it not been for the grille over the mouth of its jar, it would by now have climbed across into mine and set to work on me.

'Hey!' said a voice above me. 'Up here.'

I looked up. Homuncolossus was abseiling down from a shelf overhead. He straddled the mouth of my jar and peered in.

'So *there* you are,' he said reproachfully. 'In trouble again, eh?'

Before I could remonstrate with him, he lowered the rope.

'Tie that round your waist,' he whispered, 'and leave the rest to me.'

I did as I was bidden. Vigorously and with no sign of effort, Homuncolossus hauled me out as if I were no heavier than a sack of feathers. Then he lowered me down the outside of the jar, slid down after me and landed safely on both feet.

'Right,' he said, 'let's tidy up in here.'

Going to the jar containing the frightful insect, he threw his weight against it and pushed it off the shelf with surprising ease. It hit the floor with a loud crash and disintegrated. I hurried to the edge of the shelf and peered down. The horrific creature was climbing out of the shattered remains unscathed.

'Are you mad?' I cried. 'Don't you realise how dangerous these creatures are?'

'Of course,' said Homuncolossus, and proceeded to push the next jar off the shelf. It landed with a crash that sounded as if a whole glass factory had fallen from the sky and a huge, fat black snake came wriggling out of the debris.

'The giant will hear you!' I protested.

'Let's hope so,' said Homuncolossus, launching a third jar into space. Another crash, and a Crystalloscorpion was now at liberty. I could hear the giant whistling angrily in the distance.

Homuncolossus had picked up a huge gold pin and was levering away at the next jar. Like a skittle, it toppled sideways on to its neighbour and knocked that over too. They rolled off the shelf together and shattered on the floor. I didn't look to see what evil creatures had regained their freedom this time.

'What on earth are you doing?' I hissed. 'How are we ever going to get out of here?'

Homuncolossus paid no attention. He was looking at the shelves across the room from us, apparently well pleased with what was happening over there. Encouraged by his vandalism, the jars' inmates had begun to racket around, leaping or flying at the glass sides in an attempt to knock their prisons over as Homuncolossus had done. A few of them succeeded, with the result that another three or four jars fell to the floor and smashed.

The room was now filled with venomous hisses, menacing clatters and the whirring of wings. A red insect not unlike a monstrous grasshopper was zooming round the room, buzzing aggressively.

The infuriated giant reappeared in the doorway, his many trunks sniffing in a feverish manner. Then his membranes began to pulsate violently, filling the air with his noxious, stupefying scent.

'Now we're done for!' I cried. 'We'll pass out!'

'Wait,' said Homuncolossus. 'This I must see.'

The giant squelched to the middle of the room, whistling and trumpeting hysterically. As if in response to a secret word of command, the liberated creatures promptly fell on him. The frightful insect clambered up his body on sucker-feet and hacked away at him with its numerous beaks, the flying grasshopper transfixed him with its long sting, the Crystalloscorpion sank its pincers into his grey flesh.

The giant defended himself as best he could. He gave vent to a long-drawn-out, ear-splitting bass note as his violently throbbing membranes diffused the stupefying vapour, but the frenzied creatures were undeterred; they continued to attack him from all sides and by all available means. The black snake seized one of his trunks in a stranglehold while a monstrous rat tugged at another with its sharp teeth. The giant staggered into a bookcase and clung to it for support, only to send more jars crashing to the floor. More flying insects of horrific appearance – iridescent wings and bright green stings – arose from the debris.

The giant emitted a last, despairing, almost pathetic whistle as he slowly sank to the floor.

His stupefying vapour had drifted over to us by now, and I was struggling to remain conscious.

'Let's get out of here,' said Homuncolossus. Gripping me by my cloak, he steered me over to a hole in the wall behind the shelves and pushed me through it.

'This passage leads out of the cellar,' he said. 'We've seen enough.'

For once, we were of the same opinion.

A Good Story

'Well,' said Homuncolossus, 'you've had an experience. Now write it down.'

We were back in the dining hall at Shadowhall Castle, having completed our strenuous ascent from the cellar.

'Eh?' I said.

'Not this minute,' he said. 'Tomorrow. Sit down tomorrow and write about it. If that isn't a good story, what is?'

'I will,' I promised. 'By the way, did you know that Shadowhall Castle is really a ventilation system?'

He gave me a long look.

'You've learnt a lot already,' he said at length.

'No, no, I'm not making it up. Shadowhall is an ancient ventilation system. The giants used it to feed air into the lower reaches of the catacombs. That's the whole secret.'

'Of course.' He smiled. 'I envy your wealth of imagination. You must definitely include that in your story. It's really good.'

The next day, when I awoke feeling rested but aching all over, I promptly got down to writing an account of my recent experience.

I seated myself at a table with pencil and paper, and debated how to start.

Where to begin? With the Shadow King's disappearance? But first I would have to describe him, and that was a pretty tall order – it would take time. Mightn't it be better to begin by explaining how I'd landed myself in such a situation? Yes, except that then I would have to go back a long way – back to Dancelot's death, in fact. That would make a whole book, not a short story.

Hm. In that case, how about a quick impression, a brilliant little study in horror? Should I start at the moment when I awoke to find myself a prisoner? '*I woke up at the bottom of a jar.*' That was an excellent opening – no one could fail to want to read on!

Good. Next, a detailed description of those gigantic insects. That was unadulterated horror. Very well, I told myself, get on with it!

But before I could do so my heart began to race and my paw trembled violently. How close I had come to death! How recent my terrible ordeal seemed and how vivid and disturbing the images it conjured up! The giant's stench still clung to my clothes and his curious music still rang in my ears. I broke out in a sweat at the very thought of him.

No words seemed adequate to describe the horrors I had experienced. How was I to capture all the dreadful emanations of such a colossal being? How to paint a word picture of a scene as monstrous as that of the giant succumbing to the onslaught of those terrible creatures? Did I want to relive it all again? No! The pencil snapped between my fingers.

'Writer's block, eh?' said Homuncolossus.

I looked round. He was standing just behind me.

'How long have you been there?' I asked.

'Not long. You're finding it all too much for such a little piece of paper, is that it?'

'Now that I come to write the story down, I'm even more frightened than I was in that jar. I just don't understand it. I was supposed to experience something so as to be able to write about it, but now . . .'

'Writers are there to write, not experience things. If you want to experience things, become a pirate or a Bookhunter. If you want to write, write. If you can't find the makings of a story inside yourself, you won't find them anywhere.'

'Really? You tell me that *now*? Why didn't you tell me yesterday? We could have spared ourselves that trip to the cellar.'

'I needed your help. I'd been wanting to clear out the cellar for ages. I couldn't have done it without your assistance.'

'My *assistance*? You used me as bait, that's all. You might have warned me.'

'I did. I told you there was a monster down there. I said he was a huge, cannibalistic scientist, but you didn't believe me.'

'From now on I'll believe every word you say.'

'Now it's my turn to disbelieve *you*. For instance, what if I said I was going to show you the Orm? Would you believe me?'

'No.'

'You see? Still, that's just what I'm going to do. Come with me!'

'The last time you said "Come with me!" I wound up in a glass jar belonging to a gigantic scientist with a hundred noses. I'm not sure I *want* to come with you.'

Homuncolossus grinned. 'It won't be that kind of lesson. Yesterday was practice, today it's time for more theerio.'

'Theerio?'

'Theerio!'

Ꝓ℮ꝡ
The Library of the Orm

It was surprising how snug and homely Shadowhall Castle seemed after my visit to the cellar. The Weeping Shadows had ceased to strike me as sinister, the Animatomes I no longer regarded as vermin. I was among good friends! The ghostly music, too, no longer seemed ghostly now that I had fathomed its secret. I was in high spirits as I walked along behind Homuncolossus and followed him into a library I'd never entered before. Although somewhat larger than the other two I'd so far seen in the castle, it was, like them, of modest size.

'Well,' I said cheerfully, 'what kind of library is this? Do the books vanish into thin air if you touch them, or do they whisk you off to another dimension? Can they sing or dance or something? Do they yield milk and honey? Nothing would surprise me now.'

'I wouldn't be too sure,' the Shadow King said darkly.

'I survived the whistling giant's library,' I said. 'I'm past being thrown by anything down here, so tell me: what *is* this collection?'

'My personal library,' said Homuncolossus.

'Oh, really? Interesting. What criteria did you apply when selecting it? Are the books on the Golden List? Are they valuable, or more on the dangerous side?'

'More on the dangerous side.' He grinned. 'But not in the way you mean. Valuable? Yes, that too, but not in your sense of the word.'

'Wow,' I said, 'very mysterious! The Shadow King is indulging in vague allusions again. He remains an enigma!'

'What I mean is, they're books for writers, not collectors, and they can be genuinely dangerous even though they won't kill or injure you.'

'More mysterious still,' I said. 'But you can't scare me, Homuncolossus. Books can't hurt me.'

'These books can. This is the *Library of the Orm*.'

The Orm, huh? Careful, I told myself, this is a ticklish subject, so lay off the wisecracks and disrespectful remarks.

'The Library of the Orm? What does that mean?'

'It means that I selected and arranged these books according to how intensely their authors were pervaded by the Orm while writing them.'

'Aha . . .'

'I'd like you to read some of them. The choice is yours, I won't force any recommendations on you. Just a hint for your guidance: the Orm flowed most strongly through the books on the upper shelves. The lower you go—'

'The less Orm.' I grinned at him. 'I get the picture.'

'You can stay here as long as you like. I'll bring you your meals.'

'Great. Is that all? Don't I have to slay a dragon first, or something?'

'I already told you, this is the theoretical part.'

'Good.'

'Then I won't intrude on you any longer. Enjoy yourself!' So saying, the Shadow King silently withdrew.

I strolled along the shelves with my head on one side, checking the titles.

The Cloud Cuckoo by Bronsar Morello. *Recollections of the Day after Tomorrow* by Arlon Dumpsey. *A Pig in My Poke* by Nestroket Krumpf. Never heard of them, neither the books nor their authors. Were these supposed to be literary gems?

Little Enemies by Minimus Suminim. *A Cure for the Incurable* by Welgo Tark. *Warts on a Toad's Neck* by Horam Quackenbush. *Nasal Hairs* by Hazel Nares.

And those were the books on the top shelf! I'd never read any of them. They were the sort of books I usually glanced at in a bookshop and then forgot for ever. Could it be that the Shadow King's taste in reading matter was rather odd, not to say mediocre or even poor? He wasn't infallible, after all, just because he could write well.

Soft Teeth by Carius Molar. *The Joys of Gardening* by . . . What! I came to a halt and automatically removed a book for the first time.

It was Dancelot's masterpiece, cheek by jowl with all this worthless trash! I weighed it in my paws for a while. Then the blood rushed to my head!

Yes, dear readers, I felt ashamed because I had behaved as ignorantly as all the stupid fools who had spurned Dancelot's book. What made me so sure that Arlon Dumpsey's *Recollections of the Day after Tomorrow* was of no interest? Or *Warts on a Toad's Neck*? Had I ever given those books a fair crack of the whip? Perhaps I had just ignored them for the umpteenth time for reasons I myself couldn't have explained.

Shame on me! I had to make amends. Taking *Warts on a Toad's Neck* from the shelf, I sat down and began to read it.

Addicted

'No!' I wailed. 'No, I won't! I don't want to leave the Library of the Orm! I want to stay here! Please!'

But the Shadow King held me in an iron grip and dragged me off along the passage regardless of my struggles.

'I warned you those books were dangerous,' he said. 'Now you've read enough of them.'

'No!' I shrieked. 'I've only read a *fraction* of them. I hadn't the least idea such books existed. I must read them all! *All*!'

'Do you know how long you've been in that library?' Homuncolossus demanded as he continued to tow me along. 'Like to guess?'

I strove to remember. A week? Five weeks? Six? I hadn't a clue.

'I don't know either,' he said, 'but it must be a good two months.'

'So what? Two months, two years, I couldn't care less! I've got to read those books!'

'I've had to force-feed you,' Homuncolossus said. 'You never sleep, you never wash. You stink like a pig.'

'Don't care,' I said defiantly. 'No time to. Got to read.'

'You're reading yourself to death!' he roared. 'I had to get you out of there.'

'But I still haven't read *Flames of Folly*!' I protested. 'Or *Dreams of a Yellow Overcoat*! Or *The Wooden Spider*! I've only skimmed the lower shelves so far. I've got to read them all! I've simply got to!'

My eyes were burning like fire – they smarted every time I blinked – and my paws were raw from turning pages. My brain was positively bursting with innumerable brilliant ideas, magnificent snippets of dialogue, fascinating characters.

'Are you sure the books on the upper shelves are really so much better than the others?' I babbled. 'I think they're all equally superb.'

'There are some fine distinctions,' Homuncolossus growled.

'Let me go!' I wailed. 'Please! I can't conceive of life without those books!'

He came to a halt.

'That's far enough,' he said. 'You won't find your way back to the library from here.'

I fell on my knees and started to weep. 'Why are you doing this to me?' I sobbed. 'Why show me paradise and drag me back to hell?'

'You wanted to know what the Orm can do. Now you know. Any more of it would kill you.'

'Damn the Orm!' I shouted. 'What is it? I still don't understand!'

Homuncolossus helped me to my feet and held me tight.

'You'll understand the instant you sense it. Yes, you can sense it. There are moments when ideas for whole novels rain down on you in seconds. You can sense it when you write some dialogue so brilliant that actors will recite it on stage, word for word, in a thousand years' time. Oh yes, you can sense the Orm! It can give you a kick up the backside, transfix you like a shaft of lightning or turn your stomach. It can rip the brain out of your head and reinsert it the other way round! It can sit on your chest in the middle of the night and give you a frightful nightmare – one from which you'll fashion your finest novel. I've sensed the Orm myself – oh yes! – and I wish I could sense it just once more.'

So saying, he flung me aside like a wet dishrag and disappeared into the gloom.

'But I want to read some more of it!' I called after him.

'Then you'll have to write it yourself,' he replied in the far distance.

The Bargain

I spent the next few days roaming the castle as before, but not in search of an exit; I was looking for the Library of the Orm. Scores of Animatomes dogged my footsteps because I'd taken to distributing my meals among them now that food no longer interested me. They were constantly milling around me in hopes of a second helping.

All that interested me was the library. I had been addicted to it ever since reading *Warts on a Toad's Neck* and I now knew what Homuncolossus had meant about the very special form of danger it presented. The books in his private collection embodied literature infinitely superior to the rubbishy classics prescribed by school syllabuses.

I had read *Warts* first with amusement, then with growing enthusiasm and finally in a state of ecstasy. I sensed a dynamism lacking in the traditional novel, an energy that transmitted itself to me in the course of reading. When I finished the book I felt simultaneously replete and hungry – eager to absorb some more of that energy as soon as possible. So I seized on the next book.

That was how it had all begun. I don't know how long I read for at a stretch before exhaustion compelled me to take a brief nap, but it must have been after ten books or so.

I vaguely remember that Homuncolossus appeared from time to time and bullied me into eating a little food, which I reluctantly consumed while continuing to read. I *lived* more intensely than ever before. I laughed and cried, loved and hated. I experienced unbearable suspense and abysmal horror, the pangs of unrequited love, the sorrow of parting, the fear of death. But there were also moments of unalloyed happiness and triumphant exultation, romantic enchantment and hysterical rapture. I had reacted like that only once before, while reading Homuncolossus's manuscript, and here was a whole library of such books written in the Alphabet of the Stars. Although they fell far short of his own towering genius, they were infinitely finer than anything I had ever read before.

If it really was the Orm that made these books so special, I was addicted to them – addicted to every Orm-saturated line. Food? Unimportant. Washing? A waste of time. All that mattered was to read, read, read.

I read on my feet, I read seated, I read lying down. I plucked book after book from the shelves, polished it off and flung it heedlessly over my shoulder before seizing the next. I barely noticed Homuncolossus tidying up after me and replacing my discards neatly on the shelves. It didn't embarrass me in the least that I was demoting my host to the status of a servant because I never gave the matter a moment's thought.

The books that passed through my paws and brain were of every conceivable genre: novels and volumes of poetry, children's books and scientific works, thrillers and biographies, short stories and collections of letters, fables and fairy tales. They even included a cookbook, I remember. Common to them all was the mysterious power that pervaded them – a power to which I became more and more addicted the more of it I absorbed.

It was like being roused from a wonderful, intoxicating dream when the Shadow King eventually hauled me out of the library. I tottered through the castle for days, hoping to recapture that dream, but I was no more successful in rediscovering the Library of the Orm than I had been in finding an exit.

Sometimes, in the course of my hopeless quest, I would pick up and dip into one of the ordinary books that lay strewn around the castle. Whenever I did, it seemed so insipid and insubstantial that I flew into a rage and hurled it at the wall after reading the first few sentences. I was spoilt for any other form of literature, and the mental torment I endured was comparable to the agony of unrequited love compounded by the withdrawal symptoms associated with a severe addiction.

One day my wanderings brought me face to face with the Shadow King. He was lurking in a shadowy passage and his sudden reappearance scared me half to death.

'Listen,' he said, 'you can't go on like this.'

'Then take me back to the library!' I implored.

'That's no solution,' he replied. 'I'll take you somewhere else.'

'Where?' I asked anxiously.

'Up above. I'll take you back to Bookholm.'

I felt bewildered.

'You will?'

'I've done a great deal of thinking in the last few days. About your suggestion, among other things.'

That set me thinking too. What suggestion? Then I remembered.

'You mean about coming back with me and living in Colophonius Regenschein's compound?'

'I've ceased to belong among the living up there, but neither do I belong among the dead down here. Perhaps I could exist in an intermediate zone. It's worth a try.'

'That would be wonderful!' I exclaimed. Once aroused, my nostalgia for the world above was starting to displace my yearning for the Library of the Orm.

'There's a problem, though,' Homuncolossus added. 'And the problem has a name.'

'Pfistomel Smyke,' I said gloomily.

'We won't have a chance up there unless we eliminate him first. That's my one condition: you must help me to get rid of him. If you promise me that, I'll guide you to the surface.'

This time I didn't have to think twice. Enthusiasm was steadily clearing my head. 'Agreed,' I said. 'But how do you propose to go about it?'

'If we worsted the most dangerous creature in the bowels of Bookholm, we can dispose of the most dangerous creature on the surface of the city.'

'That's the spirit!' I cried. 'Let's go!'

'But there's something I must attend to first.'

'What's that?' I asked. There had to be a snag, of course.

'I must rid the Leather Grotto of those verminous invaders. I want to leave my kingdom in good order. You can help me to do that too.'

I'm bound to admit, dear readers, that my joyful sense of anticipation was blighted by the prospect of accompanying Homuncolossus back to the Leather Grotto and tackling the most vicious and ruthless of the Bookhunters *à deux*. I was already wishing myself back in the Library of the Orm, but it was too late to renege on our bargain now.

Farewell to Shadowhall

We were followed at first by only a handful of Animatomes when we prepared to leave Shadowhall Castle. The Shadow King strode resolutely on ahead, never hesitating for a moment when we came to an intersection.

'How do you manage to find your way out every time?' I asked him. 'Is there a special method?'

'I don't know what Pfistomel Smyke did to my eyes,' he said, 'but I can now see things I never saw before, even microscopically small things. These walls don't look the same to me as they do to you. I can detect every tiny little difference between them. To me it's as if they're all covered with different wallpapers. That's an aid to finding my bearings. Even though they occasionally surprise me by changing their location, they always resume their original places in the end. It takes a bit longer on some occasions than others, but I've never failed to find my way out.'

I noticed that the number of Animatomes following us had doubled in a very short time. We were now joined by a few Weeping Shadows, which sobbed as they flitted after us. More and more of them appeared, transforming our departure from Shadowhall into a regular procession. More Shadows glided out of every passage and more Animatomes came scuttling, crawling or fluttering out of every dark corner until our retinue was thousands strong.

Nor was it only the Weeping Shadows that made mournful noises: the Animatomes sniffed and whimpered as if aware that their Shadow King was leaving them for ever. My own mood darkened too. I had developed a great affection for Shadowhall Castle and its weird inhabitants; in fact, it had temporarily become my second home. Having experienced and learnt so much there, I would always remember it with nostalgia. However our adventure turned out, it was unlikely that I would ever see the place again.

The Shadow King himself was not unmoved, I could tell. His steps became steadily slower and he occasionally emitted sounds that betrayed his emotional turmoil, so it was with a combination of gloom and relief that we finally emerged from the castle. I would never have believed that this long-awaited moment would inspire me with such mixed feelings.

Once outside we were greeted by moist heat and the crimson glow of molten lava. The Animatomes, which had streamed out of the castle in our wake, climbed up its walls for a long-range view of our departure. The Weeping Shadows remained in the entrance, sobbing with such abandon that we could still hear them when we had already ascended the long flight of steps and passed through the gateway into the next cave.

𝓰◎𝓰
Back to the Leather Grotto

Ientered the Leather Grotto on my own. It was an appalling spectacle. The shelves were almost denuded of books, the furniture had been reduced to mounds of ash, the leather sheathing dangled from the walls in shreds. The book machine, which was a defunct wreck, had evidently served the Bookhunters as a source of scrap metal. Whole stairways and ladders, hand-rails and shelves had been removed and dismantled. A smell of burnt paper hung in the air.

I counted fourteen Bookhunters, all armed to the teeth as usual. They were seated on the ground in small groups, passing bottles of wine from hand to hand. One of them had climbed up the book machine and was trying to wrench off a handrail. Rongkong Koma was nowhere to be seen.

'I must request you to leave the Leather Grotto at once!' I called in a slightly tremulous voice. Those were the words Homuncolossus had told me to say. I was acting as bait again.

The Bookhunters, who appeared to be in various stages of intoxication,

noticed me for the first time. They scrambled to their feet and made noises expressive of amazement. One or two of them burst out laughing.

'It's that fat Lindworm who disappeared into the machine,' said one. 'But he isn't as fat as he was. He's lost weight.'

'Where have you been all this time?' asked another, who had sewn himself a horrific mask out of strips of leather wallpaper. 'We missed you.'

'That's a great trick of yours,' cried a third, 'disappearing into the machine and walking in at the door months later. You should perform it on the stage, except that the audience might get bored waiting all that time.'

They were now converging on me from all directions – all save the one on the book machine, who remained where he was.

'I must request you again to leave the Leather Grotto at once,' I called. 'That's an order from the Shadow King.' My voice sounded even more half-hearted this time. Where had Homuncolossus got to? He might at least have told me how he proposed to extricate me from this situation.

'The Shadow King, eh?' cried a Bookhunter. 'Why doesn't he come and tell us to leave himself? The price on your head has been increased, Lindworm. Lucky for us you've been away so long, it's boosted your value immensely.'

My repertoire was exhausted.

'I must request you to leave the Leather Grotto at once!' I said again, for want of any better idea.

'You're repeating yourself,' one of the Bookhunters retorted thickly. 'An inhabitant of Lindworm Castle ought to have a better way with words.'

The others laughed sarcastically. The individual who had remained high up on the ruined book machine was cocking a huge crossbow, I noticed. It seemed that he was planning to scoop the reward with a leisurely shot fired at long range.

'I must request you to leave the Leather Grotto at once!' I croaked yet again. Where the devil was the Shadow King? I would be dead within seconds!

The Bookhunter raised his crossbow and took aim. Just then, Homuncolossus emerged from the machine's shadowy interior without a sound. He came up behind the Bookhunter and gripped both his arms. Before his captive could say anything, Homuncolossus had aimed the crossbow at another Bookhunter and pulled the trigger. The bolt caught its target in the back, at a spot where he wore no armour, and he collapsed in the midst of his startled companions. Homuncolossus released the crossbow and leapt back into the machine.

Utterly at a loss, the Bookhunter picked up his discharged weapon. 'Listen, friends, I—' was all he managed to say before six crossbow bolts hit him. Five bounced off, but the sixth found its way through a crack in his armour and lodged there. He toppled over the handrail, crashed to floor of the cave and lay still.

The others were utterly flummoxed. They didn't know what merited their attention more: me or the corpse of the fellow Bookhunter whom they had just instinctively shot.

Then a familiar sound came drifting through the Leather Grotto. It caused the Bookhunters to spin round and grip their weapons more tightly. To me it meant I must turn on my heel and quit that scene of devastation.

It was the sigh of the Shadow King.

The Memorial

That was the prearranged signal. Homuncolossus had ordained that, as soon as the sigh rang out, I should take to my heels and hide outside the cave.

Only too glad to! I sprinted outside and hunkered down behind a boulder. If the Shadow King had instructed me to behave like a coward, I wasn't going to miss this opportunity to do so. I listened tensely.

Silence at first. Then came a startled exclamation. Someone yelled, 'Look out!' The clash of weapons, hectic words of command, a bestial cry of pain. Then utter pandemonium: the din of battle, a babble of screams and oaths, the Shadow King's hoarse breathing. An apelike bellow of fury. The clatter of a heavy suit of armour being hurled against a wall complete with occupant. Horrible gurgling sounds. The whistle of crossbow bolts. A cry of mortal agony. And another. Someone sobbed, but not for long. Another apelike bellow.

Then silence.

Again I heard the clatter of armour. Then a Bookhunter came staggering out of the cave, streaming with blood. Homuncolossus followed at his heels.

I emerged from my hiding place just as they both came to a halt.

'Why don't you kill me?' whimpered the Bookhunter.

'You should know,' Homuncolossus replied. 'There must always be one survivor left to tell the tale, or there would soon be no stories left to fill the pages of books and you'd be out of work, since books are what you live on. So go and spread the story of the battle of the Leather Grotto. And be sure to tell everyone that the Shadow King will be living here from now on, and that anyone who dares to disturb him will suffer the same fate as your cronies. And now be off with you!'

The Bookhunter tottered off, leaving a sticky red trail behind him.

Homuncolossus turned and went back into the cave.

'You stay here,' he called over his shoulder.

'What are you going to do?' I asked.

'I must erect a monument,' he said.

So I stayed where I was and waited to see what would happen.

He soon returned with a severed head under each arm. I was very glad they were wearing their martial helmets, so I was spared the sight of the contorted, lifeless faces inside them.

Homuncolossus deposited the heads on the ground and returned to the cave. He repeated this process several times until his monument was complete: a grisly sculpture composed of thirteen Bookhunters' heads in their horrific helmets.

'A pity there were so few of them,' he said. 'This monument is meant for the dead Booklings, but even more so for the survivors. No one but they will ever venture into the Leather Grotto again. I hope they'll return some day and make it their home once more.'

I now felt ashamed of having made only a chicken-hearted contribution to the battle of the Leather Grotto.

'Come,' he said, 'let's go up above. We still have a giant to slay.'

♀♀◉

The Greatest Danger of All

Go up . . . Such a simple, easy, innocuous expression for such an arduous procedure. I had begun to believe in the impossibility of ascending. How often I'd yearned to do so in the recent past, only to descend even deeper!

Homuncolossus conducted me along a series of seemingly endless passages through the rock. That they seemed endless was mainly because none of them led upwards, always straight ahead and sometimes, even, downhill. After roughly a day's march, however, we came to a shaft that really did lead straight upwards. It was a narrow chimney just wide enough to admit us and containing sufficient ledges and protrusions for us to be able to climb it.

'Are you sure it doesn't become too narrow at some stage, or simply peter out?' I asked.

'Absolutely sure,' Homuncolossus told me. 'I've often used it.'

'Colophonius Regenschein mentioned a shaft like this,' I said. 'He said it was too narrow to harbour anything very dangerous.'

'So Regenschein knew about this shaft, did he?' said Homuncolossus. 'Well, he must have done, because there isn't another one like it. He's full of surprises, even in death. Still, he was wrong about one thing.'

'What's that?'

'The absence of anything very dangerous. This shaft harbours the greatest danger of all.'

'What do you mean?'

'You'll see when the time comes.'

The Shadow King and his mysterious allusions! I couldn't imagine life without them now.

So we started climbing. It wasn't much more difficult than ascending a flight of stairs, thanks to all the footholds. Homuncolossus, with a jellyfish torch strapped to his head like a miner's lamp, took the lead. He climbed fast, but I found to my surprise that I could keep up with him quite well.

After a few hours, however, my limbs began to feel a trifle heavy with fatigue. I wondered how much longer the ascent would take. Not much longer, I surmised, in view of the distance we had already covered. Although I hadn't asked before, not wanting to be thought a weakling, the question now seemed appropriate.

'Another three days,' I was told.

My legs turned to jelly and I stopped climbing. I realised for the first time how deep the shaft was. It stretched away above us for miles.

'Three days?' I said, aghast. 'How am I supposed to manage it?'

'No idea,' he said. 'I myself have only just realised what an impossibility it must seem to you. Nowadays it never occurs to me that someone may not be as strong as I am. What do you think?'

'What do I think?' I wailed. 'You're crazy, that's what!'

'Shouting won't help,' he said. 'Better save your strength, you'll need it.'

'I'm going back down,' I said defiantly.

'I wouldn't advise it. Even I use a different route for going down. Know why climbing up is so much easier than climbing down? Because our eyes are in our heads. You don't see where you're putting your feet.'

I was incapable of moving in either direction.

'It's there already, isn't it?' said Homuncolossus.

'What is?'

'The greatest danger of all.'

'The greatest danger of all? Here? Where? Where is it?' Panic-stricken, I looked round for some fat snake or venomous tunnel spider, but there was nothing to be seen.

'It's inside you,' said Homuncolossus. 'Fear.'

True, I was terribly frightened. I dared not advance or retreat. It was like a form of paralysis.

'You must conquer it *now*,' he said, 'or it'll conquer you.'

'And how am I to do *that*, pray?'

'Simply go on climbing. It's like writing a novel. Everything's quite straightforward at first – the early chapters go with a tremendous swing, but sooner or later you begin to tire. You look back and see you're only halfway through. You look ahead and see you still have as much again to write. If you lose heart at that stage, you've had it. It's easy enough to start something. Finishing it is the hard part.'

That was simply great, dear readers! It wasn't enough that the Shadow King had placed me in a life-threatening situation – no, he now insisted on spouting facile words of wisdom.

'If Regenschein knew about this shaft he must have climbed it,' said Homuncolossus. 'That means it can be done. We've already come a fair way and you've coped pretty well so far.'

For the first time, I became aware that I wasn't as fat as I had been when consigned to the catacombs. I'd taken a lot of exercise lately and I hadn't had much to eat. Even one of the Bookhunters had remarked on how much weight I'd lost. Hadn't I kept up with the Shadow King until now? Yes, I had never been in better shape.

'All right,' I said. 'Let's keep going.'

We climbed for hour after hour without my having to request another breather. It was Homuncolossus who eventually paused and told me we had completed the first third of the ascent. We took a longish rest, just sitting on a ledge in silence, then resumed the climb.

The second stage proved more strenuous. It had been a mistake to rest, I thought, because my limbs now felt heavier and less supple than before. I was also conscious of all the cuts and abrasions my paws had sustained from contact with the jagged rock. It wasn't long before I felt as if I were wearing a suit of lead armour. My legs were so numb, I couldn't feel where I was putting my feet.

This sensation stole gradually up my body until it reached my head and I wondered whether to ask for another rest. Still debating this question, I dozed off in mid climb. By the time I started to fall I was already in the land of dreams.

♀♀♀

The Fire Demons of Nether Florinth

I tried to move, but it was impossible. Every bone, every muscle hurt as if it had been smashed or torn apart. Then I remembered: I'd fallen down the shaft. Now I was lying at the bottom, breathing my last.

I strove to raise my head. That, at least, I found I could do. Homuncolossus was sitting beside me, leafing through a book. Beyond him I saw a tunnel whose walls were lined with bookshelves.

'Maybe you should write poems instead of novels,' he said. 'Verse might be better suited to your constitution.'

'What happened?' I asked.

'You fell asleep while climbing. I only just managed to catch you.'

I looked down at myself. I was still in one piece but suffering from the worst aches and pains I'd ever experienced.

'You carried me the rest of the way? For two whole days?'

Homuncolossus tossed the book aside. 'Hear that?' he said.

'What?' I listened. True, I could hear noises – lots of noises. A medley of gurgles and crashes, rumbles and roars, clatters and bangs.

'That's the city,' said Homuncolossus. 'They're the sounds of Bookholm.'

I sat up, wide awake in an instant.

'Are we there?'

'Not quite, but close beneath the surface. From here it would be child's play to reach it by way of some second-hand bookshop.' He looked at me with a cryptic expression. 'But my own route goes via Smyke's library.'

'Mine too.'

'You don't have to come with me. I wouldn't feel hurt if you preferred to take an easier route. I can show you one.'

'As long as Smyke's still around I wouldn't get much further up there than you. There's a price on my head, remember?'

'In that case, let's go.'

Homuncolossus left his torch behind. This part of the catacombs was lit by jellyfish lamps. They were everywhere, those lamps I hadn't seen for such a long time, and so were books. Not ancient, malodorous tomes written in indecipherable runes, but normal second-hand books. Taking one from a shelf as we walked on, I flicked through it.

It was *The Fire Demons of Nether Florinth*, a thriller set in the Graveyard Marshes and featuring at least one large-scale conflagration in every chapter, so the blurb bombastically confided. Nothing could have interested me less than the literary glamorisation of the abnormal proclivities of the dwarfish Fire Demons, a tribe of disreputable arsonists. What interested me far more was the age of the book. It was a *pyromanic excitation novel*, a peculiarly nasty offshoot of Zamonian light fiction designed to appeal to readers who got their kicks from descriptions of huge, all-consuming fires. This literary genre had existed for only a century. I replaced the book, took out another, opened it and read the first few words aloud: *'The world is a jagged, rusty can of worms – if you ask me, not that anyone ever does.'*

'Is that your philosophy of life?' asked Homuncolossus.

'No, it's from Glumphrey Murk, the superpessimist,' I replied. 'This is another book that can be found in every modern Zamonian bookstore. We really must be quite close to the surface.'

'I told you so,' Homuncolossus retorted.

'Have you worked out a way of getting to Smyke's library?' I asked.

'Not really. I only know where the labyrinth surrounding it begins.'

'How will you recognise the entrance?'

'Oh, you can't miss it. It's signposted. There's a corpse sitting outside.'

'A corpse?'

'A mummified body. It looks a bit like . . . But you'll see what I mean when we get there.'

'Are mysterious allusions a legitimate literary device?' I demanded slyly.

'No. Only second-rate authors make use of them to hold their readers' attention. Why do you ask?'

♀♀♂

The White Sheep of the Smyke Family

Walking around so close to the surface of Bookholm was almost more claustrophobic than being somewhere deep down in the catacombs. I now knew why Homuncolossus had ended by burying himself as far away as possible. You could not only hear the life of the city but feel it. The incessant rumbles and bangs overhead made the books tremble on their shelves. Once I even thought I heard the voices of children. To hear and feel all this while imprisoned below ground was far more intolerable than being exiled to distant Shadowhall Castle.

In spite of the city's proximity I would probably have failed to get out unaided. The catacombs here were just as confusing, if not more so, as those further down, not least because they were so cramped. The passages were low-ceilinged and narrow, with countless forks and intersections, small rocky chambers and flights of steps, and there were piles of books everywhere. Books! At this juncture, nothing could have interested me less. I had got to know every type of book at first hand, whether 'Dreaming' or 'Hazardous' or 'Animatomic', and if I ever did get out my first act would be to make straight for some uncivilised wilderness where no one could read or write at all.

'Don't be scared!' Homuncolossus said suddenly. He had been striding resolutely ahead all the time. 'The mummy is in a cave round the next corner. It looks quite lifelike at first glance, perhaps because of the skeletons in its vicinity. They're probably the remains of people with weak nerves who died of heart failure at the sight of it.'

Thus forewarned, I peered cautiously round the corner – and jumped back despite myself. A familiar figure was sitting there.

'Smyke!' I gasped.

'Yes, he does look a bit like Smyke, doesn't he?' Homuncolossus whispered behind me. He had stepped aside to let me go first.

'No, not like Pfistomel Smyke,' I said. 'Like Hagob Salbandian Smyke.'

We entered the little cave together and examined the mummy. Yes, it really was Hagob Salbandian Smyke, Pfistomel's great-uncle. He looked exactly as he had in the oil painting I'd seen – well, *almost* exactly, because his corpse was completely desiccated. He had resembled a corpse in his lifetime, however, so this made little difference.

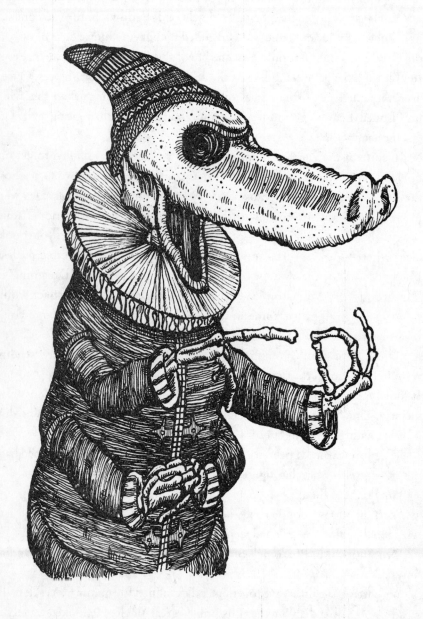

He was seated on the floor of the cave with his back against an overflowing bookcase, his dead eyes staring into space. In addition to books the cave contained two skeletons – their bones were strewn all over the floor – and suspended from the roof was a jellyfish lamp whose half-dead occupant emitted only a feeble, irregularly pulsating orange glow. The strangest aspect of the scene was that the uppermost pair of the mummy's fourteen hands was raised and that one skeletal hand seemed to be pointing to the other. It was a mystery to me how Hagob had managed to die in such a pose.

'You knew him?' asked Homuncolossus.

'Not personally, but I know who he is: a member of the Smyke family.'

'He looks pretty thin for a Smyke.'

'Yes, Hagob was a bit of a one-off. He was Pfistomel's great-uncle. He left him all he owned and then disappeared. They say he was insane.'

'He certainly looks it. What's he doing down here?'

'He probably lost his way and died of thirst and starvation, then shrivelled up into a mummy.'

'What about his hands? Why is he holding them in such a funny way?'

'He's pointing to something,' I said.

'Yes, his own fingers.'

'He really was insane.'

'No, wait,' said Homuncolossus. 'He isn't pointing to his fingers, he's pointing to something in them.'

'You mean he's holding something?' I said. 'I can't see anything.'

'Yes. There's a hair between his finger and thumb.'

I looked more closely. 'You're right,' I said. 'It's an eyelash.'

Just then I remembered how Smyke had discoursed about his great-uncle while we were standing in front his portrait: *'Hagob was an artist. He produced sculptures. My home is full of them.'*

'Really?' I had interposed. *'I haven't seen a single sculpture on your premises.'*

'No wonder. They're invisible to the naked eye. Hagob made microsculptures.'

'Microsculptures?'

'Yes. He began with cherry stones and grains of rice, but his works steadily diminished in size. He ended by carving them out of the tip of a single hair.

I'll show you some of them under the microscope when we get back. He carved the whole of the Battle of Nurn Forest on an eyelash.'

'It's a microsculpture,' I said.

'You mean this hair has been worked on in some way?'

'Possibly. Smyke claimed that Hagob could produce the tiniest sculptures imaginable. But that doesn't get us anywhere. We'd need a microscope to see it.'

'I wouldn't,' said Homuncolossus. 'I could see it unaided.'

'You could?'

'I already told you: I've no idea what Smyke implanted in me instead of eyes, but I can see as well as a Gloomberg eagle looking through a telescope. Or a microscope, whichever.'

'Really? Then take a look! Perhaps this eyelash bears a clue of some kind.'

Homuncolossus carefully plucked the hair from between Hagob Salbandian's bony finger and thumb, then held it close to his cavernous eye sockets for several seconds. I seemed to hear a series of faint clicks and whirrs.

'You'll never believe this!' he said.

'What won't I believe?' I exclaimed impatiently. 'I'll believe anything you tell me!'

Homuncolossus looked at me.

'Really? A bit sudden, isn't it?'

'Tell me what you can see!'

'You'll never believe it.'

'Please!'

Homuncolossus concentrated on the eyelash again.

'It's a will,' he said. 'Engraved on this hair.'

'No!'

'You see? You don't believe me.'

'You're driving me crazy! Read it out! *Read ... it ... to ... me!*'

'**Will**,' said Homuncolossus.

'Yes, yes, I know!' I croaked. 'It's a will, you already said that.'

'No, that's what it says here: "**Will**". It's the heading. Shall I read the rest or not?'

'Please!' If any word could sound as if it were down on its knees, it was that 'Please!' of mine.

424

Homuncolossus cleared his throat. 'Will,' he read,

'I sincerely hope that the first person to read this does not bear the name Pfistomel Smyke. If that should be the case, however, be advised, Pfistomel, you confounded rogue, that I hereby curse you! I curse you to the end of time and I shall anoint your grave with my ghostly piss until our planet collides with the sun!

'But, should you not bear the name Pfistomel Smyke, unknown stranger, listen to the following sad story. Pfistomel is, alas, my misbegotten grand-nephew and a scion of my equally degenerate family. When he knocked on my door one day – probably on the run from creditors or guardians of the law – I hadn't the slightest notion of the depths of villainy to which he could sink. Like many other people before me, I succumbed to his innate charm. I opened the door and bade him welcome, and it was not long before I was treating him like my own son. I shared everything with him, my home, my food – everything with one exception: the secret of our family library, which had been handed down for centuries from generation to generation. I was the first of the Smykes to break the chain. Instead of misusing that monstrous possession for my personal aggrandisement, I decided simply to ignore it altogether.

'For I am, as you will perhaps see from my stature, rather different from the rest of my corpulent family. There is good and evil in all the Smykes, but it must unfortunately be stated, in view of our family history, that reprehensible characteristics predominate.

'In contrast to most Smykes I tend towards asceticism, have artistic leanings and abominate power in any form. It must truly be said, therefore, that the Smykean bequest went astray when it came into my hands. On inheriting the library I resolved that it should not, while I lived, be used for any nefarious purpose – indeed, for any purpose at all. On one occasion I even briefly considered setting fire to it, but could not bring myself to do so. It was only rarely that I visited the place to read a book there.

'Many people may think it insane of someone endowed with such a potential abundance of power to spend his life producing works of art which no one can see. Well, my own ideas of morality prescribe that only a lunatic would aspire to subordinate the fate of others to his own wishes. I leave it to a higher authority to decide which view is the right one.

'Pfistomel must have grasped the truth one day. I now feel sure that he had discovered the secret of the library by keeping my movements under constant surveillance. That was my death warrant. He drugged me with a poisoned book and consigned me to the catacombs. I fear I am only the first in a succession of luckless individuals who do not accord with his diabolical dreams of absolute power.

'My strength is failing fast. I have been repeatedly foiled by the cunning mechanism that cuts off the library from this side of the catacombs, nor have I succeeded in finding another exit. All I can still do is to formally disinherit Pfistomel Smyke and unmask him as my murderer. The library of the Smykes shall belong to whomsoever finds this document and makes it public. It only remains for me to hope that he is a person of integrity.

'Hagob Salbandian, the white sheep of the Smyke family.'

'This is fantastic!' I cried, when Homuncolossus had finished reading. 'We can destroy Smyke with this – quite legally! If we make it public he's finished! He'll be branded a murderer, a liar, an embezzler. This is a document whose veracity no one can doubt. No one could have forged it. Hagob was the only person who had mastered this art.'

Homuncolossus was still staring at the eyelash.

'*You* can inherit the library, being the first to read Hagob's will!' I went on. 'I'm your witness! They'll strip Smyke of all his official positions. Everyone will turn against him. He can count himself lucky if they banish him to the crystal mines or Demon's Gulch or the labour camps of Ironville.'

'You think that's an adequate punishment for what he has done?' asked Homuncolossus. 'And for what he's planning to do?'

'No punishment could be adequate,' I said, 'but that would do for a start.'

'Whom do you propose to show the will to? Whom can you trust in Bookholm? Whom do you know that isn't on Smyke's payroll?'

That pricked my bubble of enthusiasm. We gave each other a long look.

'Perhaps you could try us?' said a piping, quavering voice. 'Even though your previous experience of us hasn't been of the best.'

We spun round and stared.

Standing in the mouth of the cave were Ahmed ben Kibitzer the Nocturnomath and Inazia Anazazi the Uggly, the Bookholm antiquarians who had told me to get lost.

They stood there at a respectful distance, trembling like deer poised to flee. I could almost smell the fear that gripped them at the sight of the Shadow King.

'You lose, Kibitzer,' the Uggly said in a tremulous voice.

'You're right,' said Kibitzer, his voice sounding even feebler than hers. 'I would never have believed that an Ugglian prophecy could prove so accurate.'

Then they clung to one another and fainted.

♀♀Ψ

The Renegades

I told Homuncolossus to remain in the cave with Hagob's mummy, or the pair of them might fall into another swoon as soon as they recovered consciousness. They quickly came round after I'd propped them up against the wall and fanned them for a while.

'Good heavens,' Kibitzer gasped, 'that's never happened to me before. I pictured him quite differently.'

'Me too,' croaked Inazia. 'I've never seen anything more frightful.'

I secretly wondered when the Uggly had last looked at herself in a mirror.

'He doesn't seem half as frightful once you've become accustomed to his unusual appearance,' I whispered, although I knew perfectly well that Homuncolossus was listening, and that his phenomenal hearing would enable him to pick up every word we uttered, however softly. 'Looked at in the right way, he's really quite handsome.'

'We didn't mean to offend him,' said Kibitzer.

'No,' the Uggly put in, 'far from it. As a matter of fact, we came to do the exact opposite.'

'So why *are* you here?' I asked.

'I'd like to recapitulate a little,' Kibitzer replied, 'if I may.'

'The thing is,' said the Uggly, 'we're sure we can shed light on certain matters you still find inexplicable.'

'That would certainly be of interest to me,' I said.

'To enable you to understand what an awkward position we're in,' said Kibitzer, 'I must go back to a time before you arrived in—'

'Will this take long?' the Shadow King demanded darkly from the cave next door.

'I'm afraid so,' I called back and he heaved a sigh.

'I'll be as brief as I can,' said the Nocturnomath. 'It all really started when Pfistomel Smyke attained a certain popularity in Bookholm. The city had previously been dominated by a form of – well, creative chaos, let's say. Nothing worked properly, but it did work after a fashion and no one was particularly dissatisfied with that state of affairs. Bookholm attracted the kind of people who didn't hanker after strong leadership, if I may put it that way. A touch of anarchy had always been more to their taste than a well-swept pavement. Then, in recent times, an alarming change occurred.

'When he first turned up in Bookholm, Pfistomel Smyke made an extremely favourable impression on us all. By "us" I mean the literary fraternity, the inner circle, the handful of antiquaries and publishers, booksellers and artists who provided the city with its intellectual cohesion. From the first, Smyke cut a good figure at our various social functions in spite of his incredible obesity. He could waddle into a room – a literary salon, for instance – and ten minutes later all present would have formed a circle round him. He was witty, humorous, a gifted literary scholar and an antiquarian bookseller with a highly specialised stock of choice volumes, yet he behaved modestly. He lived in a tiny listed building, maintained it with loving care and presented Bookholm's leading citizens with honey from his own beehive. He seemed to have no ambitions outside our circle. In short, he was a person of private means whom anyone in Bookholm with any self-respect would gladly have numbered among his circle of friends.'

'Anyone!' croaked Inazia. 'Even us Ugglian booksellers, who don't have any circle of friends.'

'He was a public benefactor, too,' said Kibitzer. 'In every respect. He was always donating valuable books from his stock to help finance some project or other; for instance, the renovation of the municipal library or the restoration of the oldest houses in Darkman Street. Even a single one of those books was sufficient to preserve an urban district from dilapidation. Above all, though, he was a patron of the arts.'

The Uggly gave a venomous laugh.

'One day,' Kibitzer went on, 'he founded the *Friends of Murkholmian Trombophone Music.* That, I think, was when conditions in Bookholm started to undergo a gradual change – not that anyone noticed it at first. The trombophone concerts became an absolute must where Bookholm's intellectual and literary élite were concerned. Everyone wanted to attend them, but only the most important citizens were invited.'

'You went to one of those concerts yourself,' the Uggly reminded me, 'so you know what they can do to a person. Please bear that in mind before you condemn us for what follows!'

I nodded. I still had a vivid recollection of that trombophone music.

'We didn't notice what was happening to us,' said Kibitzer. 'I was a little more resistant because of my three brains, but they too went soft in the end. Smyke's psychological hold over us grew stronger with each successive concert. The music's hypnotic power wore off after a certain length of time, but for several days we went around like remote-controlled machines and carried out the posthypnotic commands Smyke had instilled in the music. We did the most idiotic things without questioning them subsequently. I was there when we desecrated the Ugglies' cemetery.'

'Even I was there too,' said the Uggly, hanging her head in shame.

'And so was the mayor!' Kibitzer added. 'But those were just test runs on Smyke's part. Before long he induced us to do some really important things for him. Successful booksellers sold him their businesses for a song. Many bequeathed him their stock and then committed suicide. Others, like us two, joined the Triadic Booksellers' Association, whose members have to pay him fifty per cent of their takings. The city council passed nonsensical laws whose sole beneficiary was Smyke himself.'

The Uggly took up the thread. 'The intervals between the concerts steadily diminished until we never came to our senses at all. Smyke directed the destinies of Bookholm like a conductor directing an orchestra. And then your, er . . . your friend here arrived in the city.'

She glanced towards the cave in which Homuncolossus was lurking. The groan of impatience that issued from it made her and the Nocturnomath flinch.

'We first heard of him when he was already in Smyke's clutches,' Inazia went on. 'Smyke showed us and one or two others what this young genius had written. He also initiated us into his disgraceful plan to transform him into a monster and banish him to the catacombs, so that he could rid them of Bookhunters.'

'You knew of his plan?' I asked in horror.

'Not only that,' Kibitzer replied quietly. 'We made an important contribution to it. Listen carefully, because now comes the really shameful part of our story and we're here to make amends. The fact is, Smyke could never have fulfilled his plan without our active assistance.'

'You ought to add that we cooperated with pleasure,' the Uggly put in, '– indeed, with fanatical enthusiasm. Our brains were so addled, so manipulated, that we considered Smyke and his paranoid ideas to be infallible. We gave him all the help he requested. Take the paper your poor friend consists of. Do you know who supplied it?'

'No,' I said. 'How should I?'

'I did!' she gasped. 'It comes from some ancient Bookemistic tomes of which only my bookshop possesses a stock.'

The Uggly's eyelids flickered at the sound of a faint rustle from the cave next door. She was too scared to continue, so the Nocturnomath took over.

'And I constructed his eye mechanism,' he said, 'using a book on the optics of nightingaloscopes by Professor Abdul Nightingale. His eyes have diamond lenses ground by me personally. I also made a few other contributions to his body. His liver is good for a thousand years.'

'You mean you helped to put him together?' I asked in disgust.

'No,' said the Uggly, 'we only supplied the components. We never set foot in Smyke's secret laboratory, nor did we ever see the Shadow King completed. Until today.'

An angry growl issued from the adjacent cave. The pair of them exchanged anxious glances.

'We're almost done – I'll make it quick,' Kibitzer said apologetically. 'Well, that was that for the moment. The Shadow King became a legend and Smyke became more and more powerful.'

'And then you arrived in the city and jolted us out of our stupor,' said the Uggly. She uttered the words like a curse.

'We both recognised the handwriting of the person we'd helped to transform into a monster,' said Kibitzer. 'It was like awaking from a nightmare. We were in shock at first and it was a while before we could really rouse ourselves to help you. But by then it was too late.'

'You'd already disappeared,' the Uggly went on. 'Smyke made no secret of what he'd done with you – he blithely told his inner circle about the Lindworm he'd consigned to the catacombs. He cherishes a special hatred for Lindworm Castle. Once he has extended his power beyond the confines of Bookholm, it will be right at the top of his list for destruction.'

'So we took to plugging our ears with wax whenever we went to a trombophone concert,' said Kibitzer. 'We still belong to the Triadic Circle, but Smyke has lost his power over us. We've become spies and renegades.'

'We used to be Smyke's accomplices,' Inazia said. 'Now we're traitors. That's our story in a nutshell.'

I needed time to digest all this, but there was one thing I still failed to understand.

'How did you know exactly when we would turn up here?'

The Uggly cleared her throat with a horrible retching sound. 'I foretold your future the first time we met,' she said. 'Don't you remember?'

'I vaguely recall some fanciful remarks that might have meant anything,' I replied truthfully.

'*He will descend into the depths*!' Inazia snarled. '*He will be banished to the realm of the Animatomes, the Living Books! He will consort with Him whom everyone knows but knows not who He is*!'

Yes, I thought, those really were the words she had uttered – a rather puzzling prophecy at the time. But that still didn't answer my question.

'It isn't a gift,' she went on, 'it's a curse. That prophecy was just a typical Ugglian reflex – nothing special, utterly imprecise – so I performed an oneiromantic analysis on myself. That's one of the most accurate prognostic methods in existence, but it's also an exceptionally painful procedure. It makes you weep blood and can drive you insane. Kibitzer had to hypnotise me, strap me to a bed of nails and sprinkle me with ox gall all night long.'

'It was awful,' Kibitzer said with a shudder.

'But that combination of nightmare visions and confession under torture represents the most accurate and honest forecast of the future any Uggly can make. I foresaw your fate in every detail, down to the present moment. Kibitzer didn't believe me either, not at first, but here we are: in the right place at the right time. Now he's lost his bet. He owes me a signed first edition of Nightingale's treatise on constructing submarines out of nautilus shells.'

'It's worth a fortune!' sighed Kibitzer.

'How much longer are you going to be?' Homuncolossus bellowed.

'Well,' Kibitzer whispered, 'here we are. We've admitted our guilt. It would be only right if the Shadow King killed us for our misdeeds, but perhaps we can atone for them by doing him a favour.'

'Hm,' I said. 'He sounds pretty peeved. What have you got to offer?'

'The route to the Smykean family library,' said Kibitzer. 'Would that do?'

'You know how to get there?'

'I didn't build the labyrinth myself,' he said, 'but I completely renovated it three years ago.'

The Nightingalian Impossibility Key

'Are you sure we can trust them?' Homuncolossus asked, loudly enough to be heard with ease by Kibitzer and the Uggly, who were walking on ahead.

'Who *can* be trusted down here?' I rejoined.

'I can,' said Homuncolossus. 'For instance, when I vow to rip the brains out of anyone who tries to hoodwink me. Even if he possesses three of them.'

Kibitzer gave an agonised groan. 'I know what a burden of guilt we're

433

carrying,' he said, 'but we really mean to do our utmost to make up for it. At least give us a chance to do so.'

'What choice do we have?' I asked Homuncolossus. 'Have you a better idea?'

He didn't answer.

'Here we are,' said Kibitzer, coming to a halt.

We looked around. There was nothing special about this narrow passage lined with books.

Kibitzer half withdrew an unremarkable-looking book from the shelves and stepped back. The spine of the book opened to reveal a glass mechanism.

'That's the lock of the labyrinth,' said the Nocturnomath. 'And I have the key that fits it.'

'There's a key to the labyrinth?' Homuncolossus asked.

'Every labyrinth needs a key,' Kibitzer replied. 'Sometimes it exists only in the mind of its inventor. In this case it's a *Nightingalian impossibility key.*'

He felt in his pocket and removed a tiny object. We had to bend down to see it at all. It seemed to consist of glass or crystal, but for some absurd reason it defied close examination however hard I looked. I can't put it any other way: that key was a sheer impossibility.

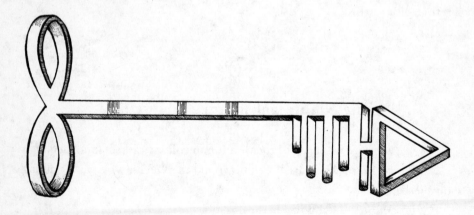

'Fascinating, isn't it?' Kibitzer asked in a dreamy voice. 'I cut it myself out of a single diamond, following the instructions in Nightingale's manuals.'

The Nocturnomath inserted the tiny key in the glass lock.

'I used it to activate the mechanical labyrinth after renovating it. Now I can deactivate it. Watch!'

He turned the key. The glass mechanism emitted a series of melodious clicks and ticks and the passage began to move. Bookcases slid forwards and sideways, rotated 180 degrees or changed places. Within seconds the passage looked completely different. Even if one had memorised a few details, none of them would now be in the same location.

'That's the whole secret,' said Kibitzer. 'Every passage automatically reconstructs itself once you've walked along it. The mechanism has now been turned off.'

'It's even more ingenious than Shadowhall Castle,' Homuncolossus said admiringly.

'Shadowhall Castle?' Kibitzer asked eagerly. 'You mean it really exists?'

'It's a ventilation system,' I said.

The two booksellers stared at me.

'Er, yes, it's a ventilation system installed by a giant with a hundred noses,' I tried to explain. 'It's inhabited by Animatomes and Weeping Shadows, and – oh, all right, forget it!'

They nodded, looking relieved.

'Right,' said Kibitzer, 'the labyrinth has now been delabyrinthised. You need only follow your noses and sooner or later you'll come out in Smyke's family library. Then our job will be done.'

'Good,' said Homuncolossus. He removed the Nightingalian impossibility key from the lock, threw it on the ground and stamped on it. 'Just to be on the safe side,' he said. 'Now we're quits. Goodbye.' He turned to go.

'One moment!' Inazia called. 'Are you really sure you want to go there?'

'Is there any alternative?' I asked.

'No,' she said. 'I'm not saying this because I want to stop you – destiny is unstoppable – but I've foreseen your future. And believe me, it wasn't a pretty sight.'

'I know what my future looks like,' Homuncolossus said firmly. 'We're going.'

I nodded.

'As you wish.' The Uggly heaved a deep sigh. 'In that case, Kibitzer, we must hurry back and leave Bookholm at once.'

'Why?' asked Kibitzer.

'Because it's our destiny,' said the Uggly. She took him by the arm and dragged him away.

♀♀♋

The Beginning and the End

It was a thoroughly agreeable sensation, dear readers, walking through a delabyrinthised labyrinth after spending so much time in labyrinths that functioned only too well. No confusing intersections, no dead ends, no more racking one's brains as to which turning to take, just a winding passage that would sooner or later bring us to our destination.

'Have you kept that will somewhere safe?' I asked Homuncolossus.

'I have,' he replied.

I forbore to ask where someone without any clothes or pockets would keep an object as tiny as an eyelash 'safe'.

'What will you do to Smyke when we see him?' I pursued.

'I shall kill him.'

'I'm not sure that's the best form of punishment for him,' I said. 'Do you really think it's appropriate? He tormented you far more ingeniously. He locked you up in a dungeon and threw away the key. You could pay him back in the same coin.'

'I know what you're getting at,' said Homuncolossus, 'but you're wasting your breath. My mind is made up.' He raised his head. 'Do you smell that?'

We came to a halt and I sniffed the air. 'Old books,' I said. 'So what?'

'A large number of old books,' said Homuncolossus.

I took another sniff.

'A very, very large number of very, very old books,' I said.

We quickened our pace. When we rounded the next bend we were confronted by a spacious cave overgrown with stalactites and stalagmites. Lined with books and generously lit by numerous candles, it was clearly an annexe of the Smykean family library.

'We must make for the central cave,' said Homuncolossus.

We traversed several more caves, each bigger and more brightly lit than the last. The candlelight conveyed the reassuring impression that they were outposts of civilisation, but I knew only too well that we were nearing the nerve centre of Pfistomel Smyke's budding empire.

And then, at long last, we entered the central cave. I almost wept at the sight. The library of the Smykes! This was where my troubles had begun and this was where everything would end. Well, not everything, or so I hoped, but at least Pfistomel Smyke's reign of terror. The library looked just as it had when the Toxicotome knocked me out: the countless shelves hewn into the rock, the wooden and iron bookcases as tall as bell towers, the incredibly long ladders, the barrels, crates and massive piles of ancient volumes. And there – yes, there was the Toxicotome! It still lay open on the ground where I had dropped it. Smyke hadn't even bothered to put it away.

'What a waste,' Homuncolossus said contemptuously. 'To think of this intellectual treasure chamber. in the hands of a criminal!'

'It could be yours,' I whispered, 'if you go about it the right way. Legally, I mean.'

We surveyed the subterranean mountain range of books, still over-whelmed by its sheer extent. Then I gave a start: one of the untidy mounds of books appeared to be stirring. I thought it was some Animatomes that had somehow found their way here and been awakened by our presence, but it was just a few ordinary books slithering to the ground. Less reassuring was the fact that the mound continued to stir.

'Homuncolossus!' I hissed.

He had noticed the same thing long ago and was watching intently. Book after book slid to the ground. Moments later a figure emerged from the summit of the mound. It was a Bookhunter! He was dressed from head to foot in black leather, wore a mosaic death's-head mask and was armed with a heavy crossbow, which he levelled at us. It was the one who had threatened to hack off my paws in Bookholm's black market.

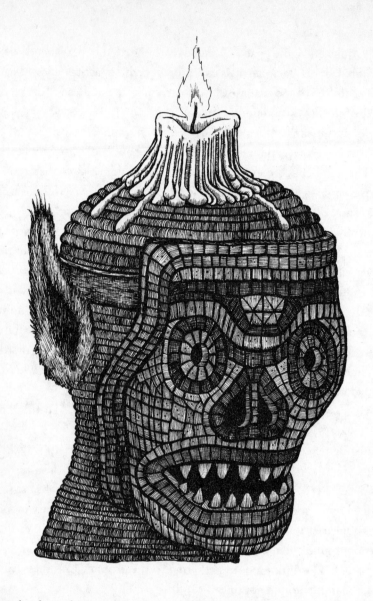

Not far from him a second Bookhunter emerged from another pile of books. His armour was made entirely of brass and he was fitting an arrow into the string of the huge bow he carried.

And then the process was repeated in quick succession. A big barrel of books started to sway, toppled over and disgorged another Bookhunter, likewise armed to the teeth. The books in one of the rock-hewn bookcases fell out, shelf after shelf of them, and on each shelf lay a Bookhunter. Seven tall bookcases butted up against the wall of the cave fell forward, one after another, to reveal two armed figures standing behind each. Like a corpse arising from a coffin, a mailed warrior emerged from the midst of an untidy heap of tattered volumes on a big wooden table.

There were far more Bookhunters than there had been in the Leather Grotto – scores of them, in fact. Numbering well over a hundred, they probably included every surviving Bookhunter in the catacombs.

Finally, a heap of yellowed parchment scrolls enclosing an enormous stalagmite collapsed and a mighty cloud of dust went billowing into the air. When the dust subsided, there stood Rongkong Koma, the most fearsome Bookhunter of all. He had put on an especially festive-looking suit of red-lacquered armour but wore no helmet as usual. His frightful face wore a triumphant smile.

'Welcome,' he called to me. 'It's a long time since we saw each other. You're looking well. You've lost weight.'

He rested his hands on the hilt of his weapon, a monstrous cross between an axe and a sword, which was stuck in a broad leather belt. Then he mounted a wooden platform that afforded a clear view of the library.

He pointed to Homuncolossus. 'That creature beside you – that ugly monster – can only be the Shadow King. It's good to see you at last, Shadow King! We've only met in the dark until now. What a hideous gargoyle you are!'

'I should have killed him while I had the chance,' Homuncolossus muttered.

'My Bookhunters weren't prepared for your cowardly attack on the Leather Grotto,' called Rongkong Koma. 'But we're all the readier for you this time and we're ten times as many.'

Several Bookhunters were holding the tips of their arrows in candle flames, I saw. They must have been soaked in oil, because they caught fire at once.

Rongkong Koma was still pointing at the Shadow King. 'I suppose you thought your treacherous attack had scared us into abandoning our profession. I'm bound to admit that my followers' morale really did take a dive – it was all I could do to remotivate them. In the end, though, you only achieved the opposite of your intention. Now all the Bookhunters in the catacombs have banded together – under my leadership! – to put an end to you, Shadow King! We've never been stronger!'

The Bookhunters uttered a bellow of assent and clattered their weapons.

'I should have killed them *all* while I had the chance,' whispered Homuncolossus.

'After your appearance in the Leather Grotto it was only a matter of time before you turned up here,' Rongkong Koma went on. 'Pfistomel Smyke guessed you would do so as soon as we told him. And here's something else you should know before you die, Shadow King: you're going to make us all, every last one of us, immensely rich. Once we've disposed of you, Smyke is allowing each of us to take as many books from this library as he can carry.'

The Bookhunters gave another yell.

'What do Kibitzer and Inazia get out of this?' asked Homuncolossus.

Rongkong Koma stopped short. 'You do your only friends in Bookholm an injustice,' he said. 'No, they genuinely wanted to help you. The Nocturnomath and the Uggly were behaving so suspiciously, Smyke kept them under surveillance. We gave the two of them free rein. Someone had to let you into the library, after all.'

'I don't believe it!' I called. 'The Uggly can foresee everything. If she's on our side, why should she let us to walk into a trap?'

Rongkong Koma deliberated for a while. 'Hey, that's a really good question! You think she foresaw you getting out of this mess after all? You think there's still some hope for you?'

The Bookhunters roared with laughter.

He raised his hands for silence. 'The other possibility is, it may be true what everyone says about Ugglies: that they're a couple of books short of a library!'

Rongkong Koma positively basked in his followers' yells of approbation.

'*Is* there a way out?' I asked the Shadow King in a whisper. 'Are you in possession of some secret power you've been keeping from me?'

'No,' he replied, 'I'm afraid I can't help you there. I'm strong but not invincible. One arrow and I'll go up in flames.'

'Then we're done for?'

'It seems so.'

'Kill the Shadow King!' Rongkong Koma commanded suddenly and the tumult died away. 'Set him ablaze! Skewer him with a hundred flaming arrows and scatter his ashes in the labyrinth! But let the lizard live – cripple him and leave it at that. I claim Smyke's reward for myself!'

'You're in luck,' I told Homuncolossus. 'You'll only burn to death, whereas I'm to be crippled first and *then* killed.'

'I don't think you'll be killed,' he said.

'What, then?'

'Smyke has greater things in store for you. You'll become the new Shadow King.'

That idea scared me even more than the prospect of death.

'We'd better say goodbye,' said Homuncolossus. 'It's been a pleasure and privilege knowing you.'

'And it was an honour to be your pupil,' I replied. 'Even though it's pointless now.'

The Bookhunters kindled some more arrows and took aim. Thin threads of black smoke rose into the air, which was filled with a sound like solemn humming.

'Who's making that noise?' asked Homuncolossus. 'Is it the Book-hunters?'

'No,' I said, 'it's someone else.'

Strange, ghostly lights were appearing among the library's vast store of books. They emerged from behind the crates and stacks of paper, the bookcases and stalagmites. There must have been hundreds of them, all slowly rising like little yellow moons. They were the eyes of cyclopean creatures, and the light in them pulsated in time to the humming that accompanied their appearance.

'It's the song of the Booklings,' I said.

⚲⚲⚲
Out of Breath

I spotted Al, Wami and Dancelot Two. Dolerich Hirnfiedler and Evsko Dosti were also there, as were Rasco Elwid, Hornac de Bloaze, Perla la Gadeon, Inka Almira Rierre and many, many others. Considerably more Booklings had survived than I'd dared to hope.

The Bookhunters were thrown out of their stride. They lowered their weapons and stared at each other in bewilderment.

Rongkong Koma raised his hands in entreaty.

'Take it easy, all of you!' he cried. 'It's only those harmless dwarfs from the Leather Grotto. They aren't even armed.'

'I've heard they're capable of witchcraft,' shouted someone right at the back.

The Booklings stayed where they were, humming ever more loudly and insistently. I began to feel all warm and sleepy, and I could see that even the Shadow King's head was drooping.

'*Mmmmmmh . . .*' went the Booklings.

One of the Bookhunters raised a crossbow loaded with a flaming bolt and aimed it at Al, who was standing nearby.

'*Mmmmmmh . . .*' went the Booklings.

The Bookhunter squeezed the trigger. The crossbow bolt whizzed past Al, missing him by a hand's breadth, found its way through the slit in another Bookhunter's helmet and hit him right between the eyes. He toppled backwards on to a stack of paper and lay still.

'*Mmmmmmh . . .*' went the Booklings.

A Bookhunter armed with a huge executioner's sword raised it high above his head and decapitated the fellow warrior in front of him – the one wearing the mosaic death's-head mask.

'What's going on here?' Homuncolossus asked drowsily.

'It's the Booklings' speciality,' I said. 'Just relax.'

'I *am* relaxing,' he replied.

'*Mmmmmmh . . .*' went the Booklings.

By now a battle was in progress such as the catacombs had never witnessed before. A contest of Bookhunter versus Bookhunter, each against all, it was fought without mercy and heedless of self-preservation. The warriors fell on each other with a contempt for death which suggested that they didn't know the meaning of the word. Arrows whistled through the air, swords clashed, limbs were lopped off, axes bisected helmets and the heads inside them. And, in the midst of it all, the motionless Booklings kept up their peaceful humming.

'This is the most incredible sight I've ever seen,' Homuncolossus mumbled.

'It's the cyclopean song that's doing it,' I said thickly. 'Think yourself lucky you aren't a Murch.'

'*Mmmmmmh . . .*' went the Booklings.

Hargo the Humungous stove in Iguriak Dooma's skull with a nail-studded club. Roggnald of Lake Blood transfixed Boolba the Heart-Eater's throat with his spear. Tibor Zakkori's helmet went up in flames because his hair had caught fire. Urchgard the Uncouth was slain with ice axes by the Botulus Twins.

I had no idea whether those Bookhunters were really called that. I simply made up the names while dazedly watching them at their mutual butchery. In any case, their real names would soon be forgotten.

'*Mmmmmmh . . .*' went the Booklings.

The din of battle was already subsiding, to be replaced by the groans and moans of the dying. Very few Bookhunters remained on their feet. One by one the last of them sank to their knees or toppled over like felled trees.

Only Rongkong Koma was still standing on his balustraded platform. He hadn't budged an inch throughout this time.

'*Mmmmmmh . . .*' went the Booklings and their humming increased in volume.

Rongkong Koma drew his gigantic sword-cum-battleaxe from its sheath.

'*Mmmmmmh . . .*' went the Booklings.

He hurled the weapon high into the air. It gleamed as it rotated in the candlelight.

'*Mmmmmmh . . .*' went the Booklings.

He bent over and bowed his head.

'*Mmmmmmh . . .*' went the Booklings.

The blade came down, severing Rongkong Koma's head from his body as neatly as a guillotine. It fell over the balustrade and landed in a basketful of books, but his body took two or three steps backwards, blundered into a heavy wooden chair, flopped down on it and sat there motionless.

The battle was over.

'*Mmmmmmh . . .*' The Booklings' humming slowly died away.

I awoke from my trance. Beside me, Homuncolossus shook his head in a daze. The Booklings crowded round us, but they seemed to be in a distressed, exhausted condition.

Al, Wami and Dancelot Two elbowed their way over to me.

'Phew . . .' said Al. His breathing was laboured and asthmatic. 'So you, er . . . made it.'

'What are you doing here?' I asked. 'So near the surface, I mean?' I well remembered Al telling me that the oxygen-rich atmosphere in the upper reaches of the catacombs didn't suit them.

'We . . . followed the Bookhunters . . . after the attack on the Grotto,' Al wheezed.

'Each Bookhunter . . . was trailed by . . . one detachment of us,' Wami chimed in, also breathing with difficulty. 'We planned to wait until they . . . reassembled somewhere and then . . . dispose of them all at once.'

'Our opportunity came here . . . in the library,' Dancelot Two went on. 'They're good at hiding . . . but we're better.'

'We can hardly breathe,' gasped Al. 'We must get back below . . . as soon as possible.'

The Booklings round us were listening like a bunch of patients in a tuberculosis sanatorium. The light in their eyes had dimmed alarmingly.

'The Leather Grotto has been cleared,' I said. 'You can go back there. *He* did it.' I pointed to the Shadow King.

'We know,' said Al. 'We heard the Bookhunters . . . talking about it. We wanted to express . . . our gratitude.'

'You already did,' said Homuncolossus. 'And how!' He gave the gnomes an appreciative bow.

'What . . . do you intend to do now?' asked Dancelot Two.

'Make for the surface,' Homuncolossus replied.

'We still have a giant to slay,' I added.

'Be careful,' said Al. 'From all I've heard . . . the person you plan to tackle is . . . a veritable ogre.'

'You'd better be going now,' I said, 'before you all die of asphyxia.'

'But first we'd like to . . . introduce someone,' said Dancelot Two. He beckoned to the back of the crowd.

The gnomes stepped aside and thrust a tiny Bookling towards me. Pale green in colour, he was shuffling timidly from foot to foot.

'Who's this?' I asked.

'It's . . . Optimus Yarnspinner,' Al wheezed. 'Our youngest.'

That was too much. My eyes filled with tears.

'But I haven't written anything yet,' I sobbed.

'We're . . . counting on you,' said Al. 'We await your first book with . . . the keenest anticipation.' He took the little creature by the hand.

I turned away and walked off in silence with the Shadow King. I couldn't have endured a grand farewell scene.

'Always remember,' Dancelot Two called after me:

'From the stars we come, to the stars we go.
Life is but a journey into the unknown.'

The Shadow King Laughs

Dancelot Two's quotation from Dancelot One was the last straw from my point of view. I sobbed unrestrainedly, and Homuncolossus had to support me for a while after we'd left the library and set off for Smyke's house.

The overconfident Bookhunters had neglected to secure the door with the incantatory lock, which was open. As we passed through the Smykes' ancestral portrait gallery, Hagob Salbandian's likeness glared insanely after us as if urging us on and cursing us at the same time.

We could already hear Smyke's voice when we reached the damp little cellar, even though he was speaking in a confidential undertone. That was how close we were!

'Rongkong Koma is next in line,' he was saying. 'As soon as he's cleared the deck down there I'll convert him into ink. Then I'll use it to write a sequel to *The Bloody Book*. It'll make a sensational addition to the Golden List.'

Someone gave an idiotic laugh. 'Good idea! And I'll get fifteen per cent!' It was the Hoggling, Claudio Harpstick.

The trapdoor to the typographical laboratory was open, so we only had to sneak up the ramp. It had creaked under my weight the last time. This time it didn't make a sound.

Here, too, everything was just as it had been: the spacious hexagonal room with the conical ceiling; the big window obscured by red velvet curtains adorned with the Zamonian alphabet (impossible to tell whether it was day or night outside); the shelves laden with alembics and flasks; the papers, quills and inks of every colour; the rubber stamps and sticks of sealing wax; the ubiquitous flickering candles; the lengths of knot-writing suspended from the ceiling; the druidical runes on the marble floor; the absurd Bookemistic contraptions; the novel-writing machine.

Pfistomel Smyke and Claudio Harpstick were standing beside an antiquated printing press, turning out handbills in the old-fashioned way – invitations to a trombophone concert, I'd have staked my life on it. They were so preoccupied, we'd reached the middle of the laboratory before Smyke swung round.

Harpstick uttered a shrill squeal like a stuck pig, but Smyke didn't lose his composure for an instant. He flung out all fourteen of his little arms and cried, 'My son! You've come home at last!'

It was only in these relatively cramped surroundings that Homuncolossus's size became truly apparent – in fact, I almost felt scared of him all over again. I noticed that he had positioned himself so that he could easily intercept the pair if either of them attempted to open the curtains.

'Yes, here I am at last,' he said quietly. 'It's incredible how much resistance one has to overcome in order to get to you – *father.*'

Smyke clasped his numerous hands together with a look of dismay. 'I trust you didn't run into any Bookhunters on the way?' he said. 'Those criminal individuals stop at nothing these days – they've even invaded my library! I don't dare go down there any more. I hope nothing untoward happened to you?'

'Oh, that problem has been dealt with,' I said. 'They're all dead.'

Smyke looked genuinely impressed.

'All of them?' he asked. 'Really? Did *you* . . . ?'

'No,' said Homuncolossus. 'They disposed of themselves – very thoroughly, too.'

'Phew,' said Smyke, 'that's a weight off my mind! They were a regular pest. Now we can breathe freely again. Did you hear that, Claudio? The Bookhunters are dead.'

'Thank goodness,' Harpstick said hoarsely. I noticed that he was slowly edging towards a candelabrum with six lighted candles in it.

'Listen to me, *father!*' Homuncolossus said in a thunderous voice that made the glass retorts rattle. 'I'm not here to play games with you. I've brought you something. A souvenir from the catacombs.'

He raised his right hand, keeping the thumb and forefinger pinched together. Surprise reigned for a moment. Even I felt puzzled. Then I remembered: the eyelash.

'I, er, can't see anything,' Smyke said, smiling. His eyelids quivered.

'It's the smallest last will and testament in the world,' said Homuncolossus. 'You'd need a microscope to read it.'

'This is a joke, isn't it?' said Smyke. 'If you'll only tell me when, I'll laugh in the right place.'

Harpstick took another little step towards the candles.

'No, it's no joke,' said Homuncolossus. 'Unless you consider it funny that Hagob Salbandian Smyke left a will.'

Smyke gave an almost imperceptible start. 'Hagob left a will, did he? Well, well.'

'Yes,' I said. 'You may have more skeletons in your cupboard than you suspect.'

Homuncolossus held his hand under Smyke's nose. 'You're aware of your great-uncle's artistic talents. This will bequeaths me his entire estate. Your estate, in fact. He engraved it on a hair.'

'I can vouch for that,' I chimed in. 'I'll testify that Homuncolossus was the first to read this will. That makes him the legitimate heir to all your family possessions.'

Smyke winced – perceptibly this time.

'There's more,' Homuncolossus went on. 'This hair – just imagine, Smyke, it's only an eyelash! – also bears a statement to the effect that you killed your great-uncle.'

'That's absurd,' said Smyke. Beads of sweat were forming on his brow.

'You need only fetch one of your microscopes,' I put in.

Smyke had started to perspire profusely. 'For simplicity's sake, perhaps you'd tell me what you really want, the two of you.' His spuriously urbane manner was slipping.

'Very well,' said Homuncolossus. 'The civilised world offers a host of opportunities, fortunately, so I'll list the possible alternatives.'

Harpstick was now only a yard away from the candelabrum.

'The simplest thing, of course, would be for you to disappear,' Homuncolossus went on. 'Together with that fat pig of a crony of yours. You would simply leave the city like an evil spirit, never to return. That would be the simplest way out. Neat, painless and straightforward.'

'That's one alternative,' Smyke said with a smile.

'But only one!' Homuncolossus held up the invisible will. 'Alternative number two: we make this public. You would probably be banished from the city and sent to the lead mines with your accomplice. Your estate would pass to me in that event too. That alternative would be the one most in keeping with Zamonian law.'

'Probably,' said Smyke. His face had turned to stone by now.

'The third alternative would be simply to make the will disappear.'

Smyke laughed woodenly. 'Oh, that would suit me best of all!'

'I'm aware of that – *father*. And so, being a loyal son, I'm now going to do you a favour.'

The Shadow King spread his fingertips and blew on them. I gave a start, although I still wasn't sure he'd really been holding the eyelash. No, of course not – he was only toying with our reluctant host.

'Very amusing,' said Smyke, 'but let's stop fooling around, shall we? I couldn't see, but I'm certain there wasn't any eyelash there – if such a thing as a will engraved on an eyelash ever existed. You're simply tormenting me for

449

everything I've done to you, right? And shall I tell you what I think? Very well, I will: I deserve it.'

'Ah,' said Homuncolossus, 'everything in life is rather more complicated than one would wish. In the first place, Hagob's will exists whether you believe it or not. And it doesn't matter whether or not I've blown it away. Thanks to the new eyes with which you, father, in your inestimable goodness, have equipped me, it would be child's play for me to rediscover that hair among the millions of grains of dust on your floor.'

'Would you kindly get to the point?' Smyke snapped, clearly losing patience. He was bathed in sweat now.

'The fact is', said Homuncolossus, 'I really did have that will at one time, but I threw it away days ago, somewhere down in the catacombs. Not even I could find it again. Even if I wanted to.'

'That's not true!' I exclaimed.

'Yes,' he said, 'it is.'

'You really did that?' asked Smyke. He was smiling again. 'Why?'

'Because I share the opinion of your great-uncle, Hagob Salbandian,' Homuncolossus replied. 'Because I believe that your family library should belong to no one at all. Because I believe that it should be wiped off the face of Zamonia – together with you. Because I'm going to kill you – *father*.'

Smyke gave Claudio Harpstick a signal. I can't think why I noticed – it was only a twitch of one of his many little fingers – but I was instantly on the alert.

I was going to warn the Shadow King, but he had also spotted the movement and forestalled me. With remarkable agility for someone so fat, Harpstick seized the candelabrum and raised it above his head. Before he could hurl it at Homuncolossus, however, his intended target pounced on him with a bestial snarl. It all happened as quickly as a door being slammed by an unexpected gust of wind. Homuncolossus dodged behind the Hoggling and, like a barber shaving a customer, slit his throat with one neat blow of his razor-sharp paper hand. Harpstick stood there for a few seconds, gargling with the blood in his gullet, and then collapsed. The candelabrum went rolling across the floor, the candles went out. The Shadow King had already returned to his former place and was thoughtfully inspecting his fingertips, from which Harpstick's blood was dripping.

'Well done, my boy!' cried Smyke, clapping his numerous hands. 'Did you see? He meant to set you on fire! He must have lost his wits! What incredible reflexes you possess! How strong I made you!'

Homuncolossus ignored him.

'Where you and I are concerned,' he said, turning to me, 'I've never pretended to you, never lied to you about my intentions. I once aroused your hopes unfairly by suggesting that I might exchange one prison for another, but that was only to get you away from Shadowhall Castle.'

He gave an almost imperceptible shake of the head.

'But I won't return to the darkness,' he said. 'Never again, whatever the circumstances.'

He turned and stared at the red velvet curtains.

'There's one more thing you should know about the Orm. If you wish to experience its power you must be able to see the sky, the sun and the moon. Down there I was dead because that power could flow through me no longer, and once you've experienced it you can't live without it.'

'What's he talking about?' Smyke demanded. 'The Orm? Where does the Orm come into this?'

'Don't do it,' I implored, my eyes filling with tears.

'*What* mustn't he do?' Smyke asked helplessly. 'Listen, friends, we need to talk! There's nothing that can't be talked about. Whatever you have in mind, let me in on it! Just think: Homuncolossus with his unique genius, Optimus with his youthful dynamism and me with my connections. Together we could rewrite the history of Zamonian literature!'

'I told you once', Homuncolossus said to me, 'that it all depends how brightly you burn, remember? Till now I've been no more than an aimlessly roaming agglomeration of paper, but now I'm going to inscribe that paper with a message the city of Bookholm won't forget in a hurry. My spirit will blaze more brightly than it has ever done; it will exert an influence no intellect, no writer or book has ever had.' He walked towards the window.

There was no way of dissuading him, I knew. I could only stand watching through my tears.

'What's he up to?' cried Smyke. 'What are you doing, my son?'

'I want to feel the sun once more,' Homuncolossus said quietly. 'Just once more.'

He was now standing in front of the curtains.

'Don't do it!' I cried.

Smyke had grasped the truth at last. His face transformed itself into a malign, twisted mask. 'Yes!' he hissed. 'Go on! Do it!'

Homuncolossus wrenched the curtains apart, and brilliant sunlight came streaming in. It surged over him like a wave and flooded the whole room, so bright that it hurt my eyes and made me cry out.

'No!' I shouted.

But the Shadow King welcomed the midday sun with head erect and arms outstretched.

'Yes!' he said.

'Yes!' Smyke whispered, wringing half a dozen of his hands in delight. 'I never thought you'd bring yourself to do it. That's true strength, true greatness!'

My dazzled, tear-filled eyes perceived Homuncolossus only as a dark figure silhouetted against a glaring expanse of light, just as I had seen him for the first time when he danced alone amid the fires in Shadowhall Castle. Thin grey threads of smoke were rising from his body. I could hear crackling, hissing sounds, and all at once the air was filled with an acrid smell. Homuncolossus turned round. His face, chest and arms were a mass of scorched, incandescent paper. Sparks leapt from the cracks in the ancient parchment and black smoke streamed up his body like rivulets of ink flowing upwards in defiance of every law of nature. Then, very slowly, he advanced on Pfistomel Smyke.

Smyke's triumphant smirk vanished. In his mind's eye he had probably seen the Shadow King go up in a sheet of flame and turn to ashes beside the window, but now he was horrified to find that his creation still possessed the strength to move.

Sheet after sheet of alchemical paper caught fire, hundreds of lambent flames were already writhing in the air, each a different colour. With a menacing hiss, sparks shot out of the multicoloured inferno and adhered to the surrounding wood and paper, setting them ablaze. Tiny fire devils flickered along the laboratory's shelves and up its walls, igniting the wallpaper.

The Shadow King strode on, steadily closing the gap between himself and Smyke, who had at last found the strength to retreat.

'What do you want of me?' he cried in a reedy falsetto.

But Homuncolossus grew and grew, becoming ever brighter, an

incandescent figure from which liquid fire was dripping. And then he started to laugh the rustling laugh of the Shadow King. It was a long time since I'd heard it and suddenly my tears ceased to flow, for I sensed that he was happy at last. Happy and free.

He paused once more as he passed me and raised his hand in farewell, a crackling torch with white sparks gushing from it. He was now a single flame, a sight of unforgettable beauty. And for one brief moment, the space of a heartbeat only, though it might also have been my imagination, I thought I saw his eyes for the first and last time. They were sparkling with the unbridled happiness of a child.

I too raised my hand in farewell and he turned back to Smyke, who was now slithering down the wooden ramp in a panic.

'What do you want?' Smyke called shrilly. 'What do you want of me?'

But the Shadow King merely followed him like a vortex of hissing flame that ignited all it touched. And he laughed as he descended into the cellar – he laughed with all his might. I could still hear him long after he had disappeared below ground.

A flask exploded. I looked round as if awaking from a dream. That was when the full danger of the situation dawned on me. The whole laboratory was on fire: the tables and chairs, the wooden ramp and the beams in the walls, the shelves and books, the carpets and wallpaper, even the lengths of knot-writing suspended from the ceiling. Chemical fluids were boiling in the glass alembics, acids spurting, corrosive vapours and biting smoke rising into the air.

The heat had set many of the absurd Bookemistic machines in motion. Their cogwheels were turning, their flaps opening and shutting as if they had come to life and were eager to escape the conflagration.

Just before my cloak could catch fire I caught a last glimpse of the chest full of inestimably valuable books. It wasn't a rational act on my part, just an instinctive desire to save at least one of them from destruction: I snatched up the topmost volume and fled outside.

The Orm

The street was quiet and deserted, the air fresh and cool: it was a perfectly normal sunny day in Bookholm. I had dreamt of this moment for so long, and now it meant nothing to me.

I paused outside Pfistomel Smyke's house and waited for the first wisps of smoke to seep through the shingled roof. Then I turned and walked off – slowly, because I had no further need to hurry. It took some time for any alarming noises to make themselves heard – bells ringing, a babble of agitated voices, the clatter of horse-drawn fire engines – but the smell of smoke soon pursued me as relentlessly as if the blazing Darkman of Bookholm himself were at my heels.

Hear the loud Bookholmian bells –
brazen bells!
What a tale of terror, now, their turbulency tells!
In the startled ear of night
how they screamed out their affright!
Too much horrified to speak,
they can only shriek, shriek . . .

Those lines from Perla la Gadeon's poem kept running through my head as I walked on, passing house after house, street after street and district after district until the City of Dreaming Books itself lay behind me. I had reached the city limits, where Bookholm and everything else had begun so unspectacularly. But I didn't stop even then. I simply walked on staring doggedly ahead, further and further across the deserted plain.

At last, dear readers, I summoned up the courage to pause and look back. The sun had set by now, and the burning city was surmounted by a cloudless, starry sky and an almost full moon.

The Dreaming Books had awakened. Miles-high columns of black smoke were rising into the heavens fraught with paper transformed into weightless ash: the residue of incinerated thoughts. Swirling within them were myriads of sparks, every one a fiery word ascending ever higher to dance with the stars.

And then I saw it up above: the Alphabet of the Stars. It sparkled in the firmament, clear and distinct, a spider's web of silvery threads entwined amid the celestial bodies.

Below, the bells continued their senseless tolling. The rustle of the countless awakening books reminded me sadly of the rustling laughter of my friend the Shadow King, the greatest writer of all time. It occurred to me only then that I had never asked him his real name. He, too, was ascending in the biggest, most terrible conflagration Bookholm had ever undergone. He, the original spark and author of that conflagration, was soaring heavenwards to become a star that would shine down for ever on a world too confined for a spirit as great as his.

That was the moment when I first felt the Orm. It surged over me like a hot wind, but not from the fires of Bookholm. Originating in the uttermost depths of space, it swept through my head and filled it with a maelstrom of words that swiftly, within a few excited heartbeats, arranged themselves into sentences, pages, chapters and, finally, into the story you have just read, my faithful friends!

And I joined in the Shadow King's laughter, which now seemed to resonate from all directions, from the all-consuming flames of Bookholm and the stars of the firmament. I laughed and wept until no vestige of that frenzied feeling of joy remained within me.

I recalled Al's farewell recitation in the Leather Grotto, which now at last made sense to me. It was as if the author whose spirit lived on in that little Bookling had looked into the future on my behalf and foreseen this moment, the moment when I received the Orm:

> *Had I but died an instant before this chance,*
> *I had liv'd a blessed time; for from this instant,*
> *there's nothing serious in mortality;*
> *all is but toys; renown and grace is dead,*
> *the wine of life is drawn, and the mere lees*
> *is left for Bookhunters to brag of . . .*

Now, for the first time, I examined the book I had snatched from the inferno in Pfistomel Smyke's laboratory. I could not repress a shudder when I saw that it was, of all things, *The Bloody Book*. Averting my gaze from the sight of the burning city, I walked on without another backward glance.

And now, dear readers, you courageous friends who have so fearlessly accompanied me thus far – now you know how I came into possession of *The Bloody Book* and acquired the Orm. There is nothing more to tell.

For this is where my story ends.

Translator's Postscript

Although I esteemed it a privilege to select material for translation from Optimus Yarnspinner's oeuvre, it proved to be an intellectual marathon. I devoted years to the task, overwhelmed and intimidated by the sheer magnitude of his output. Yarnspinner produced hundreds of novels, thousands of short stories and poems, and a score of monumental stage plays that took months to perform. He also wrote a number of books under pseudonyms: Thelonius Orm, Wilfred the Wordsmith, Hildegard Mythmaker and Oscar van Tripplestock, to name but a few.

I eventually decided to proceed chronologically. The earliest book by Yarnspinner to be published in Zamonia was *Memoirs of a Sentimental Dinosaur*, but the first edition encompassed over 10,000 pages and would have taken me a lifetime to translate had it been published unabridged. That being so, I resolved to extract the first two chapters from the aforesaid novel and lump them together under the title *The City of Dreaming Books*. I trust I shall be forgiven for having taken such an editorial liberty, but I firmly believe that these fragments possess all the makings of a book in its own right.

Walter Moers